"What were you thi[n]king [going over] those falls?"

She should have expe[cted this from] Ryan. Tori kept her voi[ce calm.] "That's not exactly what happened."

"So you weren't kayaking alone? You didn't go over the falls?"

Tori locked eyes with him. "I went to the river to travel in Sarah's path the day she died." She held back the furious tears that surged unexpectedly. "So I went kayaking."

"Why do you torture yourself?" His expression twisted into one of severe pain. "Is that why you went over the falls?"

"How could you even think that? I planned to turn back. But someone shot at me and hit the kayak. I tried to get away, and in the end, I had nowhere else to go. The falls grabbed me. I thought I was going to die."

Ryan's mouth hung open as if he couldn't quite absorb the full meaning of her words, and he appeared to search for an adequate response but came up empty.

"Someone tried to kill me."

TARGET ON THE MOUNTAIN

ELIZABETH GODDARD

&

USA TODAY BESTSELLING AUTHOR

MARY ALFORD

Previously published as *Deadly Evidence*
and *Standoff at Midnight Mountain*

LOVE INSPIRED
INSPIRATIONAL ROMANCE

LOVE INSPIRED®

INSPIRATIONAL ROMANCE

ISBN-13: 978-1-335-46916-8

Target on the Mountain

Copyright © 2021 by Harlequin Books S.A.

Deadly Evidence
First published in 2019. This edition published in 2021.
Copyright © 2019 by Elizabeth Goddard

Standoff at Midnight Mountain
First published in 2018. This edition published in 2021.
Copyright © 2018 by Mary Eason

This edition published by arrangement with Harlequin Books S.A.

For questions and comments about the quality of this book, please contact us at CustomerService@Harlequin.com.

Love Inspired
22 Adelaide St. West, 40th Floor
Toronto, Ontario M5H 4E3, Canada
www.Harlequin.com

Printed in U.S.A.

CONTENTS

Elizabeth Goddard is the award-winning author of more than thirty novels and novellas. A 2011 Carol Award winner, she was a double finalist in the 2016 Daphne du Maurier Award for Excellence in Mystery/Suspense, and a 2016 Carol Award finalist. Elizabeth graduated with a computer science degree and worked in high-level software sales before retiring to write full-time.

Books by Elizabeth Goddard

Love Inspired Suspense

Mount Shasta Secrets

Deadly Evidence
Covert Cover-Up

Coldwater Bay Intrigue

Thread of Revenge
Stormy Haven
Distress Signal
Running Target

Texas Ranger Holidays

Texas Christmas Defender

Wilderness, Inc.

Targeted for Murder
Undercover Protector
False Security
Wilderness Reunion

Visit the Author Profile page
at Harlequin.com for more titles.

DEADLY EVIDENCE

Elizabeth Goddard

Thy word is a lamp unto my feet,
and a light unto my path.
—*Psalms* 119:105

To the One who lights my path

Acknowledgments

Many thanks to my family, who put up with the many hours I spend on my computer crafting stories. Also a big thanks to my writing buddies, who encourage me along the way and patiently listen to my wild ideas and offer suggestions. My sincerest gratitude to my editor at Love Inspired Suspense, who gave me the opportunity to indulge my imagination, and to my agent, Steve Laube, who never stops working on behalf of his clients.

ONE

Wind River, Northern California

Victoria "Tori" Peterson glanced over her right shoulder as she rowed in her kayak, enjoying the view of the Wind River as it traversed through the shadow of Mount Shasta in beautiful northern California. Sweat rose on her back and beaded at her temples. Her muscles burned with each row of the double-bladed oar, but she welcomed the pain as the kayak glided on the river.

The exercise invigorated her. Got her heart pumping and the oxygen flowing.

It reminded her that she was alive.

Still, the uncanny sensation that someone was following her clung to her.

Another glance told her that no one was behind her. No one was on the river as far as she could see in the middle of a Monday afternoon. The weekend was over and summer was ending—students were back in school.

She was utterly alone out here. Just how she wanted it.

This stretch of river was calm and slow and perfect for relaxing, contemplating and easing her troubled mind after the tragedy that had brought her all the way from Columbia, South Carolina. And for which she'd taken bereavement leave from her job as a special agent with the FBI.

She shrugged off the heaviness and focused on the sound of the oar cutting through the gentle flow as the current carried her forward. She needed this moment of solitude to get her through the next few weeks. Before the river became agitated and the current too strong—before Graveyard Falls—she would urge the kayak upstream against the current and back to where she had parked her car.

Sarah's car, actually. The thought of her sister brought on a surge of tears.

Focusing on the environment instead, Tori held them back and guided her bright blue kayak forward. The river twisted through the designated wilderness area and opened up into forests at the base of the mighty mountain—an inactive volcano. Mount Shasta could be seen from nearby Rainey, where she'd grown up.

The serene setting belied the violence that had taken place along the river only a few days before. Maybe it was the weight of that memory that punctuated the brisk mountain air and the combined scent of pine, hemlock, fish and fresh water with the feeling that someone had followed her.

Or maybe someone was really there.

She'd only taken leave last week in order to attend the funeral and hadn't so quickly forgotten to listen to her instincts. Still, she pushed the fears aside for the moment. Let the memories surface as she floated on the river that would eventually travel through Rainey on its way to empty into the Shasta River.

Growing up, she and Sarah had kayaked here all the time and camped in the area close to Mount Shasta—the mountain that had hovered over them their entire lives. Those memories made her laugh with joy even as she cried with grief. Those peaceful memories would forever be spoiled for Tori now.

But life went on around her. Nature blossomed and gloried in beauty as though nothing tragic had happened. The sun shone down on her. An eagle floated on the wind above her, its high-pitched whistle underscoring the wild environment around her.

And that eerie yet glorious sound nudged her with the very question that had nagged her since her return. What had driven her to join the FBI, move across the country and leave behind the most beautiful place on earth? Leave behind her family, her sister and even a guy she could have married? Whatever those reasons, she couldn't quite remember them now. Instead, she would give anything to have stayed and gotten more time with her sister, Sarah.

She squeezed the oar and released her fury, taking it out on the river with each cut into the water.

The report of a rifle resounded, echoing through the woods and bouncing off the water.

Tori flinched and her gaze flicked to the woods behind her. She took in her surroundings again. Was someone simply out for target practice? She couldn't think of any hunting season open just yet, but she wasn't up-to-date on hunting season laws.

A thump shuddered through her kayak as another shot resounded. Her kayak had taken the hit. Someone was targeting her kayak.

Targeting her!

Her heart lurched as panic swelled. Pulse pounding, she pushed harder and faster with the oar.

She should have listened to her instincts. This was one of those moments when she hated to be right. Even if she hadn't wanted to believe it, someone had been following her. Somehow. Someway. They had waited here to ambush her. They'd planned their attack well. She couldn't possibly paddle fast enough or move out of the crosshairs if someone intended her harm.

Another bullet slammed into her kayak. Tori took hope in the miss. It seemed that whoever was shooting wasn't a trained sniper. Given the recent murders, she doubted they were just trying to scare her or warn her away. No, they were trying to hit her—and she couldn't count on them missing forever. Their next shot might hit the mark and injure her, or worse, kill her.

Her arms burned and lungs screamed as she sliced from the right to the left. Right, left, right, left, her body twisting with the movements, until it felt like she was one with the kayak.

God, please, please help me!

I can't die now! I have to find Sarah's killer!

Despite her efforts, she would never make it out of range if the shooter's rifle could handle the distance.

And if the shooter was determined.

Somehow she had to make this harder for the shooter. But how?

Ideas. She needed ideas. If she left the kayak and swam to the opposite shore, then what? She'd be stuck over there at the shooter's mercy. She'd have to dash a hundred yards before she could hide in the tree line.

She couldn't count on being able to make it to safety that way. No. Tori needed to push farther on the river.

Get much farther away and downriver and then she could possibly make her way to the trees before being gunned down. She'd be safe once she put enough distance between her and the shooter…except she had no idea how far the long-range weapon could shoot.

She had a feeling one of the shooter's shots would hit its mark if she stayed in his sights.

Another idea came to her. Tori gasped as she continued to push, putting more distance between her and the shooter. Hope built inside her that she would soon be out of range.

Would her idea work or would it kill her in another way? Before another bullet could slam into the kayak or into her body, she made a decision. Sucking in a big breath, Tori flipped the kayak as if to make a wet exit, only she remained in the kayak, floating on the river upside down, hoping instead to confuse the shooter. Make him wonder if she was planning to swim to shore, or if she'd drowned.

If he couldn't see her, she reduced his ability to kill her. Maybe.

He might still take a few shots, hoping to kill her under the water. But she knew from her training that water distorted bullet trajectories, especially if the shooter wasn't experienced enough to compensate.

Holding her breath, she urged the kayak forward and out of range. Eyes open, she worked to avoid the outcropping of rocks thrusting toward her, but she wasn't quick enough. Pain lanced through her as the jagged edge of a broken rock gouged her shoulder. Her need to cry out almost cost her the last of her breath.

Lungs burning and screaming for oxygen, she held on to the last of her air a little longer, refusing to draw river water into her lungs. Had the shooter stopped, convinced he'd successfully shot her? Could he confirm that through his scope while she was beneath the water?

Her lungs spasmed. She was running out of time. The current grew stronger, the water more agitated. The kayak was getting closer to the falls.

Two options remained. She could exit the kayak and swim for it—or she could remain in the kayak and try to make the riverbank. She'd be on the opposite side from where she believed the shooter had perched to take his shots, and she'd be farther downstream by several hundred yards, but if the shooter had a good long-range rifle, he could still pick her off.

Using her hips and oar, she rolled the kayak back so she was above the water and sucked in a long breath. Her pulse raced.

Graveyard Falls roared in her ears and fear constricted her chest.

Too close. She was much too close to the falls. Had sending her over the falls been the shooter's intention all along?

Idiot. She'd been such an idiot!

She paddled backward, but the strong current had seized the kayak in its grip and wouldn't let go. The current was much too powerful for her—especially since she hadn't practiced this water sport in a long time. Tori groaned with the effort as she fought the current, the violent rapids and rush of water that would soon take her over. She fought to steer clear of the outcroppings of boulders that caused the water to boil even more. The river ensnared her, leaving her gasping and choking as she fought to survive.

Had another report sounded? She couldn't tell. Her

chest swelled with fear. Good thing she hadn't exited the kayak—at least it could offer a measure of protection against the buildup of boulders and rocks near the falls. She desperately hammered the water in an effort to free the kayak but it was no use. The river pushed her forward toward the deadly waterfall. Despite her best efforts, she was going over the falls.

This wasn't called Graveyard Falls for nothing. Her breaths came fast, unable to keep up with the oxygen demand of her rapidly beating heart. Would these be her last breaths?

Graveyard Falls propelled the kayak, along with Tori, over the rapids, tossing her like she was a rag doll in a toy boat.

"Oh, no, no, no, no, no!"

Tori clung to her kayak as the waterfall took her over.

In those moments, every regret, every mistake she'd made, clung to her heart.

Ryan...

Detective Ryan Bradley's footfalls echoed down the sterile white hallway of Rainey General Hospital. Ten minutes ago, while in the middle of questioning someone in an ongoing investigation, he'd been informed that Tori Peterson was here and had asked for him.

She'd been injured, pulled from the river after going over Graveyard Falls. That news shocked him, to say the least. He was still stunned. Beyond concerned. He'd finished his interrogation, but unfortunately, he doubted he'd remember much of what was said. That was what he had a recorder for. At this moment, nothing mattered to him but Tori.

As soon as he'd heard that Tori had gone over those

falls and survived, he'd wanted to rush to her side as if the last four years—and the all-important FBI job that she'd chosen over him—hadn't come between them. Ryan wanted to see for himself that she was all right. He wanted to hold her in his arms and feel her warm body against him and know deep in his soul that she was truly okay.

That was how he found himself rushing down the hallway toward her room—*whoa there, boy*—when what he really needed to do was slow his steps way down. That would give him time to decelerate his too-rapidly-beating heart and *get a grip*! Ryan had to find a way to redirect his mind away from his spiraling emotions that threatened to overtake him.

And most of all, he needed to focus on the facts. He didn't even know why she wanted to speak with him. Had she asked for him as a detective, or was this much more personal? Ryan should hope for the former, but his heart wished for the latter.

Traitorous heart.

He knew Tori was in town because of her sister's murder. Tori had attended the funeral last week, and she had obviously remained in town, perhaps to help her parents go through Sarah's things, or maybe just to comfort her parents.

Those were probably the excuses she told her family. But honestly, he could guess the real reason why she remained. He ground his molars and fisted his hands as aggravation churned in his gut. He'd figured it was just a matter of time before she sought him out—after all, he was the major crimes detective investigating the multiple homicides that had occurred two weeks ago and that had unfortunately involved her sister. He still couldn't believe it himself.

Tori's sister. Sweet Sarah Peterson. Gone forever.

Still, it was strange that Tori had asked for him after being pulled from the river. He was grateful she'd survived the falls, but he wanted answers about what was going on.

Spotting a vending machine—his salvation—Ryan stopped to grab coffee. He should join Procrastinators Anonymous, or was it United? After inserting and reinserting the cash into the slot until it finally pleased the machine, he pressed the appropriate buttons.

Coffee. *Give me coffee, black and strong*, he mentally demanded as the vending machine took its sweet time, for which he should be grateful. He needed a few more minutes to compose himself and appear like the disinterested, detached and impartial detective he strove to be.

His efforts were failing because he was definitely anything but detached and impartial. He couldn't believe how the mere thought of seeing Tori again affected him, especially knowing that she'd come so close to death. What was the matter with him? He let his thoughts sift through the last couple of weeks and focus on Tori and her family—their needs. Not his personal issues that had no bearing in the present.

Tori had lost her sister. She had to be a wreck. Ryan had been the one to give her parents the news, and it had been all he could do to keep his composure. Those were the moments when he hated this job.

A warm cup of coffee finally in hand, he downed the contents, then steeled himself. Enough procrastinating. He walked the rest of the way to room 225 and pressed his fingers against the partially open door. Voices drifted out. Tori's mother sounded upset. He leaned against the wall, deciding he'd give them a few moments. He popped in a piece of gum and skimmed his emails on his cell, except his mind was far from his cell phone.

Tori Peterson.

Once upon a time in the past, he'd thought he and Tori were on the same path. The same life track. He'd let his heart hope for something long-term between them. Then, when a door opened offering her the job of her dreams, she'd chosen that over him. Good for her. Bad for him. At the time, he'd been furious and hurt, and they hadn't parted on good terms.

Four years had changed his perspective. Now, he didn't blame her or hold anything against her. Instead, he saw it as a cautionary lesson not to set his heart on anyone. Time could heal all wounds, the saying went, and with time and experience, he'd learned his limits.

Ryan couldn't take that kind of heartache ever again.

The voices in the room died down and the room went quiet. Time for him to make his presence known. He knocked lightly on the door as he said, "Detective Bradley. Is it all right for me to come in?"

The door swung open to reveal Sheryl Peterson. She blinked up at him, relief in her face. "Come in, Ryan. I mean… Detective."

She eyed him as if to ask if it was okay that she called him by his first name. He smiled and gave a slight nod as he entered the room. He had known the Petersons for years—there was no need for formality with them.

Sheryl caught his arm, preventing him from going farther. She leaned in and spoke in a low tone. "I'm so glad you're here. She's not ready to listen. The doctor wanted to keep her another day. But she's planning to leave anyway. Can you talk some sense into her?"

Tori stepped out of the bathroom fully dressed. Next to the bed, she swayed a bit. Ryan rushed forward and caught her. He assisted her to the bed, where she should have stayed.

"I heard you lost a lot of blood during your fight with a waterfall," he said, his voice coming out gentle and caring. Not exactly what he'd been going for. He'd wanted to make it clear to her—to *both* of them—that he'd finally left their relationship in the past.

She lifted her gaze as if just now realizing he was there, that he'd been the one to assist her to the hospital bed. "Ryan. What…what are you doing here?"

Really? He'd been told that she'd asked for him. Maybe someone had made a mistake.

"I need to run an errand." Sheryl pursed her lips, still upset with her daughter. "I'll be right back. Ryan, please keep her in this room until I get back, okay?"

He nodded, but he couldn't promise anything. Sheryl disappeared and left Ryan and Tori alone in the room. It shouldn't feel awkward but it did.

"What were you thinking, taking that waterfall?" he asked. "Kayaking alone and going over the falls?"

Was she so devastated from the news of her sister's death that she had a death wish of her own? No. The Tori he'd known before would never take her own life—no matter what.

He fisted his hands, controlling the fury over her choices and fear for her safety that he had no right to feel. Swallowed the lump in his throat at the thought of what could have happened.

He was over her. Had been for a long time. But apparently the emotional equivalent of muscle memory hadn't gone away. When she was putting herself in danger, it was his instinct to worry.

Dumb instincts.

And he was done playing games or wasting time. "Why did you ask to see me, Tori?"

But he had a feeling he knew exactly why. Tori was here to find the person behind four murders, behind Sarah's murder, and as lead detective on this investigation, Ryan was about to get swept up in Tori's fast-moving current.

TWO

Ryan Bradley. Detective Ryan Bradley is in my room...

Blood rushed to her head.

Sitting on the edge of the hospital bed, Tori squeezed her eyes shut and breathed steadily. She had to regain her composure and stop her head from spinning. Enduring the guy's pensive gaze hadn't been in her plans for the day. She'd asked to see him? She didn't remember that part.

Tori focused on what had happened, mentally replaying images from her fight to survive the crushing falls. The helplessness as she tumbled through the air while water enveloped her. That suffocating, painful, drowning feeling of trying to catch enough air to live while unable to stop the force that could dash her against the rocks. All of it thrashed around in her thoughts even now.

Goose bumps rose on her arms.

Then she remembered... One of her last thoughts had been about Ryan. Her whole life—her decisions, mistakes and regrets—had flashed in her heart, and some of those biggest regrets revolved around him. No way could she tell him any of that here and now, if ever. She was embarrassed that she'd asked for him...but now that she thought of it, it was good that he was here. They *did* need to talk—not about her feelings, but about facts. But not here. "Can we go somewhere and talk?"

He studied her, obviously trying to decide if she was coherent or was suffering, both physically and emotionally, too much to think clearly.

He crossed his arms. A sentinel complying with her mother's demands to keep her here? "I don't think they want you to leave yet," he said.

Ah. He'd made his decision—the wrong one—and had sided with her mother. Tori didn't want to waste time at the hospital. She needed to find out who had killed her sister and why.

Then he shifted his posture, shoving his hands in his pockets. The way his jacket bunched up, she could see his department-issue weapon at his belt. "We can talk here," he said. "I'm assuming you want to talk about your sister's murder."

Amazing blue-green eyes stared down at her. His dark blond hair was slicked back and made him look far more serious than she remembered. He sported a Vandyke beard now, as was the style. In spite of herself, warmth flitted over her as she looked at him. How had he gotten more attractive since she'd seen him last?

Though maybe what really attracted her was that Ryan had that look of someone who knew what they were doing. The experiences of life shone on his face along with an intensity he hadn't had before. Not really a hardening, but more the look of someone focused and determined, who knew what he wanted and how to get it.

Just being in the room with him was almost too much.

A shiver ran through her.

She steadied her nerves and pushed to stand. "Yes. What I have to say has to do with Sarah, though not in the way you might think. But first you should know that I'm leaving. I've asked for discharge papers. I'm waiting on those now. Mom was wrong about them keeping me—she's the one who thinks I need more time here, not the doctor. So I'm leaving and I don't want to talk about my sister here."

His frown wasn't unexpected. He had to know she wasn't satisfied with his investigation into the four murders, including Sarah's.

A social worker entered. "Ms. Peterson, I have your discharge papers and instructions. If you'll just sign and initial here." She laid out the yellow papers for Tori's signature and went over the instructions for the care of her wound.

After the social worker left, Tori smiled up at Ryan. "See?" Her mother would be furious when she got back here to find Tori had gone, but at least this way, she couldn't try to stop Tori from leaving. "But now I have a problem. I don't have a way out of here."

She thought to offer Ryan an innocent grin and blink as if to give him a hint—something she'd done in the past with him—but she had to steer away from giving him the wrong impression. No need to remind him of their past. Still, why wasn't he offering her that needed ride?

Instead, Ryan watched her. She never liked being analyzed. She supposed that was hypocritical since she did that a lot to others in her role as an agent. But being on the other end of that wasn't pleasant.

Finally he said, "I'll give you a ride. We can talk on the way. Where would you like to go?"

"Thanks. I'll text Mom and let her know that I'm with you and I'm okay."

"Are you really okay?" His wary eyes showed just how worried he was. His concern went deeper than what he'd have felt for a fellow human being, or that of a detective who cared about people and bringing justice.

Ryan still cared about Tori.

Before panic could swell, she tore her gaze from him to text her mother. "I'll survive," she said.

At least, she hoped she would. And she would survive being in Ryan's presence, too. As for surviving the attempt on her life—would there be more attempts? Would one of them succeed? Her sister hadn't survived when someone had tried to kill her. Tori almost sagged under the weight of loss.

A tear trailed her cheek as she stared down at her cell. She wasn't sure what she was going to do without her sister in her life, but the truth was they hadn't exactly been in each other's lives that much since Tori had moved across the country. She'd told herself that they'd make up for lost time later, with phone calls or visits. That chance no longer existed now.

The knowledge that Sarah was gone, taken from this world by a murderer, flayed her and left her raw and bleeding.

She finished the text and looked up at him again. Waves of remorse and a thousand conversations she wanted to have with him rushed through her. Tori tried not to shudder. She didn't think he'd missed that, because Ryan had always been sharp and could read people even when they tried to hide something. *Especially* when they tried to hide something.

And years ago, he'd had an uncanny ability to read her. Had that changed?

Fifteen minutes later, they sat in a booth at a coffee shop. Tori had suggested they have their talk over coffee. Ryan had obliged. Coffee ordered, Tori resisted the need to take painkillers. Her shoulder had been wrapped, and she'd been given blood. She'd heal, with or without the painkillers, and she wanted her mind to stay clear. Somehow, she had to toughen up and see her way through this.

Ryan studied her. Scrutinizing her again?

"Would you please stop?" She rearranged the condiments.

Frowning, he shook his head. "Stop what?"

"Please stop looking at me like you're dissecting me. I'm not a frog. This isn't Biology 101."

"Sorry. I didn't mean to make you uncomfortable."

"No? I see you making mental notes that Tori Peterson doesn't like to be studied. I'm not a suspect, so you can quit with your intimidation tactics."

He shrugged. Then he shifted forward in the booth, a frank expression on his rugged face. "I'm worried about you."

"This is just a gash in my arm." He had no idea yet of the real reason why he should be worried. She vaguely remembered the pain of that rocky outcropping gouging her, but at least she wasn't dealing with a bullet wound to her head or her chest.

"What were you thinking, going over those falls?" He'd asked the question before and wanted an answer.

She kept her voice low and said, "It was not exactly my choice."

The waitress brought their coffee. Tori poured half-

and-half in hers. Ryan sugared his up too much for her taste.

"What are you saying, Tori? That you weren't kayaking alone? That you didn't go over the falls?"

"See, this is what I wanted to talk about." She took a sip of coffee and let it warm her belly, then leaned back. She shut her eyes and calmed her breathing. Let herself remember.

Tori opened her eyes. "I thought I was going to die when I went over the falls. I fought to survive and somehow…somehow I did survive. I woke up and coughed up water. Maybe the couple who pulled me from the river revived me. I don't know. But I do remember now that I said your name, Ryan."

Deep lines carved into his forehead and around his mouth. "Tori, I—"

"I went to the river today to travel in Sarah's path." That, and she'd needed to remember what it was like to be on the river at the base of Mount Shasta. She'd needed to remember Sarah. "I'm staying in her house. I'm on bereavement leave now." She held back the furious tears that surged unexpectedly. "So I went kayaking along the river. That's what the four of them were doing that day, wasn't it? They were camping and had their kayaks, so we know they had planned to go down the river."

"Why would you torture yourself like that?" His expression twisted into one of severe pain. "Is that why you went over the falls?"

Her heart felt like it might just rip open at the realization that he really seemed to believe it had been a suicide attempt. She'd thought he knew her better than that. "How could you even think that? I planned to turn back. But someone shot at me and hit the kayak. I tried to get away and in the end, I had nowhere else to go but into the water. I thought I could get to shore once I put some distance between me and the shooter, but the falls grabbed me and wouldn't let go. You know how strong the current is the closer you get to Graveyard Falls."

Ryan's mouth hung open as if he couldn't quite absorb the full meaning of her words, and he appeared to search for an adequate response but came up empty. Tori decided to fill the silence herself.

"Someone tried to kill me."

Stunned at her claim, Ryan somehow found the strength to close his mouth. Then to form words. "Are you sure?" Entirely lame and inadequate words. He knew as soon as they escaped his lips, but especially after the glare she gave him. She didn't like that he'd questioned her.

As an FBI agent, she thought herself superior to him. He knew that with certainty because that was why she'd wanted to join the feds to begin with. And suddenly he was thrown back in time. He'd never been good enough for Tori Peterson. Nor would he ever be good enough.

But he didn't care to be good enough for her now. Finally, he could let go.

Keep telling yourself that.

"Of course I'm sure. Why would you doubt me?" She narrowed her eyes and studied him. Must be her turn to analyze him.

He wasn't intimidated by her FBI-schooled expression. Instead, he was terrified that her words could be true. "I didn't say I doubted you. You've been through a lot. You've suffered a great loss. I'm concerned, that's all." He wanted to believe that her memories of what happened were false memories brought on by the trauma and her injury. Ryan didn't want to even entertain the possibility that someone had actually tried to kill Tori.

"You don't believe me? I can prove it to you, Ryan. Let's go find the kayak. You can look at the bullet holes yourself. We can gather evidence together."

"You're not part of my investigative team."

She pursed her lips. "But I *am* going to investigate, whether you want me to or not, so wouldn't it make more sense to work together? Especially if the attack on me is in any way tied to Sarah's murder. What do you think, Detective Bradley? That Sarah's death was a random act of violence—four kids killed by someone out on a shooting spree while camping? Or that maybe they stumbled upon something they shouldn't have seen? Or did someone kill four kids to cover up one murder? On any of those possibilities, do you think the murders are drug-related?"

Okay. Well, sure, that it was drug-related was his working theory for now. Wasn't it almost always drug-related no matter the crime? He said nothing, wondering what she'd say next—what she'd reveal. She'd called the victims kids, but they had been in their twenties. Still, Tori considered Sarah her kid sister growing up and that obviously hadn't changed. He understood because he had three siblings himself.

Katelyn was his twin sister, then there was his brother Reece, who was two years older, and Benjamin—Ben—who was three years younger. He couldn't imagine losing any of them.

How was Tori even holding it together?

"Fine. You don't want to answer now. We can talk on the way to the river. Are we going or not?" Her determined tone and severe frown left no doubt as to her resolve.

Of all the times for him to crack a smile—but he couldn't control himself. He'd always loved it when she got fired up over something she believed in. So feisty and determined. Did she realize how much Sarah had idolized her? Sarah had wanted to be just like her sister, and had found her own passionate way to serve people by involving herself in social justice issues. Tori had taken a different route but fought for justice all the same. And when she was on the hunt for answers, nothing and no one could make her stop. He knew she was right that he wouldn't be able to stop her from investigating, but he'd torture her a few moments longer with a wry grin before he'd announce his decision.

Meanwhile, he took his time admiring her new look. She'd cut her long brown hair shorter so that it hung to her shoulders, and she'd dyed the silky tendrils a soft golden blond that was growing out and revealed hints of brown. Ryan remembered her smile—she'd always had the most amazing dimples that drove him wild and made him want to kiss her.

Even now, with the mere thought of it.

He cleared his throat and forced his impartial face in place. He was such a liar. "Let's go."

In his unmarked utility vehicle belonging to the Maynor County Sheriff's Department, he drove toward the river. He would radio for assistance once he got a look at the kayak himself to confirm Tori's claims. He wanted to see the bullet holes first. Ryan held on to the small hope that her memory of today's earlier events was off. If Tori really was being targeted for some reason, that would terrify him but also change the investigation.

As if sensing his need to contemplate what she'd told him, she kept quiet and left him to his own thoughts. He gripped the steering wheel too tightly as he steered the SUV through the small town of Rainey, the town where he'd chosen to live. Rainey had proven to be peaceful and quiet—a place he could go home to at the end of a long day of facing crime puzzles and criminals and simply relax and breathe in the fresh air.

But the murders two weeks ago—just outside of Rainey—had rocked his world. In fact, the whole town of Rainey had been shaken.

Ryan kept driving until he was on the long, curvy road that followed the Wind River. Tall trees hedged the road to either side on this part of the drive and he could barely make out the peak of Mount Shasta as he headed toward the camping and river rafting/kayaking area where Tori told him she had parked her vehicle.

Not far from where four people had been murdered.

He knew the spot well. Had been there too many times to count—with her, no less. He made to turn into the parking area but she touched his arm.

"You need to go all the way down to the base of the falls," she said. "My kayak is probably downriver, unless someone already picked it up."

She dropped her hand, but he still felt the spot where she'd touched him.

Of course the kayak would be downriver of the actual falls. He should have thought of that. Being this close to her, he couldn't think straight. But he'd give himself a break—he hadn't seen Tori in so long and now she'd been injured and could have died on those falls. He was allowed to be a little distracted under those circumstances.

"Maybe whoever shot at you already grabbed the kayak." And with the words, he realized he'd lost all hope that she'd been mistaken. He believed that someone had, in fact, shot at Tori Peterson.

Tori was a good agent, and despite the trauma and the grief of loss, she would know exactly what had happened. She'd been trained to have an excellent memory. She glanced his way with an arched brow as though she thought his words were simply more sarcasm.

"What? I believe you."

Her brows furrowed.

"No, really. I had hoped you were mistaken, I'll be honest."

His response seemed to satisfy her and her expression relaxed. "Let's hope we can find it."

"Agreed." He sighed. "We need to talk this through. I take it you think that whoever shot at you is somehow connected to Sarah's murder." And also Mason's, Connie's and Derrick's. Four people in their twenties just out camping and having fun, murdered.

"I think it's highly suspect, don't you?" She fumbled around in that big bag she called a purse.

Unfortunately, yes. He nodded and maneuvered the road. "I don't usually believe in coincidence. That's why I held on to the smallest of hopes that you were wrong about what happened."

He felt her glare again.

He glanced at her and then focused on the road. "A detective can hope, can't he? I didn't want to think that someone had tried to kill you, Tori. And the fact that they did brings up another question." How did he word this?

"Well, what is it?"

Might as well try. "Someone killed four people, leaving us to speculate on the reasons and focus a lot of resources on finding answers. Why would they draw more attention by shooting at you? What could they hope to gain with that attempt on your life? It doesn't make sense." Though when did murder ever make sense?

"I don't know. I think… I was close to the falls. Honestly, I think they had hoped to send me over to die and make it look like an accident. Maybe they had planned to make sure I was dead, but the couple found me first."

"But again—why?"

"Maybe they don't like Sarah's FBI sister digging into things and planned to head me off before I found out the truth."

Ryan did not like to hear those words. They meant Tori's life was in ongoing danger. Man, did he wish this wasn't happening. Those kids were gone and that was tragic news. It was his job to find their killer, but how did he also prevent another murder, and Tori's at that? His insides twisted up in knots. Tori was an FBI agent and had faced dangerous situations in her job, but that didn't make him feel any better about her safety. On-the-job danger was one thing—someone actively trying to kill her was another.

Finally he came upon the sign for the trailhead and boat launch at the bottom of the falls. He parked at a gravel parking spot near the river, just down from where it spilled over Graveyard Falls. On weekends and during tourist season, the place would be crowded. People liked to hike along the narrow path between boulders, to get closer to the waterfall and watch the majesty of the beast, as well as feel the spray hitting their faces and getting them wet.

Tori reached for the door. He touched her arm and she held back from opening the door. "What is it?"

"Before we get out, there's more I want to say." Before finding Tori's kayak with a bullet hole or two in it messed with his head. "My working theory has been that the murders are drug-related. Sarah's boyfriend, Mason Sheffield? Turns out he had some priors. Mostly the usual stuff with drugs. Maybe he was dealing or stole something. Sarah got involved with the wrong guy. It happens, Tori, you know it does."

She shifted in the seat to face him. "So they take out a group like that? And the law comes down on them?"

"I agree. That wasn't smart."

Tori shook her head vehemently. "I'm not buying your theory. Or rather, I'm not ready to settle for it."

Ryan held his temper in check. Did she realize she'd insulted him? But he was curious, too. "So let's have it. What do you think happened?"

"Killing several people in a group out camping could be a ploy to take the focus off just one murder."

"You brought that up earlier. That doesn't mean drugs aren't involved."

She stared straight ahead and heaved a sigh. "It's not like Sarah to date someone who was into drugs."

"I hear you. I didn't want to believe it, either, but in the world we live in, our loved ones are getting involved in dangerous things left and right. And family ignores it, chooses not to believe it, or somehow they live in complete ignorance." He drummed the console between them. They needed to get out and find the kayak. This wasn't getting them anywhere.

"If it was all stuff from years ago then I can see Sarah giving him a second chance," Tori said. "Maybe he wanted to change. Maybe she was helping him to get clean."

"I can see that, too."

When Tori said nothing more, he finished what he'd started. "Bottom line is that, regardless of the reasons, the murders are heinous crimes that make no sense. But even if we manage to find answers, making sense out of the murders won't bring Sarah back. It won't change anything."

"Is this your way of suggesting I stay out of it?"

He shrugged. "You have a job and a life back in South Carolina, Tori. It's my job to solve this. Staying here won't bring her back." He braced himself for her reaction and when it didn't come like he expected, he released the breath he'd held. The truth was that he understood why she felt she had to stick around and try to find Sarah's killer. If he were for some reason assigned to another case and removed from this one, he would still work to solve Sarah's murder. He wanted to make sense out of her death, too.

"Look—" she released a sigh "—murder can never be resolved, not really. Finding out who did this and why will be enough for me. But nothing we've said here explains why someone shot at me."

She was right. Taking her out, too, made no sense. But if that was what had happened, then he doubted the danger was over. He knew she wouldn't leave until the murderer was caught, which meant he would have to figure out how to protect a capable special agent who didn't think she needed protection. And the worst part?

Ryan feared he would fail.

THREE

Making their way to the falls, they trekked alongside the fast-moving river, Tori leading Ryan, who trailed a few paces back. The roar grew louder with their approach. The force of the falls up ahead compelled the river forward, causing it to be swift and dangerous. The memories of the moment Graveyard Falls pulled her down and over lashed at her insides.

She hesitated for a moment, unsure if she could keep up the search for her kayak, and stopped to watch the river. While swirling in that vortex, she'd feared she would die.

Had Sarah known she was going to die? What were her last thoughts? Tori hated to think of the terror her sister must have endured. Had Sarah also spoken someone's name in those moments before her death? And if she had, whose name would she have said?

A loved one's?

Or the killer's?

A shudder crawled over her.

"You okay?" She was freed from her musings by the arrival of Ryan's sturdy form next to her.

"Sure."

Tori shook off the morbid thoughts and started hiking again. She turned her focus instead to this path next to the river and the unbidden memories floating to the surface. She and Ryan had hiked this trail on multiple occasions when they were seeing each other. Probably like the young couple who had pulled her from the river earlier in the day.

Back then, it had been just the two of them. Hand in hand. Falling deeper in love with each passing day.

And they'd shared more than one amazing kiss right here when no one else was around. Her chest grew tight.

Was he thinking about those kisses, too? She hoped not, but when she glanced over her shoulder and caught his pensive gaze, she knew where his mind had gone— to them as a couple before she left.

Pain cut through her at how different things were now. Instead of a couple in love enjoying a nature walk, they were now joined together only by the need to find a killer before he struck again. Was that why she'd said his name earlier? Because he was the investigator on Sarah's case? Tori had thought she was going to die, and maybe she'd wanted to somehow let Ryan know that her death hadn't been an accident. She'd thought of him—her last coherent thought before the greatest struggle of her life, and then, she'd huffed out his name when she came to.

If she hadn't said his name, they would probably be here together now anyway, since she would have gone to him to report the attack on her as soon as she left the hospital. That she'd said his name shouldn't matter so much, but it bothered her and she wanted to know why. She would have to think about that later, though. Much more pressing matters needed her attention.

She hiked forward, closing in on the falls.

The flash of color on the other side of a rocky out-cropping drew her attention. "There. I see a kayak."

"Fortunately it's not across the river," he said. "Are you sure it's yours?"

"It looks like mine, and if it's not, then that could mean someone else went over the falls." She didn't think that was the case.

Spotting the kayak exhilarated her. Now they were getting somewhere. Not that she feared he doubted her words—not anymore, at least—but the kayak with a bullet hole or two in it would go a long way to boost her theory, one she hoped Detective Bradley was also formulating.

They made their way around boulders and roots, and then to the edge of the riverbank where the broken kayak had wedged between rocks. Tori gasped at the sight. She wrapped her arms around herself.

That could have been her body. Broken and lifeless.

Ryan's frown deepened. He appeared shaken as he pressed his hand over his mouth then rubbed his chin.

Then, seeming to pull himself together, he reached in the pocket of his jacket and tugged out a small camera. "Don't worry. We'll get Jerry, our tech, out here now that we know it's part of a crime scene, but I want to take my own pictures just in case."

Ryan walked around the kayak and took photographs from various angles.

She peered at the front portion. "See, just there. A bullet hole."

"Here's another." He pointed, then crouched and took close-ups of the holes.

Tori looked around for the oar, but she doubted she'd

find it. "I'm surprised a bullet went through the material, but I guess it all depends on the caliber of bullet and the quality of the kayak materials."

"Right."

"We'll have to go up above the falls to look for rifle shells," she said. "It's a big area to search."

"Finding a shell doesn't mean it belonged to this particular shooter," he said. "We need bullets, too."

"Your lab can get ballistics, can't they?" Tori had to be careful what she said. Ryan was probably kind of touchy about the limited resources of his job compared to hers, and she didn't want to sound superior. But, well, the FBI had superior training, facilities and labs. The best, in fact.

He pursed his lips and eyed her as he got on his radio and asked for evidence collection and retrieval of the kayak. "We'll need to wait here to make sure no one disturbs it intentionally or otherwise, although if they had intended to do that, I think the kayak would already be gone."

Tori started toward the falls. "I'll hike up topside and look for rifle shells. There were more than two shots fired, even though there are only two bullet holes in my kayak."

Ryan grabbed her arm and gently squeezed as he pulled her toward him. "Are you serious? What makes you think whoever shot at you won't try again? You're not going up there."

"In that case, what am I even doing out here with you?"

"Good question." He worked his jaw as if angry with her. Angry with himself.

His concern for her chipped away at the wall around

her heart. She reminded herself that his reaction didn't mean that he cared for her on a personal level. Of course he would be this concerned for anyone. Right?

"I don't think the shooter is still here," she said. "When I got on the river, I had an eerie feeling. You know the one. I felt like someone was following me. Like someone was watching me. But I don't sense that now."

He scraped a hand through his hair, messing with the slicked-back look. "Come on, you can't trust a feeling like that. Not saying you should ignore it when you sense that someone is watching you, but you can't be certain you're safe just because it doesn't feel like anyone's watching you." He searched the ground near the kayak. For footprints? Too many hikers had been by the kayak today for forensics to find anything. After a minute, he lifted his gaze to look at the woods. A group of senior citizens hiked up the trail toward them, lost in their conversation. They smiled and bade them a good day as they passed.

The shooter wouldn't try again here today with people out on the trail, would he? The couple who'd found her hadn't been at the top of the falls where she'd been forced over. She'd been alone up there when he'd shot at her. Tori rubbed her arms and stared at the woods. She absolutely wouldn't let fear take hold of her or stop her. "We have to find who did this, Ryan."

Her comment drew a severe look from him, one that she knew well. Tori averted her gaze.

"Don't you have a job back in South Carolina to get back to? How long are you staying again?" The friction between them edged his tone. "Bereavement leave doesn't give you but a week or two, does it?"

"I... I don't know," she said.

"What?"

She hung her head. Closed her eyes. "You're right. Officially, I only have two weeks, but I'm considering taking an indefinite leave."

"Why would you do that?"

A feral emotion flashed in his gaze. She understood the deeper meaning behind his questions. She'd given him up. She'd left him for an FBI career—now he wanted an answer as to why she would give it all up for this investigation when she wouldn't give it up for him. She offered a one-shoulder shrug. "Mom and Dad are devastated. They've lost a daughter, Ryan." She looked in his eyes and took in the blue-green hues. "I need to be here for them and..."

Something shifted behind his gaze—and for the life of her, she couldn't tell if it was good or bad. Again, she had the strong sense that he still cared about her. That he'd never stopped. Her next words would drive an even bigger wedge between them. She'd hurt him terribly when she'd chosen her career with the FBI over a relationship with Ryan. She'd wanted more than working law enforcement in a northern California county. She could have taken a job and worked with him, but she'd taken the FBI's offer.

Tori drew in a breath. She might as well say it. "I need to make sure her killer is caught."

He lifted his chin to search for words in the bluest of skies. "And you don't trust me to do that."

"That's not what I said."

"But it's what you meant. You can't go home because you don't think we'll find the killer without your help."

"Ryan, please tell me that you understand. You would

do the same if it was one of your siblings, someone you loved dearly, no matter who was investigating."

When he looked at her again, she saw resignation. "You're not here in your capacity as an FBI agent, so I'm going to ask you not to interfere. Trust me to do my job, Ms. Peterson."

The air rushed from her lungs. *Oh, come on.* She took a step toward him, trying to think of what to say to get him to see, though she wasn't sure why she wanted him to understand. "Ryan, please. I… I trust you to do your job. I promise I won't interfere with your investigation."

He nodded and huffed, then surprisingly gave her a wry grin. "I hear what you're saying. And what you're *not* saying. I know you, Tori. You have your own investigation going."

Sarah… "While you're looking for the person who killed four people, I'm looking for the person who killed one person. Sarah. You can't get in her head like I can. You can't walk in her shoes or think the way she would have thought. That's all I'm doing." She and Sarah were sisters. No one could know her better, even with the fact that Tori had lived far from Sarah for four years.

His forehead furrowed. Eventually he would come to the same conclusion about whom the murderer had intended to kill—the one target—if he hadn't already.

In the distance, they saw two county SUVs pull up behind Ryan's unmarked vehicle.

"Looks like the wait is over." He sounded relieved. "I can't stop you from investigating on your own. But don't make me charge you with obstruction. If you find evidence, please call me."

Even a private investigator looking into a major

crime like murder could get charged with obstruction if he or she wasn't careful. "I will, I promise." She eyed him. "I trust you with this case, honestly." More than he would ever know or believe. "And you're a good detective. You're a good man, Ryan."

He stared at her as if he didn't know how to take the compliment, but she saw the doubts swimming in his eyes. Being a county detective hadn't been good enough for her. Before emotions rushed through her, she looked at the river. She shouldn't think about the past, but she almost regretted the choices she'd made that caused her to lose him.

Almost.

Because truly regretting her choices would mean she'd made the wrong ones. And she couldn't accept that.

While Ryan spoke to his team of deputies and his techs who would process and then transport the kayak, Tori waited near the river. Was the shooter out there somewhere, watching?

Two techs began processing the kayak—taking pictures and documenting everything. Tori was glad Ryan hadn't just hauled it in his SUV as if it had no importance. The slightest detail could be vital in a case like this.

He left his team to work and approached her. "You ready to go?"

"I thought we were going to look up top for rifle shells. We could help those deputies search for evidence. We aren't doing anything."

"Let the county sheriff's department handle it. I'm taking you home."

Though she didn't need the lead investigator acting as a chauffeur, how else would she get home? Dad had already gotten her car from the river. Back in his SUV, Ryan steered them toward town.

"Is there any remote chance that the fact someone targeted you has to do with something unrelated to Sarah—maybe one of your past cases?"

"I suppose anything is possible, but it's not probable."

They remained quiet for the remaining miles back to town. As he drove down Main Street in Rainey, her mind constantly flashed to memories of them together. It seemed so strange to be with him again, only for an entirely different reason than because they simply wanted to be together.

A gut-wrenching reason. Her breath hitched and she squeezed the hand rest.

"I keep asking if you're all right." He steered into the driveway of Sarah's small bungalow and parked. "You keep telling me that you are. But you're not okay. I'm worried about you, Tori."

"You've said that." Tori hung her head. She didn't want to get into this conversation with him. Why did he have to keep asking? Why did he have to care? Of course she wasn't okay.

"Is it me?" he asked.

That question brought her head up to look at him. "What do you mean?"

"Is being here with me too much for you? Too awkward? I know we're both trying to stay focused on the case, but maybe it's too much. Maybe it's just too hard to work together."

And you want to avoid me, Ryan? She kept the question to herself. "Even if it's too hard, we have to push past that. We can't change it."

"We can. You can go back to work in South Carolina. Be safe. Let me find who killed these people. Your sister. I don't need your help."

Tori had no response to that. She got out of the vehicle, slammed the door and stomped up to the home that reminded her so much of Sarah. She remembered when her sister had picked it out. Sarah had emailed so many pictures to Tori. She'd been so excited to find such a cute place to live in on her own.

Oh, Sarah...

What had happened to her was wrong on so many levels. Why couldn't Ryan understand that Tori could not leave this alone? She wanted to look Sarah's killer in the face. And deep in her heart, she wanted to be the one to bring him down.

At the door, she fumbled for the keys in her purse with shaking hands and then finally unlocked the door. Ryan remained in his vehicle, making a call, waiting for her to get safely inside. She wished he would hurry up and leave.

Inside, she slammed the door and pressed her back against it, her heart pounding for no other reason than she was upset with Ryan. Upset with herself. Upset that this nightmare was real. Tears leaked out the corners of her eyes.

She swiped them away. No time for grieving.

Tori needed an escape from the events of the last weeks, days and hours. Unfortunately, Sarah's home was full of reminders instead. She shoved herself away from the door and dropped her bag on the table in the foyer. Dad had retrieved it from the car and Mom had brought it up to the hospital. Mom. She'd better text—

Clank, clank...

Tori froze. She listened.

The hair on her arms rose. Someone was in the house just down the hallway.

She pulled her weapon from her bag. Even on leave, she was required to always carry her FBI-issued weapon with her.

Weapon at the ready, she crept down the hallway toward where the sound had come from and cleared the first room. That left only one more room. Heart pounding, she whipped the weapon around as she stepped through the open door. "Freeze!"

A masked man stood much too close—her mistake—and he knocked the SIG from her grasp. She fought him, but with her injured shoulder, she struggled. Still, Tori was determined to best him. Somehow, she needed to get to her gun on the floor. Tori punched him in the solar plexus for good measure, then slammed his throat.

He coughed and gasped, but pulled out his own weapon—a nine-millimeter Glock.

Oh, no...

Tori dove into the hallway as gunfire exploded.

At the crack of gunfire, Ryan's heart jackhammered.

He tossed his cell aside and radioed dispatch that shots had been fired and to send backup. But with Tori in danger, he couldn't wait for them. He jumped from the SUV and pulled his Glock from his holster all in one smooth motion.

Please let me be wrong, please let me be wrong.

But it was hard to mistake the sound.

He sprinted up the driveway toward the front door. The distinct sound of glass shattering resounded from the back of the house.

Weapon held at low ready, he quickly crept along the side of the bungalow, cautious near the bushes in case someone hid behind them. At the back corner, he peeked around, prepared to face off with a possible perp.

But he saw no one in the neat backyard that included a blue-and-white-striped hammock. His heart kinked as he pictured Sarah relaxing in that hammock. But there was no time to think about what had been lost. Ryan kept his weapon ready to aim and fire and continued all the way into the backyard to make sure it was clear.

At the back of the house, he found the shattered glass and the window that had been broken.

"Tori!"

While he didn't want to destroy any evidence, his primary focus was on finding her. He approached the window carefully and glanced inside. He saw nothing. "Tori?"

There was no response. His heart rate ratcheted up. *Lord, please let her be okay.*

He ran around to the front of the house and, shoving the door open, forced his way inside. "Tori! Are you okay?"

"Here. I'm in here."

Following the voice, he rushed into the hallway and found her on the floor. His pulse thundered in his ears as he crouched next to her. "Tori, honey…"

Sweat beaded her face and blood soaked her arm. His heart pounded. "You're hurt! Someone shot you?"

"No, it's just my wound broke open."

He wanted to reach for her but was afraid to make her pain worse. "What happened?"

"First, help me get up."

He assisted her to her feet.

She bent over her thighs as if to catch her breath, then leaned against the wall, her hand pressed to her chest. "Someone was in the house. A masked man. I walked in on him. We fought, but my shoulder isn't so good, so he got the best of me."

Blood soaked her shoulder and arm now. While she talked, he grabbed towels from the bathroom, then pressed one against her shoulder. "We need to stop the bleeding."

"I made a mistake and he was too close to me when I confronted him. He was able to knock my gun away. We fought and I almost had him, but then he pulled a gun of his own. That's when I dove into the hall. He broke the window and climbed through it to the backyard."

Tori pressed the towel against her shoulder, relieving Ryan of the task.

"He didn't pursue you into the hallway?" *Thank You, God.* He couldn't bear to think of how this could have ended—and on his watch, no less.

"No. I'm not sure why he didn't just flee out the front door, but maybe he was afraid he would run into you. I'm also not sure why he didn't try to…" She trembled.

Kill her? Was that what Tori would have said had she completed her sentence?

"I'm not sure why he didn't finish the job," she said.

His insides quaked. Ryan never ever wanted to see his Tori, tough FBI agent Tori Peterson, this shaken again.

His Tori?

"Oh, honey." He took her into his arms, careful of her shoulder.

She cried into her hands against his chest, the bloodied towel pressed between them against her shoulder. Tori had always been the strongest person he knew—but she'd been through so much. These latest attacks meant she'd barely had time to grieve over the loss of her sister. But he supposed that this *was* how she'd chosen to grieve—by fighting back and trying to find Sarah's killer. Tori's job was all about law and justice, and for her sister to be murdered chafed in every way.

Sirens rang out in the distance and grew louder.

Finally...

"I called reinforcements when I heard gunfire." His chin rested on the top of her head, stirring memories of him holding her in his arms—but those times from their past couldn't be more different than the current situation.

She sniffled and stepped away. Swiped at her eyes. "I'm sorry. I don't know what came over me."

Strong Tori was back again, and strong Tori refused to show any weakness. She left him standing there and stomped into the bedroom. The guest bedroom...he knew that because he was the detective on the case, and he'd already been through the house in search of clues. Ryan trailed her.

"This is my FBI-issued gun." She pointed at the weapon lying on the floor on the other side of the room. "He knocked that out of my hands. He was wearing gloves, but maybe there could still be DNA. Certainly not prints, though."

"Jerry will look it over first to make sure."

"Okay. I want it back as soon as possible." She moved

to the window. "You already know that he broke the window getting out. While your people sweep this place for prints and evidence, I'll canvass the neighborhood."

Right. He fisted his hands on his hips. "You really can't let it go, can you?"

She scrunched her face but her gaze swept the room. "What are you talking about?"

"You are not the law around here anymore. You gave that up, remember? Your FBI credentials don't change the fact that this murder case isn't in your jurisdiction." Nor would she be allowed to work it professionally because Sarah was her sister.

"Fine. I'm going for a walk then. I need to get my head together."

Ryan grabbed her arm. "You're not going anywhere."

"Get your hands off me."

He released her slowly but stayed close. "Tori, just calm down. You're bleeding, remember?" He lifted the towel and held it out to her.

She scrunched her face and took the towel, pressing it against her shoulder again. She wasn't thinking clearly, either, or else she would suggest looking at the rest of the house. Maybe the intruder had been in Sarah's home searching for something. Was anything missing? But Ryan wouldn't bring that up just yet. Tori needed to see the doctor again, and she'd only insist on looking through the house if he brought that to her attention. Discovering if something was missing could wait. Her well-being came first.

Deputies finally entered the home. Tori appeared pale and remained shaken, so Ryan stayed near as he explained what had happened. Her official statement could be given later. Ryan escorted her out of the house.

"I need to take you back to the hospital so you can get that looked at."

"I'm supposed to replace the bandage anyway." She shrugged. "I'm fine to take care of it myself."

He'd expected her resistance and knew the best method to counter it was to redirect the conversation. "I'm considering this more than a simple break-in."

"You mean…"

He nodded. "Yes. I told you I don't believe in coincidence. My working theory—which I'm hoping the evidence will confirm—is now that Sarah was the primary target, not Mason or any of the others. For now, I'm going to investigate as if the rest of them were in the wrong place at the wrong time or killed to throw off the investigation. Satisfied?"

She offered a tenuous smile. "Yes."

Outside, he ushered her back to his SUV. "I'll take you to the ER first."

"Ryan, I was serious when I said I would be fine. My shoulder just needs a new bandage. There's nothing more the doctor can do, really. It needs time to heal."

"So let it heal and stop fighting criminals. Do we have a deal?" He tossed her a wry grin, and was rewarded with a half smile.

"If you stop insisting on taking me to the hospital."

"Fine. Then is it all right if I take you to your parents' for the night?"

She nodded.

"Once we're finished processing the bungalow and release the crime scene, you can go back to staying there, but I wouldn't advise it. Whoever broke in can try again. Next time you might not be so fortunate." He hated saying those words. Hated that Sarah had somehow made an enemy, and Tori had put herself in the line of fire to find the person responsible.

Tori said nothing more, which troubled him. Normally she would have objected or put forth her opinion, but even the strongest FBI agent could become traumatized when they had lost a loved one *and* been personally targeted. A female officer would pack a small bag of clothes for Tori's stay with her parents and deliver it. He drove the SUV from the quiet neighborhood where Sarah had lived to the Petersons' home only a mile away. After parking in the driveway, he ushered Tori to the house.

Tori knocked softly and then opened the door, peeking her head in. "Mom? Dad? It's me."

She stepped through the door, and Ryan remained on the porch, unsure if he was invited. Tori glanced at him.

"Tori?" Sheryl appeared in the foyer. "I thought you were with—" Her eyes caught on Ryan. "Well, don't just leave him standing there. Come on in, Ryan."

He looked at Tori, searching her eyes for reasons he couldn't explain. He should get back to his investigation. He couldn't read her. Did she want him to stay or…

"Are you coming or what?" she asked.

He shrugged. "I can only stay a few minutes."

Sheryl gasped when she saw Tori's arm. "See, I told you they let you out too soon! We need to take you—"

"Mom, please. I just need some fresh bandages." Tori headed down the hallway like she was a disgruntled teenager, Sheryl on her heels.

Arms crossed, Tori's father stepped from the kitchen area and watched them go. "What happened?"

Ryan was glad he'd stayed for a few minutes, after all. He wasn't entirely sure how much he was ready to share with her parents, but since it appeared that Tori truly was in danger, they needed to know what was going on for their safety and hers. He was glad for the opportunity to explain things to her father; then David could figure out the right way to tell Sheryl.

As Tori's father listened to Ryan detail the events of the day, his face paled. Ryan almost regretted telling him, but he needed all the help he could get to protect Tori.

Tori and her mother stayed in the bathroom redressing the wound and Ryan bade David goodbye. He had work to do. On their porch he took in the surroundings of the middle-class neighborhood and hoped Tori would be safe here.

But he knew that once she was able, Tori would stay at the bungalow again—tracing Sarah's steps, she'd said. Those steps could lead her right to her own death.

Ryan couldn't let anything happen to her. For her sake, for her parents' sake and for his own sake.

He was a homicide detective, but he'd give that up in a heartbeat to be her bodyguard. If she would let him.

He knew Tori would say she didn't need him.

She never needed him—not in the past, and not now.

But this time, that wouldn't stop him.

FOUR

The morning sun broke through the crack between the drapes, startling Tori awake and away from the grips of her nightmare. Heart pounding, she bolted upright and reached for her weapon—but it was gone.

Just calm down. She drew in a few long breaths. They'd taken her gun to look for fingerprints.

It took her a breath or two to remember that she was in her old bedroom in her parents' home—the home where she and Sarah had grown up. Mom hadn't changed much in the room. She'd taken down the posters of teenage idols and replaced them with Scripture-laced nature pictures. Tidied up the room a bit and, oh, replaced Tori's bed with a smaller twin bed. No wonder she hadn't slept all that well. She was accustomed to spreading out in the queen-size bed she'd purchased for her apartment back home.

Home.

And just where was home exactly? Was it here in California or was it back in South Carolina? She pushed aside the complicated musings—too much to think about at seven in the morning.

She eased back down in bed, surprised her mind had

finally let her sleep. She tried to recall the nightmare, but nothing clear came to mind and she was grateful she couldn't remember. Still, the dream had left her unsettled. Her shoulder ached, and even itched a little. That was good. That meant it was healing.

The aroma of bacon and eggs pulled her all the way out of bed. She might as well get up to face the day. She slipped into comfy sweats and a T-shirt and meandered down the hallway with a yawn, then made her way to the kitchen, where she found Dad cooking breakfast.

He glanced up from frying bacon. "Hey, sleepyhead." No matter that she was in her thirties and was an FBI agent, he still talked to her like she was his little girl. Tori wasn't sure she would have it any other way.

"Morning." She wouldn't add the word "good." Nothing about it was good. She grabbed a mug from the cabinet and poured the rich dark coffee blend they all preferred. Tori breathed it in as she shoved onto a tall seat at the counter.

Dad smiled as he moved bacon from the pan to a plate, but despite the smile, a persistent, aching sadness poured from his gaze, and that, she understood completely. Her heart ached with the pain of loss they all shared.

She took a drink of coffee, hoping her thoughts would come together. "Dad, you don't have to cook me breakfast. Or even sound cheery for my sake. We're all still shaken over what happened. It's going to take us a long time to get over…" She couldn't even say her sister's name.

He plated the eggs to go with the bacon and set the dish on the counter in front of her. "You're still alive and with us, Tori. I intend to make the best of every moment with you. You need your energy, so eat up."

Tori obliged and crunched on a bacon strip. "Where's Mom?"

"She went to the store to grab orange juice."

Tori's favorite. Mom had done that for her. Oh, man. She sighed. This was going to be a long day. While on the one hand she appreciated what her parents were doing, she knew they would smother her if she let them. Hadn't the whole reason she'd come back to stay for a while been to comfort *them*? Still, maybe they could all comfort each other. Tori knew she often wasn't willing to admit when she needed emotional support. But maybe this time she should give in to it. Their encouragement could very well sustain her through trying to find Sarah's killer.

Tori heard the sound of the front door opening, then closing, and in rushed her mother with a few plastic sacks of groceries. She set them on the counter and smiled at Tori—that same pain was raw and unfiltered behind her gaze.

"That looks like more than orange juice," Tori said.

"Well, you know how it is. You go in for one thing and leave having spent a hundred dollars more than you intended." Mom poured juice into a glass and sat it in front of Tori. "Drink up."

Tori finished the eggs and bacon and drank the juice while her father ate his breakfast quietly and Mom cleaned up the mess he'd made. Tori carried both their plates over to the sink, rinsed them and then stuck them in the dishwasher. She turned to find her mother wiping down the counter.

Still no words. No one knew what to say.

"Thanks, Mom. Thank you both, but you don't have to do this."

Mom's eyes teared up as she shrugged. "What? What are we doing? We almost lost you, too."

Dad gave Tori a warning look, as if she'd said something wrong. Truth was, anything she said would be the wrong thing.

Tori rushed around the counter and hugged her mom. "I'm sorry," she said.

Dad hugged them both. As warm and comforting as the embrace was, it was also steeped in sadness. She could drown in all this grief, and she had to somehow stay afloat.

Finally she backed away and wiped at her own eyes. "I can't... I can't find out what happened to Sarah like this. I need to focus."

Tori headed for her bedroom. A female deputy had brought a few of her belongings over to the house from Sarah's bungalow last night. Tori should shower and get dressed for the day.

"Wait, Tori, please." Mom rushed after her.

Tori hadn't meant to upset her mom. She turned to face her. "I'm here, Mom, for as long as you need."

"Please, come back to the living room and sit down. Your father and I want to talk to you."

Uh-oh. Tori followed Mom down the hallway to the comfortable living area and the sectional sofa. "I'd prefer to stand."

Dad made his way to the living room and joined them. Mom was the only one to sit.

Dad crossed his arms. "You mentioned that you were considering an indefinite leave or quitting your job so you could stay here. Now that we know your reason for staying would be to look for the killer, we want you to go home. Go back to your job. Please, Tori. We can't lose you, too, and if you stay here, you're in danger."

"What?" She hadn't realized she'd made her decision yet until this moment. "I can't go back, Dad. I can't go back to work on investigating other crimes when my mind will always be on finding Sarah's killer. Don't you want justice for her?"

"Ryan can give us that, Tori," Mom said. "You should trust him."

"I do trust him." She rubbed her arms. But apparently not as much as her parents did. What was the matter with her anyway?

Dad approached and hugged her again. He released her and gripped her shoulders to level his gaze at her. "Mom and I will come to stay out there in South Carolina with you. We'll do anything we need to do."

They were overreacting, but could she really blame them? They were terrified for her, and she hated doing this to them.

Mom tugged tissues from a box on a side table. "We considered moving even before yesterday. There are just too many memories here. I don't know if I can stand it. We could move to be close to you."

A lump grew in Tori's throat. "But you don't have to move to be close to me. I'm here. And you don't want the person who took Sarah from us to scare us away. Sarah wouldn't want you to leave one of the most beautiful and amazing places in the world because you don't want to be reminded of her." The words sounded more cruel than she'd intended.

But I moved away from the most beautiful place... And people who loved me. A man who loved me.

Mom's eyes teared up again. "Please, just consider it."

She nodded. "Okay. I promise I will." That was the least she could do.

Tori turned and hurried back to the bedroom. She fell onto the bed.

"God, what am I going to do?" *They're going to drive me up the wall.*

When all was quiet in the house, she snuck out of her room to snag another cup of coffee. Dad had made another pot and left her mug out for her, knowing her too well. She hurried back to the bedroom and set her laptop up on the desk. Working to figure this out was the only way to move past the grief.

She waited for her laptop to boot up. If she'd needed more confirmation that Sarah had been the main target, she'd just gotten it with the break-in at Sarah's home. After the attempt on her life on the river, she hadn't needed the confirmation, but she was glad Ryan now seemed convinced.

She realized now the burglar hadn't entered the home and waited for her return in order to kill her, the way the shooter on the river had. No. She'd stumbled upon a simple break-in. That left her confused about what was going on. But she feared that whoever had been searching the house might have gotten what they'd been looking for. If so, she wouldn't have that clue to know what had gotten Sarah killed.

Her laptop booted up, Tori pulled up the emails she'd received from Sarah. She never deleted an email, for which she was now grateful. She started reading as far back as she could retrieve the emails. Distance hadn't diminished Sarah's relationship with Tori, but Tori's job had prevented her from being as engaged as she should have been with her family.

Tears burned down her cheeks and she accepted they wouldn't be the last, as she continued to read, searching for that one email that could possibly give her a clue.

Her cell rang. Ryan. Her heart warmed with the thought of him—which aggravated her. She needed to stay focused on the case, not get distracted by an old flame. Still battling annoyance with herself, she answered, "What have you found?"

He snorted. "Can we back up to hello or hi or how are you?"

"Why waste time?" She leaned her forehead against her hand. "I'm sorry. Hi, Ryan. How are you?"

"That's more like it. Rough morning?"

"You could say that." She kept what had happened with her parents and their suggestion of moving to South Carolina to herself. "So, was this just a friendly call to check on me?"

She hoped not, though at the same time, she liked the idea.

"Yes and no. Now that I've checked on you, I have some news. First, your dad called me and asked me to keep the bungalow under crime-scene lockdown."

Dad! She sucked in a breath. "What?"

"He doesn't want you moving back there. I can't blame him. I advised you against it."

"So when do you think I can move back in?"

He exhaled loudly. "It's ready now. The crime scene techs worked late into the night and finished up this morning."

"I'm so glad. Did they find anything?"

"Time will tell, Tori. Please be patient. You know these things take a while."

"Right. Okay. Thanks for letting me know. And thanks for releasing the crime scene. I'm going to move back to the bungalow. I need to be in town for Mom and Dad, be accessible to them, but living with them is…hard."

"I understand."

Ryan had three siblings and they, along with his parents, lived in the Mount Shasta region. Close enough to be together for important events, eat Sunday dinner or hang out, but not too close.

"It's worse now because they're smothering me." Tori squeezed her eyes shut. She hadn't meant to reveal so much of what was going on.

"Honestly, Tori, I don't blame them." The tone in his voice made her think he would like to do the same. But she must be hearing things.

"Thanks for calling to let me know."

"Wait, don't hang up yet," he said.

"Is there something else you want to tell me?"

"Yes. I'm standing at the front door."

After ending the call, Ryan stood at the front door waiting. He didn't want to knock or ring the bell and disturb her mother and father, especially after what Tori had just told him. Plus, they would ask questions for which he had no answers. Tori might do the same. She was taking her time answering the door. Maybe she had decided she wasn't going to open it, after all.

Just as he lifted the phone to text her, the door swung open.

Tori rushed out. "Okay, let's go."

She walked right past him without a glance. Her purse slung over her shoulder and her briefcase and small duffel at her side, she hurried down the sidewalk to stand next to his vehicle, which he'd parked at the curb.

"Wait." He held back a laugh as he caught up with her and opened the door for her. She tossed in her things. "Where are we going?"

"You're taking me to Sarah's."

That was what he had in mind. Sort of. He'd wanted her to look at the house to see if anything was missing. More than that, he'd wanted to see her.

He climbed into his vehicle on the driver's side and started it. "Aren't you even going to say goodbye?"

"To my parents? I already told them you were taking me back to Sarah's. That's all right, isn't it? It was providential that you showed up when you did. Really, I appreciate the ride, Ryan."

"You're welcome." Tori's car, or rather Sarah's car that Tori had been driving while staying here, remained parked at the bungalow. "As a matter of fact, I had hoped to take you there to have you walk through and see if anything obvious was missing."

He pulled away from the curb. Sarah's bungalow was only a couple of neighborhoods over—barely a mile away. Her home was in the same neighborhood as Ryan's and was actually only a few houses down.

"Why the big rush to get out of there?" He glanced over as he drove. She must have recently showered. He could still smell the shampoo. She was beautiful as always, but she looked like she hadn't slept well last night. That was understandable. He stifled the desire to reach over and grab her hand to reassure her.

"I didn't mean to come across like I was in a hurry to leave." Tori stared out the passenger window.

He took a right at the intersection. "You could have fooled me."

She blew out a breath. "Okay, well, maybe just a little. I love Mom and Dad, but they're pressuring me to leave town. They've even offered to come with me."

"You mean visit you?"

"They talked about moving to South Carolina."

Wow. He drove slowly down the street, passing his house on the way to Sarah's. "And you're not encouraging them with their plans."

She jerked her head to him. "Of course not. They aren't thinking clearly, Ryan. Once they have gotten past the initial grieving process, they'll realize that they don't truly want to leave their home or their friends. They'll realize that they cherish the memories of Sarah here. A permanent move would be a rash decision based on emotions."

"While I agree with you that they need time to grieve before they make such big decisions, maybe they need some new scenery, at least for a little while. Something that doesn't remind them so much of Sarah until they've grieved enough." He pulled to the curb in front of Sarah's bungalow as he said the words. Great timing. Seeing the bungalow gave him a sick feeling in his gut. He could use a change of scenery, too.

Sarah had painted her home a light grayish blue to brighten it up, though the huge windows and the cozy front porch did a great job of that already. But Sarah wasn't here anymore to enjoy the work she'd put into her home. He shifted into Park and turned in the seat, facing Tori to talk more about her parents.

"Thanks." Tori opened the door. She stepped out but leaned back in to grab her briefcase, duffel and purse, and then said, "You don't have to come in with me."

He quickly got out and rushed around to walk with her. "Oh, no, you don't. You're not getting rid of me so easily. After what happened the last time, I'm going to clear the house before you go inside. Then I'll walk with you to see if anything is missing. I want to be here when you look through it all."

"That's not necessary," she said and closed the car door. "I can always give you a call later if I notice something." Tori hiked up the sidewalk lugging her things.

Ryan caught up with her and tried to relieve her of the duffel. "You'll hurt your shoulder."

Grimacing, she relinquished the bag. "Thanks. You're probably right."

"You're welcome. Oh, by the way—" he reached inside his jacket and grabbed her gun that he'd tucked in a pocket, then handed it over "—Jerry said no prints. You can have your weapon back. But I'm still going in first. Don't argue."

Ryan unlocked and opened the door. "Wait here in the foyer for me. You might try using the alarm next time. Turn it on when you leave but also while you're here in the house. If you'd armed it maybe the perp would have been deterred."

"I didn't know the code before, but Dad gave it to me this morning. But you and I both know he could disarm the alarm if he set his mind to it. You can learn how with an online tutorial."

Ryan frowned. "Then if you're going to stay here, we should get you set up with a state-of-the-art system."

"We?" she arched a brow.

Ryan didn't respond to her jab at his intrusion in the details of her life. Instead, he drew his weapon and moved through the home to make sure no one else had broken in. "Make sure to call for the window replacement today!" he called over his shoulder.

"Dad already did," she yelled from the foyer.

They were so familiar with each other. Maybe he was too close to this investigation, getting too involved with Tori, but he didn't think so. He was a professional and could compartmentalize his past relationship with her while he investigated Sarah's murder and the obviously related attacks on Tori.

After Ryan cleared the house, he found her dutifully waiting in the foyer, which surprised him.

Arms crossed, again she arched a brow—and a lovely, well-defined brow, at that. "Well? Find anyone suspicious?"

He tucked his weapon away. She would already know if he had. "Funny." He lifted her duffel, but she held her briefcase close. "Where do you want me to put this?"

"On the bed in the master bedroom. Sarah's room." Anxiety edged her words.

He moved down the hallway with Tori on his heels, glad she'd allowed him to help her if only a little. Her shoulder must be still be bothering her.

In Sarah's warmly decorated room, a pang struck his heart. He could only imagine what sleeping in her sister's room would do to Tori. When given the choice, Tori had chosen the guest bedroom to begin with. Interesting that the burglar hadn't been in Sarah's room searching but had instead been in the room where Tori was staying. He would keep that tidbit to himself for the time being.

He set the duffel on Sarah's bed, grief weighing on him. When he turned to face Tori, he caught her staring at the photographs neatly hung on the wall.

"Might as well start here," he said. "See anything missing?"

"I haven't been in her room yet. I… I was avoiding this moment, and now I'm in here looking at her stuff under completely different circumstances than I'd imagined. I thought I'd be packing up her things, not looking for anything that might be missing so we can figure out who broke in and if he's her killer."

He held back a sigh. "I know it's hard. You can do this."

She drew in a breath and stood taller, then gave him a look that said he needed to dial the reassurances and platitudes down. "I know I can do it, Ryan."

Her way of telling him she didn't need his encouragement. Or rather, she didn't want it. He wanted to argue that everyone needed encouragement, especially under circumstances like these, but he doubted Tori would be willing to listen. She prided herself too much on her ability to stand on her own two feet.

She didn't stay in Sarah's room long. He followed her through the house as she gave everything a once-over and then they ended up in the attic. Sarah had filled it with a few old boxes—memorabilia from school—but that was all.

Finally Tori finished her search in the kitchen. She shrugged. "I didn't see anything missing, but that doesn't mean it isn't."

Her staying in this house didn't sit well with him. "Look, are you sure you want to stay?"

She nodded. "If there's something to be discovered here, I'll find it by staying."

He wouldn't convince her otherwise. "Before I leave, I'll board up the broken window until you can get the glass replaced."

"Thanks, Ryan, but Dad is coming over this afternoon to do that now that you've released the scene."

"Oh, right. Okay." He squeezed the keys in his pocket—Sarah's house keys that he should give back to Tori. But he held on to them for now. "At least give your parents' suggestion a thought. Go back to your job. Years ago, you couldn't wait to get out of here. Remember? Go back and let your parents come and visit with you for a while, and then see what happens. If they move, they move. There's nothing you can do about that. But you'll all be safer there." And if she left, then she wouldn't be staying in this house. She wouldn't be here in northern California to be targeted again.

"Are you kidding me? My job there keeps me busy around the clock." She shook her head. "I wouldn't have time for them."

"Maybe it would be a good idea to be back at work so you can get your mind on other matters." And let him solve this. But he was hoping for too much.

"That's not going to happen. I can't stop thinking about finding who killed Sarah." She opened the fridge. "You want a soda or something?"

He let his gaze roam through the kitchen, dining and living area again. He knew this whole house well by now, after spending last night searching for a clue in the quaint home.

Ryan suddenly realized Tori was staring at him, Coke in hand. He took it, though he wasn't really thirsty.

"I know I can't stop you from doing your own investigation. But remember, you're not even a licensed private investigator. This isn't an FBI investigation."

"Get real."

"Exactly. I'm under no illusion that you're going to stop. I'm only going to ask you to be careful. You could ruin my investigation. Mess with evidence. Keep me from putting this person away."

She came across to plop on the sofa with her Coke. "Don't worry, you and I will be investigating on very different paths."

He fisted his hands. "Still think you're going to find this killer on your own while I'm off on a wild-goose chase?"

Opening her laptop, she popped the Coke top, and fizz nearly overflowed to her computer.

"Careful!" He quickly snatched a towel from her kitchen and tossed it her way.

"Thanks." She cleaned up the mess, drank the Coke and eyed him. "You've got it all wrong."

"My investigation is not even good enough to be on your radar, is that it?" Could he just shut up? Why did she seem to push all the wrong buttons? Or right buttons, depending on one's perspective.

"It's not a question of your skills or abilities. I just have insight into Sarah that you can't match. I'm going to walk in her steps in a way you and your team could never do. That's all."

He shoved his hands in his pockets. "Fine. Make sure you share with me when you find something."

"You've already told me that I'm not on your team."

He sighed and softened his next words. "Let's put

aside our…competition, for lack of a better word… And find Sarah's killer before he can get away."

To his surprise, Tori set her Coke on the coffee table, the other end from her laptop, and moved to stand next to him.

He could tell by the haunted look in her eyes that sadness still clung to her heart, but determination remained there, too. Good. He wouldn't expect to see anything less in her gaze. Those dark green irises could still hold him captive. Tori stood close and he caught another whiff of her coconut shampoo. Her face was clean and free of makeup. She was beautiful just like this.

"Thank you, Ryan. For being here for me. For being there for Sarah. I started reading through her emails and she mentioned how you helped a few times when her car broke down. Or she needed to borrow something. You made her feel safe."

He shrugged, grief strangling him. "Just doing my duty."

"It was more than that, and you know it. You were kind of like a big brother to her." He'd treated Sarah like a little sister when he and Tori had been together before. And he hadn't stopped just because Tori had broken his heart.

It hit him that Tori was all alone now. Where he had three siblings, she'd lost the only sibling she had.

He wasn't sure how it happened, but Tori was suddenly wrapped in his arms. It felt right and good for all the reasons it shouldn't. He knew better than to think anything lasting could come of this. Still, they'd shared a bond once, and now that bond had moved to one of deep loss. He wished he could hold her for as long as it took for the pain to leave them both. Wished he could convince her to go to the safety of South Carolina, or that she'd become willing to believe that he could solve this—that he wouldn't let her down. But that was all fantasy.

And Ryan lived in the real world.

She stepped away from his embrace and stood taller as she wiped her eyes. "I'm sorry."

"You don't have to be." Tenderness coursed through him. He wanted to pull her back in his arms. He wished they could turn back time and have another go at a life together. Maybe Sarah could still be here with them, too, if he was going to wish for impossible things.

"We both have work to do, Ryan." She opened the door and effectively dismissed him.

FIVE

He almost looked hurt. "Be sure to set the alarm."

"I will." Tori couldn't exactly slam the door in his face, so she waited for him to walk away.

He held her gaze for a moment longer, then turned and walked down the sidewalk. She watched him until he got into his vehicle and then, finally, he drove away.

Tori closed the door, locked it and dutifully set the alarm. Then she remembered the window. She headed to the room where she'd slept while here and saw that the techs had at least put plastic over the window. The frame was still in place—funny the alarm was armed but she had a gaping hole in her house, for all practical purposes.

She grabbed her cell and texted her father to ask when he would be over to board it up. She could do it herself, except her shoulder still hurt. Plus, she knew her father and he would be hurt if she didn't allow him this one small gesture of help.

Dad texted back that he was at the hardware store and would be by the house later in the day. She loved her parents so much and was glad that she could be close to them at this difficult time—just not *too* close. They each needed space to grieve in their own way. And her way of grieving was working to find Sarah's murderer. She needed to help Ryan. She settled on the sofa and set her weapon on the side table, glad to have it back.

Finally she could focus—at least until Dad got here. She concentrated on reading through Sarah's emails to her over the last several years.

It seemed like a long shot, but it was a good start. Some of them, she'd forgotten completely. She snacked on Doritos and chocolate and guzzled more sodas—almost as if she and Sarah were hanging out. Laughing and crying together.

Her cell buzzed. Mom. She texted her back that she'd be over for pot roast this evening but couldn't come over early since she was busy at the moment and also was waiting on Dad to fix the window.

Her phone buzzed again. Only this time it was a call from Ryan. She pursed her lips. She didn't trust her voice to sound steady just now. She texted him that she was all right, on the off chance he was calling to check up on her.

He wasn't much better than her parents when it came to the smothering, and that thought sent odd and yet familiar sensations through her.

I have work to do. She pushed thoughts of Ryan away to focus on the emails.

One email sent only two months ago made mention of an issue regarding land pollution. Sarah had said she was heading to Sacramento, California's capital, to protest. Tori sat up. With this email, she might be getting somewhere. Sarah had always been about social justice issues as well as environmental causes. Following this small clue could lead her nowhere, but Tori had to start somewhere. Though there were more emails to read, she could get back to those after a little digging on this.

After researching online, she finally found the name of a guy who had organized a protest in Sacramento over an agricultural pesticide used on commercial farms. The event had taken place around the same time as Sarah's email. Tori decided to go with it.

The guy's name was Dee James and he headed up an organization called A Better World.

It wouldn't hurt to call him to ask if he knew Sarah. Tori searched through online databases until she found the person she believed was the right man, though she couldn't be sure. There were a few listings under that name. She would try them all if that was what it took.

And in fact, she was able to narrow it down to three different Dee Jameses.

She left a voice mail for each of them.

If one of these numbers was his, he probably wasn't picking up because he didn't recognize her number. She gave him a few minutes to call her back or at least listen to the voice mail. If one of the men knew Sarah, maybe they would call back. Tori was counting on it. She needed to find something. She needed a win.

Someone knocked on the door. Tori grabbed her weapon and peeked through the peephole to see her father. She let him in just as her cell rang.

"I need to take this, Dad. Go ahead and work on the window." She smiled and then looked at the phone. Her heart jumped. Maybe it was him. "Hello? Dee James?"

An intake of breath. "Yes. I'm returning your call."

"Thanks. As I mentioned in my voice mail, I'm Tori Peterson. I'm Sarah's sister."

A few breaths of quiet, then he said, "I'm sorry for your loss."

Of course, he already knew about the death.

"Yes, well, thank you." Tori cleared her throat. "I was hoping you could help me."

Again, he was silent for a few heartbeats. This man was wary.

"I don't know how," he finally said.

"Can you meet me to talk? I'll buy you a cup of coffee." If she could get him in person she could read his expression. Plus, he might be willing to share information—that is, if he had any.

"I don't know anything about what happened to Sarah. I'm sorry, but you're wasting your time if you think I can help."

"But you were in an environmental group with her, right?"

"Yeah, so? She was in lots of groups with lots of people."

Ah. Now. So she was getting somewhere. He knew enough about Sarah to know that. Still, she had the feeling he wasn't going to agree to meet her. So she had to press her point and see how he reacted. "I read some information about suspicious activities such as… um…ecoterrorism. The FBI was checking into that. I… I just want to find out if Sarah was involved with the group, that's all."

"You already know she was involved in A Better World, and as I mentioned, many more groups besides."

Tori was going to lose him and soon. She was surprised he'd stayed on the line this long. Maybe he feared if he didn't satisfy her that she wouldn't go away. "Yes, well, I mean, was Sarah involved in any suspicious or violent activities? I'm not trying to build a case. I just want to know why someone would try to kill her."

Dad's hammering echoed through the house and she tried to concentrate on Dee's words. "I don't know anything about any suspicious activities. I'm sorry for what happened to Sarah, but I don't know anything to help." He ended the call.

Tori stared at the cell. Her mouth went dry. The call had the kind of tension that let her know she was on to something here. Dee James probably regretted returning her call. He'd probably thought he could brush her off and make her go away. Now he would be worried and maybe even try to flee—that is, if he had something to hide.

The unnatural tension in his voice told her that he did.

Dad emerged from the hallway. "All done."

"What? That was fast."

"The window should be restored tomorrow afternoon."

"Thanks, Dad." She smiled.

"I can see you're busy. Will your mother and I see you later?"

Tori didn't want to lose her momentum after that conversation with Dee. "I'll be at dinner. We can talk more then." She got up, moved to her father and kissed him on the cheek. "Thanks, Dad. I'll see you tonight, okay?"

"Okay." She knew him well enough to see he had more to say, but she was grateful when he kept it to himself and bade her goodbye. He let himself out. She reset the alarm and got back to work.

Thunder rumbled through the house. She made notes of her conversation and then read through more emails, carefully now. If she'd been reading too fast, she would have missed the mention of the environmental protest, though she should have known to look into that to begin with. There had to be a ton of environmental groups in the area. She would make a list of the groups and the major participants, but she was pretty sure Dee James was someone to question further and she would make sure to do that soon.

The sound of torrential rain soon followed.

Then, the power went out. Of course! After what had happened here, staying alone in the darkened bungalow was too creepy, and since she couldn't continue her internet search, Tori decided to head out.

She wrote down an address she'd found for this Dee James and then she shut down her laptop. She might as well make use of the downtime.

After grabbing a light jacket and an umbrella, she ran to the car but was drenched even though she'd used her umbrella. The issue came when she tried to close her umbrella and tuck it inside the vehicle. Tori wiped the water from her face and smoothed her hair. Maybe she should have waited until the rain stopped but that was a moot point now. She turned on the vehicle and activated the windshield wipers.

Though she probably shouldn't head out in the storm, sitting in Sarah's house without power wasn't a safe option, either. She thought of Ryan and his investigation.

See, I told you, we wouldn't even cross paths.

No way was he following this particular lead. He needed Tori on this and didn't even know it.

She thought back to the moment when he held her. Of them holding each other. They had been grieving together over Sarah, but there had been something more between them. Tender emotions that had nothing to do with Sarah's death. A knot lodged in her throat. She pushed those unbidden thoughts away.

It was much too late for them, and she couldn't think about that.

She had to think about her sister.

Sarah, what did you get yourself into?

Ryan trudged down the hallway in the Maynor County Sheriff's Office, feeling the effects of a long day in which he'd learned nothing new.

"Any news, Bradley?" Sheriff Rollins asked, calling to him from his office at the far end of the hallway. Ryan's direct boss was Captain Moran, who was in charge of the investigations division. Above Captain Moran was Chief Deputy Carmichael, who oversaw the patrol, court and investigations divisions. But the sheriff, who headed up the entire department, took a special interest in this case. The multiple homicide had drawn much attention and he wanted the case solved expeditiously. Ryan wanted a promotion, and he knew he'd better handle and solve this case or he could kiss any chance of that goodbye.

Sheriff Rollins headed toward him, change jingling in his pocket. Ryan scraped a hand down his face. He hadn't yet shared with his boss, Captain Moran, that he was leaning toward Sarah being the primary target. Sheriff Rollins still believed the Mason kid's years-old drug involvement had spurred the homicides. Ryan had spent the day trying to close up those loose ends before he could present his theory to Moran in a way that couldn't be doubted or ignored. He didn't like disclosing this to the sheriff without Moran weighing in.

After measuring his response, he opened his mouth to speak—

"Ryan?" Hope Rollins was the office receptionist and the sheriff's niece.

He turned to see Hope approaching him. "Sarah Peterson's father, David, is here. He wants to speak to you."

The sheriff's cell buzzed. He gave Ryan a harried look. "Go ahead. You can add this conversation with Mr. Peterson into your reports. We'll talk tomorrow."

Ryan hoped he hid his relief and turned to the receptionist. "I'll get him. Is the conference room available?"

"I'll check. If not, I'll find you another room."

What could the man want besides answers Ryan didn't have? He buzzed through the door into the lobby. "Mr. Peterson, come on back."

The man barely smiled. "No need for formalities with me, son. We've been through too much for that. You can call me David."

He'd prefer the formalities while at his place of employment, but he didn't want to argue. Saying nothing, Ryan offered a tenuous smile and led the man to the conference room. He gestured to a chair. "Coffee? Water?"

"Nothing for me, thanks. I would have called you, but I wanted to have this conversation in person."

"I could have stopped by the house. I don't live that far from you."

"I didn't want Sheryl to know that I talked to you. Or Tori, for that matter. She's coming over for dinner tonight, by the way." His eyes brightened with the words, if only slightly. "Please join us, if you like."

"Mr. Peterson. Um… David, please tell me what's

on your mind. Have you remembered something about Sarah that could help the investigation?"

David clasped his hands and hesitated, then finally said, "This is about Tori, not Sarah."

Ryan had figured as much. "Go on."

"Her mother and I, we don't want her to stay here. I can't lose another daughter."

Ryan measured his words. He wanted Tori to go, as well, but he had to tread carefully here and not get into the middle of a family disagreement. "I'm confused. How can I help?"

"I'm hoping as a detective you can discourage her from trying to find Sarah's killer, that's how. Isn't there something you can do to keep her out of the investigation? If she can't look into things, she has no reason to stay."

Ah. "There's nothing I can do to stop her. I've already tried to talk her out of it. She's determined to find the killer. All I can do is keep her close. Work with her as much as possible."

David crossed his arms and leaned back in the chair. "We need her to be safe. What can we do?"

"Maybe she needs *you*," Ryan said. "She needs the familiarity of her home and the people she loves."

"We've thought of that. That's why we offered to move with her. Or at least visit her where she lives in South Carolina for months, however long is necessary."

Ryan's heart went out to the man. There were no easy answers. "What you need is a therapist or a counselor. Someone who can help you all work through this time of grief. I take it you're not seeing one."

He shrugged. "Even thinking about that…it just hurts

too much. We don't want to talk about our feelings with a stranger."

Ryan refrained from scraping a hand down his face. "I'll talk to Tori, but you know she probably won't listen to me."

"Thank you. And, son, you have more influence over her than you know, despite what happened in the past. She still admires you and I believe she'll listen to you." David blew out a breath, relief apparent on his face.

As if Ryan alone could make Tori change her mind. David was about to be disappointed.

"I'll give it a try," Ryan said. "Was there anything else?"

"No. That's it." David stood. "I appreciate you taking a few minutes to listen."

Ryan was surprised David didn't ask if they had made any progress on Sarah's murder case. "Of course. I'll walk you out."

After Tori's father had gone, Ryan headed to his cubicle. He still needed to finish writing up his reports, but that would have to wait. He rubbed his eyes. He'd already tried to call Tori this afternoon and she was ignoring his calls. She'd texted him to let him know she was okay, so at least there was that.

He needed to maintain his emotional distance while still keeping his finger on the pulse of her little private investigation. The other side of the equation—he hadn't been able to stop thinking about her since she'd returned. Opening a drawer, he slammed it shut to vent his frustration with himself, earning a few looks from his fellow county employees. How had he gotten to this place in his life? He thought he had finally moved on from her but instead, he was right back to square one. It made no sense!

He exited the county offices and got in his vehicle. If she wasn't answering, he should check up on her.

The sky had been gray and rainy this afternoon and he turned the windshield wipers to the highest setting as he steered through town toward home. He would stop by the bungalow first; he hoped she was there and not out in this weather.

To his surprise, Tori steered right past him, going in the opposite direction.

Ryan made a quick U-turn in the middle of the highway as he grumbled under his breath, although he didn't know why he bothered to keep his voice low. He was alone in his vehicle as he followed Tori.

She would be furious when she found out he'd tailed her. *If* she found out.

Following her hadn't been his intention, but she'd ignored his call, choosing to text him a short message instead. And her father had paid him a visit.

Still, the investigation into the multiple homicides needed to be his top priority, not Tori herself. But after the two attempts on her life, he remained concerned about her safety. And she was tangled up in this investigation whether he liked it or not.

The rain wasn't helping matters. His windshield wipers couldn't keep up with the torrent.

Tori drove out of town and just kept driving along the freeway. What business could she have out here? Tension built up in his shoulders as he followed Tori for a good forty-five minutes, and she never noticed him on her tail—he could thank the weather for that.

In Shady Creek, Tori parked her vehicle at the curb

near a cluster of apartments. Across the street was a laundromat, an insurance office and a coffee shop advertising free internet. The downpour continued as if the storm had traveled with them to the next town. The rain had probably ceased in Rainey—he laughed out loud at that. But in Shady Creek, the storm kept up.

Shady Creek was in Maynor County, so it was still part of his jurisdiction, but if she'd gone as far as Shasta County he would have continued to follow her as part of this investigation.

She'd learned something. He knew it. But what?

The thought soured in his stomach. He thought they had an understanding and had agreed that she would share whatever she learned so that he could more quickly find the murderer. He parked across the street from where she'd parked and noticed she had remained in her vehicle so far. He was down a ways, too, and needed to think through his next steps. Should he follow her from a distance or should he make his presence known? If he did reveal himself, would she be forthcoming with what she'd discovered?

Though it was still raining, Tori got out of her vehicle, wearing a hooded jacket. She started down the sidewalk of the quiet two-way street.

Ryan tugged his wind jacket on and pulled the hood up. Looked like he was getting out in the rain, too. Hoodie covering his head, he tried to follow her. He decided that once he knew her destination, he'd make his presence known. Unfortunately, he wasn't certain she would give up what she knew, even though he was the detective on the case.

Unease crept up his spine and his senses kicked into high gear.

Something wasn't right. Call it instinct or a gut feeling, but he'd learned to never ignore it.

Tugging her jacket tighter, Tori glanced over her shoulder at the slow traffic as if to rush across the street. She started across and Ryan made to cut her off, done with trailing her.

An engine revved behind them as a vehicle rushed forward, heading directly for Tori.

"Look out!"

SIX

The grille of the blue crossover filled Ryan's peripheral vision as he propelled himself forward. Tori twisted around as he grabbed her. Gripping her arms, he dove with her out of the vehicle's path. Together they slammed against the sidewalk, though Ryan rolled to absorb the bulk of the impact. Pain stabbed through him, but he ignored it.

Protecting her, he held her on top, his back against the asphalt. Tires squealed as the vehicle sped away. Gasping, he tried to jerk his gaze around to catch the license plate, but he couldn't see it as it turned the corner. Still, he had the make and model. He would radio the information in for law enforcement to be on the lookout.

Would the vehicle come back? Had the near collision been intentional or had he overreacted? He didn't think he had.

As if it hadn't been pouring hard enough, the ground began to crackle with drops. The rain wouldn't give them a break.

"Ryan!" Tori's voice startled him.

He'd been focused on the vehicle and only now realized she'd been calling his name. She stared down at him. "You can let me go now."

What? Oh, he still gripped her tightly to him. "Are you all right? Are you hurt?"

"No, I'm not all right." Her dark green eyes pierced him. Her frown deepened. "What are you doing here?"

"Saving you, apparently." He opened his hands, releasing her.

She got to her feet, then offered her hand to assist him up. Her grip was slick with rain and his hand slipped free, but he got to his feet anyway.

"I'm good." Was he? His back might never be the same, and for sure he'd have a few bruises. But rushing Tori out of the way had been worth it. No doubt there.

He glanced around them. Was someone else watching and waiting? The rain kept everyone inside, and if someone had witnessed what happened, no one had stopped to help them.

"I don't understand. Why are you here?" Water droplets beaded on her weather-resistant hoodie.

"Let's get out of the rain and go somewhere safe and dry," he said. "Maybe you can tell me where you were going."

Hands on her hips, she angled her head. "And you can tell me why you were following me."

"You know, it's kind of hard to have a meaningful conversation in this downpour." He offered a grin to defuse the tension.

"Come on." She took his hand, and they rushed over to the café across the street.

Tori stepped through the glass door first and a jingle announced their presence. The small internet café was empty except for an employee—the barista—arranging mugs. The space felt warm and welcoming, and the aroma of fresh coffee filled the air.

The barista glanced up and waved them over. "What'll it be? And it's on the house."

"Really?" Ryan angled his head.

"Sure. You two look like you could use a free cup of joe today."

Tori chuckled.

Ryan's shoes squeaked as he made his way to the counter. He glanced at the menu, his mind on anything but coffee. "A regular coffee for me."

"Cappuccino macchiato for me." Shivering, Tori hugged herself.

"Give me a minute to make a call." Ryan tugged out his cell, grateful it had remained dry, and moved to stand by the glass storefront.

He stared at the gray sky's relentless payload while he made his call. Would he see the vehicle again? Was someone following Tori—someone *else*? He contacted dispatch and reported the type of vehicle that had tried to run her down. He didn't think he'd mistaken the vehicle's intent. Still, without a license plate there wasn't much more to go on. Deputies could be on the lookout in the area and they would go from there.

When he ended the call, he turned his attention back to the café and spotted Tori in a booth against the wall, a fusion of bar towels wrapped around her. She'd taken off the jacket, which hadn't exactly been waterproof enough for this deluge. The blue T-shirt she wore was soaked. He approached and smiled down.

"The guy was really nice." She gripped the mug with both hands to warm herself. "He brought me this towel and is bringing some more. Said business had been slow today."

"I'd think more people would be here getting coffee in this weather," he said.

She shrugged and sipped on her cappuccino. He slid into the booth, next to her, forcing her to scoot over, then reached over to grab his plain coffee placed across the booth.

"What are you doing?" She scooted closer to the wall. "You're supposed to sit across from me."

His preference, too. "I can't see the door from that side. Would you like to sit over there instead?"

"No. Then *my* back would be to the door."

"Then I guess you're stuck with me sitting here."

Weren't they a cute law enforcement pair? Except they weren't a couple at all. Still, sitting next to her like this, he could almost pretend they were. But he would steer clear from thoughts like that.

"Actually, now that you're here, I could use your warmth. You can stay." She smiled. "For now."

"Funny. You do realize that I'm blocking your escape. You have to go through me to get out."

She arched a brow. "Is that a challenge?"

He chuckled. *What am I doing sitting here with Tori and laughing?* "No."

There was a killer out there. At least one. Maybe more than one. He took a swig of the hot coffee and focused on the situation.

Ryan stared out the window, watching for any other anomalies. Anyone else who might want to hurt Tori. He let the anger of the situation sober him. He needed something to create resistance to the warmth he could feel coming off her.

Tori positioned herself at an angle against the wall so she was half facing him, half facing the table. He felt her green eyes on him but continued to watch out the window. He almost wanted the driver to come back so he could detain him. Or her. He honestly didn't know if it had been a female or a male.

Then again, maybe they shouldn't stay long enough for whoever it was to come back. It might be better if he ushered Tori home. She didn't seem to realize that someone had just tried to kill her. Again.

Or maybe she didn't want to accept it.

"What happened back there?" she asked.

He turned to look at her. The wet ends of her hair were finally drying.

"Why were you following me?" Tori stared at him over the rim of her mug.

"I wasn't *exactly* following you."

"Oh, yeah, what would you call it? You showed up here. How did you get here if you didn't follow me?"

"You didn't answer my call, for one."

"No, but I texted you that I was okay."

"After what happened, I wanted to make sure that was true. For all I knew, someone else could have stolen your phone and sent that message. I headed home and thought I'd stop in to make sure you were all right, plus find out if you learned anything today. You sped right past me. So yeah, maybe I turned around to see where you were going." He'd leave her father out of it for the moment. She had enough issues going with her parents.

"And followed me."

Ignoring her indignation, Ryan watched the slow traffic through the big plate glass window. Time to re-direct her. "Why don't we focus on the more serious issue? You haven't said one thing to me or asked me about why I pushed you out of the way. Did you realize that someone tried to run you over?"

He turned to see her reaction. Her face paled and she shifted her position. She was entirely too close.

"I thought... I thought I had somehow stepped out in front of a car. I didn't realize... Are you sure?"

"Yes. It caught me off guard, too, but I was approaching you to make my presence known when I heard the engine rev and the vehicle pulled from the curb and headed straight for you. I yelled for you to look out."

"I turned to see who was yelling."

"I didn't have time to explain. I only had time to shove you out of the way. Didn't you hear the vehicle speeding up?"

She stared into her cappuccino macchiato. He knew that admitting that she hadn't been aware of someone following or targeting her would be hard for her. She hadn't even known that Ryan was following her. He suspected Sarah's death was clouding her mind and impacting her usual perceptiveness. More now that she realized Sarah had been the intended target. The grief and stress were pressing in on her. That was why a bereavement leave was given. But instead of using this time to cope with her loss and work through her feelings, Tori refused to give herself time to process Sarah's murder. He wouldn't press her on what she'd missed today, but there was something else he would press her on.

"So, what's here? Why did you come to Shady Creek? I have a feeling you're following a lead."

She had hoped he wouldn't go there. "Back up. I'm still reeling over the fact you claimed someone tried to run me over."

Tori squeezed the bridge of her nose and took a breath. What was the matter with her? If what Ryan said was true and someone had tried to run her down, then this latest attack meant that two people had been following her and she'd missed that. Or one person had followed her and one had waited for her here. Either way, she was getting careless. Her hand shook as she tried to lift the now tepid drink to her lips.

Ryan still waited for an answer to his question and Tori wasn't ready to give him one. She eyed him over the rim of her cup. She wished she had opted for sitting across from him now. He was much too close.

She tried to shake off the effect his nearness was having on her. How had she found herself so close to him twice in one day? She shivered again, the still-damp clothes fighting against her attempts to get warm. She almost wished she could lean into Ryan and soak up some of his body heat, but she was drawn to him for other reasons, too. Reasons she wouldn't indulge.

But he was waiting on an answer. "Clearly, I didn't make it to the place where I could learn something, as you put it."

"Come on, Tori. You know we'll get to the bottom of this faster if we work together."

"As soon as I know anything solid, I'll share it." She angled her head to look at him. She knew a little but it was mostly a feeling she was going on here. "I don't have any facts worth your time."

He worked his strong jaw back and forth. His slicked-back hair was now mussed, even though he'd tried to shove it back into place. His blue-green eyes held both appreciation and…something more. Affection. Getting a glimpse of that sent longing coursing through her.

And she absolutely couldn't act on any part of that. She couldn't afford to miss what she once had with this man, or think about how much she wished she hadn't had to make a choice between him and a career she'd wanted.

The barista—Tom—approached the table, interrupting her thoughts. "Some more towels if you like. They're just small dish towels, but they're dry."

"Thank you, Tom," Tori said. She didn't want to reach over Ryan to take them. "That's very kind of you."

He set them on the table, smiled and left. She wished he would bring her another cappuccino macchiato.

As if he weren't close enough, Ryan leaned closer to Tori after Tom left. "I think he's a great guy, but he's also looking for a big tip since there are so few customers today."

Tori smiled. "I think he deserves one."

Ryan smiled back and held her gaze for a few breaths. "Me, too."

"Maybe we should leave that tip and get out of here." Tori needed to escape her proximity to Ryan.

"I had hoped that whoever tried to run you over might come back." They had either followed her and had parked when she parked, or had been lying in wait for her.

"Oh, really." She feigned outrage.

"Yes. We could get a license plate. A face. Something to find out who is behind this." He guzzled the rest of his coffee and set the empty cup on the table.

"But now you want to leave?" She did, too, but if she could keep him talking about something else, she might be able to prevent him from pursuing information about why she'd come to Shady Creek. She didn't want to share too much. At least, not yet. If she got Ryan involved too early then she'd stand no chance of getting more information out of Dee James. James knew something.

"Yes. The towels aren't doing enough to warm you up."

"And how do you know that?"

"Your lips are still kind of blue." His gaze lingered on her lips.

Tori's heart skipped erratically. She needed to escape from where he'd purposefully pinned her so he could protect her. While he'd been serious about not sitting with his back to the door, she was sure protecting her was the real reason he'd sat beside her. She knew that much about Ryan.

The thought stirred her heart and made her miss him and what she'd left behind all the more.

"Okay, then, let's get out of here." After all, if she couldn't lean against him to get warmer, she needed to get home so she could get out of the wet clothes. Her jeans hadn't dried at all and the cold and wet chilled her to the core.

She'd have to come back to talk to Dee James another time. Ryan and Tori both pulled bills out and left them on the table for a more than adequate tip, and thanked the barista.

At the glass doors, Ryan tugged her aside. "Be careful. I'll walk you to your car and stay with you until you get in. Then I'll follow you home."

She gave him a wry grin. "I wouldn't expect any less of you." She still wasn't entirely sure how she felt about the way that he'd been following her at all, not counting the fact that she'd missed her tail completely to begin with.

The rain had slowed while they were in the café but

now it came down in sheets again. "Really? It's like it was just waiting for us to finish our coffee. Can we run?"

He frowned and subtly shook his head. "I've got a bad feeling that I can't explain. I got that right before the vehicle went for you. Let's take mine instead. I'll send deputies to bring yours back."

"What? No, that's not going to work for me." Tori reached into her bag to dig for her keys.

When she glanced up, Ryan's eyes had widened.

Tori turned in time to see the grille of a vehicle heading right toward them!

As if in slow motion, she and Ryan gripped hands and ran toward the back of the building. He yelled at Tom. "Get away. Move out of the way!"

Tom looked up, startled, and then his expression filled with horror. He dropped the glass mugs he was holding and then ran to the door that led to the kitchen. He opened the door and waved them in. "In here! Come in here!"

The vehicle crashed through the plate glass window and it shattered behind them as the engine revved and the ceiling crumbled. Tori and Ryan ducked as they ran forward and propelled themselves through the door that Tom held open for them.

Tori feared their efforts to escape wouldn't be enough as the three of them kept running, continuing to the back of the kitchen. Tom held another door wide for them that opened up to the alley behind the strip of buildings. Still running, they rushed outside and into the rain.

Ryan got on his cell and called emergency services and then the local police, as well as the sheriff's department, to let them know his version of what happened, all while he peered at her. Done with his business, he tucked his cell away.

"I need to check on the driver," he said. "But I also need to keep you safe."

"I'm going with you to see who was driving," she said.

Ryan scowled.

To Tom, he said, "Sorry we brought trouble to your workplace, Tom. Please hang around so we can take your statement."

"Cool, man. I'm sorry this happened, too."

"Please don't go back inside the building."

"I can just wait in my car. It's over there." He pointed to a small gray sedan parked in the alley.

"Okay. Someone will come for you to take your statement, if you want to wait there."

Ryan started jogging around the building.

She followed him around to the front to get a better look at the damage.

"It's not stable," he said. "I don't want you anywhere near that building."

She peered inside without going in. "I don't see anyone in the car."

"He or she could be unconscious, but I think you're right. The door is open. Looks like the perp fled."

"Was this the car you said tried to run me over?"

Frowning, he nodded.

"Ryan?" Tori sniffed. "I smell gas. Do you think the crash severed a gas line?"

He tugged her across the street as a concussive force slammed into them and drove them forward.

SEVEN

Ryan weighed her down. Once again he'd protected her. She was grateful, but she also couldn't breathe. She pushed against him and squirmed.

"Ryan, I'm okay." She croaked out. "Can you let me up now? We have to quit doing this."

"Funny. And no, I don't ever want to let you up again."

"Stop joking. This isn't the time. I… I can't breathe."

He crawled from her, stood and assisted her up as he looked her up and down. "Are you okay? Did the blast hurt you?"

She sucked in a few gasps for breath. "No, I don't think so. You knocked the air from me, that's all." Or the blast had done that, but if that was the case, she would have some organ damage, too, except she felt okay. It wasn't the blast but Ryan's protective nature that had caused the minor issue.

Concern and regret filled his features. "I didn't hurt you, did I?"

Despite the dire circumstances, Tori offered him a soft smile. "I'll probably be sporting a few bruises tomorrow—" she glanced across the street "—but those are nothing compared to what Tom's café will look like after the fire is done with it." Flames shot through the front and licked the roof. The insurance office next to the café didn't have any noticeable damage yet, but the structures could be unstable. Still, they were far enough away that they could be all right.

Ryan's cell rang and he answered, but he kept a grip on her arm.

A crowd started to gather, probably including the insurance staff, those in the laundromat and people who lived in the apartment complex. Was Dee James among them? Early on, she'd searched for his picture and found him—a redheaded guy in his late twenties. But she didn't see him among those watching the explosion.

Of course the rain had stopped right when it could have been useful dousing the fire. She shook her head, unable to understand the weather or the events that led up to this moment.

Sorrow and anger gutted her. Could the café be in flames because she and Ryan had chosen to drink a cup of coffee in there? She covered her mouth to hold back sobs. Reminded herself she was an FBI agent and needed to act the part. And as an agent on leave, here unofficially, she wanted to help. But how?

The best help she could offer at the moment was to get out of here. Ryan needed to focus on this situation and not hover around her to protect her.

When he ended the call, she said, "Ryan, you need to do your job and I need to leave. I'm just going to go home."

Instead of letting her go, he gripped both of her arms and turned her to face him. Tori wanted to shrug free, but the pure terror in his eyes kept her frozen.

"You need to take this threat on your life more seriously. Sure, you're trained and know how to protect yourself, but have you ever had someone actively trying to kill you? Someone who is relentless in seeking you out?"

Her mouth suddenly went dry. "No. You're right. This is...this is different."

"You probably need to tell your superiors about these attacks, if they don't already know." He rubbed a hand down his face. "In the meantime, you're not taking your car home today. You're riding with me. I'll take you home. We already decided that, remember?"

"That was before the explosion. You're needed here now."

Ryan ignored her comment and took her hand, kept her closer than she would have liked as they hurried down the sidewalk. He led her over to his vehicle. Opened the door for her and waited as she climbed in. Fire trucks and other emergency vehicles had arrived and were blocking the street.

"What about Tom? Don't you need to go get his statement?" she asked.

Before he could reply, a fireman headed for Ryan, who'd repositioned his badge to hang around his neck so it was visible. Ryan met the fireman halfway, standing only a few yards from her. Ryan spoke with the fireman in the street, explaining what had happened, as police officially blocked it off. Then he instructed another county deputy, mentioning Tom the barista—Tori heard that much—who would still be waiting in his sedan in the back alleyway. Two firemen rushed around the alley toward the back of the building, she presumed in search of Tom.

Though Ryan had just been through a traumatic experience or two, he was still the man in charge today and appeared confident and experienced.

And Tori was reminded more strongly than ever of what she'd lost when she'd left Ryan behind. A lump grew large in her throat. She could hardly swallow.

Ryan suddenly jerked his attention to her, his eyes both searching and piercing, then he jogged around his vehicle to the driver's side. A month ago, Tori would have wanted to be the one in charge. She would never have allowed him to herd her into this vehicle. She would have been very much hands-on in processing this crime scene. But today she'd acquiesced to his demands and was even glad for his overprotective concern.

If he hadn't been there earlier today, she could have been mowed over before she'd even realized she was in danger. She would be in the hospital with injuries. Either that or she'd be in the morgue. Maybe she'd lost her edge.

When Ryan climbed in, she said, "Thank you."

"You're welcome."

She expected him to comment that he was only doing his job. Instead, he started the vehicle and steered out of the cordoned-off block.

"Hey, there's Tom, talking to a deputy. He must be giving his statement." She sighed. "I feel so bad. The café was destroyed because we decided to go there to get warm. Tom was so good to us, and now he's out of a job. We should check in on him later."

"I agree," he said. "We should definitely do that."

He steered onto the main road leading out of Shady Creek and back to Rainey.

Tori suddenly realized she'd used the word "we,"

and in his reply, Ryan had, as well. Uncertain what that meant, if anything, she turned her attention to watching for anyone suspicious.

"If the place hadn't exploded we could have checked for video footage. I noticed they had a security camera. That could have given us an image of the driver. But we do have the plates now."

"That we do, but I suspect since the driver was so willing to crash it into the café where there would be no retrieving it, they weren't concerned about the license plate tracking back to them."

"You're saying the vehicle was probably stolen."

"Yes."

Both of them caught up in their own thoughts, they drove in silence the rest of the way back to Rainey, where, thankfully, the rain had also stopped, and the sky was clearing.

Who besides Detective Ryan Bradley had followed her all the way out of town to Shady Creek? Or had they been waiting there for her? The thought gave her the creeps. Maybe she'd been capable of taking care of and protecting herself before, but she was having some serious doubts about her abilities now, in a way that left her feeling vulnerable. She wrapped her arms around herself and wished she had a blanket, even in the warm cab. The weather added to her dreary mood. What happened to the beautiful summer days of northern California? The weather seemed unusual.

She feared that someone might have figured out where she'd been heading and why. Her call to Dee James could have been the catalyst to today's events. She would keep that to herself for now. She didn't want Ryan looking into him and scaring off her only lead.

Still, did Dee James have anything to do with what happened to her today? Had he sent someone to follow her? Or had it been him?

She sat up taller. "You didn't even get a glimpse of the driver?"

"No, why?"

Too bad. If Ryan had said anything about red hair that would have told her something.

"Just wondering."

When Ryan turned onto the street and then parked in front of Sarah's house, Tori realized she'd been so caught up in her thoughts that she'd barely noticed the ride going by.

A deputy waited in a vehicle at the curb. She got out of Ryan's and headed for the house, though she fully expected Ryan would want to clear the house first. She would wait at the door for him. Honestly, she wanted a hot shower and to relax for a few minutes before she had to head over to Mom and Dad's for dinner.

"Tori," Ryan called. He stood next to the vehicle and spoke with the deputy inside.

Tori trudged over.

"Deputy Jackson needs the keys to your car. He'll get it back to you tonight."

Tori nodded and dug through her purse. As her fingers grabbed onto the large key ring that used to belong to Sarah, a pang shot through her heart.

Ryan walked her to the door. "I'm not so sure you should be driving Sarah's car around since we know she was targeted."

"I don't think it matters what car I'm driving. Are you sure you want to use the extra manpower just to bring mine back?" Finding the house key, she thrust it in to unlock the door.

He pressed his hand over hers on the knob. She gazed up at his taller form. She'd once had a thing for him. Might *still* have a thing for him because his nearness seemed to suck the air from her.

"I'll use all the manpower available to me to protect you, Tori."

And she believed him. That thrilled her, when it shouldn't. Warmed her to her toes, despite her cold, damp clothes.

"Now, I'm going in first," he said.

He pulled his weapon as they entered. She disengaged the alarm to allow them entry, then armed it again for protection while they were inside. Like always, Tori waited in the foyer, her own weapon out while he cleared the bungalow again.

Mom texted her.

Dinner ready within hour.

If Mom only knew what Tori had just been through. She would have to keep that from her or else Tori would never hear the end of it.

Ryan returned. "It's all clear, but—" he hesitated "—are you going to be all right? It's been a harrowing day."

She shrugged. "Mom texted that dinner will be ready in an hour. I should be good until then."

His lips flattened into a straight line as if he didn't believe her.

Tori didn't want him to leave yet. Was it only the dangerous situation getting to her? Or was it something more?

"Until then, I'll build you a fire. It'll take the chill off."

She could build her own fire, thank you very much, but if it would keep Ryan here, that was fine by her.

"Still worried about me?" Now why had she asked that? It sounded entirely too much like flirting.

From the way he looked at her, it seemed he'd noticed that, too. A half smile lifted one cheek. "As a detective on this case, yes, I'm worried about you."

His words might have hurt her, if she'd bought into them. With the emotion behind his gaze, she didn't believe his concern was a simple matter of a detective doing his job.

"Okay. I'll just change into clean clothes and then... and then... I'll make us some coffee while you make a fire." That sounded way too romantic, and yet she was walking into this with her eyes wide open.

What are you doing, Tori Peterson?

A few minutes later, as she settled on the sofa with a nice warm fire in front of her and hot coffee in her hand, Tori felt so relaxed that she could fall asleep. She was warm, and with Ryan sitting at the far end of the sofa, she knew she was safe. When was the last time she'd actually felt safe like this? When was the last time she'd allowed herself the *need* to feel safe? It was foolish for her to be here with him now like this, but she needed this.

"You should know that I've been invited to dinner with you and your parents tonight, too." His voice was husky.

The news surprised her. "Oh? Are you going to come?"

"Don't worry," he chuckled. "I have reports to write."

"You sound like you think I wouldn't want you

there." Tori sank deeper into the sofa. She was actually considering not showing up, either, but then again,
that would hurt Mom and part of the reason she'd stayed
in Rainey was for her parents.

"Are you saying that you would?"

She could feel his eyes on her as she stared into the
fire he'd made.

Would she? What exactly was she thinking? She
edged forward on the sofa and rested her elbows on
her knees. "Ryan, believe it or not, I do have regrets
about..." *us* "...regrets about everything."

When he didn't respond, she risked a glance at him.

He stared into the fire as if he was afraid to hear what
else she might say. The flames flickered softly and the
ambience was more than romantic. She should get up.
Move around. Ask him to leave. Something.

So she did. Tori moved to stand closer to the fire and
rubbed her arms. Maybe she should explain her comment about regrets. "Sarah's death has given me a different perspective on life."

As it well should.

A few seconds ticked by, then Ryan's voice was gentle. "Don't tell me you regret taking the FBI job."

She heard no antagonism or resentment in his tone,
which invited her to share her deepest thoughts. "The
work has been fulfilling. But now I see that my family
should have mattered more to me."

Tears freely leaked from the corners of her eyes.

That you *should have mattered more.*

Suddenly Ryan was there, next to her by the fire. He
gently wiped one tear away before turning her to face
him. "Your family knows how much you love them,

Tori. They're so proud of you. Sarah…she was proud of you."

Why did he have to be so kind and sensitive?

He cupped her jaw and brushed away the tears. Though her mind screamed warning signals, she felt equally compelled to stay right where she was. She ached for his touch, his gentleness. Her heart was like parched, cracked ground and Ryan was a pitcher of cool water.

His lips pressed against hers. She expected a quick kiss of reassurance, but he lingered. Her hands slid over his shoulders and around his neck, pulling him closer. Heart pounding, she soaked in this man. Everything about Ryan that she'd thought she loved at one time.

Oh, how she'd missed him.

He was the one to ease away first, but then he pressed his forehead against hers. She kept her eyes closed while she steadied her heart and held back more tears. Stupid, uncontrollable emotions.

She hated being so vulnerable.

When he released her and stepped away, she opened her eyes. His tortured expression spoke volumes. He was as confused by their kiss as she was.

"I'm so sorry, Ryan," she said. "Kissing you doesn't help. We're trying to work together on this, unofficially, and I don't want to make things more complicated." She should stop talking if all she was going to do was fumble around.

Ryan scraped both hands through his hair, his frustration evident.

Oh. Now she'd hurt him. That hadn't been her intention. Would she ever be anything to him but a huge pain? Surely he didn't want a second chance with her.

"Look, Ryan, not that you're asking me, but I don't deserve a second chance with you." Especially since she wasn't sure that she wanted one.

Far more than the words themselves, Ryan was stung by the tone in her voice, and the complete lack of warmth in her eyes. This was her way of trying to brush him off. He blamed himself for getting in this situation in the first place. He could have put another deputy on the house while Jackson got her car. Ryan didn't have to personally sit in the house with her on the comfy sofa with a fire. And he definitely should never have kissed her—a woman whose sister's murder he was in charge of investigating. He should have never kissed her—the woman who almost destroyed him four years ago.

And he should walk out now, but he couldn't leave without addressing her comment. "Don't worry. I learned my lesson long ago." He grinned, hoping to dial down the tension. If he let it get the best of him, this wouldn't end well.

But he wouldn't let her hurt him again. He would never trust her with his heart. He'd known better than to get his hopes up, which was how he knew he was going to be okay, despite her rejection today.

Regardless, he had to rein this conversation in before it became a full-blown argument. He needed to keep this civil because of what he was about to tell her. So far, he'd kept his distance from her personal investigation into Sarah's murder, but now he needed to shut her down.

First things first. "Your father came by the county offices to see me today."

That brought her chin up. "What did he want?"

"He wants what I want for you. Your safety. That's only going to happen if you stay out of this."

"You told me earlier you knew you couldn't stop me," she said. "And you can't."

"Yeah, well, there was another attempt on your life today, remember? That's two in one day. Someone tried to run you over and when that didn't work, they plowed right into the café! So that changes everything. I can't imagine what Sarah was into that someone is so determined to hide, but so far they've killed four people and now they're going after an FBI agent. This isn't an investigation you can handle as a private citizen. It's just too dangerous."

"They might not know that I'm FBI, Ryan. You give them too much credit when it seems they are becoming careless, which is good for us. We can get the killer sooner."

He took a step closer and tried to skewer her with his eyes. "I'm telling you right now, do not think about continuing to look into her death. Step back from it and hand over everything you've learned so far."

She stepped closer as well and stood taller, unwilling to back down. "Maybe I can never get her back, but I can find her killer. Please don't try to stop me."

"You're exasperating, you know that? Let me do it, Tori. This is my job, not yours."

"Who's stopping you from doing your job? Not me." She thrust her hands on her hips, as if to dare him to stand in her way.

"You've always doubted me. Doubted my abilities. You think you're more qualified to find her killer than I am." His gut twisted as he laid his insecurities out there for her to tromp on.

She raised her arms into the air and moved away to pace behind the sofa. "It has nothing to do with that, Ryan. Nothing at all. I explained this to you. Why do we keep coming back to this?"

"You're right. It does feel like the same old argument." Like the one they'd had when she left him to move and take a new job. He'd thought he'd gotten over that. But it was painfully obvious to them both that that wound remained and still festered.

Why hadn't he gotten over that hurt? Gotten over her? He must somehow shove aside those forbidden feelings to stay focused on this investigation.

He crossed his arms. "If you're going to do this then I insist you share information with me or I'm going to slap you with obstruction charges."

She narrowed her eyes. "You wouldn't."

"Try me." Ryan set his jaw.

Releasing a slow breath, she said, "I haven't learned anything that could be useful to you, Ryan."

"You were in Shady Creek to follow a lead. That much is obvious. Someone tried to kill you while you were there—to prevent you from finding out more? Don't lie to me."

Her throat moved up and down with her swallow. "Okay. Okay. It's a slim lead, at best. I found out that Sarah participated in an environmental protest in Sacramento with a group called A Better World. Did you know about any of that?" she asked.

"No. My investigation hasn't gotten into the victims' hobbies or personal causes yet. We've been confirming alibis of all those nearest to the four. Talked to families, significant others, people at their places of employment. I questioned those who worked with Sarah at GenDynamics." Before the attacks on Tori, he was looking into all possibilities for the four victims but looking more closely at Mason's life.

"Her part-time work as an accountant didn't matter to her nearly as much as her volunteering. Sarah was always into social justice and protecting the environment."

"What was the protest about?" Ryan tugged out his pad and pencil.

She arched a brow as if surprised that he was taking this lead seriously, but this could all be important. She obviously thought so, and he wanted to know everything.

"Pollution. I don't know all the details. I think this protest had to do with pesticides used on commercial farms. I haven't spent a lot of time on that. Not yet."

No. She had to go to Shady Creek because she'd found something else. "What triggered you to look into that?"

She scrunched her face. "I've been reading all her emails to me. I never delete emails, so I started as far back as I could find, searching for any hint of activity that might seem suspicious or indicate danger. She doesn't always tell me everything, of course, especially these last few years. I'd been—" she shoved back tears "—My job kept me fully occupied."

Groaning, she rolled her head back and stared at the ceiling and swiped at the tears, clearly frustrated with her emotional state.

His heart kinked. He'd never seen her like this, but then she'd never endured such a tragic loss.

"She mentioned marching in a protest with the environmental group. So I contacted the guy who ran the group. It was clear he knew Sarah, but he didn't offer me answers. Just said he couldn't help me. The conversation had a nuance to it that told me he knew something."

"So you drove out to see him today?"

She nodded. "I had hoped to meet with him, but he'd refused. I figured if I found him and saw him face-to-face, he might be more willing to give me information."

"And what is this guy's name?"

"Dee James."

"Tell me the conversation exactly." Ryan waited with pen ready.

Tori shared as much as she recalled. On the one hand, the guy could be telling the truth about not knowing anything, but Ryan agreed with Tori. There was the hint of something more and it was worth questioning him.

Going there alone to do that had been a dangerous move on her part, but he pushed down his fury at the situation. Beating her up now wouldn't serve any purpose. Still, Ryan couldn't help the admiration that swelled inside at her ability to find a promising lead while he'd only hit dead ends. He simply didn't have enough investigators to dig so deeply. It would take time.

"Good work, Tori."

She hung her head. "Look. I know you don't have the manpower to do this kind of searching. Nor do you have access to communications from Sarah like I do, so please, let me help. I'm sorry… I'm sorry about—"

The kiss.

"It's not your fault, and I'm sorry, too. Let's just forget it ever happened and move on." He was the one to approach her and kiss her, after all. He wouldn't let her carry the blame.

Arms crossed, she shrugged, her right cheek rubbing against her shoulder. The familiar action brought back a flood of memories. "Listen, are you coming to dinner then?" she asked.

"I think I will." It would mean he'd know when she was coming back to the bungalow afterward—that way, he could clear her home again before she settled in for the evening. He would also make sure someone watched her home at all times. "If that's all right with you."

He half expected a frown, but she offered a tenuous grin. "Only if you promise not to say a word to my parents about what happened today. All they need to know is to remain cautious for their own safety because Sarah was a target, which they already know."

"You drive a hard bargain." They might see something on the news channels, but that was in Shady Creek so who knew if it would make the evening news.

Her parents were likely to ask a million questions about the investigation. Maybe eating with them was a bad idea. "Let's make sure to let them know we don't want to talk about the investigation and that it's just a pleasant meal between friends."

Except if they connected just as friends, without the investigation as a distraction, that would mean dredging up the past and too many memories.

EIGHT

Roast beef, potatoes and carrots had been served and eaten. Oh, and homemade rolls, too. Tori's mother had outdone herself, but Tori thought the dinner would never end. She had made it clear that she and Ryan didn't want to discuss the murder investigation.

Besides, she didn't want to scare them or make them worry more than they already were.

So they'd talked about Sarah. Rehashed old but good memories of life growing up. When the conversation had finally waned, Tori yawned.

That had been a perfect segue into announcing it was time to leave. She and Ryan said their good-nights to her parents. This felt far too much like the good ole days when they had dated and grown serious, and her heart was heavy with memories. Add to that, she'd had a hard time shaking thoughts of the earlier kiss she'd shared with Ryan by the fireplace.

At least she had her own vehicle—she'd insisted on driving it to Mom and Dad's rather than riding with Ryan. After they left, Ryan followed her back to Sarah's house in his vehicle. The deputy who had delivered her car remained parked next to the curb. His presence would presumably serve as a deterrent to another break-in or something even more nefarious.

She hoped.

Tori parked in the driveway and waited for Ryan. After parking at the curb he jogged over to her. "Deputy Jackson will stay here and watch your house this evening. He'll be trading off with another deputy close to midnight. I'm not sure whom yet, but I wanted you to know."

At her porch, she nodded. "I truly didn't mean to cause you problems by staying in town. You probably don't need to waste manpower on me, though I appreciate it. I realize that your investigation would be easier without having to worry about me being here."

Ryan said nothing. But he studied her.

Averting her gaze from the handsome detective she might have married, she stared out at the streetlights that barely illuminated the neighborhood and rubbed her arms against the chilly night air. "I know you think it would be easier for you if I went home to South Carolina and maybe even took Mom and Dad with me. But I would be no use to my employer in my current frame of mind. I won't be until this is over. If this is all resolved before my bereavement leave is over, then that's different. I'll be settled and can be of use to my employer." But she had a feeling that she would end up staying no matter what.

"I don't think my investigation would be easier without you," he finally said. "Obviously you've run across information that could help us, but I'm worried about you, Tori. I can't..." His frown lines deepened, then he appeared to rein in his emotions.

What was he going to say? *I can't lose you, too?*

She wasn't sure her heart could take this painful dance she and Ryan found themselves in. Bad enough she might not come out of this ordeal unscathed beyond the agony she already suffered at losing Sarah.

"I promise I'll stay alert," she said. "In fact, I'll try to go through Sarah's home again and be more thorough this time. If I can't find anything to help us, then I'll move to a safer location."

"Good. In the meantime, we'll bring Dee James in for questioning."

"No, please," she said. "Let me handle him."

Ryan stiffened.

She'd better reel him in. "If you want me to share information then please let me handle gathering it. I think this guy is spooked. If you bring him in, he'll lawyer up and you won't get a word out of him. But if I approach him alone, he might be willing to talk. I don't think he had anything to do with what happened today."

"How can you be sure?" Ryan asked.

"I can't, but something in his tone on the phone let me know that he cared about my sister. As I've already said, I got the feeling he knows something, but he could be scared and might even run. In fact, he could already have disappeared." She hoped that wasn't the case.

"All right," he said. "I'll give you two days to try to make contact again."

"Come on. You know it could take me that long to hear from him. Give me a week."

He huffed an incredulous laugh. "Are you kidding me? A week is too long. Two days, plus you have to bring me with you if you arrange a meeting. Anything face-to-face and I'm there with you, Tori. It's much too dangerous otherwise. Do you understand?"

She chewed on her lip. Could she agree to that? "Fair enough."

"I'm only agreeing to this because I believe that you're right that he could clam up if I brought him back to the sheriff's offices for questioning."

She saw in his eyes that he hoped she wouldn't make him regret this decision. Tori turned and unlocked the door, disarmed the alarm system. Ryan conducted his usual bungalow clearing and this time, he didn't linger but instead wished her a good evening and left.

She closed the door and locked it, rearmed the system, then peeked out the window. Ryan was talking to the deputy through the vehicle window, his gaze searching the area as he talked. The neighbors had to be wondering what in the world was going on. But that was good. They would be more vigilant about keeping their eyes on the house. That way, they could spot anyone lurking around looking for trouble, out of view of the deputy parked at the curb.

Tori kept all the rooms dimly lit. Nothing harsh and bright, but just enough so there were no dark shadows. She wanted to see every corner. This way she'd prevent any of those too-stupid-to-live moments she often saw in movies when someone crept forward from the shadows.

After the day she'd had, Tori should crash along with the adrenaline in her body, but she wanted to dig back into Sarah's emails. Might as well make a big pot of strong coffee.

She'd contact Dee James tomorrow.

Propped in Sarah's cushiest chair, Tori opened up her emails again and started reading where she'd left off, looking for more about the environmental activities or any other interesting and potentially suspicious mentions.

It was right to stay here and do this. Ryan couldn't investigate this like Tori could. So they would solve this case as a team. And that also felt good and right.

Unfortunately, warm feelings for him flooded her at the thought. She recalled the gentle kiss they'd shared earlier that day and knew without a doubt they both still cared deeply for each other, though neither of them could afford to act on those feelings. Somehow she had to shut down any rekindled emotions that remained for him, which would be hard to do given their current collaboration.

Tori focused back on the emails. She struggled to stay awake, despite the strong coffee. She imagined Sarah's fingers typing the emails, or her smile and eyes as she stared at her laptop. Sarah had been a loving, giving person. The best person that Tori had ever known. The saying that only the good die young seemed true in Sarah's case. Her death was such a huge blow, such a wrongful loss. Tori sniffed to rein in her emotions and the resulting leaky nose.

If Tori was going to help in securing justice for her sister she had to push past the melancholy.

Then she spotted it.

An email sent three weeks ago. In the email, Sarah had added a short line at the bottom about sending Tori a package in the mail. A small intake of breath escaped. She remembered seeing the email now, but just hours after she'd received it, she'd been assigned to a stakeout that lasted for days. Tori—the amazing sister that she'd been—had completely forgotten about the email regarding a package.

Then she'd gotten the shocking news that Sarah had been killed. In a grief-stricken daze, Tori had packed a few belongings and left as quickly as possible. She'd been in a hurry to get to California, so she'd just grabbed the stash of mail she'd yet to go through after her stakeout and crammed it into her briefcase. Whatever didn't fit, she'd put in her luggage to go through later or never.

Tori set her laptop aside and shoved her face into her hands.

I let you down, Sarah!

She shoved from the cushy chair and grabbed her briefcase. She dumped the contents out on the kitchen table and rifled through the envelopes of bills and a few padded mailers, but found nothing at all from Sarah. Next, she moved to the bedroom. She'd hung up her clothes in Sarah's closet next to Sarah's things after the break-in—a pang shot through her—but left the stash of mail in her suitcase.

She dumped the contents of her luggage on the bed and skimmed through more mail—almost all of it junk.

Again she found nothing from Sarah. If Sarah had mailed Tori a package it should be in the stash she brought. She'd left nothing of importance behind in her apartment in South Carolina.

So…whoever had broken into Sarah's home could have found the envelope and taken it. It seemed they had been searching for something, given they had taken nothing else that she could see. The only reason Tori could think that someone would go to that much trouble for the package was because it could contain incriminating information. What Sarah had mailed to Tori could hold the details over which she'd been murdered.

And now, whoever had taken it *could* believe that Tori knew why Sarah had been killed, and it was only a matter of time before she connected the dots to the killer. And only a matter of time before Tori met the same fate as Sarah.

To survive, she would have to beat them at their game before the clock ran out.

The next morning Tori woke up to bright sunshine breaking through the cracks in the mini blinds. Maybe the rain was finally gone and wouldn't return for a while. She stretched and breathed a sigh of relief.

Well, what do you know? I survived the night.

She'd been so exhausted and distraught she was surprised her mind had allowed her to sleep without nightmares, but her body's need for rest had overruled everything else.

Still, her mind remained foggy this morning. If she could have slept another hour or two she would have, but she needed to get busy. Grabbing a cup of coffee from the single-cup coffee maker, she guzzled it before she bothered to get dressed.

She thought about the package she was supposed to have received from Sarah. Was it small or large? What? She didn't know. Sarah hadn't left her any details.

One thing she did know—she'd have to tell Ryan about the package.

She crunched on a breakfast bar and stared at her cell phone. She noticed that she'd received a call during the night but the caller had left no voice mail.

She recognized the number. It belonged to Dee James.

Tori had better fully wake up, and fast. Had she brought trouble to him by going to his address? Did he have any idea that the café's explosion was because someone had tried to kill her? That had all happened right across from his apartment complex. He could know about the explosion but still not know the cause or that she'd been there at all.

Or…he could have been the one to try to kill her. She hoped not. Tori cleared her throat and focused her thoughts, then pressed his number to return the call.

He answered on the first ring. "Hello."

"It's me. Tori Peterson." As if he didn't know the number he'd tried to call.

Per usual he was quiet for a second or two before responding. "I'd given up on you calling me back."

Dee hadn't left a message but obviously assumed that she would recognize his number and eagerly return the call. Maybe he was spooked and didn't want to leave messages.

She responded in kind and made him wait for her reply. Then she said, "You called me in the middle of the night. Sorry, but I just now saw the missed call."

"I'll get right to the point." He responded without waiting. "I've been thinking."

Tori's heart jumped. "So you remembered something that could help me find out who killed Sarah?"

"Yes," he said. "I think we should talk, after all."

"I'm glad you decided to talk, but we're talking right now. What can you tell me?"

"No, I mean…in person."

Okay. "Name the time and place."

"No cops," he said.

"No cops," she repeated and grabbed a pen and a pad. He didn't know she was FBI? Sarah hadn't shared that detail? "Where and when do you want to meet?"

He gave her the address. He was staying at a motel just outside of Shady Creek, toward Redding. She decided she wouldn't mention that she knew where he lived and had been on her way to meet him when she'd been attacked. She suspected she knew why he didn't want to meet at his apartment. He was running and scared. Someone could be after him, too.

"I can be there in two hours," she said.

"I'm not going to wait for you that long. Make it one."

What was with this guy? "Okay. I'll be there."

She ended the call and scrambled to shower and get dressed quickly. Now to get out of here without tipping Ryan off. The guy had said no cops. Ryan had given Tori time to make contact and now that she'd made it, Ryan would also want information out of him. Though Ryan had insisted he needed to come with her to meet Dee James, the guy wasn't going to talk with Ryan there. Tori needed answers.

She peeked out the window. The deputy Ryan had stationed outside her house was still there. Of course. But did that mean that she would be followed when she left the house? Or was the deputy there to watch the property?

Tori got into the car and pulled her cell out in case Dee called. Or in case Ryan called. Dee had sounded scared and had wanted a secret meeting with no investigators—no cops, as he put it. But was this a trap? Did he intend to hurt her?

Even so, she had a weapon and knew how to protect herself.

Backing from the drive, Tori headed down the street, surprised the deputy didn't follow her. He must just be assigned to prevent anyone from entering her home, not necessarily protect or shadow Tori. Good. It wasn't liked she needed a bodyguard.

Tori wouldn't go into this situation if anything raised an alarm or if someone followed her.

A half hour later, she pulled into the parking lot of the Shasta Motel, fifteen minutes early. Good. That would give her time to assess the situation. This time of morning the parking lot was only half full. Either most everyone had checked out, or they hadn't had many guests in the first place. The motel wasn't near any theme parks or anything worthy of entertainment. A family exited their room and climbed into a Suburban. Other than that, the place was quiet.

She drew in a breath.

God, please help me find answers about who killed my sister. You know who it is. Please help me to find the killer and bring them to justice.

Okay, she'd told Ryan she wouldn't do this alone. But as soon as she spoke with Dee and found out what he knew, she would contact Ryan to fill him in. She just wanted to wait until she finally had some answers. Everything she'd discovered so far had only caused her to have more questions. Her weapon hidden beneath her jacket, she headed toward the opposite end of the motel and then made her way down the walkway until she stood in front of the room number Dee James had given her.

She knocked softly. Nothing.

Then she knocked again. "Mr. James? It's Tori."

The door cracked open. She could barely see the redheaded man in the shadows staring out. Hadn't she just last night thought about stupid people walking into the shadows?

"Dee James?" she asked. "I'm Tori. Sarah's sister."

He swung the door wide so she could easily see into the room, for which she was grateful.

She stepped inside and flipped on all the lights to chase away the shadows. "Do you mind leaving that door open while I check the bathroom?"

"Who do you think I have hidden in there?"

She pulled her gun out. He threw up his hands. "Whoa, whoa."

She scrunched her face. "Don't worry, Mr. James. This is for my protection only. I'm checking the bathroom, that's all. I want to make sure this isn't a trap. Is that okay with you?"

He relaxed. "Knock yourself out."

Dee moved to stand in the corner opposite the door he'd left open, which she appreciated. This wasn't the best scenario and she hoped she hadn't just lost his trust.

She glanced at him before clearing the bathroom, then took in the small space in the wall that passed for a closet. He swiped a hand through his hair and fidgeted. Then did it again. Rinse and repeat.

She gestured that he could close the door.

"I don't like guns. Why did you bring a gun? I should have said no guns along with no cops."

"I didn't mean to scare you or upset you. But a girl can't be too careful. My sister was killed. Murdered. I'm only trying to protect myself. That said, I'm going to keep my weapon out and close, if you don't mind." Tori sat in the only chair in an effort to dial down the tension. She hadn't meant to spook him.

"I understand. You don't trust me."

"It's not you." Though she couldn't be sure that he was safe. "I've been attacked a few times since I arrived in California. Now, please tell me what you can about Sarah and what happened to her. It's obvious that you know something."

Sweat beaded his temple to go with his constant fidgeting. Dee began pacing the small room.

"Why don't you have a seat on the bed and calm down?" Tori suggested.

She noted that he acted like someone who was sitting on explosive information and she wanted the information so she could get out of here before things blew up. She would pull pen and paper out, but she didn't want to take the time to write things down. She had a great memory. She had a feeling he wasn't the kind of guy who would allow her to record their conversation.

"Okay. Okay. Sarah…she was always so radical. Outspoken. I think she made some people mad in Sacramento. Some of the legislators."

"You mean when you protested about the pollution issues? Why do you think that *she* made someone mad, specifically? She wasn't the only one protesting."

He shrugged. "She might have threatened someone."

A chill ran over her. "Who did she threaten? How and why?"

"I don't know. Look. I told her to use a secret email. To get an alias, if she was going to be so in everyone's face."

Her sister had used an email to threaten someone. That was what Tori was hearing.

"But isn't that part of the point of belonging to an activist group and protesting? To stir things up and be in-your-face, as you said, in order to affect change?"

"I guess so, yes. I just thought she would take more precautions."

He wasn't giving her enough information to make heads or tails of this. "When I read up about A Better World, I found a few articles that loosely linked eco-terrorism back to your group. What can you tell me about that? Was Sarah involved in ecoterrorism? Is that what you're telling me—that she threatened politicians with violence?" No way would Tori believe that Sarah would actually hurt someone, but if her targets thought she was dangerous, they might have decided to strike first. Or had Sarah decided to use more subtle tactics to perhaps change laws, like blackmail? There was much more going on here.

Dee's face reddened. "Look. I'm telling you all I know, all right? When I heard about the murders and that Sarah was killed, I wanted to believe that someone hadn't targeted her specifically—that she was just in the wrong place at the wrong time."

"But now you think she *was* targeted. You know something you're not telling me. What did you bring me here to tell me, Mr. James?"

He leaned closer and lowered his voice as if someone could hear them in this room. "She told me that she thought someone had been following her. That she was in danger."

Tori bolted upright then, startling him. "And you're just now telling someone? Why didn't you come forward earlier?" Okay, she was downright angry now.

"I didn't want to get involved—I still don't! I'll deny talking to you or telling you that if questioned. I'm only telling you because you're Tori's sister and I wanted you to know." He stood from the chair and pulled car keys from his pocket. "That's all I wanted to say."

Did he want her to leave or was he the one leaving? Either way, she wasn't done with him yet.

"Why would you deny what you told me to law enforcement? What are you hiding?" Tori put her gun away. It wasn't helping him talk. "Look, I only want to find out who murdered my sister. Are you afraid to admit to some criminal behavior of your own? I already know that Sarah was involved in ecoterrorist activities with you. That's already on the table—you're not helping yourself by keeping quiet about it."

He swiped the sweat from his forehead. "I'm scared. I don't know who I can trust."

"Then come in and let us—" she cleared her throat "—let Detective Bradley and the sheriff's department protect you." Better not to mention her own job title. He probably already knew that the FBI would want him if he was truly involved in ecoterrorism.

"Get real," he said.

"Who did she threaten? I need a name."

"Look, if I knew who Sarah had threatened I would tell you. It happened right after the protest. She got into an argument with a state legislator coming down the steps. A couple of days later, she told me she thought someone was following her. That she'd done something she hoped would make a difference. That's all I know."

"Okay, then, who is the legislator she argued with?"

"Look, there were a lot of people there that day. I only heard about the argument later. I don't know who it was."

Right. Tori wanted Ryan to bring this guy in for questioning. Maybe he could get more out of him. She was running out of patience.

She crossed her arms. This wasn't adding up. This

man made it his business to terrify organizations, though he hadn't been caught yet, and now he was running scared? "What's her email alias?"

He shook his head. "I don't know. I told her to use one and that I didn't want to know about it. So she didn't tell me and she didn't communicate with me."

Hmm. "Then what was the point? Who did she need to email while keeping her identity a secret?"

"I've told you all I know."

Well, that was it. He'd shut down on her. Mr. Dee James was about to meet Detective Ryan Bradley.

"I appreciate you calling me and what you've told me. I wish it was more. If you think of something else, please tell me. I want to get to the bottom of this."

"You should be careful. If what you said is true and someone has attacked you, then you could end up like Sarah. You should stop digging things up and asking questions."

Tori put her hand on the doorknob. That sounded more like a threat. Had Mr. James been playing her?

Gunfire resounded on the other side of the door.

From behind the brick wall where he took cover, Ryan returned fire. He'd already called for backup, but unless they arrived soon, they would be of no help.

He couldn't believe he found himself cornered in the alley next to the motel. He'd followed Tori after the deputy watching the house had contacted him to say she'd left. He'd caught her on the highway leaving town and followed from a good distance so she wouldn't see him. He'd spotted a gunman approaching the motel room and then the man had positioned himself behind a vehicle to shoot her as soon as she exited the room.

Ryan knew he would have to stop the ambush meant to kill Tori. He'd identified himself and tried to detain the man, who then shot at him.

He'd returned fire but had to take cover and now he was pinned behind this wall. This wouldn't help Tori at all, but by now she had to have heard the gunfire. At least she wouldn't be ambushed.

Peering around the wall, he prepared to take another shot. Tori stood opposite him behind a car and fired her weapon at the man.

Ryan reloaded his clip.

"You can come out, Ryan," she called. "He took off."

Ryan stood and cautiously left the cover of the brick wall in time to see that Tori had run after the man and now sprinted down the alley, the rush of adrenaline giving her the boost she'd needed.

Ryan burst from the wall and ran to catch up with her. She paused at the end of the alley.

Gasping, he asked, "What do you think you're doing?"

"I'm going after him." She prepared to peer around the corner.

"Please, let me." He looked both directions. "Clear."

They ran from the alley. "Which way did he go?"

"Not sure. But he couldn't have gotten far. I'll go south, you go north."

"No, we're sticking together." They jogged across the street to a shopping center parking lot.

Ryan stood at Tori's back as they both searched. "We've lost him."

"No, wait." She tugged on his sleeve. "That van is starting up. Can you see who's in it?"

"Not yet. We can watch it drive by." He pulled his

cell out to take a picture. Sometimes he wished the sheriff's department had enough funds for the deputies to wear body cams. Maybe next year. That could make his life so much easier. The van passed them.

"I can't tell if it was our guy. The driver was wearing a ball cap. Could have pulled that on as a disguise." Ryan took the photo of the license plate anyway. "We'll run it and see what we come up with."

Tori put her weapon away.

He shook his head and urged her back to the motel until they stood at her vehicle.

"I don't like this. You shouldn't be questioning potential witnesses. You could ruin our case. You know that, right? I was supposed to go with you."

"What case? You wouldn't even have this without me."

"I thought we were working together. You were supposed to call me if you set an appointment with him. It was too dangerous for you to come here by yourself. If I had not followed you then you would have been ambushed. If I hadn't been here, that guy would have shot you the minute you walked out that door."

"Okay, you got me. But I can't say I'm sorry for jumping on the chance to talk to the guy. I appreciate that you saved my life. But Dee called me. He was willing to talk, but he said no cops."

"And we could have kept you safe while you talked to him. You know all this." What had gotten into her except her hazardous need to find Sarah's killer at any cost? "Well, what did you find out?"

She told him everything, including Sarah's email about the package. "But we're here now, and I suggest you question Dee. We don't have time to play games."

Ryan put his gun away for the moment. Together they headed for Dee James's room and knocked on the door.

"Mr. James? It's me again," Tori said. "Detective Bradley would like to speak to you."

They waited but no one answered.

"Mr. James," Ryan said. "You could be in danger. Someone tried to shoot Tori as she exited your room."

A maid pushed a cleaning cart toward the rooms. Ryan was glad she hadn't been in the vicinity of the shots fired. Sirens resounded as other law enforcement showed up.

He flashed his badge and gestured for her to open the door. They didn't have a warrant, but he was concerned that a stray bullet could have hit Mr. James—exigent circumstances. The maid opened the door and they found the room empty.

"He's gone," Tori said. "He must have left as soon as you and I chased after the shooter."

A police officer stepped up to the room. Ryan explained what had happened and contacted Deputy Jackson to bring Dee James in for questioning.

Ryan then walked her back to her vehicle.

Tori lingered at the door but didn't open it. "He said he was scared and didn't know who he could trust. And he definitely won't trust me after this."

"I hope the feeling is mutual and you don't trust him," Ryan said. "That was an ambush."

"So what if it was? It doesn't mean that Dee James arranged it." Despite her words, uncertainty flickered in her gaze.

"We'll get to the bottom of this," he said. "I'm going to follow you home."

Tori made to climb into her vehicle, but he stopped her. "I forgot to thank you for saving me back there."

She shrugged. "You can handle yourself."

"No, really. You had my back. I got cornered. I honestly hadn't expected to see someone gunning for you like that, even after everything that's happened so far." His heart tumbled around. He wanted to pull her to him and hold her—to comfort himself. He pushed aside the ridiculous thought.

"You're welcome, Ryan." She slid into the seat.

"Tori?"

She lifted her gaze to meet his, her green eyes flashing at him. If he understood the timeline, her bereavement leave would run out soon, and then what would she do? Would she really give up her career to stay here? He just couldn't see that happening. If her goal was to be there for her parents then maybe she could somehow transfer to be closer. There was a field office in Sacramento, and resident offices. But he understood agents were often assigned and had few choices.

And why did he care?

"Yes, Ryan?"

"Let's work together. I mean…closely. You can help us with what you know and learn about Sarah, but I can't have you rushing in on your own, ruining our chances of charging someone or getting a conviction."

Subtly nodding, she looked at the ground. "I understand."

Then she started her vehicle. He got into his and followed her back to Rainey. As soon as they pulled into the drive, his cell rang.

Deputy Jackson. He answered.

"Dee James is dead."

NINE

Tori had wanted to go to the scene where Deputy Jackson had found Dee James, but Ryan wouldn't let her. He was letting the techs gather the evidence first, he'd said.

She'd almost been killed. Again. Now she had to wonder if Dee hadn't been the true target. Ryan had assumed the attacker was waiting for her, but what if he'd been waiting for Dee? Or for both of them?

In the meantime, she was back at the bungalow. Another eventful morning to process through, and the day wasn't even over yet. She'd shared with Ryan all the information she'd gathered from Dee, which left her with more questions than answers, and yet, it had sent her in a direction. She would try to find out who the legislator was that Sarah might have threatened.

Getting Sarah's email alias and accessing those emails was critical.

So Tori peered at her own laptop again, but her mind was far from Sarah's emails. She analyzed everything that Dee James had said from their initial phone call through to their meeting at the motel. She tried to think if she'd missed some nuance in his words. Some important information.

Because now he was dead and he couldn't tell them more.

At least, Dee couldn't tell them more in person. But maybe there was something at his apartment, on his cell, or on his computer to help them. Maybe someone else within his environmental activist group knew something to help them. They would need to track down all those involved to question them.

Oh, wait. Ryan had said he would put someone on that. Translation: Tori should stay out of it.

So while she sat in Sarah's comfy chair, on her laptop, Ryan paced in her kitchen. She'd damaged his trust in her when she'd gone to see Dee James alone. Now he was here at the house with her and she wasn't sure he would let her out of his sight again. And she couldn't blame him. He'd refused to leave her side, despite her insistence that she could protect herself. She wanted him out there, working the case, but instead, he was doing his job in her kitchen, speaking on the phone, trying to get a warrant and tech people to retrieve Sarah's digital evidence on top of another possible murder to investigate—Dee James's.

Her heart ached at the thought of his death. The cause of death was a drug overdose, but she and Ryan both believed he'd been forcibly injected—murdered.

She wished she could be officially assigned to work this case. She could almost wish that she worked for Maynor County with Ryan, but even if she did, she would never be assigned her sister's murder case. At least this way, with no official role in the investigation, she had some freedom to look into things in her own way.

Tori concentrated on her conversation with Dee.

There had to be something more that he hadn't told her, something that would explain who had killed him—and Sarah. It was all interconnected and Tori focused back on trying to figure out Sarah's alias— she didn't have time to wait on Ryan and his team to get the proper warrants to look through Sarah's computer. Even as her sister, Tori could only give consent to search her own belongings. Anything more could be challenged in court by a defense attorney. Ryan was covering all his bases.

Admittedly she had already been on Sarah's computer, but now Ryan had a reason to search for digital evidence in his investigation.

Still, Sarah wouldn't have bothered with an alias only to use that on her personal computer. It was like Dee had said—if she was going to email someone with the alias, using her own computer, then there wasn't much use for it.

Who was the person she didn't want to be able to track her down? Whom had she emailed using the alias? And how had they found her?

Ryan approached from behind. "What are you doing?"

"I'm trying to figure out her alias."

"I'm waiting to hear on the warrant for the digital evidence. That includes her alias."

She shoved up from the chair. "You're not going to find anything about the alias on her computer. And we don't have time to wait on warrants. Think about it, Ryan. Someone got to Dee James already. They might already know Sarah's alias address and they could be in the process of erasing the emails. I'm not hurting anything by looking."

He sighed.

"Besides," she said. "Someone keeps trying to kill me. They must think I know more than I actually do. So they want to kill me to keep me from figuring the whole picture out. They don't seem to understand that attacking me only drives me to try harder."

"All the more reason you need to be somewhere else." He held up his cell. "I've been on the phone to make all the arrangements. I'm moving you to a safe house."

It wasn't a request or even an argument. He'd already made his decision and the arrangements without involving her. He crossed his arms as if he expected a confrontation.

Tori rose to face him, crossing her arms, as well. "I might be a lot of things, but I'm not stupid."

"Meaning?"

"Though staying in Sarah's home has been good for me, and I think it could still help us, I know I should move somewhere they can't find me. That said, I do need to stay here until I can figure out her alias."

Ryan huffed out an incredulous chuckle. "First, you can look for her alias anywhere you can get internet on your computer. Second, what makes you think *you're* going to find it?"

Ryan still didn't get it? "Because I know my sister. She would choose a certain kind of email handle— something with personal significance. That's why, no, I can't just figure it out from anywhere. I have to be here. Just being here in her home, surrounded by her things, her photographs and knickknacks—everything that has Sarah all over it—can trigger that for me."

"But then you'll still have to figure out her password, and how long will that take?"

"Nah. Sarah always used the same one."

Ryan flinched as his eyes widened. "You're kidding."

"Nope. She said she only had so much mental band-width, so why try to remember a kazillion passwords." Tori completely understood that thinking, even though she knew it was practically begging a hacker to dive into all of your accounts. "Okay, so you go do your thing. Call someone or something. I need to look through her house and see if I can figure out her email."

The incredulous but amused look Ryan gave her was kind of cute.

Tori started in the kitchen, looking at the placards of nature and verses from the Scriptures. She skimmed through a couple of cookbooks Mom had given Sarah for Christmas.

Lord, please give me some direction.

Hours later, technicians arrived to retrieve Sarah's computer. Apparently Ryan had gotten the warrant to search for digital evidence. Tori had pulled everything from her sister's closet in search of ideas and now she felt ridiculous. Why had she thought this would work?

Ryan approached. "It's time to move, Tori."

"I haven't figured it out yet. I can't leave." He was right about going, and she knew it, but she wanted a few more minutes. Maybe then...

He shrugged. "You might never figure it out."

Tori turned and Ryan was much too close.

"In the meantime, I want you out of danger, Tori." His nearness tugged at her.

Her breath hitched. She wanted to feel his arms

around her again. Tori put a hand on his chest and gently shoved him back so she could get by.

"You can still work on it at the safe house," he said. "Sometimes you have to get some distance to get a fresh perspective."

The way he said the words, she wondered if he'd meant something more. If he was talking about their past relationship. And their recent kiss. What would her perspective be on that kiss when she finally got any distance from Ryan? She lifted her eyes to look at him. He studied her. He'd shuttered away the emotions she might have seen earlier. What was he thinking? A better question—did she really want to know?

"All right." She blew out a breath. "I'm going to pack. I don't have much, so it won't take long. But I might need to come back here if I think of something to look into."

He lifted his palms and then dropped them. "If that happens, we'll do what we can. But I think we both know there's nothing here to find or you would have found it already."

"Maybe I can help your computer tech with Sarah's computer."

"We'll see," he said. "Now it's getting late. I want to get you to the safe house before dinnertime."

"What about my parents?"

"I'll inform them that I'm keeping you safe. That's what they want, and they need to trust me for now."

Wow. "But they'll want to see me."

"We'll arrange for that." Ryan's brows knitted. "You know how this works. Why are you wasting time? Let's just get out of here."

Tori couldn't take his intensity and headed toward the bedroom to pack.

She turned to shut the door only to find him standing in the doorway, blocking her.

"Please give me privacy so I can pack," she said.

"I'm sorry. I thought we were still talking." He shrugged. "Thank you for agreeing to this, and also, for what you've learned to help the investigation."

Admiration swam in his eyes. Tori wanted that from him much more than she should. "You're welcome."

He nodded and stepped back enough for her to close the door. Grumbling to herself, she removed the few clothes she'd put in Sarah's closet and dresser drawers. She was accustomed to living out of her luggage when she traveled, but she'd put her stuff away as if she truly intended to stay here.

Uncertainty about her future gnawed in the back of her mind. Those permanent, life-changing decisions were too big, too important to make while she was in this frame of mind. And yet wasn't it because of the current set of circumstances she was even considering leaving her position?

Tori sighed as she finished packing far too quickly to clear her thoughts. She hadn't brought much. After all, she'd only come out here on bereavement leave. It was only after she'd gotten here that she began to consider extending that indefinitely. She plopped on the edge of the bed and pressed her hands against her face.

Should she go back to work? Ask for a longer extension, or simply resign? She'd need to make that decision over the next couple of days. She wanted to stay close to her parents, but she was in danger, herself, and couldn't be very close to them anyway, since she would be staying at a safe house. Nor could she be as free as she needed to be to conduct her own investigation.

"Oh, Sarah." She lifted her gaze and, through teary eyes, spotted the framed photograph on the dresser. Her sister stood in front of the marina sign in Crescent City with Tori. The picture had been taken before Tori had moved to South Carolina.

The window exploded with shards of glass.

The bedroom door flew open.

"Get out!" Ryan grabbed her and threw her in the hallway as he covered her.

An explosion ripped the air.

His ears rang and dizziness swept over Ryan as he used his body like a human shield to protect Tori. Anguish engulfed him. He should have somehow run farther with her and completely escaped the house before the explosion. But instinctively he'd known there wasn't time and had chosen to cover and protect her.

At least the ceiling hadn't caved in and crushed them.

Shouts resounded and broke through the continuous buzzing in his ears. He needed to get up and get Tori out of here, but his mind and body couldn't agree on how to do that.

Hands gripped Ryan, tearing him from Tori. His first instinct was to fight the assailant, and he reached for his weapon, prepared to battle and save her.

Deputy Jackson. The breath rushed from Ryan. "I… I could have shot you."

"No, you couldn't. You're moving too slow, Bradley. Are you okay?"

"Yeah. Sure." Ryan glanced down at Tori.

Unmoving, she remained on the floor.

Oh, no!

Ryan knelt down next to her and pressed his hand against her carotid artery. She was still alive. Relief whooshed through him.

"Tori." No response. Fear corded his throat. "Tori, are you okay?"

"We called emergency services," Deputy Jackson said. "Looks like it was a pipe bomb someone tossed through the window."

"Is anyone in pursuit?"

"No. I rushed inside to help."

"Did you see who did this?"

Jackson shook his head. "I only heard and saw the explosion."

Ryan wanted to ask Jackson how someone had been able to approach the house and throw a bomb inside with a sheriff department vehicle parked out front. Had Jackson been snoozing or otherwise engaged? Why hadn't he prevented this? But he would save those questions for a better time.

He was worried about Tori.

Tori groaned and rolled over. Her lids fluttered and then opened, and her green eyes focused on him.

He pressed his hand gently against her cheek. "You scared me to death." Had he thrown her to the ground too hard? Maybe she'd hit her head.

"Are you okay?" Her voice sounded weak.

"I'm fine, but you were out for a few seconds."

"No, I wasn't."

"What? Don't you know that you blacked out?"

"Ryan, I was fully aware. I just took my time responding, okay? I feel pommeled by someone's determination to kill me."

Hmm. He wasn't sure he bought that, but then again, Jackson had said Ryan had been moving slowly.

"Okay. Well, good. I'm glad you don't have a concussion. Regardless, an ambulance is on the way." Ryan glanced at the ceiling. "I don't want to move you, but I'm not sure of the house's structural integrity."

She sat up, then pressed her hand against her forehead as if her head hurt. Ryan and Deputy Jackson reached down to assist her to her feet, but she refused their help.

Ryan took that as a good sign.

Sirens rang out in the distance. But Ryan knew emergency services could sometimes take much too long to arrive. "Let's get out of here," he said.

He, Tori and Deputy Jackson quickly exited Sarah's bungalow. He gripped Tori's arm as he ushered her toward his vehicle.

"I'm okay, you can let me go now." She twisted out of his grip.

"You don't look okay."

At the look of sorrow on her face, Ryan wanted to pull her to him.

She pressed her fingers over her eyes. "Sarah's home is destroyed now."

"Maybe only her bedroom—it's too early to say. But it can be repaired, Tori. The house is just a thing. It's not a life."

"Her bedroom is the most important room. There were photo albums. Things I still needed to go through. And what about my things?"

He frowned. "We don't know about the damage yet. We'll have to wait and see. At least you left your laptop on the coffee table." But he knew her suffering had less to do with the material things than with the emotional weight of losing another piece of her sister.

"Come here." He wrapped his arms around her. He should be more concerned about her and less about protecting his own heart and keeping his distance.

He held her a few moments, then urged her to sit in his vehicle until the ambulance arrived. Ryan turned to his deputy, who stood waiting with him. "Have our techs check the house for cameras and bugs of any kind."

When he focused back on Tori, her eyes were wide and clear.

Good. Maybe she really hadn't blacked out. "Next time, we might not be this fortunate."

"Someone knew I was in my room and threw the bomb through the window. They knew I was there."

"Exactly what I was thinking. It could have been a coincidence that you were in the room when the bomb came through, but you know I don't believe in those."

"That means either they were watching me through the window—" she glanced across the street "—or the initial break-in could have included someone installing a camera or listening devices. The creeps." She shuddered.

"They could be searching for the information Sarah had, and hoped you would find it. That would be a reason to watch you."

She scrunched up her face. "That makes no sense. If they want me to find something for them, why try to kill me?"

"It could be both. They want you dead, but they also want to know if and when you learn something. In this case, they might have heard our discussion of moving you and decided to try to take you out before it was too late."

A chill crawled over Ryan and he hovered near her to protect her. "You should wear a vest at all times now."

"What makes you think I don't?" She lifted her sleeve enough for him to see a light body armor.

Any other time and he would have chuckled. He'd hugged her, so he knew that she had one on now. The body armor served as a reminder that if he had gotten her out of the house and somewhere safe sooner, Sarah's house would likely still be intact, and Tori wouldn't have almost lost her life again.

If he hadn't lingered in the hallway, he wouldn't have been there to yank her out. Would she have reacted differently and died in the explosion?

A fire truck finally arrived, as well as an ambulance for Tori. Ryan allowed a paramedic to check him out but refused the full exam at the hospital. He insisted that Tori go, and then from there, they would head to the safe house. His biggest fear at the moment was her safety on the way to the hospital and while she remained there. Whoever was behind these attacks was determined, and they had stayed ten steps ahead of his investigation.

A familiar vehicle steered up to the curb. Oh, no. Tori's parents. They couldn't have come at a worse time. Had they heard the sirens or maybe been on their way home and followed emergency vehicles here? Or maybe they just wanted to check on their only living daughter.

David Peterson jogged around his vehicle as Sheryl got out, and together they crossed the street. Both their faces were pale and somber. David kept a protective arm around Sheryl.

The ambulance drove away with Tori.

"Ryan?" David asked. "What's happened here? Where's Tori?"

"She's in the ambulance, but she's fine."

Tori's mother started sobbing. "She's not fine if she's in an ambulance. What's going on?"

"I assure you, she's okay. She got knocked to the ground, so a doctor should take a look at her, but mostly I wanted her out of here. I'm going to meet the ambulance at the hospital." He wanted to reassure them, but he wouldn't lie or pretend that Tori wasn't in significant danger.

"You didn't answer my question. What happened?" David asked.

"An explosion of some kind. Listen, you two, we have everything under control, but you should know I'm moving Tori to a safe house."

David's mouth dropped open. "What?"

"You wanted me to keep her safe, remember?"

"And now that you've failed again, you're finally doing something?" Anger had replaced Sheryl's whimpers.

He wanted to reply that their daughter was nothing if not stubborn, and very capable—he couldn't protect her if she insisted on running directly into danger. But arguing with her parents over whether or not he was at fault wouldn't do any of them any good. "I'll call you later."

He climbed into his vehicle.

"We're coming to the hospital, too," David said.

Ryan groaned inside. His biggest concern at the moment was Tori's safety, and if her parents were there then he only saw them getting in the way. Their interference wouldn't help. But their daughter had come by her stubbornness naturally—he could tell they wouldn't back down, so he didn't bother trying to convince them.

He radioed for law enforcement to meet the ambulance and a deputy to remain with Tori at all times until he got there. His job as an investigative detective had suddenly morphed into him doubling as a bodyguard.

TEN

Tori was getting tired of seeing the inside of a hospital, especially since her parents and Ryan were having a confab in the hallway without her. Unfortunately, the doctor had insisted he keep her for overnight observation. She hadn't convinced Ryan that she hadn't been knocked unconscious. She couldn't be 100 percent sure herself. And her shoulder was giving her fits.

But morning was here. She'd stayed overnight and she was ready to go. She found new clothes her mother had bought for her and put them on. Jeans and a T-shirt and a zippered hoodie. Perfect.

Ryan was much too focused on Tori's safety, for which she knew she was partially to blame. She hadn't done such a great job convincing him she could protect herself. But it was like he'd told her—under normal circumstances she *could* protect herself, but being targeted was far from normal.

Sarah had thought someone was following her—and in that way, she'd even done a better job of staying alert to danger than Tori had. Had she experienced any other kind of threat to her life that they hadn't uncovered?

Tori squeezed her eyes shut. *God, please help us to*

find who did this to Sarah. Please... Help me. Show me the way.

The door opened, startling Tori from her prayer. The nurse handed over the paperwork for Tori to sign, which she quickly did and met her family in the hallway.

She took in their expressions. Uh-oh.

Ryan's face had grown even more somber. Mom's face was paler than she'd ever seen, and Dad's was red and twisted with anger.

How she wished they could have been spared.

Tears formed in Mom's eyes and she hugged Tori to her and sobbed. At this moment, Tori wished she was two thousand miles away. She'd only brought them more heartache by being here.

"I'm so sorry, Mom. I didn't mean to put you through this on the heels of..." She couldn't say Sarah's name when referencing her death. Not to her parents. It hurt too much. "I only meant to help."

Mom released her, then Dad stared down at her, his expression stern, as if she were still a child. "I insist you go home to South Carolina now. Go back to your job and leave the investigation to the authorities."

Tori frowned and fought the need to defend her decisions. She wasn't a child, even if her father insisted on treating her like one. "I can't have this discussion with you. Not here. Not now." Maybe not ever.

Turning her back on them, she walked away, hating herself for the seemingly heartless action. It was anything but heartless—too many emotions were getting in the way of her talking to them, causing an abyss to expand between them.

She stopped at the elevator, hoping for an escape. She had considered remaining in Rainey even after the investigation concluded because she believed her parents needed her. They all needed each other after Sarah's death. But now she wasn't sure she could tolerate her father's attitude. Would he always be this overprotective, this controlling if she stayed? She couldn't be sure—and she knew it wasn't fair to judge him based on his behavior right now, when emotions were running far too high. They all needed a little bit of grace and mercy for each other right now.

Footsteps approached from behind. She knew that cadence.

Ryan.

Unbidden, her heart danced around inside. She shoved those nonsensical feelings away, or rather, tried to.

He sidled up next to her. "So you're just going to leave them like that?"

Tori pressed the elevator button, then angled her head toward him. "It's an argument that can go nowhere and might escalate into something truly hurtful. I'll call them later. They'll get over it. You should know how it works in families. You have a bigger one than I do."

He hung his head and shrugged, then lifted his chin, his eyes pinning her. "He loves you, that's all. He's worried about you."

And so are you.

"I know. You feel the same way he does. You want me gone."

Ryan said nothing in response as the elevator door finally dinged and then opened.

Together they stepped into an empty elevator, but not before Tori noticed her parents chatting with the doctor,

Rick Hensley, whom her dad knew. Good, they were distracted. A pang shot through her heart.

The elevator doors closed them in. "I'm at the end of my rope, Ryan. That's all. Now please take me somewhere safe so I can get busy again. If my laptop and purse can be recovered, I'm going to need those, too."

"We're going to find him, Tori, I promise."

"Don't you think you're a bit overconfident? You can't make that promise." The words came out sounding harsh, which she hadn't intended.

She caught a bit of her contorted reflection in the small mirror in the corner. She was a wreck. Tori combed her fingers through her hair so she could look more presentable.

Ryan said nothing at all, but in the reflection she saw his lips had flatlined.

"Look, I'm sorry," she said. "Your retort should have been, 'And you're the one who's going to bring him down?'"

He chuckled.

Good. She liked the sound of it. That was exactly what they needed more of around here. She allowed herself to laugh, too.

"I can't say I wasn't thinking it," Ryan said, "but it's been a rough day and tensions are high. I don't need to add anything inflammatory."

She shifted to face him. These elevators could take an eternity. "I'm glad we've at least come to the place where we can laugh about our ridiculous…competition, I suppose—though that doesn't seem like the right word."

"We're not competing," he said. "We're working together. I'm working closely with you, the person who knew Sarah the best, to find the answers, so my team and I can build a case and get this guy behind bars. But in less than a couple of days, you'll have to return to work because your bereavement leave will be over. And I know you, Tori. You'll go back."

The way he grinned with his words, he was simply letting her know what he knew to be true, even if she didn't feel she knew it herself yet.

She lightly punched his arm. Tori hadn't officially left the feds, though it had been in her heart and mind. But she didn't want to make such a drastic decision when she was grieving.

Finally the elevator doors opened.

"Tori." He held her back. "Let me go first. We'll meet a plainclothed deputy in the lobby and get into that vehicle. We'll change to another vehicle a few miles down the road, just to be sure."

His words took her aback. "Wow," she said. "I'm impressed."

"Believe it or not, impressing you wasn't my goal."

Oh, he was being funny again. She walked with him to join a deputy she hadn't met yet and the three of them climbed into an unmarked SUV. Someone could follow them from the hospital, so the deputy drove around town for fifteen minutes until they were certain no one had followed, then they turned into a parking garage at the local bank building, where Tori changed into a wig and cap. Ryan simply wore a hat and different sunglasses for his disguise.

"You've thought of everything." She climbed into the new vehicle.

From the driver's seat, he glanced at her, dimples

carving into his cheeks. "Were you expecting anything less?"

She couldn't help smiling at him—gone was the animosity between them. He'd resented her for the longest time, believing she thought she was better than him because she was a federal agent. But while she'd wanted something different from the Maynor County Sheriff's Department, she admired Ryan and his abilities. "No, Ryan. I wasn't."

That brought a satisfied grin to his face.

The easy camaraderie between them made it that much harder for her to keep to herself what she'd learned moments before the pipe bomb had been tossed through the bedroom window.

Ryan finally steered the vehicle up the winding drive to the home loaned to him by Jasper Simmons, who was away on vacation. Ryan had saved Jasper's son from drowning when the boy had fallen into the Wind River and then been whisked away by the swift current during a fishing trip. Ryan, who had been on the river in a boat at the time, had been able to reach the ten-year-old boy before he went over the falls. Afterward, Jasper had told Ryan to call him if he ever needed anything, anytime. Day or night. Ryan had made that call and now Tori had a house in which she could be safe for the time being.

Tori sat up taller as the long drive continued to wind around and Mount Shasta came into view. White patches could still be seen on the peak in the summer—glaciers remained at the highest points and never melted. Up close and personal, the mountain was breathtaking.

"Would you look at this view." She moved the visor

so she could see better out the window. "Okay, now I really do think you're trying to impress me."

He parked the vehicle in front of the sprawling log cabin. "Now why would I want to do that?"

Tori said nothing to his question. It was only light banter, so she shouldn't be offended. Impressing Tori hadn't been his intention. All he'd wanted to do was to keep her safe.

Hopping out, he jogged around to open the door for her, but she had already climbed out.

Hands on her hips, she stared at the mountain as though she hadn't grown up in the shadow of Mount Shasta. Still, unless you hiked to the summit or lived in a place like this, this view wasn't something you saw every day.

"The Karuk tribe call it White Mountain," she said. "Did you know that it's the second highest peak in the whole Cascade range?" She turned to look at him and laughed.

"I didn't realize you were so fascinated with it," he replied.

"So there are still a few things you don't know about me. I'm glad I can still surprise you."

She was glad about that? He tried not to consider the implications.

"And now, I have a surprise for *you*." He smiled.

"Oh, yeah? What's that?"

He opened the back of the vehicle. "Your stuff's in the back."

Tori pressed a hand to her forehead. "I'm so relieved, Ryan. Thank you!"

She strode over to the back of the vehicle to stand next to him.

He handed off her laptop, a duffel bag of newly purchased clothes—since her others had been destroyed—and her purse that seemed to survive everything. "We've taken the liberty of going through your belongings in search of listening, visual or tracking devices."

"Of course. I'm glad you did." She shouldered her purse and held the laptop under her arm.

When she reached for her duffel bag, he snatched it. "I've got this."

"Thanks." She waited for him to shut the back. "Well, are you going to give me the grand tour of this place?"

"You and I will get the grand tour together. I don't know my way around, either. We'll have to go exploring. I hear it has two ponds and a creek. But, of course, I'll need to make sure the area is safe. No going off the property. Understood?"

"Understood."

Together they hiked to the porch, up the steps and to the door. Ryan fumbled around in his pocket and found a key. Jasper's mother kept a spare and Jasper had instructed her to hand it off to Ryan for the time being.

Inside the home, Tori set her things on the floor, her gaze traveling up and over the log walls and ceiling. The home featured a large open kitchen with soapstone counters and stainless steel appliances.

In the living area they found custom wood-carved furniture to go with the cabin. Tori sighed. "Okay, now this is my dream home. I never had a dream home before. Sarah wanted a house like the bungalow she got."

No, you didn't have a dream house—just a dream job...

Crossing her arms, Tori strolled through to the great room, where she stood in front of the panoramic window with a view of Mount Shasta. "Yeah. Dream house."

Ryan moved to stand next to her and take in the view.

"Just breathtaking," she said, then eyed him. "Okay, Ryan. You've ruined me. I didn't know I was missing anything until you brought me to this house."

Tori smiled. Her golden hair and green eyes with that mountain in the background... Um... Yeah... Breathtaking. The mountain alone couldn't do that for him. A knot lodged in his throat.

Why had he let this woman get away from him? In his heart, he'd known that she had to leave and take the opportunity presented to her, but it made his heart ache to think of how he had let her go and not tried to persuade her to stay. She'd never even asked him to come with her, so he hadn't presumed she wanted him to.

There was the old adage—*If you love something, let it go. If it comes back to you, it's yours forever. If it doesn't, then it was never yours at all.*

Tori obviously hadn't been his to begin with.

She'd had to make her dreams come true. So he'd been right to simply let her go, even if he'd been crushed and then allowed anger and resentment to take root.

But he was done with that, he hoped. He was glad that she'd achieved so much. Not many people had the strength to go after their dreams with such single-minded determination.

Ryan didn't trust himself to speak, so he kept quiet.

Tori angled to look at him and offered a soft smile that did uncontrollable things to his heart.

"All I know is that I'd better not get used to this place because I'm not going to be here that long and it might be painful to leave if I get too attached."

He chuckled. "Sometimes you can't help getting attached."

No matter the effort put in to stay disentangled. Her eyes flashed with emotions, and he sensed that she'd understood his deeper meaning. See, he shouldn't have trusted himself to speak.

Her expression turned serious. "You're going to find the person responsible for Sarah's death and the attacks on me just like you've reassured me repeatedly."

She was obviously trying to redirect him. Refocus him back on task. No pressure there. He found himself searching for the right response when the doorbell chimed. Perfect timing.

"Ah, that must be your protective services," Ryan said.

Tori's eyes narrowed. "I thought *you* were my protective services."

Was she disappointed? He had the strong feeling that she was, and that was too much to process. He had the sudden urge to kiss her, which just told him he needed to step away. "I have to investigate, remember? And find this guy, just like I *reassured* you."

Emotion swirled in Tori's eyes and she appeared speechless, which might be a first. Wow. Entirely too much chemistry brewed between them. Was it because they had nearly lost their lives multiple times? Traumatic events had a way of pushing people together, making them closer under pressure.

He opened the door to let in a female deputy who would stay with Tori. Admittedly, he'd brought Deputy Shawna Reiser into this to free himself up not only to investigate, but to put distance between himself and Tori. And now part of him wished he hadn't, but that was only because his emotions were getting in the way, which should never happen. Tori had to know that his heart was getting involved when it shouldn't, and as much as he wanted to protect her personally, it was more important that he solve the murders. An emotional involvement on his part would jeopardize the investigation.

Now he was glad he'd made the decision ahead of time. He found Tori in the kitchen eyeing the bananas. "I thought you said they were on vacation. Why are there fresh bananas on the counter?"

"Jasper's mom knew we were coming and stocked a few items." Ryan hadn't liked that even one more person knew about their current location but it couldn't be helped. "I'm heading out. Remember to let me know if you learn anything new."

She peeled a banana. "I'd appreciate the same consideration. That will help both our efforts."

"Will do." He left her in the kitchen and headed for the front door. Shawna stood there, waiting. "Don't forget to lock up. Check all the windows and doors and keep an eye out. I don't expect any trouble, but this guy is determined and we can't be too careful."

He opened the door to step outside.

"Detective Bradley," Shawna spoke in low tones. "Ryan..."

Shawna and Ryan had some history—a short time of seeing each other before they'd realized that they would make good friends but nothing more. She'd been hurt in the past, as had Ryan, and neither of them had been truly ready to move on.

Hesitating, he shut the door. "Is there a problem?"

"Yes. This house is far too big to adequately protect

someone, don't you think? And the windows? She's far too exposed here. Whose idea was this?"

"I understand your concern," he said. "But it was the only house available and you have to admit that it's far off the beaten path. She won't be easy to locate. This will give us some breathing room since we know she can't stay in Sarah's home or with her parents. Besides, if someone actually finds her, it's not going to matter how many windows there are."

He opened the door again, though he had more to say. "Don't worry, I'll check in on her. But I don't want a lot of people going back and forth here. Other than Jasper and his mother, only you, me and my captain know that we're using this location. Let me know about anything suspicious. Anything at all."

Frowning, she nodded, clearly not happy with the location. "I'll do my best, Detective."

"That's all any of us can do," he said and turned again to leave.

"Ryan…" she shifted to a more personal tone "…it's her, isn't it? This is the woman you hadn't gotten over yet back when you and I dated."

He subtly nodded. He was afraid to ask her what gave him away. Not wanting to get any further into that conversation, he took another step out the door, officially shutting any more questions down. "I'll check the perimeter before I leave."

With that, Ryan finally closed the door behind him. He got a pair of binoculars out of his vehicle and then hiked around the house. The log cabin was positioned on a ridge on the north side, so at least they didn't have to worry about an intruder from that direction. No one was going to climb the ridge to enter the house. Still, he peered through the binoculars in all directions and saw nothing but nature and wildlife for miles around.

Satisfied they were utterly alone out here, he marched back to his vehicle and made to open the door.

"Ryan!" Tori called as she jogged over.

"Something's wrong already?" He left the door open but didn't get inside.

"No." She shook her head, then said, "I mean, yes."

He crossed his arms and waited.

"Right before the explosion in the bedroom, I found something. Remember I mentioned looking for a trigger?"

"I remember."

"I found a picture of Sarah and me together in Crescent City. She'd wanted to spend time with me on the coast before I moved."

"And that's the trigger?"

She nodded vehemently. "I thought it could be her alias."

"And you're just now bringing this up to me, why?" He dropped his arms and fisted his hands.

Tori blinked. "I couldn't know for sure."

His heart rate jacked up. "And now you do."

"Yes." Her right cheek hitched up with her half grin. "I found her alias, and I think you should stay."

ELEVEN

Tori couldn't read Ryan's expression. She had hoped he would be as excited by this breakthrough as she was. Was he disappointed in her for not telling him right away?

"Look, an explosion got in the way of me telling you right when I noticed the picture. Okay? That and, well, I wanted to make sure. Why waste your time if it was a dead end? You understand, don't you?" Why was it so important to her that he did?

He shut the door and locked up his vehicle, then walked with her back to the house. "It's not important now. But next time, please share anything with me right away, whether you think it has merit or not."

Shawna held the door for them, and Tori led Ryan through the house to the spacious breakfast room, which had a view as amazing as the one from the great room. Her laptop sat open on the table.

At the stern expression remaining on Ryan's face, Tori tried to lighten his mood. "If only I could have this view every day while I have my morning coffee." Ugh. She really had to come up with something better to say than going on about the log cabin.

He shifted a bit to look her full in the face, and then offered a weak grin. "I couldn't agree more."

His words pushed into her and through her, along with certainty that he wasn't talking about the view through the window. Her pulse kicked up. *This isn't happening. This can't happen between us.*

Tori forced her eyes to her laptop while she calmed her heart. She pulled out a chair at the table to sit in front of the computer so she could show him what she'd found. But Ryan remained standing.

"Well, are you going to sit down?" she asked.

"I'm fine here, thank you."

And she had the distinct impression he was working hard to keep space between them. She understood completely.

She awakened the laptop and showed Ryan the webmail screen. "She used the server she was familiar with, only she probably always logged in from a public computer when she was using this email. Like I said, she always used the same password. And if she was using an alias that no one should associate with her, why come up with a new password?"

"I think it would have been better to give the tech guy the alias, Tori. You're stepping onto shaky ground here since we have the warrant for digital evidence. We want things processed correctly."

"You said you wanted my help."

"I do."

She could feel his warmth, his breath against her face as he leaned close to peer at the screen.

"Do you want to look at her emails or not?" Her voice sounded too tremulous.

"Let's see them." Ryan's voice, however, was firm and confident.

Still, she sensed that her nearness affected him the same way his impacted her. Time to focus on the task. She blew out a breath.

Together, they opened and read several emails.

"I can't believe this," Tori said. "It sounds like she was digging around in the environmental group. Like she was involved as an activist to find out about their ecoterrorism activities." Tori let out a sigh. "Honestly, that sounds more like Sarah. I can't believe she would ever be involved in illegal activities even for a cause she believed in, or threaten anyone, like Dee James suggested."

Ryan finally pulled up a chair to sit next to Tori. "I don't understand why Dee told you he was the one to suggest she use an alias for an email, since she was looking into *his* group and activities. But it looks like he told the truth when he said she never contacted him from this account. She *was* emailing someone else, though. We need to know who this person is."

"He also said she thought someone was following her," Tori said. "Could it have been someone with the environmental group? Except that doesn't make sense— Dee was scared himself. Obviously for good reason because someone killed him." Maybe Dee had turned against the more violent extremists in the group after they killed Sarah? Maybe that was why he was willing to talk to Tori—and why he was killed?

She scratched her head, wishing she could figure this out.

"Right. There's that, but let's focus on these emails. Who is she talking to here?"

"Ned Hundley. We can't know if that's also an alias, though," Tori said. "Wait a minute."

She turned to look at Ryan, realization reflecting in his gaze.

"She was an informant," they said simultaneously.

Tori shoved from the table.

"And who investigates ecoterrorist groups?" Ryan asked, though he already knew.

"The FBI." Fury boiled through her veins. "I can't believe this!"

She rushed from the breakfast room to the living area with the panoramic view of Mount Shasta and then finally settled to stare out the window.

Ryan approached from behind, then stood next to her. "You think both of them should have told you."

"Whatever my employer did or didn't do, whatever the Bureau's involvement, I think *she* should have told me." Grief and anger twisted inside.

What was the purpose in working for the FBI if she couldn't keep her own family safe? How had Sarah ended up working with the FBI as an informant? Had she been caught for being involved in something illegal and then forced into becoming an informant to clear her own record? That was how it often went down. Nausea swirled in Tori's gut and she pressed her hands against her midsection.

Knowing her sister, Tori felt it was more likely they somehow convinced Sarah that she was going to help them to prevent something terrible from happening. That would be very in character for Sarah. The queasiness eased up a bit.

Still next to her, Ryan sighed. "Maybe she was approached and then once she agreed, she was instructed not to share the information with anyone. Not even you."

"I need to contact this Ned Hundley. If that's even his name," Tori said.

Ryan started pacing along the large, panoramic window. "This has shifted into a new investigation. If she was killed because of her informant status, the FBI should be investigating her death. They would also be investigating Dee James if he's tied into this, too. So why aren't they?"

Tori pulled out her cell. "I'm going to find out."

Ryan urged her hand down. "You're on bereavement leave, remember? You're not supposed to be working a case. Let me reach out. In fact, I need to send what we've learned over to computer forensics techs working on Sarah's digital evidence. Maybe they can also find out more about Ned Hundley, if that is his real name. Let's work this through the proper channels so we can build our case."

Reluctantly she put her cell away. He was right. She turned to face him and looked into his intense blue-green gaze. She'd been such an idiot to leave him behind to pursue her dream job. The FBI might have resources that took her work to a higher level…but the Maynor County Sheriff's Department had a degree of trust and respect among colleagues that the Bureau was clearly lacking, especially since it looked like someone within the ranks of that organization had used her sister and gotten her killed. The bitter truth of it stung.

Tori didn't know how to process the information. She wished she was back at work and in her office now so she could face off with someone as anger boiled through her. On the other hand, it was better that she was here now and with Ryan.

"I'm glad you're in this with me." She couldn't believe she'd admitted that to him. Now the fact that she'd said his name after she'd been pulled from the falls made so much more sense. But deep inside, she also knew that her need for him in this investigation went much deeper than the simple fact that he was the investigating detective.

She hung her head and hugged herself.

"Tori…" The way he said her name curled around her heart.

He pulled her into his arms and Tori soaked up the strength of Ryan's broad shoulders and sturdy chest, when she shouldn't. She savored the comfort that poured from his heart, when she shouldn't. She had no right to take from him when she had nothing to offer in return.

But she needed to feel his arms around her, if only for a moment.

"Detective—"

Deputy Reiser abruptly entered the living room, startling them both, and Ryan suddenly stepped back. He hadn't meant for the deputy to see him holding Tori.

Shawna cleared her throat.

"What is it?" Ryan's tone was sharp with frustration.

"I think someone is lurking in the woods."

His shoulders stiffened. "Tori, get away from the window."

He pushed a button that lowered the enormous shades. Shawna's earlier words about the size of the home and the windows came back to him. He hoped she was wrong about a lurker.

"Show me," he said to Shawna.

She rushed around the house and through the kitchen to look through the window in the breakfast room. Tori tried to follow Ryan and the deputy, but he turned and gently grabbed her arm. "I want you to stay in a room without windows for now. Please."

Tori nodded and fetched her laptop from the table and then disappeared down the hall.

Shawna studied the woods. "Whoever it was is gone. I don't see him now."

"It was a 'him'?"

"Yes. I think it was a male but from this distance I can't be positive."

Ryan scraped a hand down his face. "Are you sure he was lurking? As in, watching this house?"

She shrugged. "What else would you call it when someone gets that close to a house on private property and seems to be hiding in the trees? You said to tell you if I saw anything."

"I'm glad you did, but I need all the facts, Shawna. Are you sure he was on the property? Not just in the public woods?"

"I haven't actually gone out there to mark off the property line." Shawna was growing irritated at his questions. "But even if he wasn't on the property, if he was standing behind a tree to watch the house, that's something to note."

"You're right."

But he couldn't fathom that someone had found Tori yet. He didn't want it to be true.

Ryan retrieved his weapon from his holster. "After I leave, lock the door. If you haven't already checked all doors and windows, please do so now, and then stay with Tori and keep her out of sight. Remain aware and on the lookout for someone outside trying get in. I'll communicate with my radio."

"But what about you?" Shawna asked. "Do you want me to call for backup?"

"I'll check it out first. It could be nothing. If you hear gunfire, then you can call."

Weapon ready, he made his way to the back of the house in search of an exit. Then he carefully slipped out through a door in the mudroom. The surrounding woods were vast, offering way too many opportunities of places to hide.

He waited and listened to the sound of wildlife—insects and birds. A squirrel jumped from a tree branch. A golden eagle screeched in the sky. If someone was close, they could disrupt those sounds, but the natural world gave him no hint of a man's presence. Ryan calmed his breathing.

If someone had come for Tori, that meant this safe house was no longer safe.

Please let Shawna be wrong about this.

But despite his wishes, he knew that Shawna was no fool. Keeping to the shadows, he crept to the other side of the house, his eyes searching for movement in the woods. These woods were thick with evergreens—red-and-white fir, Douglas fir, a variety of pines. Mountain mahogany and junipers also thrived. Underbrush was thick here, as well, and would make getting to the house difficult.

It could also make tracking someone easier. If someone was in those woods, he had to find them. It didn't matter that he didn't want to leave Tori behind.

Holding his gun at low ready, he left the house behind him and entered the forest of evergreens, watching the pine needles and underbrush for signs of humanity. After half an hour of traipsing through the woods, he found no evidence that someone had been lurking.

In the nearby distance, a vehicle roared to life. Ryan took off running through the woods, jumping over underbrush where necessary, dashing around trees and pushing his way through underlings. He ran toward the sound until he made it to the river.

Gasping for breath, he watched a Jeep utility vehicle driving away on a dirt path. He wished he had his binoculars so he could catch the license plate, but he had left them in the house. Still, he made note of the make and model, and the kayak sticking out the back.

Ryan hiked his way back to the house, palming his pistol. How could he know if someone had simply taken that path to kayak the river, or if someone had intentionally crossed the river to try to get closer to Tori? And if they had made their way to the house deliberately, then how had they found out where she was staying so quickly?

By the time he made it back to the house he was frustrated and breathing hard. Ryan spotted a vehicle through the trees exiting on the long drive. Panic spiked through him. He sprinted to the door and tried the knob. Fortunately, it remained locked. He rang the doorbell.

Shawna let him in. "Did you see him?"

"No. But I spotted someone exiting the drive. Did anyone come to the house while I was gone?"

She shook her head.

Despite her reply, Ryan knew one thing. "That's it. This house is obviously compromised. I can't be sure that Tori will be safe here. Would you mind helping her get her things? I'll take her somewhere else."

"But where?"

"I'm the only one who will know this time."

"I promise you, I told no one," she said.

"I know I can trust you," he reassured her. "There are at least three other people who know we're using this house for a safe house, and there are many other ways to find out."

He was most worried about those other ways.

TWELVE

Tori couldn't believe that she was standing in the living room of Ryan's home.

"Your house? Really, Ryan? What are you thinking? I might as well move back to Sarah's bungalow since it's only a few houses down." That is, as soon as the crime scene was released and construction work made the place livable again. Oh, she couldn't believe any of this.

"It's temporary, okay?" Ryan scraped a hand down his face. An action she'd noticed him doing an awful lot of lately.

"Okay." She tried to soften her earlier incredulity.

"It's just until I can figure something else out. And don't worry about—"

A door opened and shut somewhere in the house, interrupting what he might have said. Ryan palmed his weapon, and Tori grabbed her own. Had whoever found her at the big dream house followed them here?

"Hi, honey, I'm home," a lilting female voice proclaimed.

Jealousy snapped through her. Ryan… He had someone? Who was—

Ryan's twin sister, Katelyn Bradley, strolled into the

room with a large reusable grocery sack that she set on the counter with a thunk.

Tori relaxed and put her gun away.

"You nearly gave me a heart attack." Ryan returned his weapon to the holster at his waist. "I forgot you were coming over."

"See," Katelyn said. "This is why we never get together. You forget about me. I'm your twin. How could you possibly forget?"

"It's been one of those days, okay?" He winked at his sister. To Tori, he said, "I texted her earlier when I knew we had to move again."

Tori nodded.

Katelyn's long brown hair pulled back in a flattering ponytail, she flashed a brilliant smile, letting them know she was teasing. "Hey, Tori. It's good to see you, though I'd prefer it were under much different circumstances."

Tori looked from Ryan to Katelyn. So he'd brought in a chaperone? He didn't trust himself to be alone with Tori? Oh, she wished that thought hadn't even occurred to her.

"It's nice to see you, too. So why exactly are you here, if I may ask?" The question sounded kind of rude, but she wanted to know what was going on.

"I can see those wheels spinning in your head." Ryan's wink brought on a blush.

That he could read her mind made her cheeks all the warmer.

Ryan cleared his throat. "Katelyn can take you where you need to go, if you actually *need* to get out. Let's hope we get this guy, and soon. Things seem to be ramping up."

"You mean whoever killed Sarah is becoming desperate to find and kill me for whatever they think I know. Their actions seem counterintuitive to me. Escalating the murder attempts only increases the heat on them."

Arms crossed, he nodded. "Agreed. But it doesn't seem likely the guy is going to back down now, even if he could better protect himself by hiding rather than attacking. In the meantime, we're on the lookout for the two vehicles that approached the original safe house, so I hope we get a hit there. Jasper has security cameras so we can use those to see if we can get more details. But if solving this case takes much longer, then we'll have to make different arrangements for you—that is, unless you're willing to go back to your job on the other side of the country."

Katelyn appeared thoughtful, her blue-green gaze startlingly similar to Ryan's.

"I'm here to help you, Tori," Katelyn said. "As a friend, of course, but also to help out my twin brother. But I should mention he's paying me, too." She offered a silly grin. "I'm freelancing right now."

"Freelancing?" Katelyn worked in law enforcement in the town of Shasta, Tori had thought. What happened to that?

"Let's just say I'm in between law enforcement jobs." Katelyn lifted her jacket to reveal she was armed, then unpacked the groceries. Looked like they were eating Italian tonight. "And I can also cook a mean pot of pasta."

Tori chuckled. "Well, this should be interesting."

Ryan opened the fridge. "Three heads are better than two."

"Three heads?" Tori asked. "What about your entire sheriff's department? What about the FBI?"

"When it comes to you, Tori," he said, "I'm holding your safety close."

Meaning this time, no one besides Ryan and his twin sister knew where Tori was staying. That is, unless someone had followed them here. Maybe someone had followed them to the last house, despite their best efforts to conceal their travel destination.

"Fair enough."

Ryan had grabbed three sodas and set them on the counter. "You thirsty?"

"Sure, but…" She shifted the purse on her shoulder and eyed her duffel and laptop case. "Can I put my things somewhere?"

He studied Tori for a moment, the hint of his grin barely revealing his dimples. "Pardon my manners. You'll find the guest bedroom down the hallway. Second door to the right."

Tori found the room decorated in shades of sage and brown. Comforting and practical. Had Katelyn been the decorator? When Tori and Ryan had dated years ago, he hadn't owned a house. He'd lived in an apartment.

An image flashed through her thoughts of her and Ryan together. Married. Living in a home of their own, busy and active with their law enforcement careers. A small framed picture sat on the side table. She lifted it to get a closer look. The picture was older and portrayed his parents and siblings—they were all much younger. Ryan was probably only ten.

Kids.

Sarah had wanted that life. She'd wanted to get married and have a family.

Tori had kept pushing that part of her dream further out each year. She might have even put it off until it was too late. She chewed on her lip. Focusing on her career first had made sense at the time…but Sarah's death had changed her perspective and, in fact, was still changing the way Tori viewed life. The way she viewed everything.

Ryan.

She set the picture down. What about Ryan's brothers? What were they doing now? Oh, why was she feeling so nostalgic when there was work to be done? Tori shoved the mushy feelings over to the far side of her heart so she could concentrate on helping Ryan get to the bottom of this.

Plus, Tori had a decision to make. Should she ask for a longer leave and stay or go all the way and give up her job? Or when her bereavement leave was up, should she go back to her job and leave Ryan to find Sarah's killer and Tori's attacker without her help? Thoughts of stepping away from the investigation left her unsettled. Not that she didn't trust him, but she was worried about him, too. The killer had already murdered five people. If Tori got far enough away, she should be safe, but Ryan would still be here in the midst of it. Touching the image of a young Ryan in the photograph, she pursed her lips.

Uncertainty weighed on her, though she needed to make a decision. She would need to know the answer to her own questions soon.

She left her duffel and purse on the queen bed and snatched her laptop from the case. She brought it with her back into the kitchen and set it on the table. Katelyn had already filled the room with the delicious smells of Italian food. Tori's stomach rumbled in response.

"Where's Ryan?" she asked.

"He's on a call. Something about the FBI and eco-terrorists." Katelyn gestured toward the front part of the house.

"Good." That meant they wouldn't lose more time than they'd already lost today. She crept forward, not to eavesdrop, but to let him know she was available to participate if needed.

She saw him standing there, cell to his ear as he peeked through the mini blinds, out the front window. For a few seconds she studied his profile. A strong jaw and well-defined masculine features. A few whiskers had erupted on his cheek where he shaved to form the Vandyke beard. Finally he turned his head to look at her, as though he'd been aware of her presence all along. He didn't appear disturbed with her for intruding on his call.

"I understand," he spoke into the cell. "Yep. We'll be there."

He ended the call.

"We'll be there?" she asked. "What's going on?"

"I just spoke with an FBI agent. He sounded perturbed with us. We're meeting with him in twenty."

"What?" Hands fisted on her hips, Katelyn stared at them as she strolled into the room. "And miss my pasta? I was cooking it up special, just for you."

Ryan chuckled and glanced at his smartphone. "If it's ready we can eat fast and make it."

"No way," she said. "You do your meeting and then we'll have a nice relaxed meal when you get back. No rushing through a meal I'm taking my time to make." Katelyn leaned close to Tori and squeezed her arm. "Besides, I want to catch up with Tori."

Tori and Katelyn had been friendly, but not all that

close. Still, Katelyn's friendliness warmed her. With Sarah gone, Tori's heart ached with loneliness, and even the smallest of gestures meant so much.

"I'd like that, too," Tori said.

"That'll work, then," Ryan said. "I don't think we'll be that long." Ryan glanced at Tori. "The plan for coming and going will always be the same. You have to duck down in the vehicle before I exit the garage. Wear the cap and the wig, just in case."

Tori stared at the ceiling and shook her head. "Like that worked so well the last time. Whoever is looking for me is not going to be fooled."

"We do all we know to do, Tori. Just work with me on this, okay?"

"Okay, fine. Let's do this."

Ryan sat in the passenger seat of the special agent's big black SUV parked under the overpass of a bridge in an abandoned industrial area. The agent remained in the driver's seat. Tori sat in the back seat. This clandestine meeting was like something from a movie. Ryan didn't like it.

Why couldn't they be up front and out in the open?

His cell had buzzed a few times. His captain was calling him.

Special Agent Sanchez remained stoic, but Ryan suspected that beneath the surface he was fuming. "Sarah Peterson's murder had nothing to do with her involvement in the ecoterrorist group."

"You can't know that. I think you're trying to deflect your responsibility in this." Tori wasn't hiding her own frustration.

"Ecoterrorists aren't profiled as murderers. The extent of their activism typically involves property damage. Sarah's murder was part of a multiple homicide. Your investigation has taken a wrong turn, Detective."

"How do you explain Dee James's murder?" Tori asked. "He was murdered because he knew something about Sarah."

"I'm sorry, are you investigating, Special Agent Peterson? Because it was my understanding you're on bereavement leave." Sanchez's unemotional features suddenly shifted. He was losing his patience. "What's going on, Detective Bradley?"

"I'm in charge of this investigation," Ryan said. "Since Tori has insight into her sister that we wouldn't otherwise have, I've asked her to offer her expertise. Her knowledge of her sister's life led us to Sarah's involvement with Dee James, which led us to her email alias, and then finally to you."

"You were not led to me. I contacted you because you could have cost us months of work. Do you know that?" Now was the moment when the agent would come unhinged.

Instead, he blew out a breath. "We took down the ecoterrorist activists within A Better World at four this morning. We raided the homes of eight people and brought charges against them for planning to bomb a factory."

"But not murder?"

"No. But if we learn more about Sarah's death from our perpetrators, you can learn about that on the news. Now if you'll excuse me, I have someplace to be."

"Wait, Special Agent Sanchez," Tori said. "Please tell me that Sarah wasn't involved in violence. That she wasn't an ecoterrorist who got caught and had to make a deal."

He pursed his lips for a couple of breaths, then said, "She was working with us the whole time, Peterson, if that eases your mind. As for her murder, I suggest you get back on track with your investigation, Detective, and focus on a different target and motive. You've missed the boat on this one."

The agent was dismissing them.

Ryan suspected that Tori wanted to argue more. How could the arrogant Agent Sanchez know that someone within A Better World hadn't found out that Sarah was an informant and decided to take revenge? Did Dee James know what Sarah was up to? Tori made it sound as if the guy liked Sarah and wanted to help. But Sarah had taken his idea of an alias email and used it against him.

He stood with Tori under the bridge and watched Sanchez drive away in his slick black Suburban. Again, just like in the movies.

"Well, that was weird," Tori said.

Ryan would keep his thoughts to himself for the moment.

Back in his county vehicle, Ryan started the ignition, and let Tori process the meeting, as well. Ryan said nothing as he absorbed the news shared by the agent.

Tori pressed her head against the seat back and released a soft sigh. "It could be over, then. They've arrested the main threats in the group and will obviously find out more by questioning them. The FBI will know if there was some reason they could have had to kill Sarah, her friends, and then also Dee. I just know that Dee was scared. If only he had shared everything he knew with me. But maybe someone in this group they've arrested will share more—like who found me at the safe house today."

"I hope you're right." For Tori's safety's sake. "Let's hope they discover the true reasons for Sarah's murder now that they have made some arrests, but it doesn't sound like they're connecting those dots the same way we are. I'll do what I can to find out more, even though this guy made it clear he wasn't going to share the information with us. Maybe when your leave is over, you can somehow use your connections within the FBI to find out more."

"You're assuming that I'm going back to work for them. I told you that I was considering staying even if only by extending my leave. You didn't believe me?"

"No, actually. I believed you would come to your senses."

"Can we just get out of here?" Irritation edged her tone.

"Yes." He glanced at her. "But first, pull your cap on."

She flicked her green eyes his way, and though she tried to send him a severe look, dimples broke out on her cheeks. And at the sight of them, his heart was in his throat. He reined in his emotions before he spoke.

"Tori, please. You agreed to work with me."

"Fine, but I'm not ducking." She tucked the hat over the wig of long black hair. "Even if Sanchez believes the killer is still out there, since he doesn't believe the activists murdered her."

"We can't know for sure, and I, for one, don't want to take any chances. There are too many unanswered questions." He steered from the parking lot. "So let's do this. Let's relax and eat with Katelyn when we get back to my house. She's going to be upset if we don't, I know that much. So please just try to enjoy the dinner that she cooked. Sometimes we have to get away from the investigation long enough to clear our heads."

"Agreed. And I assure you I won't have to work hard to enjoy her dinner. It smelled amazing. Besides, I need a break. I've been overthinking. Whatever Agent Sanchez says, I still believe Sarah's murder has something to do with that group—or at least her environmental activities, which just leads back to them. Maybe there's another group she was involved with. Something we missed. At least the ecoterrorist faction has been effectively shut down for the time being. But after I eat Katelyn's pasta, who knows what I will think."

God, please let this be over.

And if it truly was over—if Tori was right and Agent Sanchez was wrong—then she would probably go back to her job in South Carolina. Maybe she wouldn't go back now, or even next week, but eventually. His throat threatened to close up on him at the thought.

"Look out!"

Tori screamed.

The vehicle filled his vision. He accelerated and swerved in hopes of a near miss. But he had no time to escape the vehicle as it slammed into them.

THIRTEEN

A loud blast filled her ears as a force propelled her forward. The next thing Tori knew, she sat in the vehicle, stunned, a deflated airbag in her lap and a weird smell filling the air. Seconds ticked by before she shook off the daze and gathered her wits. The airbag had exploded and the impact happened much too fast for her to comprehend.

And screams.

She'd heard screams.

Tori realized the screams had come from her. But she wasn't screaming now. She was absorbing the fact they'd been in a car crash and she was still alive. She gasped for much-needed oxygen as her heart pounded. Dizziness tried to swallow her but she fought it. She remembered a vehicle had headed straight for them.

A hand gripped her. "Tori. Are you hurt?"

Ryan. Ryan had been driving.

"No, I'm not hurt. I'm… I'm okay." She looked at him, a deflated airbag in his lap as well, but he had a cut across his forehead, and the sunglasses propped on his head were broken. "But *you're* hurt."

She touched his head and then looked at the blood on

her fingertips. Ryan checked the rearview mirror that barely remained intact on the cracked windshield. "I'll live. We have to get out of here."

Tori reached up to touch her own head to see if she, too, was bleeding. Then she realized she was no longer wearing the wig. The impact had dislodged the disguise she'd donned moments before. She disentangled herself from the airbag and unbuckled the seat belt to search for the wig. The move ignited a throb across her chest. She'd have a bruise from the seat belt, if not the airbag.

"Get ready to run." Ryan's tone was urgent. "Tori, are you listening?"

"Sure." She tried to shake off the daze.

"I need you to stay down until I can get you out." Ryan grabbed her chin and forced her to look at him. "The wreck was deliberate. Your life is in jeopardy." Ryan had his weapon out. "Get down, please."

He urged her downward in the seat, which was hard because the front end was crunched inward, giving her less room. Again her chest throbbed. Tori did her best to remain down and out of view.

"Wait here," he said. "I'll be back."

Ryan tried to open his door, but it wouldn't budge. He shoved against it repeatedly. Then he shifted his body around, putting himself practically over her, and kicked the door open. He slipped out of the vehicle.

"We should stay together, Ryan."

But he was gone. What was he doing? Panic spiked through her. Tori tried the passenger door. It wouldn't budge. She reached for her own gun.

She could possibly crawl over the console and out of Ryan's opened side, but then that would expose her if someone was aiming to shoot her. Tori remained crunched down in the seat.

Gunshots exploded around her in an exchange. Between Ryan and who else? Was he up against one person or many?

Her breathing accelerated. She needed to help him. *I have to get out of here. I'm a sitting duck.*

"Where are you, Ryan?"

With all the gunfire, he could be shot and injured or worse… Dead.

He'd told her to wait, but she couldn't.

Then she heard him.

"Tori, get out of the vehicle! I can't make it to you!" he called, his voice sounding distant. "I'll hold him off!"

More gunshots resounded.

Time to move.

She kicked against her door again but it still wouldn't budge. Tori crawled across the console to the driver's side. Keeping low, she slid out, her weapon ready to fire. She needed somewhere to go, but she was stuck hiding behind the door of the vehicle as she tried to figure out where to go. She wanted to call out to Ryan but didn't want to give herself away. He had to know she had climbed out, because he'd been shooting at someone to keep them from shooting at her.

If someone wanted her dead, wasn't there any easier way to go about it? What a ridiculous thought to have at this moment.

Footfalls pounded the ground.

Two sets now.

Her heart hammered. Someone was running, but in which direction? Away from her, or toward her? She risked a peek down the alley and spotted Ryan giving chase.

That was it. She was going, too. Tori shoved from the vehicle, propelling herself forward and running after the two of them. The man he was chasing turned a corner.

"Ryan, wait up!" she called.

Ryan hesitated at the corner and then turned to wait for her. She caught up with him and didn't miss a step as together they bounded around the corner and into the service vehicle access behind the buildings.

But the guy had disappeared. They continued forward until they made the end of the access behind the buildings that opened up to another alley.

She gasped for breath. "Déjà vu. This happened before. We can't lose him this time. I'm going right, and you go left."

"No." Ryan held his weapon ready to aim and fire at the first sign of trouble. "We'll go together."

Tori didn't argue and crept down the alley, Ryan at her side. She held her weapon ready to lift and fire at a moment's notice. As she moved, she looked in every direction, waiting for the perp to jump out of the shadows or a corner. Ryan did the same but she had the uncanny sense that he was guarding her, as well. What a strange situation to be thrust into. At least Tori trusted Ryan to have her back, though she wasn't giving him much choice at the moment.

A door slammed in a vacant building up ahead. She gestured toward the building. "In there."

"I don't like this, Tori," Ryan said.

"I don't like it, either, but we have to catch this guy. I'm not going to be safe until this is over." Clearly she'd been completely wrong to believe she was safe with the ecoterrorist group in custody. Sanchez had been right on that point. That chafed. Unless Sanchez had been wrong and they had missed someone. But she couldn't think about that right now.

Ryan grabbed her before she entered. "I'm lead on this. I'll give chase."

"And I'll watch your back."

He opened the door and stepped inside. "Police. Give it up."

Slowly and methodically they cleared rooms on the lower level of a forsaken, multi-floor commercial building, then moved to the next floor. Neither of them spoke as they worked together. Very well together, she noted.

When they approached the last door in the building, Ryan hesitated and they shared a knowing look. The guy had to be in this room. And the perp had to know this was the end of the line for him.

Ryan positioned himself to safely enter the room, then called out in his official law enforcement tone, "It's all over. I'm going to open the door. If you're holding a weapon—"

The man fired off three shots. Bullets passed through the door. Tori's pulse roared in her ears.

"I think he's out," Ryan said.

"He could have another clip," she said.

Ryan nodded. "Give it up," he called through to the shooter. "I'm with the Maynor County Sheriff's Office, and I'm going to open this door. I'm going to shoot you if you are still holding a weapon. Understand?"

"Understood." The response from behind the door surprised her.

Except, what did that really mean?

"Be careful, Ryan," she said. "This could be a trap."

Ryan kicked the door open and pointed his weapon. "Police!"

Tori came in low behind him.

A man stood at the far side of the room with his hands in his air. A gun lay on the floor in front of him. "I'm out, man. Don't shoot me. I'm out." Oddly, tears leaked from his eyes.

He was scared? That didn't fit with the cold-blooded killer she'd been imagining. There was more going on here than she'd realized.

Finally a break in this case. The break they needed. Finally she could learn what happened to Sarah.

The window shattered. The perp's face scrunched and then he crumpled as gunfire rang out.

Lights flashed from the emergency vehicles parked near the car accident that had taken out Ryan's unmarked car. The wrecked vehicles had been moved to the side of the road to allow for traffic to flow.

The county coroner had already examined the perp's body, and the building across the street from where the kill shot had been fired had been swept for evidence. Ryan hadn't been informed on what had been discovered yet.

Medics had checked both Ryan and Tori out because neither of them wanted to sit in the hospital again. Not with a killer out there. With the attacks ramping up, they had to be getting close to the truth about who was behind this. And that meant Tori was in even more danger.

Ryan and Tori had already given their statements. It was getting late and Ryan was exhausted, but he'd grown somewhat accustomed to the long and odd hours as a detective. What was unfamiliar—and uncomfortable—was the hands-on scrutiny he was facing. Ryan shifted back and forth on his aching feet as he filled in his boss, Captain Moran, as well as his boss's superiors, Chief Deputy Carmichael and Sheriff Rollins. It was a rough day when the heads of the sheriff's department came to the scene of the crime to question Ryan on the events of the evening, including the clandestine meeting with the FBI agent. Sheriff Rollins was none too happy about the turn in Ryan's investigation, the threats on Tori's life or the FBI agent's attitude.

Ryan's investigative tactics were being scrutinized, as well, for everyone to hear. Couldn't they take this back to the office to discuss?

"I get the feeling from you that Special Agent Peterson has been working this investigation, perhaps even leading you, the lead detective on the case," Captain Moran said.

The chief deputy watched and listened.

Ryan knew when to speak, and when to keep quiet. Now wasn't the time to reply. His boss hadn't finished with him.

"Maybe I need to have a few words with Agent Peterson's boss," Sheriff Rollins said. "It's time for her to leave. She's a distraction to you, Ryan, and her life's in danger, and almost cost you yours."

"Where is she now?" Captain Moran asked.

Ryan was more than relieved Katelyn had picked Tori up and carted her away from the scene so she wouldn't have to endure more questions. "Safe."

The captain eyed him. "I asked you a question, Detective."

"In light of the fact that someone knew where to look

for her at my original safe house," Ryan said, "I prefer not sharing her location information here." He gestured to the law enforcement presence and the public gathered at the scene. "Add to that, the Jeep that slammed into us was seen at the original safe house."

Captain Moran lost his tough stance, his features softening a bit. Ryan hadn't known him to be harsh, but maybe the captain was under pressure with his two superiors here, as well. He had to perform his duties or be scrutinized himself.

"That was the correct response," he said. "Lets me know that you've got your head on straight."

Tension eased from Ryan's shoulders.

"Yes, sir," Ryan said. "We have the name of the man who was driving and who was subsequently shot and killed. Eddie Slattery. We've run a background. I'm still looking for his connection to the other murders—of Sarah Peterson and her friends, and Dee James. Or a connection to anyone who would want to harm Tori."

The sheriff nodded, only half listening as he answered his cell.

Ryan released a slow sigh of relief. He fisted his hands by his sides, impatient to finish the inquisition and answer their questions—all of which would be written up in his reports for them to read later. He understood the investigation of four murders, now six, had taken several turns and the public also wanted the killer caught. The entire sheriff's office was being scrutinized, not just Ryan as the lead investigator.

But all he wanted, all he could think about was to get out of here and check on Tori. They needed to talk through the implications of what happened tonight. This could mean they had been following the wrong leads.

Did Sarah's murder have something to do with her social justice activities or not?

Captain Moran squeezed Ryan's shoulder. "All right. I think we're done here. Carry on, Detective Bradley. You're doing a good job staying on top of things, considering all that's happened so far. But I do agree with the sheriff that Sarah's sister needs to be out of the investigation."

"She has insight into her sister's goings-on and has provided me with important information."

"I understand. She's offering assistance, but she's also interfering with your investigation, I hope you realize that. When is she heading home to her real job again?"

"I'm not sure. I've tried to persuade her to leave."

"Well, try harder." With those words Captain Moran left him, to join the sheriff and chief deputy.

Captain Moran had effectively dismissed him. That was fine, because he wanted to leave and find Tori.

Except, to get out of here, he was going to need a new vehicle.

His cell buzzed. He looked at the text.

To your right.

Ryan turned and spotted Katelyn's car parked a distance away from the wreck. He jogged over and climbed in on the passenger side, painfully aware that Tori was not in the vehicle with his sister.

He stiffened. "What's going on? Why aren't you guarding Tori like I'm paying you to?"

She steered the vehicle around the corner. "I can't protect someone who doesn't want to be protected. When we got back to your house, Tori called a cab and left."

FOURTEEN

Tori dropped her briefcase, duffel and purse on one of two queen beds in the airport motel. She still couldn't comprehend the chain of events that had propelled her here.

Maybe she had this all wrong.

Maybe she shouldn't have walked away from Ryan's attempt at protection. But someone had seemed to know their every move, no matter what they did. And this evening, Ryan had almost been killed along with Tori. Sure, he was accustomed to dangerous situations, but like he told her—it was harder to stay safe when someone was targeting you, even if you were trained law enforcement.

Tori might not have listened to his words before, but they hit harder when it concerned Ryan. After the deliberate car crash, she made the decision she wouldn't put him or his sister in the line of fire. She'd already lost her own sister. The Bradley family didn't need to lose anyone because of Tori.

Besides, she was due back in the office the day after tomorrow. If she returned to her job, it would take her a day of travel and recovery at her apartment as it was.

Uncertainty about her plans had plagued her for the last few days, but now she knew exactly what she would do.

She would go back to South Carolina and hope she could find out more about Sarah's murder when she was back at work. Right now, it was time to get her things ready for flying. Tori dumped her purse to clear it of anything that wouldn't clear security, and she spotted a small round device. She lifted it to examine it.

A GPS tracker.

Tori groaned.

"Idiot! I'm such a stupid idiot."

A knock came at the door. Panic swelled in her chest and she gripped her weapon. Tori didn't ask who it was, she simply waited quietly in case it was the man who had shot Eddie Slattery—the perp who'd drive his Jeep into them and shot at them. She'd just found a GPS—was that his? Had he somehow gotten access to her things to plant the tracker and then followed her here where she was all alone?

Sweat beaded on her temple.

"It's me."

Ryan.

Tori released a slow breath.

Ryan's tone wasn't gruff like she would expect, but instead he sounded…desperate? Whatever. She was both relieved and perturbed. Him finding Tori here meant one thing. She marched to the door and opened it, leaving it wide for Ryan to enter. He shut it behind him.

She held the GPS tracker up for him to see. "Really?"

He shrugged. "That wasn't me."

"Katelyn." Tori squeezed her temples. "How could I have been so stupid?"

Ryan's sister had advised Tori against leaving, at least until she could talk it out with Ryan. Katelyn had known that Ryan would be furious with the both of them—Tori for leaving and Katelyn for allowing it. Tori had known that, too, but at the time she hadn't cared. She was thinking about their safety. Tori had gotten into the back seat of the cab with her laptop and Katelyn had handed off her duffel and purse. She would have had the opportunity to place the tracker then. Katelyn had been thinking ahead. She was a smart cookie.

"She wanted to make sure you were okay," he said. "That you got to the airport safely."

"And that you could find me."

Leaning against the wall, Ryan crossed his arms. "Right. She meant to help, that's all. What if something happened to you, Tori? You're in danger. Running off like this wasn't a smart move."

"And you think the tracker would help you to find me if I were abducted or left for dead? If the bad guys nabbed me, I don't think they would let me bring my purse." She sent him a wry grin.

"You might have found a way to convince the nabber you needed to keep it. That said, he might still look inside, so you'd need a backup tracker." Ryan responded with his own grin.

"No…" Katelyn hadn't! Tori shrugged out of her jacket and searched. She removed her shoes and looked inside and out.

"Relax. I don't know if that's the only tracker Katelyn planted, but we do know that someone has known where you've been. Like the bedroom in Sarah's house."

"And the first safe house—the dream house."

"And like tonight. Eddie drove that Jeep right for

you. He aimed at your side of the vehicle. I couldn't stop the collision but I tried to swerve so he wouldn't crush the passenger side." He scraped a hand down his face as it paled.

The implication got to him as it did her. A chill crawled over her.

She palmed her weapon. "And you think they could have followed me here."

"I think if you're heading back home then you shouldn't stay here tonight. You should get an earlier flight and wait in the airport beyond the security checkpoints. Take the red-eye, even. I'm happy to take you to the airport. But if you're not going to stay with me, then go there and be safe. You know you're not safe until whoever is behind this is caught."

"Unfortunately, I do know that." Tori sat on the edge of the bed. "Listen, I'm sorry I left without at least saying goodbye. I just didn't want to endanger you or your sister, or anyone who is near me."

He gave her a look, and then she suddenly remembered his words to her—he'd told her that she would go back. She was glad he didn't say, "I told you so."

"So yes, you were right about me, after all. I'm not staying here like I had been considering. I think I can do a better job finding answers for us if I'm back at work and can gain access to information we need. Special Agent Sanchez isn't going to share with you, that much is clear. I don't even know if I can get anyone to share with *me* even if I put pressure on them from within, but I'm going to work that angle. Katelyn will be safe because she won't have to protect me. I don't want you to be in danger, either." Tori didn't want to keep having to dodge bombs and bullets until this was over.

"She's pretty miffed at you, you know. She would have helped me protect you for nothing, but she needed the work." He frowned.

"You don't need to lose your sister, too, especially because of me. Besides, it's not just her I'm worried about. You could have died tonight, too. This way, you won't be in danger, either—at least, not because of me."

Her words surprised herself. She hadn't realized how deeply she cared for Ryan's safety. But her worry for him hadn't only been about his safety. Her concern took her through forbidden territory. She and Ryan already had their chance at something special once before.

"You know that comes with the job, right? And if you're worried about Katelyn, if that's why you're leaving, then we can do something about that. Because... I'm the one who's supposed to protect you." Now his tone had turned gruff.

Maybe he'd been right in the first place—about leaving. She'd go to the airport and hang out there. See about getting an earlier flight. She began stuffing everything back into her bag.

"You're confusing me, Ryan. You've continued to insist that I leave. Insist that I go home where I'll be safer. Now you sound like you want me to stay. The truth is, I'm only a distraction to your investigation. That's all I've ever been. You need to focus. I'm sorry, I thought I could help."

He stepped closer.

That made her heart beat all the harder.

"You *have* helped." Deep need resonated through his tone.

Tori fought her trembling hands. "No. I sent us both in the wrong direction."

"But Dee James knew something," he said. "That was not the wrong direction."

"I think… I think he was truly concerned for Sarah's safety and Dee was killed for the same reason someone is trying to kill me. For something they thought he knew. Something they think *I* know. And now tonight the guy who followed me to the safe house and who rammed us, another of our leads in addition to Dee James, is dead."

Ryan took a step toward her, as if he wasn't already much too close. "Tori…"

Her heart skipped around inside at the way he said her name. She pressed her fingers over her eyes. "I can't think clearly with you standing so close."

In the room.

In the house.

In her life.

She huffed out a breath. "Just… I need to go. You were right all along. I shouldn't have stayed. I've only messed everything up."

"Tori, I—"

She avoided looking at his face or into his eyes. That was the only way she could keep from melting right into his arms. "Go, Ryan. I'll call a cab. I can take care of myself."

Her words had the wanted effect. He took a step back. "I'll wait until I see the cab pick you up."

"Fine. Do what you need to do."

Still, she didn't look at him as she moved to peek through the door and window to make sure it was safe to exit. Then she held the door open for him, hating this whole scene—but she had to be cold and calculated to let him go.

For herself and for him.

Finally she lifted her gaze to meet his. Ryan studied her, then his striking features turned severe. "Safe travels, Tori. I hope you'll share with me anything you learn."

He turned his back on her and exited the room.

Tori shut the door and leaned against it. She calmed her breathing. The room seemed to spin a little and felt lonely and empty with him gone. She'd been fine before he'd shown up. Hadn't she?

She concentrated on getting her act together and getting herself to the airport. Once she was back on the job, she would be safer.

At least, Ryan had kept telling her that, and now she believed it, too.

She needed distance between herself and her attacker—and access to the FBI's resources. That was the best way to catch this guy. She wouldn't truly be safe until she'd discovered whatever this person thought she knew, and then she would take him down.

I'm coming for you!

Tori dug through all her belongings in search of another possible tracking device—Katelyn's or someone else's. Her belongings seemed clean. Not that it mattered, since Ryan knew exactly where she was at the moment. She had no doubt that he would follow the cab to the airport, and that was his choice, but she wouldn't ride in a vehicle with him again and put him in danger.

She wouldn't stay here any longer and put her heart in danger, either.

Ryan had borrowed Katelyn's vehicle and waited inside. He'd have to pick up a new one tomorrow at the office when he went in to file reports. He really didn't have time for all the paperwork, with everything going on.

Like now. He should be back at the station, writing up his reports, but instead, he watched the motel near the airport for signs of suspicious activity. Anyone who might be sitting and waiting on Tori, like he was.

Waiting on Tori.

Had that been what he'd been doing for the last several years? Had he been keeping busy with his job and pretending to find satisfaction in that while deep inside, he secretly hoped and waited for the day when Tori would come back to him? Pathetic. He'd let her go, and like the adage claimed, if she came back to him then she was his. And now that she was, in fact, back, had Ryan been harboring a hope that Tori would stay because of him? That she wanted to be with him?

He rubbed his eyes to push back the ridiculous thoughts. His reaction to her cutting out on him blindsided him. He should have been encouraging her to leave instead of desperately trying to keep her here. His motivations were purely selfish. He'd own that, sure. But they'd worked together well, he thought, and they could *still* work together well once on the other side of this investigation. When Sarah's killer was caught and Tori was safe and sound. That had been a secret dream of his long ago—the two of them solving crimes together, and going home together. But she'd taken a different path.

Together until death do us part.

He coughed up a chuckle. Ryan truly loathed himself at this moment. A few more seconds and he might have found himself begging her to stay. It all proved to be a real eye-opener regarding his own character.

He could berate himself in the weeks and months to come, but right now he focused back on the situation. He had to keep Tori safe while she headed to the airport. He didn't blame her for not wanting to ride with him.

Twenty minutes later a cab pulled into the parking lot.

Ryan stiffened. If someone had followed her here, this could be the moment they took action.

He started his vehicle and watched her get into the cab. The white minivan then steered slowly through the parking lot, which seemed to take an eternity. Ryan just wanted her at the airport—checked in and through security, where she would be safest.

Finally the cab turned onto the street and Ryan followed closely behind, hoping to provide a deterrence to anyone who thought about attacking her again.

The cab's driver seemed to inch along the freeway and Ryan thought about calling Tori to have her ask the man to speed things up. But she'd made it clear she could and would take care of herself. Ryan followed the cab around the airport drive. Then he pulled up behind it when the cab stopped in front of the drop-off. Ryan didn't get out but simply watched from the inside of Katelyn's vehicle.

He watched Tori, waiting for the moment when she would glance back at him. He planned to give her a little wave. He also planned to follow her inside—from a distance. But she didn't look back as she carried her duffel and laptop case into the terminal. Ryan left Katelyn's vehicle at the drop-off zone and followed Tori inside. Until she was through the security gate, someone could still cause her problems. Even after she was through, they could try to harm her, but the chances were much lower considering no unauthorized personnel could carry a weapon through the security screening.

Inside the terminal, he stood back and watched and waited. If Tori knew he'd followed her inside, she didn't let on. That she didn't acknowledge him squeezed his heart, leaving him sick to his stomach.

Get a grip, man. Why had he let her get so deeply under his skin again?

Finally she moved through the security gate. He would have expected to breathe a sigh of relief, except he'd just let the love of his life get away from him again.

He made his way back to Katelyn's vehicle, which he'd left illegally parked. Captain Moran called and Ryan gave him an update, relieved he could actually tell his captain that Tori was at the airport, waiting to board a plane. When he approached his vehicle, an airport cop was writing him a ticket. Ryan flashed his Maynor County Sheriff's detective badge and explained his business and then got in.

Katelyn called as he pulled away.

He answered with "No, your vehicle isn't wrecked. And yes, Tori is at the airport, checked through security. I'm heading home now."

"I wasn't calling to check up on you. Not really. You can take care of yourself, little brother."

"Hey, I'm not your little brother just because I was born two minutes after you."

"Uh-huh." Katelyn chuckled. "I was calling because I've found an interesting connection that you're going to want to look into."

FIFTEEN

Tori found a seat at the gate. She would go standby on the next flight back to South Carolina, which included a lot of connections. Still, that didn't take off for another three hours, so this could very well turn into a long night. She decided she would put that time to good use, doing the same thing she would do in the motel room, only here she wouldn't be constantly listening for someone approaching the door.

She could easily spot an approaching threat from where she sat at the gate, her back to the window and facing the inside of the terminal.

Ryan had been right to suggest she hang out at the airport, though part of her felt like a coward. But she didn't want to die before she could solve the mystery of who killed Sarah. That person needed to pay for what he'd done to six people now, adding Dee James and Eddie Slattery to the group.

Sorrow for their loss left her hollowed out. If she and Ryan had solved the first murders sooner, then the others might still be alive.

Or...if Sarah hadn't gotten involved in something

that turned her into a target, all six people might still be alive. But it did no good to take that perspective.

While she waited to gain access to the flight home, she could work on her laptop. She sent her supervisor an email, notifying him that she was returning and would be back in the office tomorrow. She also thanked him for the flowers the department had sent for Sarah's funeral, though she planned to send a handwritten note, as well. She had to tread carefully in how she explained the FBI's possible connection to her sister's death. She tried to focus on how best to word her email, but her thoughts kept going back to Ryan.

She'd been painfully aware of his vehicle following the cab, and that he'd gotten out and followed her inside, watching until she made it through security. A thousand times she'd considered approaching him or at least acknowledging his presence, but what would that solve? Nothing. It would only stir up the same old argument of whether she should stay or whether she should go, and those same unwanted emotions would erupt.

She had to put what being with Ryan for the last few days had stirred inside her back into a locked box. She sent an email to Dad, letting him know of her departure and why she'd had to leave. Tori explained that she would be back for a short visit or they could come out to see her, once the person responsible for Sarah's death and Tori's attacks was incarcerated. He would be hurt that he didn't at least get to say goodbye in person—which was the reason she chose to email rather than get into the emotional drama over the phone—but he would have to understand. He would then break the news to Mom. Together, they would console themselves with the fact that Tori was doing what they had wanted her to do, and that she would be safer. They wouldn't lose another daughter.

Tori sat taller and shoved the sudden tears away.

She let the fury at this killer wash through her and leave her as a force to be reckoned with.

Dad replied to her email sooner than she would have thought, stating that he was glad she would be safe and he looked forward to hearing from her when she arrived. Phew. Relieved at his response, she read more. He said they would discuss coming out for a visit when she had time.

And that was another issue, wasn't it? In her job she hardly had time for family, especially when she lived halfway across the country.

Her cell rang.

Mom.

Tori flinched. Mom would stir up her emotions, and she needed to stay levelheaded as she remained on guard.

Groaning inside, she answered the call. "Mom, hi."

"Hey, honey. I know you can't tell me where you are, where the safe house is. I understand all that, but I wanted to hear your voice. I miss you."

Disappointment sank in Tori's gut—Dad hadn't told Mom the news yet. Her mother could very well figure her location out when she heard the background noise. Tori pinched the bridge of her nose, wishing now that she hadn't answered. Why hadn't she simply let it go to voice mail?

"I miss you, too, Mom. Let's pray this is over soon and we can spend time together without having to worry."

"I can't lose you, too, Tori." Mom's words sounded warbled, but Tori suspected she was doing her best to control her emotions.

"You won't, Mom. I promise." She might as well go ahead and tell her she was leaving.

"I meant to ask, what was in that package Sarah sent you?"

Package?

"What package?"

"You didn't find it? It came to our house a few days ago—they forwarded it from your apartment. I stuck it in your briefcase when they gathered your things from Sarah's house. That was after the explosion. You were in the hospital."

"Right. They took me to the safe house from there. I didn't see a package, but I haven't rifled through my briefcase—" though she had pulled her laptop out of its pocket several times "—Listen, Mom, I have—"

An announcement for an incoming flight came over the intercom.

"Where are you, Tori? It sounds like you're at the airport. What's going on?"

Air whooshed from Tori's lungs. "I'm heading home, Mom. I emailed Dad to explain that in order to be safe, I need to leave."

"But—"

Mom would have at least wanted to see her off. To say goodbye. Give her a hug. Tori got it. This wasn't how Mom had imagined Tori going somewhere safe.

Dad's voice sounded in the background as he explained to Mom what was going on. *A little late, Dad.*

She'd wanted to avoid the drama. While she listened to the secondhand conversation, she dug through her briefcase and spotted a small package—the one from Sarah?

"Mom, I think I found the package. I have to go." Tori ended the call abruptly. Mom would have to understand, and Tori would make up for it later.

Gripping the orange-colored mailer, she stared at the handwriting—Sarah's writing—and the date it had been sent. The day before Sarah's murder. Tori had made sure to forward her mail to Mom and Dad's, and it had taken time to find her here.

Without a doubt she knew what she held in her hands was the information that had put a target on her head. They thought that she already knew. That she had already received the package.

She slid it over her keyboard to hide it behind her laptop and looked around the terminal. The rush and madness to make the next flight had died down and only one person sat in the waiting area with her. Few people walked the halls.

Tori ripped the package and a USB drive fell out. She peeked inside the package and found a sealed envelope, too. She opened it to find a handwritten note from Sarah.

Dear Tori,
I got myself in too deep and I'm not sure where to turn, so I'm sending this to you. I thought it would be easier to mail and have you look at it first, and then we can talk later. But no email. I'm concerned that someone could find out what I've been up to. I think someone has been following me.

That's it? Come on, Sarah. At least you could have explained what this was about.

But then again, Sarah had probably been scared to say too much, and with good reason, given the danger she was in. Only it had gotten her killed anyway.

Tori detested the anger that surged through her. Anger at her sister for getting herself killed. She pushed down that hateful emotion—this wasn't Sarah's fault.

Goose bumps rose on her arms as she stuck the USB drive into the slot on her laptop.

She stared at incriminating documents about the company GenDynamics—the place where Sarah worked. And then it hit Tori. GenDynamics was an agricultural company. Of course! Now it was all beginning to make sense.

Tori should have looked into this from the beginning. She'd been too distraught to see clearly what was right there all the time.

Tori sat up and did a quick search on the company. GenDynamics produced pesticides and GMOs—genetically modified organisms. She'd heard the term repeatedly, but what exactly did that mean?

Tori read further. Gene splicing. That was what it was all about. DNA from a variety of species were forced into genes of other plants or animals. She cringed at what she read, and then went back to the information Sarah had gathered. Sarah had taken photographs of documentation that showed the company was purposefully mislabeling and selling an unapproved pesticide. If that was discovered, it could cost them tens of millions of dollars in fines, lawsuits and government penalties.

Comprehension slammed into her, and she flattened against the seat back.

Oh, Sarah...

She'd been part of an environmental group, and Tori had a feeling Dee knew about these other activities, but he'd been afraid to tell Tori. GenDynamics was a huge company with deep pockets. Maybe Sarah's run-in with the legislator was her way of trying to get someone to listen to her about what was going on there. And when they wouldn't, she'd gathered this information herself.

Sarah had turned into a major whistle-blower. Whistle-blowers were supposed to be protected by laws, but they were often persecuted.

And in this case, she had been murdered before the whistle could be blown.

Tori's cell rang. Dad this time.

Tori grimaced. She couldn't talk to him at this moment. She had to process what all of this meant. Why hadn't Sarah given this information to Sanchez? She already had a working relationship with him. Instead, Sarah had sent the information to Tori so she could take action, and Tori had failed her sister.

Monumentally.

She couldn't go back in time to change any of it. All she could do was go forward and try to fix it now. She would find out who was behind Sarah's murder, thanks to this information she now had in her hands.

Tori's cell rang again. She would need to text Dad that she would call back in a bit. She opened the texting app to tell him and then stared at a text that had come through from Dad's cell.

If you want to see your parents alive bring me the package.

She replied with her own text. Wait. I'm at the airport. You'll have to give me time. I don't have it with me.

I know you have it with you.

Tori stared at her cell. Had he employed a listening app on her phone or on her parents'? Or was he watching her even now, here in the airport? Tori glanced around her. Goose bumps crawled over her.

If you want them to remain alive, you must tell no one. If the information in the package ever comes to light, their deaths will be on your hands. And then you'll die, too.

The street was dark and quiet when Ryan finally turned into his driveway and parked in the garage. He'd had to go back to the office to catch up on his reports and update his boss again, which meant he'd had to wait to find out what Katelyn wanted to show him. He found it was best to ferret out the truth before presenting anything to his boss.

Now he was ready to hear what she'd learned. He hadn't asked her to stay and help, but he'd take any assistance he could get.

Ryan entered his home through the garage entrance and found the breakfast area dimly lit. Katelyn sat at the kitchen table, the light from her laptop reflecting on her face.

"Sorry I'm late. Captain Moran wanted a face-to-face with me." It had been good to be able to reassure his boss that Tori was no longer part of the investigation.

Now that Tori was at the airport, he realized just how

glad he was that she was headed home. Maybe he would have caught the murderer by now, without her proximity and the fact she was in danger scrambling his brain.

And now he could focus on dousing what her presence had kindled inside of him.

And douse he would, though he wasn't sure how yet. Starting tonight.

He grabbed sodas for each of them from the fridge, then pulled out the chair at the end of the table to sit. Ryan popped the top, drank and savored the fizz, then guzzled the rest. He sat the empty can on the table.

Katelyn finally responded.

"And you couldn't update him with this new information because you didn't have it, is that it?"

"Pretty much." He'd called her on the way to the office, but only got her voice mail. "So please enlighten me."

"You're still in love with her."

Her words struck him in the chest. "What?"

Katelyn finally pulled her attention from the laptop. "You heard me."

"Why are you saying this to me?"

Laughter burst from her. "So you admit it?"

"No. I admit nothing." He scraped a hand down his face. "That just came out of the blue." And it wasn't what he wanted to hear from his sister.

"Not out of the blue. You asked me to please enlighten you. So I did. I told you something you're ignoring."

He couldn't listen to this. Tori was gone and he had to get over her once and for all.

"I'm not in love with her," he said. "That ended a long time ago. How I feel has no bearing on finding

Sarah's murderer and whoever is behind the attacks on Tori. She's going home now. Going back to work, where she'll be surrounded by FBI agents and be safe." He hoped. "Please explain your phone call to me. You said you found an interesting connection. Could you have been a little less cryptic? No, don't answer that. What have you learned?"

She rubbed her eyes. "I was looking into Eddie Slattery when I came across a connection. I thought he could be connected to Sarah's place of employment, GenDynamics. He's not, but that's when I came across this interesting information."

Ryan stared at her laptop, at the two faces she'd pulled up.

"It could be nothing," she said.

"Or it could be everything."

SIXTEEN

Tori's palms slicked against the steering wheel. She'd taken a cab back to Sarah's to get her sister's car, and now she sat parked on the side of a dark road and looking at an empty building that had been condemned.

This monster had her parents in there?

Oh, Mom...

Anger raged in her veins. How dare he do this to her family? How dare he bring them into this?

Lord, please help me know how to play this. How do I get them back, safe and sound, and take this guy down?

If only she hadn't sent Ryan away, maybe he would be following her now as he had on multiple occasions, saving her from danger. She'd given him the cold shoulder in her need to get away from the situation, believing it was for the best.

But now her parents' lives were at stake.

Gripping her weapon, Tori quietly exited the car. She would likely be forced to give up the weapon, but she had another tucked away at her ankle.

Creeping forward, she held her weapon ready, prepared to use it if necessary. Wouldn't it be nice if she could surprise the kidnapper and killer and get the best of him...not that she thought it would ever be that easy.

She'd tucked the package in her purse. Maybe she shouldn't have brought it so she could have strung this guy out a little longer while she tried to save her parents.

At the building, she hesitated, mentally preparing herself to face whatever evil lurked inside with her parents.

Footfalls approached from behind. She stiffened.

"Don't move," a distorted voice said. "Toss the weapon and hold your hands up where I can see them."

Tori tossed her weapon, but not terribly far. "My parents?"

"In due time. Now, toss the other weapon, the one you keep at your ankle."

She heaved a sigh and removed the smaller pistol from the ankle strap, then shucked that, as well. Again, not too far. In a pinch, she might be able to reach it.

The distorted voice creeped her out. Then again, he was hiding his identity, which offered her hope that she and her parents might actually make it out of this alive. If he planned to kill them, there would be no reason to take such precautions to disguise himself.

"Keep walking and go inside the building."

Again Tori complied, her mind racing with how she could overtake this man. But she had to make sure her parents were alive and then get them someplace safe before she took action that could get them killed.

She stepped up to the doors.

"Open it."

"Look, there's no need to involve them."

"Open the door and go inside."

Tori did as she was told, stepping into a condemned

and dark building, even though that went against every
bit of instinct she had and all her training. But the threat
to her parents trumped everything else.

A flashlight came on from behind, lighting her way
ahead.

"Keep walking to the end of the hallway and then
take a right."

Tori feared that her parents weren't here at all and
she was only walking into a trap.

Lord, help me to get us out of this. Please save us.

In the long, dark hallway, she could see light up
ahead of them, coming from beneath a doorway. A
room in the middle of the building so no lights could
be seen on the outside. No sniper shots to take out the
person or people orchestrating the abduction.

She paused at the door from which light beamed.
"This one?"

"Yes. Go inside and see your parents."

Tori opened the door and stepped inside. Her parents were both gagged and bound, sitting in chairs.
Their eyes widened when they saw her. Short-lived relief rushed through her.

She started to move toward them to hug them.

"Stop."

Tori stopped, fear and anger surging through her.
The terror in her parents' eyes nearly stole her breath.
They both subtly shook their heads as if they wished
she had stayed away. It shocked her that they expected
her to save her own life and leave theirs to this monster.

"I assume the package is in your bag. Empty the
contents on the floor."

She dumped everything out, suddenly wishing
she'd done a more thorough search. What if Katelyn

had planted another tracker and that was revealed now? She and her parents could die for that mistake. Who was she kidding—they would die anyway. Even if the abductor hid his identity, they still knew too much. Sarah had known too much and had died for that.

Still, the thought of a tracker gave her hope. What if there really *had* been another tracker she hadn't found? That meant Ryan would know she had left the airport and wasn't on a plane to the far side of the country, if Katelyn still followed the tracker's data and shared that information with her brother.

"Kick the envelope away from you."

Tori kicked it away. The man morphing his voice stood behind her. She still hadn't seen his face. "All right. You have your package now. If you're thinking of killing us now, then you'd better think again."

He didn't respond.

"You told me if the information ever comes to light, then my parents' lives will be threatened again. The reverse is true—if something happens to them or to me—then I've made arrangements for everything to be revealed to the authorities. Do you understand?"

The words she was trying to use to gain their safe passage from this situation fell flat to her own ears.

"You're bluffing."

"I'm not. But if you kill us, you'll find out." Would he kill them and dump them in the river, or try to tie their murder to drugs like he'd tried with Sarah's death? He'd tried to make it look like she'd been in the wrong place at the wrong time and with the wrong group of people.

Whatever happened, she trusted Detective Ryan Bradley to discover the truth about their deaths.

Except Tori had no intention of letting it go that far.

She slowly began turning around.

"Stop!"

She continued turning, because if she wanted him to believe her about her threat, then she'd better start acting the part. Soon she faced off with a smallish figure dressed in black and wearing a mask.

Something looked strange about him.

He pulled off the mask.

Only he was a she. Blond hair spilled out over her shoulders.

"Who are you?"

That she'd revealed herself didn't bode well for them. Tori had pushed too far.

"You think you're so smart." The woman turned off the voice-distorting device. "I'd let you try to figure out who I am, except you're not leaving."

"What? That was our deal. And you know what's going to happen."

"It'll be too late by the time they figure it out, even if your threats are true."

Tori didn't get it. Why would it be too late? Unless... "You're leaving the country." Could Tori reach and disarm this woman in time?

"None of that is your concern any longer. Don't worry, I'm not going to kill you." The door opened and in stepped a muscular guy. "*He* is. Meet Vincent. It's easy to hire an assassin online these days. I'm glad he was around to finally get rid of Eddie, who botched everything, starting with those four murders."

The woman turned and then glanced back, tossing her hair over her shoulder. "Have fun, Vincent, but not too much fun. I want this all erased within the hour."

And she was gone.

Tori would have to face off with Vincent, but at least she had a chance to survive. A chance to save her parents. She wished she had called Ryan in, but it was too late for regrets now. Tori accepted the fact that Ryan wasn't coming. He wasn't following her.

She was on her own.

"It's just you and me now, big man. Drop the weapons and let's do this mano a mano." *Hand to hand.* "Or are you afraid to fight without your gun?"

His big arms still crossed, he grinned as if to say, "Challenge accepted."

This fight would test Tori in ways for which she hadn't prepared.

Her one advantage—this was a fight for her life and the lives of her parents.

Tori's kicks and punches didn't have the impact she'd hoped for. At least she was dodging the big man's attempts to harm her. Or was he simply toying with her?

With her efforts to hurt him, she slowly lured him away from her parents, hoping to give them a chance. A way out if they were able to take it.

She found herself situated between shelves filled with boxes of who knew what. Using her good shoulder, she rammed herself into the shelf. It toppled onto the beast.

A paint scraper slid across the floor. She grabbed it. She could cut her parents free.

Hurry. They had to hurry.

Catching her breath, Tori grabbed the scraper and started toward them.

A beefy hand closed around her ankle and squeezed. She cried out in pain as she fell to the floor. Twisting around, she tried to slice at him with the scraper, but she wasn't getting anywhere.

"Here!" She slid the scraper across the floor to her parents.

It stopped just short of her father's reach. Gripping her ankle, the mercenary pulled her closer while he slid from under the shelf.

In his eyes, she saw that he was done with the games. Now he would kill her.

Ryan stepped into the fray as the big man was taking entirely too much pleasure in choking Tori, strangling her to death in front of her parents. With distance between them, he pointed the weapon at the man's head.

"Police! Release her now or I'll shoot!"

The man just held on tighter. Did he consider himself invincible? Ryan had called for backup, but he couldn't wait for them. Nor did he think he could wrestle this guy to the ground alone.

He fired his weapon, the sound exploding in his ears. The sight puncturing his heart as the man fell off Tori. Ryan removed his limp body completely and crouched next to her. Her hands around her throat, she sucked in air, then coughed. He gently assisted her into his lap and held her.

"Are you okay?" He was tired of asking that question and hoped this would be the last time for a good long while.

She nodded but couldn't speak.

Deputies and police officers streamed into the room and freed her parents. Ryan would have gotten to them, but concern for Tori filled all his thoughts.

She rested her hand against his shoulder. Relief

surged inside. Relief and something he repeatedly tried to bury.

"How… How did you find me?" she croaked out. "Another tracker?"

"No. Please, don't talk. An ambulance should be here soon."

Her parents would have to be checked out, too. Right now they were giving their statements about their abduction, which gave him a few needed moments with Tori.

"Katelyn discovered that Suzanne Sanchez Tate, the owner of GenDynamics, where Sarah worked, was Agent Sanchez's sister. She married the man who started the company decades before and ran it with him until his death."

"That must be why Sarah sent the information to me instead of Agent Sanchez," Tori once again croaked out the words. "She was afraid she couldn't trust him with information on his sister. I wonder if he's guilty of playing a role in his sister's crimes or in covering up the real motive for the murders. But that still doesn't explain how you found me. Is there another tracker that I don't know about?"

"I think that your cell phone has been hacked and then tracked and that's how Mrs. Tate was able to follow you. She hired Eddie to kill you, but he failed. As for how I found you, I went to Mrs. Tate's home to question her. When I got there, she was driving away and I followed her instead—all the way here—and waited. Anyone who goes to an abandoned building in the middle of the night is up to no good."

Tori peered up at him, the admiration in her eyes overwhelming him.

"Thank you," she said. Her eyes widened. "But what about—"

"When I saw her forcing you down the hallway into this room, I called for backup quietly. I didn't want this to turn into a hostage situation—more than it already was. When she was on her way out, I cuffed her to a post in the building to hold her until I could check on you.

"Then I made my way to the room where she'd taken you. I missed the assassin going into the room. I'm just glad I got here in time." Ryan looked at Tori.

She appeared frazzled, with smudges on her face. Wild hair. Bright eyes.

He loved her so much.

God, will I ever get a chance with her?

He knew the answer to that. No. No, he wouldn't.

Finally the paramedics arrived and took Tori from Ryan, not for the first time. He didn't want to let her go, but she'd sustained more injuries. Once again she was taken to the hospital. At least she was safe and had survived—her parents, too.

At least this was over.

And that would mean his time with her was over, too.

Ryan turned his focus to policing matters. Deputies placed Suzanne Tate in the back of a vehicle to cart off to a holding cell on murder charges, as well as kidnapping. There could be more charges as they dug deeper into the activities she'd killed to hide.

Three days later, Ryan sat at his desk filling out reports and completing paperwork. He'd killed a man to save Tori, and that required an investigation into the incident regardless of the circumstances. Given the nature of additional financial and environmental crimes committed by Mrs. Tate, the feds were also involved in peeling back the layers. Agent Sanchez's activities were under scrutiny, as well.

It was hard to accept that Sarah's attempt at whistle-blowing to expose harmful behavior had ultimately ended in her death and that of her friends. Harder still to deal with the fact that she'd reached out for Tori's help. The guilt that she hadn't been there for her sister when her assistance could possibly have saved her continued to distress Tori. Moving beyond that would take time, if she ever got over it.

Just like it would take Ryan time to get over her.

Although trusting Tori with his heart was a huge risk, deep down, he'd always known it was a risk he would take again if given the chance. When her life had been in danger he'd realized just how much he wanted a second chance with her.

But that wasn't going to happen, and Ryan would have to be okay with it. He would survive, just like he had before.

Tori was alive and well, and he wished her the best.

A ruckus drew his attention from his computer. Katelyn smiled as she approached.

He pushed back from the desk. "What are you doing here?"

"I have a surprise for you. Can you come with me?"

He blew out a breath. "You aren't trying to fix me up with someone, are you? I'm really not in the mood."

"No. Nothing as nefarious as that." Katelyn led him through the sheriff's department offices and out the door, then around the corner to the small coffee shop.

Sitting at a table in the back corner, Tori smiled at him.

His heart almost stopped and he stumbled forward. "What's going on, Katelyn?"

He'd told himself he would be okay going forward without her, but he couldn't take more torture.

"Come on." Katelyn pulled him forward.

Tori stood from the table. "Hi, Ryan. It's good to see you."

She wore a flattering scarf around her neck, presumably to hide the bruises that likely remained.

"You, too." He slowly sat at the table with his sister and Tori. "So what's this about?"

I thought you'd gone home.

Katelyn appeared giddy as a schoolgirl and her laugh almost sounded like a giggle. "Well, Tori and I have an announcement."

"The suspense is killing me. Really. What's going on?"

Tori pressed a hand on Katelyn's arm. "We're starting up our own private and protective services business. We need to come up with a snazzy name."

His heart jumped around inside. "Wow. Well, that was fast. Are you sure?"

"Yes," Katelyn said. "Absolutely."

He wanted to hear Tori's take on this. Had Katelyn pressured her? Not that it was easy to make Tori do anything.

"So will this business be something you do from across the country?" he dared to ask her.

"I'm moving back, Ryan," she said. "I've already handed in my resignation."

Hope surged. Hope and caution.

"Well that's my cue to give you some privacy." Smiling, Katelyn slipped from her chair. "I'll be over there, eyeing the ice-cream cones."

Ryan breathed in slowly. Braced himself for what she would say.

"Can we take a walk?" Tori asked. "It's a beautiful day."

"Sure." He fought the need to run from this torture. Run far away from what he knew she could do to his heart.

Outside, they walked over to a small park with a stream. He waited patiently for her to speak her piece. Finally they stopped, next to a thick-trunked pine. In the distance, he could see Mount Shasta, magnificent and beautiful.

But the mountain's beauty was nothing compared to Tori's. She was doing it to him again. Warmth spilled out of his heart through his chest. He wanted to let himself love her.

Katelyn had been right—he was still in love with Tori. He wanted the freedom to give in to that.

"Mom and Dad urged me to go back to my job and my life. Funny, I thought working with the FBI was what I wanted." Tori stared at the small, trickling brook for two breaths, then lifted her gaze to him. "But the job I thought I loved, the life I thought I wanted, that's all changed."

"What are you saying, exactly?"

"I don't have the right to ask, Ryan, after everything I've put you through, but I hope you'll give me another chance. Give *us* another chance. Because I would choose you, choose this life here, over anything else in the world. I know that now. I'm so sorry I didn't see that before. But if you don't want that chance with me, I'll walk away. I'll understand."

In an instant, his lips were pressed against hers. His arms were around her, and she responded with tenderness, and something more just under the surface. He eased away enough to whisper, "I love you. I've always loved you."

"I love you, too, Ryan. Forgive me."

"There's nothing to forgive." Just… Ryan eased away but held her closely. "I don't want to lose you again. Lose you to your job or—"

"You won't, I promise."

"Then why don't we make it official?" His palms slicked. He could be pushing her too fast. She might not be ready for this. "Will you marry me?"

"Are you sure about this?"

"I've never been more sure of anything." His heart pounded. What would she say?

She lifted her chin and kissed him. Thoroughly. Then she said, "Does that answer your question?"

His head dizzy, he peered at her green eyes. "I think that's a yes, but I'd love to hear that on your lips."

Your beautiful lips.

"Yes, Ryan Bradley. Yes, I'll marry you."

* * * * *

Mary Alford was inspired to become a writer after reading romantic suspense greats Victoria Holt and Phyllis A. Whitney. Soon, creating characters and throwing them into dangerous situations that tested their faith came naturally for Mary. In 2012 Mary entered the speed-dating contest hosted by Love Inspired Suspense and later received "the call." Writing for Love Inspired Suspense has been a dream come true for Mary.

Books by Mary Alford

Love Inspired Suspense

Forgotten Past
Rocky Mountain Pursuit
Deadly Memories
Framed for Murder
Standoff at Midnight Mountain
Grave Peril
Amish Country Kidnapping
Amish Country Murder
Covert Amish Christmas

Visit the Author Profile page
at Harlequin.com for more titles.

STANDOFF AT
MIDNIGHT MOUNTAIN

Mary Alford

Yea, though I walk through the valley of the shadow of death, I will fear no evil: for thou art with me; thy rod and thy staff they comfort me.
—*Psalms* 23:4

To first loves.

ONE

The still of the peaceful Wyoming morning was broken by the noise of a vehicle approaching. Rachel Simmons breathed a heartfelt sigh of relief. Alex was here. Maybe now, with his help, she could finally get some answers into her brother's mysterious disappearance.

Outside, the car came to a stop. A door slammed, followed by footsteps, then someone knocked noisily on her door, jarring her spent nerves.

She hurried to answer it. With her hand resting on the door handle, a voice she didn't recognize spoke, stopping her in her tracks. "Ma'am, I'm sorry to trouble you so early, but my wife and I seem to have lost our way." A pause followed, almost as if the man was waiting for her response, yet she couldn't manage a word. Who was this person? "Can you tell me how to get back to the highway?"

Close by, her faithful golden retriever, Callie, growled low, the hackles along the ridge of her back standing at full attention. Callie charged for the door, sniffing and barking her alarm. A chill sped down Rachel's spine, her internal radar skyrocketed. She'd been living on edge since her brother's last visit. Now, after trying to reach Liam for more than a week without avail, she couldn't shake the feeling that something bad had happened. It was the reason why she'd called in her CIA colleague, Alex Booth.

"Quiet, Callie," Rachel whispered close to the dog's ear. Callie stopped her barking and sat back on her haunches, but the ridge didn't go away.

Nothing but the tiniest rays of light from the woodstove in the great room would be visible through the curtained windows. It was four in the morning. How had this man ended up at her door so early, and why would he believe anyone in the house was awake at such an hour?

What he'd said finally registered through her troubled thoughts and she shivered. *Ma'am.* He knew she was here alone.

Rachel grabbed her constant companion as of late, the one piece from her past life as a CIA agent she still possessed: her Glock.

Her place was in the middle of forty heavily wooded acres and not even close to a main highway. No one would just happen by here, especially at this hour. She clutched the Glock tighter. The man's sudden appearance smelled of some type of setup.

"I realize it's early, ma'am, but we really need some directions and my cell phone has died." His tone had taken a turn toward sharp. He was growing impatient with her. "Can my wife and I come in and warm up for a bit and maybe use your phone?"

Rachel ticked off every tense beat of her heart while she tried to decide what to do next. Where was Alex? She had expected him some time ago. Did this man's sudden appearance have anything to do with Alex's delay? She didn't want to think about her call being responsible for harm coming to Alex.

One of the front porch boards squeaked as the man shifted his weight. He wasn't leaving and she had a choice to make. She needed to get rid of him before trying Alex's cell phone. If this man was up to no good, she could be putting Alex's life in danger. That is, if she hadn't already…

Don't let me make the wrong decision…

Rachel hurried to the window closest to the door and inched the curtains apart. A tall, bulky man dressed in dark clothing, a knit cap pulled over most of the top of his head, stood on her porch.

Callie followed her, growling like crazy. She was picking up on her owner's unease.

Rachel's gaze slid to the car parked out front. A woman was seated inside, watching the man. Was she his wife as the man had said, or was there something more going on here? "I'm sorry, but I don't have a phone," she called out in answer to his request to borrow hers. "But if you go back the way you came, you'll run into the main highway without a problem."

The man took a step closer to the door.

"It's awfully cold out, ma'am. If we could come inside just for a minute?" He attempted a smile that didn't come close to reaching his steely eyes.

Rachel spotted a bulge beneath the man's jacket. He was armed! Out of the corner of her eye, she noticed that the woman had opened the car door and was getting out, her hand tucked inside her jacket. Why would two innocent travelers need to be armed?

"How did you know I lived here alone?" Rachel immediately regretted the question. She'd given away too much.

"Must have seen it on your mailbox," he muttered, not even trying to hide the lie. The only name on the mailbox was Simmons, the alias Rachel had taken when she'd left the life of a spy behind and returned to Midnight Mountain.

Fear settled into the pit of her stomach when the man whipped his gun from its holster. Callie forgot her command of silence and began barking ferociously. The truth became apparent. These two hadn't just happened by here. They were here deliberately…for her.

Rachel hurried for the door, making sure all the locks were securely in place. Seconds later, the man opened fire, bullets riddling her door.

Rachel automatically hit the floor. Keeping as much out of the line of fire as she possibly could, she crawled on her hands and knees until she reached the kitchen, with Callie close by, growling and shaking with fear.

Behind her, she could hear the man yelling to the woman to cover him while he leveraged his full weight against the locked door, sending it rattling on its hinges.

After her brother's strange behavior before he had left to meet with his asset more than a week ago and had seemingly dropped off the face of the earth, Rachel was positive that these two intruders were somehow connected to Liam's disappearance. If she stayed here, she'd be dead before Alex could reach her. She prayed that he was safe and had just been delayed.

If she was going to live, she had to get away now. Her frantic brain tried to come up with an exit strategy, but there was really only one way out.

Once she reached the kitchen, she grabbed her coat

from where she kept it close to the back door. Keeping as low as she could, she ran out the door with Callie at her heels, before her only means of escape evaporated. What if there were more men surrounding the house? She could be walking into a trap. Holding on to what was left of her courage, she raced for the woods off to the right.

Once she reached the trees close to the house, Rachel heard the man finally break through her front door. They'd breached the house. It wouldn't take them long to realize she'd gone out the back.

"Hurry, Callie," she urged the dog as they forged deeper into the woods.

"There's no sign of *them* inside. I'm guessing they were never here." The man's voice carried through the still predawn. "They're both still up on the mountain somewhere. We know one or both are injured. Find her. We need to put a lid on this. Now. Too much is at stake and we don't know if Carlson told anyone else."

Reality shot through Rachel like a lightning bolt. He was talking about Liam. If what the man said were true, her brother was hurt…or worse. More than ever, she knew she had to find Liam, which meant she'd need to get out of here alive and before they could capture her.

Callie let out a tense-sounding growl as they continued frantically running through the dense wooded area. Low-slung branches tangled in Rachel's hair and snagged her face, making it impossible to make much progress. Every step she made jarring. The cold of the early morning chilling her to the bone.

The dog was on edge just as she was. Callie had faced down lots of predators, bears included, but she'd never been involved in a gunfight.

Rachel stopped long enough to gain her bearings. From where she stood, she could just see the back of the house through the trees. Two people emerged from inside, flashlights shining all around. She ducked when the light hit close.

"Over there," the man yelled, homing in on the area where she stood with his flashlight beam.

Rachel turned on her heel and started running again, her heart thundering in her chest with each step. She'd been out of the game for a long time. She wasn't used to being hunted.

Callie soon took the lead. They'd barely managed a handful of steps when a round of shots whistled past Rachel's head. Close enough for her to feel the breeze it kicked up. She tucked closer to the ground, almost doubled over, and ran.

"Hurry—she's getting away." The woman spoke for the first time. Rachel didn't recognize her voice either, but she detected a faint accent that she couldn't place. Who were these people and how were they connected to Liam?

Some distance behind her, the rustling of brush assured her that her pursuers had now entered the woods. Callie growled at the noise and turned back in a defensive stance, ready to charge the enemy. The dog was overly protective of Rachel, but she couldn't let her companion get caught in the line of fire.

"Come, Callie. Hurry," Rachel ordered, and the dog reluctantly abandoned her defense and followed Rachel.

Where was Alex? He should have been here by now. Had something happened to him? Fear shot through her body.

With her thoughts churning in a dozen different directions, Rachel tried to come up with a means of escape on foot. She had the advantage. She knew the area like the back of her hand. If she could make it to her neighbor's house, she could call for help from there. But if Liam's suspicions were true? What then? Liam was a seasoned CIA agent. If what he believed proved real, then she could be walking straight into the enemy's arms by calling in the authorities.

Rachel didn't dare take a direct path to the Reagans' place. It wouldn't be long before her pursuers figured out the direction she'd gone. She'd be bringing her troubles to the Reagans' doorstep. She couldn't do that.

"This way," the woman yelled. "I see her up ahead." More shots rang out; bullets flew past, one barely missing her shoulder. They were gaining! Would Tom Reagan hear the shots and come to investigate?

Please, God, no.

She had a feeling these people wouldn't be opposed to killing anyone who got in their way. Even someone as innocent as Tom.

Rachel shoved branches out of her way as she ran blindly through the woods. Just in front of her, Callie suddenly stopped dead in her tracks. Rachel almost tripped over the dog in the process. There was just time to sidestep in an attempt to avoid the mishap when she slammed headfirst into something warm and solid. A man! He reached out and grabbed her tight. One thought raced through her head. They'd found her. She had to get away if she wanted to live.

Panicked, Rachel fought with everything she had, but she was no match for the man's strength. Before she could scream, a hand clasped over her mouth and the man pulled her close.

"Don't scream, Rachel. It's me." *Alex!* He was alive and he was here.

Relief made her knees weak. She hugged him close and struggled to let go of the panic still electrifying her nervous system.

"I heard the shots from the road and guessed something had gone wrong. We need to get out of here fast. Those shots sounded close. And this place is crawling with men. My car's just over there." He pointed up ahead, then glanced in the direction Rachel had come. "They're almost here. Run for the car. I'll try to distract them. I'll be right behind you," he added when she didn't budge.

Alex gave her a gentle shove in that direction, but Rachel stood her ground. She might not be part of the CIA anymore, but one thing was still ingrained in her brain: you never left your partner behind.

Alex drew his Glock and opened fire. Rachel didn't hesitate before doing the same.

A scream of pain rang out. They'd hit one of their pursuers. Rachel didn't believe it would slow the other down one little bit.

She turned and hurried toward the car with Callie. Alex cleared the woods shortly after her and the dog.

Before they could reach the vehicle, someone opened fire on them. Rachel ducked for cover behind the side of the car. She caught a glimpse of a man holding his shoulder. He was injured but it didn't stop him from shooting at them. Alex managed to get off several rounds, forcing the man to hide behind a nearby tree to avoid another direct hit. Where was the woman?

"Hurry, Rachel," Alex yelled as he opened the driver's-side door and lunged inside. Rachel yanked her door open. Callie hit the front seat first. She followed seconds later.

"Go, go, go," she urged in an unsteady voice, reflecting the magnitude of what had just happened.

Alex put the vehicle in Drive and floored it while staying as low as he possibly could and still see where he was going.

Rachel glanced behind them. The man had stepped from his tree coverage and began shooting at them again. Several other men joined him, all firing. The back window shattered. Rachel tucked down low while from the back seat Callie let out a frightened yelp.

"It's okay, girl. Everything is going to be okay." She stroked the dog's fur, trying to reassure them both.

Alex jerked the wheel to the right to avoid another hit. The car veered close to the edge of the road. He quickly corrected and managed to keep them from crashing just in time.

Soon, at least four sets of headlights flashed behind them. The men were coming full force. Alex floored the gas pedal once more in an attempt to lose them.

"What happened back there?" he asked, the tension in his voice evident. He spared her a glance as he continued to push the car to its limit, still unable to shake the vehicles.

Numb from shock, Rachel shook her head. "I don't know." It was the truth, but she could see that he didn't believe it. Not that she could blame him. People just didn't come to your house and start shooting at you for no reason. "A man and a woman showed up at my door. He said they were lost. I could tell he was armed. When I refused to let him come inside, the man started shooting at me. Alex, I barely got away…" She stopped for a much-needed breath and glanced down at her hands. They were shaking. She'd almost died. Both of them had come close.

"There's no way they just happened to show up at my front door. This is connected to Liam's disappearance somehow. What I don't understand is how they knew where to find me?" Rachel had gone to great lengths to disguise her identity after leaving the Agency. She'd created an alias last name. Even after she'd gotten married, she hadn't taken her husband's name simply because there was always the chance that her past might come looking for her. No one would be able to track her by that association.

Rachel cast a suspicious look Alex's way. "Did you tell anyone you were coming here?"

His response came quick, his tone reflecting his hurt. "Of course not. Rach, you asked me not to tell anyone, so I didn't. But the woods were crawling with people back there. I'm surprised they didn't spot me before I was able to reach you. Or hear my car, for that matter." He shook his head. "You said on the phone you hadn't spoken to Liam in more than a week. You believe he's gone missing?" She nodded. She hadn't said as much when she'd called, but Alex had guessed. "Why do you think that? How does this ambush fit into Liam's disappearance?"

She'd been brief on the phone. Afraid to tell him her worst fears. "I don't know how this fits into it, but I know Liam, and I *haven't* heard from him in over a week." She realized how foolish she sounded right now, but she knew if her brother were able to, he would have been in touch by now.

Rachel kept a nervous eye on the vehicles behind

them. So far, Alex had been able to keep them at a distance, but they had to find a way to lose them soon if they were going to help Liam.

"We need to get off this road, Alex. It'll drop us into the town of Midnight Mountain, and who knows how many more men they have waiting for us there." She pointed up ahead. "There's a side road coming up on the right, just after we make this next curve around the mountain. Take it."

Alex nodded and turned his full attention on his driving. When the road in question came into sight, he slowed the car's speed slightly.

"Hang on," he warned. Alex was an excellent driver and yet it took all his skills to make the curve at the high rate of speed. Once they'd safely exited, he killed the lights to give them a fighting chance.

With adrenaline pumping through her body like crazy, Rachel spotted the vehicles swerving onto the same road. "They're still coming." She racked her brain to recall the layout of this less-traveled road. It had just recently opened after being closed for the winter. Even though it was late March and springtime in other parts of the country, here in the mountains snow still hung around, especially in the high places.

"Hold on. There's another less-traveled side road just past this next bend. It's pretty obscured from view. Unless you know it's there you probably won't see it. If we can make that, with the lights out, I think we have a chance of getting away undetected."

Alex slowed just enough to make the turn, then gassed on the accelerator once more. So far, none of the cars appeared to be following.

He glanced in the rearview mirror and then at her.

She could tell he believed she knew more than what she'd told him so far and he was waiting for her to talk. Did she dare voice her concerns aloud?

With everything that happened, especially after what Liam had told her, she didn't know who to trust. But this was Alex. He'd dropped everything to come to her aid simply because she'd asked for help.

"Rachel, please tell me what's going on," he asked quietly.

If what she suspected were true, had she put Alex's career, if not his life, in danger by asking for his help? In spite of everything they'd been through in the past, she still cared for him. They'd grown up here in these mountains, the three of them. She still considered Alex a friend.

"Look, these guys have proven they aren't about to give up until they get what they're after. You called me in because you needed my help. You can trust me, Rachel. Let me help you."

As she looked into his eyes, she knew, no matter what, Alex would never betray her or Liam. She *could* trust him.

She blew out a breath and shook her head. If it were anyone else, Alex might have thought she was overreacting. But she was former CIA herself. He knew she wasn't imagining things. That was why he'd come so quickly.

"Liam told me he was scheduled to meet with his asset after he left my place, but I could see he was anxious about something. I'd never seen him look so worried before. He kept checking out the window as if he were expecting someone to show up." She stopped for a breath, then told Alex what Liam had said about the newest terror threat he'd been chasing. Liam didn't say how, but he believed the person he was after might be closer than Liam had originally believed. At the time, Rachel hadn't been sure what to make of Liam's comments.

She couldn't read Alex's opinion of this. "Yesterday, I was putting away some clothes and I found Liam's phone along with a map that he'd left in my bedroom dresser drawer. The phone was turned off. He'd wanted me to find them after he left. There was a location pinpointed on the map along with an initial and a phone number on the back…" She stopped and realized how little it was to go on. Liam had been trying to tell her something. His warning had been chilling. If only she knew what he was trying to say!

"Did you call the number?" Alex asked, and she nodded.

"Although it took me several hours to work up the nerve." He smiled at this and clasped her hand for a second.

"I didn't recognize the voice on the other end. A few hours later, those people showed up at my door. It's no coincidence." She shuddered at the thought.

Rachel didn't understand what was going on, but the couple that came to her house knew about her brother. They'd known Liam had been up on the mountain along with someone else, presumably his asset. They believed he was injured and possibly still there. Would she and Alex be too late? Would they find her brother dead? She couldn't bear the thought.

Lack of sleep made it hard to keep her thoughts focused, but she had to try. Liam needed her.

"Did Liam ever mention knowing someone whose name starts with the initial *D*? A friend maybe?"

She watched as Alex tried to recollect any such name. He shook his head. "No, never. But one thing's clear. Liam would never have left those things behind if he wasn't worried about something. He wanted you to have them in case…"

He left the rest unsaid but she knew what he meant. In case Liam didn't make it down from the mountain.

"Did you check Liam's phone for calls? Maybe someone he called can help us figure out where he's at?"

She had checked, and the results were disappointing. "I did. It was as if he'd deliberately cleared out all the numbers."

Rachel could tell this didn't sit well with Alex, yet he tried to reassure her. "Maybe he was afraid the phone might fall into the wrong hands. He could have been expecting those people to show up at your place."

None of these options helped ease her fears any, and he must have seen it.

"First things first. We need to get out of sight as quickly as possible. Once we have a chance to breathe, we can come up with a plan to locate Liam." Alex smiled and then turned his attention to the road ahead while uneasy thoughts churned through Rachel's mind.

Who was this new player Liam had uncovered and how were they connected to her brother's vanishing? There had to be more to the story than what Rachel knew, because right now, all she had to go on were bits and pieces of a puzzle that might well lead them to a deadly conclusion. And every minute they didn't know the answer, Liam's life was in danger.

* * *

Alex was still shell-shocked by the things that had happened since he'd returned to his hometown of Midnight Mountain; his head burst with unanswered questions. His fear for Liam's safety wasn't eased one little bit by what Rachel had told him.

While they might have lost the men chasing them for now, they weren't out of the woods yet. Without knowing why those men were coming after Rachel and Liam so mercilessly, he had no idea what they were up against. There could be more armed men saturating the surrounding countryside and staked out in town waiting to ambush them.

Alex made several more evasive turns as a precaution before they shot out onto the outskirts of town in the opposite direction from the house where Rachel was living.

A quick glance in the rearview mirror assured him they weren't being followed—yet.

He slowed the car's speed and glanced over at Rachel. "They'll be looking for this car. It's not safe to be out in the open like this for long."

Alex tried to recall some of the back roads they'd once used as shortcuts when they were younger, but he'd been gone from the area since his parents passed away in a car wreck his senior year. He'd graduated high school and went away to college. After that, he'd joined the CIA and his work had taken him around the world. He hadn't been home since.

Rachel pointed up ahead. "There's a county road a little ways from here. And I know where we can hide out for a while. Maybe they'll think we've left the area and they'll move on if they can't find us right away."

Alex turned onto a less-maintained road filled with potholes. As much as he wanted to believe it, these men had proven themselves ruthless.

"At least we've lost them for now." He sounded much calmer than he felt inside. In the space of a less than eight hours, his life had been turned upside down. His friend was missing, and he and Rachel were working together again to try to figure out what had happened.

There was little doubt in his mind that Rachel's worry for Liam's safety was valid. She wasn't the type to jump at shadows.

"Those people were there because of Liam. They thought he'd be at my house." She turned in her seat so that she could look Alex in the eye. "He's in serious trouble. He's up there on Midnight Mountain somewhere... and I'm not sure if he's still alive."

What she said struck like a blow to the gut. "You think Liam may already be dead?" Alex couldn't allow himself to even contemplate the possibility. He and Liam were closer than friends. They'd grown up together. They were like brothers.

"I don't know." She shook her head, her tone conveying her fear for her brother.

In spite of what had happened today, one thing bothered Alex a lot. Why was Rachel so convinced that Liam was in trouble with very little to back up the conviction? Was he missing something, or was there more to the story than what she'd told him so far?

"How do you know for certain that Liam's not still on a mission? You must have something more to go on than the fact that you haven't spoken to him in a while and he left his phone and a map at your place. I know the two of you are close, but you realize it's not uncommon for an agent to go dark for a long time when he or she is working a lead."

He barely got the words out before she rejected his theory. "It's more than that, Alex, and I know it." Her words wiped away what little bit of hope he still held on to. His heart wouldn't let him go there. He couldn't imagine losing Liam.

"Have you spoken to his handler?" He sure hoped she'd overlooked something. While Alex knew the information the CIA would give out to a civilian was limited, she was different. She'd once been one of them.

"I've tried. Seth isn't answering. And when I called his boss, he gave me the company line. He said he couldn't discuss any details concerning Liam's mission. When I told him I was worried Liam might be in trouble, he pretty much dismissed me. He told me that I, of all people, should know that when an agent is on a mission, they go radio silent."

Alex felt his hands were tied as to what to do next. "I need to reach out to Liam's boss right away. Perhaps he'll talk to me."

He barely finished the sentence. "No, you can't."

Alex stared at her, his eyes wide with surprise. "Why not?"

Rachel turned away in a defensive manner. There was something she didn't want him to know. "You just can't, okay."

She didn't fully trust him yet and that hurt like crazy. Was it because of what happened between them, or who he worked for?

He blew out a frustrated sigh and agreed to go along

with what she wanted for the time being. "All right, I won't make that call just yet."

It would be up to him and Rachel to put the pieces together and bring Liam home alive.

Alex glanced in the back seat where the dog had finally settled down, although she still kept a close eye on Alex. It was clear the dog was protective of Rachel.

"Who's your friend?" He nodded behind them when she looked at him in confusion.

"Oh. Her name is Callie, and she's been my good friend for a very long time now." Something bordering sadness shadowed her eyes. He wondered about her husband. Where was he when all this was happening to Rachel? Why was she alone at her house?

Alex would give just about anything to ask that and the question foremost in his mind: Did she still hate him for the way he'd ended things between them? He glanced her way. Saw the closed-off expression in her eyes. They weren't there yet. Emotionally, she was on the other side of the earth from him. She'd put up a wall between them that didn't encourage him trying to scale it.

What she didn't realize was that he had been a different man back then. He hadn't believed in anything beyond the job. If he were being honest, he'd known she had wanted out of the Agency for a long time. When their relationship had turned serious, her desire for a normal life seemed to have doubled. Five years ago, Alex couldn't imagine life without the adrenaline rush of the CIA...and so he'd lost her.

"There's a driveway coming up on your right. Turn in there." Rachel's voice interrupted his chaotic thoughts.

She didn't look at him, and he wondered if she'd read his thoughts.

He spotted the driveway in question and exited onto a dirt road as dust boiled up in the headlights.

In front of them, an old farmhouse appeared at the end of the drive some distance from the county road.

"Whose place is this?" Alex asked as he stopped the car.

She didn't answer right away and he turned to her, curious.

"This was my husband's family home. He grew up here and I promised him I'd hold on to it after he passed away."

Shocked, Alex couldn't even begin to hide his surprise from her. Nothing prepared him for hearing that Rachel was now a widow. He glanced down at her left ring finger. She still wore her wedding ring. How long had her husband been gone?

Alex looked from her to the simple white house with its pale gray shutters barely distinguishable in the car's headlights. Something akin to jealousy seared his heart. He hated thinking of her loving another man.

Liam had told him she'd gotten married a few years after she'd moved back to Midnight Mountain some five years earlier. After that, well, Alex had just stopped checking in with his friend for a while because it was too painful.

Which was why the envelope he'd received from Liam days before Rachel's call had been so concerning. He had no idea what Liam was trying to convey. It contained ramblings about things they'd done in their childhood and some of the places they'd explored growing up. He assumed Liam had written the letter at a low point. There was no sense in telling Rachel about it and alarming her further.

Alex realized Rachel was staring at him as if she expected him to say something. He pulled himself together and cleared his throat. "I'm sorry. I had no idea your husband had passed away." She continued to stare at him with those telling blue eyes. The look in them now reminded him of when he'd told her he wasn't leaving the CIA with her.

Was she expecting him to be jealous that she'd gotten married? If so, then she should be happy. She had no idea how hard he'd taken the news of her wedding.

"Thank you," she murmured, and looked away. While a thousand questions flew through his head, he could tell she wasn't ready to discuss any of them with him. "We should probably put the car away and get inside. It's possible that whoever attacked us will connect this place with me." She stopped for a breath. "There's an old garage behind the house. We can hide the car in there."

Once they'd stowed the rental car in the rickety old garage that was a little ways from the house, Alex grabbed his gear and followed her while the dog sniffed around the yard for a bit then went after them, keeping close to Rachel.

Rachel flipped on the lights, illuminating the drop cloths that covered most of the furniture inside the home.

"Sorry for the mess," she told him. "It's just easier to keep clean this way. The place has sat empty for several years now. Brian's family raised workhorses up here for many years. I still keep a few pastured out back because he loved working with them so much. There's a neighbor who stops by each day to care for them."

He managed an awkward nod and dropped his backpack by the door. "I'll take a quick look around just to be safe." He could see she hadn't considered the possibility that the place might not be secure. She'd been away from the spy game too long.

She shook her head and smiled at him for the first time since their reunion. It stopped him dead in his tracks. "I never even considered someone might have already been here."

He loved her smile. He'd almost forgotten just how beautiful she was, especially when she smiled. She wore her golden brown hair longer now. She'd braided it and it hung halfway down her back, the overhead light catching the gold highlights. Dressed in a plaid shirt, jeans and cowboy boots, she reminded him of the young girl he'd fallen for all those years ago. Only her midnight blue eyes held a hint of the things she'd endured. There was a sadness in them that appeared embedded there.

Alex collected his straying thoughts. "Not looking over your shoulder all the time sounds like a good thing. I'll be right back." He excused himself and went upstairs, grateful for the chance to get control of his emotions. He thought he'd left Midnight Mountain behind for good when he went away to college, yet so many of his childhood memories were tied to this place. And to this woman…

After he finished checking the upstairs rooms, he was more ready to join her again. At the foot of the stairs, he noticed that the dog had settled down close to Rachel's feet.

"There's no sign anyone's been up there in a while…" He stopped when he noticed her staring strangely at the desk in the corner of the room. "What is it?"

Rachel visibly shivered. "Even though it's a half hour drive from my home, I still come here every couple of days to make sure the place is okay. I'm pretty sure that drawer was closed when I was here yesterday."

He stared at the desk and then at her. "Someone's been here." He stated the obvious. "What was in there?"

She shook her head. "That's just it. Nothing was in there. There isn't anything of value here besides the horses."

"But they weren't looking for something valuable." Their gazes locked and a new fear entangled him in its clutches. "Whoever was here was looking for something connected to Liam."

No doubt the people behind Liam's disappearance had known about his connection to Rachel all along, including this house.

"You said you keep horses on the property?" Alex's thoughts snarled together. What she'd told him about Liam was disturbing. That Liam had left her the location where he was scheduled to meet his asset seemed to indicate he had been concerned something might happen to him up there.

"That's right. Why?" she asked innocently enough.

"Because they may be our only way out of here." Alex glanced out the front window at the breaking dawn. They'd need to keep moving. Get up on the mountain as soon as possible.

"The stalls are behind the house a little ways down near the south pasture."

"Good. Then we should probably head out. Are you

ready for this?" She didn't hesitate. Rachel had been one of the best agents he'd had the pleasure of working with. She might be a little rusty, but she was more than capable.

If something had happened to Liam, each day that passed whittled away at his chances of survival. Rachel said she'd had no word from her brother in more than a week. As a former CIA agent herself, she would know that it was common practice for agents to carry burner phones as a means of communicating without being tracked. If Liam hadn't reached out to her by now, then something bad was wrong.

It bothered Alex that Liam seemed worried about something. It wasn't like his friend to show fear, but from Rachel's account, he'd definitely been concerned when he showed up at her place. He had told her he was close to bringing down a new player in the terror field. He'd mentioned something similar the last time he and Alex had talked.

Did Liam's disappearance have anything to do with what he'd uncovered about the terrorist threat? If so, then whomever he was chasing seemed determined to silence anyone who got in their way or attempted to uncover their identity.

As he and Rachel headed out into the new day dawning, with Callie at their heels, Alex could almost feel her uneasiness growing.

He touched her arm and she slowed her steps and faced him. "We'll find him, I promise. And don't forget, Liam's tough. He's been through much worse than this."

She smiled without answering. Did she believe him?

He needed to get a look at the map. It would give some indication as to where exactly on the mountain they'd be heading. "Do you have the map Liam left you handy?" he asked, and she dug it out of her pocket and handed it to him.

Once he'd opened it, he recognized the location right away. It was more than a twenty-four hike under the best of conditions and over some very rugged terrain.

"This is where Liam was going to meet with his asset?" he asked with a sense of foreboding.

She nodded. "I think so."

Even if they headed straight there, they'd still have to find a place to make camp for the night before hiking the rest of the way up. Darkness came early to the mountains. They'd never make it to the site before nightfall. The weather would definitely play a factor, especially with the mountains making their own conditions. It might be early spring, but snow and ice weren't unexpected this time of year. Up on the mountain several feet of snow still clung to the crevasses.

"I hate going into a situation blind like this, and we don't know for sure what's really happened to Liam. Maybe something went wrong with the meet and he was injured. Or maybe his asset sold him out." Alex glanced around, expecting trouble.

Rachel hesitated a second too long. Right away he could tell something was wrong.

"What is it?" He almost dreaded her answer.

"There's something else I haven't showed you, Alex. It's on the back of the map."

He turned it over and saw the phone number and initial Rachel had mention previously. But it was the words that were scribbled below them that increased his concern for Liam's well-being tenfold.

Agency. Dirty. Trust no one. Especially anyone in

authority. It was a message Liam had intended for Rachel alone.

Alex stared at it and then her. If true, the magnitude of what they now faced had grown beyond anything he could have imagined.

Rachel dragged in a breath before she delivered the worst news possible.

"Alex, I think the person Liam was chasing, this new terrorist threat that he'd uncovered… I think it involves someone from the CIA."

TWO

The expression of shock on his face told her how hard it was for him to wrap his head around the idea that someone from the CIA, both her brother and Alex's own team, might be responsible for harming Liam.

"Rachel..." Her name came out on a frustrated-sounding sigh. Alex couldn't hide his doubts. She certainly understood. As an agent, his head wouldn't let him go there.

"I know how crazy this sounds, but you weren't there when Liam came to see me. He was spooked, and Liam doesn't spook easily. I think his disappearance is in some way connected to the new threat he's been chasing. Maybe he uncovered information that connected someone in the CIA as possibly being involved with this terrorist somehow."

She looked up at him, willing him to understand. "It makes sense, Alex," she said.

Yet he couldn't hide his skepticism. After all, Alex was still part of the CIA, and there was a bond between agents that was unbreakable. In his mind, it would be unimaginable to think someone you trusted with your life might betray you in such a deadly way.

Still, she tried to make him understand. "Just think about it. Those people who showed up at my house obviously knew about Liam's meet location. They managed to connect my name to Liam, even though it's an alias. They probably knew who he was meeting with as well, and those arrangements are kept confidential for the agent's safety. So how would they possibly know about it without having some inside information?"

His gaze locked on hers; he was clearly surprised by what she'd said. "What are you talking about? You don't know that they knew who Liam was meeting."

Rachel blew out a breath and explained. "I do. I overheard something one of them said. They believe Liam and someone else, probably his asset, are still up on the mountain. Alex, I know you don't want to think it's possible, I didn't either in the beginning, but this is Liam and his life is at stake. We can't afford to discount anything. If they're right and he's somewhere up there still, he could be hurt. He needs our help, because no one else, the CIA included, is going to help him."

Before he could voice his obvious doubts aloud, a noise in the distance captured both their attentions. It sounded like a car on the gravel road nearby slowly coming to a halt.

"That seems really close." She turned her anxious gaze to his.

"You're right. If they've found us again, we'd better hurry." Rachel led the way to the pasture where she kept a couple of mares stalled.

"The horses know this terrain better than I do. They'll get us out of here, but it will be slow going. Do you still remember how to ride?" she asked with a hint of teasing in her tone.

He shook his head, managing a smile for her. "Don't worry about me. I think I can remember well enough to keep up."

The woods expanded into fertile pastureland and Rachel headed toward the barn where the horses were stabled. Behind them, nothing but eerie silence could be heard. Had the car turned around and left already or were they coming after them on foot?

Alex obviously still had concerns. "The sooner we're saddled and riding, the better."

"There are a couple of sleeping bags and some camping gear stored at the back of the barn on a shelf there. We'll need the gear for staying overnight." She pushed open the barn door and went inside. One of the mares neighed when she spotted Rachel.

"It's okay, Naomi." Rachel went over and patted the horse's head. "You ready for a ride?" Next to Naomi, Esther, the second mare, whinnied.

Alex and Rachel worked quickly to saddle the mares and within no time they were leading them out of the barn.

"Let's grab the rest of the supplies from inside," Rachel said. She and Alex went back into the barn and brought out the sleeping bags along with camping gear, then split the load between the two horses. Rachel quickly mounted Naomi and headed down one of the trails behind the house. Alex did the same with Esther.

"There's a ridge not too far from here. It has a great view of the house and the surrounding area. We can get a better idea of what's going on down below," she told him once he'd caught up with her.

Both mares covered the rocky countryside easily enough, with Callie keeping good time behind them.

Once they neared the ridge, they dismounted and tied the horses in a treed area some distance from the ridge and hiked the rest of the way up.

Rachel brought out the binoculars that had been part of the camping gear and homed in on the road near the house.

"The vehicle is parked on the edge of the road close to the driveway. There's no one inside." She frowned as she studied it. "And it's not the same one that was at my house." She handed Alex the binoculars.

"Where are they?" he murmured as he focused on the wooded area between the road and the house. "Wait, I see something." Alex zeroed in on a particular spot.

"What do you see?" She barely got the words out before he turned and grabbed her around the waist. "Get down." Alex tugged her into the shelter of his arms and hit the ground as the world around them exploded with gunfire.

Alex's body protected her from most of the blow-back from tree branches splintering and dirt kicking up around them as the bullets hit all around. Close by, Callie whined pitifully and tromped for cover.

"Let's get out of here. There's enough firepower down there to take down a small village. They could have snipers anywhere." The tension in Alex's voice somehow got through the shock that had kept her immobile.

He got to his knees and took her hand. Together they crept as close to the ground as possible until they'd reached the horses.

"Keep as low as you can," he told her as they mounted their horses once more and headed in the opposite direction from the shooters.

Both he and Rachel leaned in close to their horses' necks, almost lying flat against the beasts.

"Can we make it to the base of the mountain riding?" Alex's tone was strained. He glanced back over his shoulder, as if expecting the enemy to emerge behind them at any moment.

Rachel made sure Callie was able to keep up with them. She wouldn't leave the dog behind no matter what.

"Yes, but we'll have to go slower in that rocky terrain, and we will be using up valuable time we don't have to spare. Alex, we need help."

The path widened slightly and he rode up beside her. With no sign of the men behind them, they sat up straight once more. "Who do you suggest?"

In her mind, there was only two people she trusted other than Alex. "The Reagans are my neighbors and good friends. I can call Tom and have him meet us someplace. He can pick up the horses and bring a four-wheeler. We'll make better time with it."

She could tell Alex wasn't nearly as confident in the plan.

"Alex, you can trust them, I promise. They moved to the area soon after we all went away to the university. I've known them ever since I came back home. They're like family."

He slowly nodded. "If you trust them, so do I. Give them a call. The sooner we get to Liam's meeting location, the faster we'll be able to figure out what happened to him."

The problem was that she had no phone to make the call. "I destroyed both my phone and Liam's right after I called the number he'd written down. I phoned you from my landline. I thought that if what Liam suspected were true, and these people are somehow connected to the CIA, a rogue group of agents perhaps, they'd pull apart my life piece by piece. Probably track his cell or mine. Or both. I couldn't take the chance."

Admiration shone in Alex's eyes. She'd put a lot of thought into destroying the phones, but then, some of her CIA training was still useful.

"Good thinking. Hang on." He pulled out his cell phone and handed it to her. "Use this one. It's a burner phone and no one knows the number."

She smiled her gratitude and dialed her friend's number while praying that whoever was chasing them hadn't contacted her neighbor already.

The short amount of time it took Tom to answer did little to settle her nerves.

"Tom, it's Rachel. I need you to meet me at Willow Creek as soon as possible. And bring the four-wheeler."

"I should be able to do that," Tom said in an evasive tone that made her wonder if someone was listening in on the conversation.

Rachel glanced uneasily at Alex. "I'll meet you there in a couple of hours, then." After a second of silence on his end, she told Tom goodbye and then ended the call. She handed the phone back to Alex while praying she wasn't leading the enemy right to them.

"He's on his way. Willow Creek is due north of here. There's some pretty hilly areas between, but we should be able to make it in an hour." She hesitated. "Alex, Tom sounded strange, almost as if someone were there and he couldn't talk."

Rachel could see right away that he didn't like it. "You think they're watching him?"

She shook her head. "I don't know, but we'd better check out the area around Willow Creek very carefully when we get there. We could have unwanted company."

The trail was just wide enough for the two of them to ride side by side for a bit and, thankfully, it was mostly level.

"Where will this trail take us?" Alex asked, keeping a careful eye on the surrounding woods.

"It will dump us out at Willow Creek after we summit Plume Mountain."

She couldn't help it; she had to look at him. His gaze tangled with hers. She could see that he remembered the place, as well. They'd once spent a lot of time hiking the valley below Plume Mountain and fishing back when it had been her, Liam and Alex. Before life got complicated and their career paths took them through troubled waters.

"When was the last time you spoke to Liam?" Rachel asked, mostly because she needed a distraction to get his attention off her so that she could reclaim some of her equilibrium.

There was something in Alex's gaze that drew her in and made her wonder if he, too, was remembering their time here together. Back then their romance was just beginning. They had skirted around the edges of their feelings since they were teens. She'd often wondered what her younger self would have done if only she'd known the outcome.

"Too long ago, I'm afraid." He clearly regretted the lapse. "I'd like to say we both got busy, but I guess in truth it was just too hard." He spared her a look and she swallowed with difficulty and looked away, her heart going crazy with possibilities. Did Alex have regrets about their parting? He certainly hadn't showed it all those years ago.

When Rachel had made up her mind to get out, she hadn't realized how hard it would be. Hadn't known she'd be walking away from Alex along with the Agency. She'd been a broken person when she came back to her hometown of Midnight Mountain. She'd spent weeks crying. Liam had tried his best to console her, but Liam was cut from the same cloth as Alex. They both ate, breathed and slept the CIA.

For a long time, Rachel hadn't known what to do to move on beyond Alex. She'd gone to church with the Reagans one Sunday. She had felt a sense of peace that day, realizing that she wasn't alone in her pain. Knowing that God was with her no matter what happened in her life. It was because of this that her heart had begun to mend.

"To tell you the truth—" Alex's familiar voice interrupted her unsettled thoughts "—I've missed working with Liam…and you."

Her heart contracted painfully and she struggled to keep from showing how hard it was to hear him say those things. Why was he telling her this *now*?

She'd buried how handsome he was deep in her heart. Now it was a painful reminder of the dreams she'd given up. He was tall and fit; his dark brown hair now almost touched his collar. Those piercing green eyes still held a hint of mischief in them whenever he smiled, as they had when they were kids growing up together. Yet the years and the job had left their mark on him. Fine lines fanned out around his eyes and mouth. She'd witnessed enough horror in her years on the job to know the reason behind those lines.

Rachel shoved those dark memories back into the recesses of her heart. She needed to keep her focus on her brother.

"I called Liam a couple of months back," Alex said, surprising her. "He didn't answer, but he called me back a little after from a phone number I didn't recognize. For some reason, the number stuck in my head."

He gave it to her. She didn't recognize it, either. She shook her head. "I've never heard him use that number before."

Alex nodded. "Anyway, we talked for a bit. He sounded…tired. Distracted, maybe. He said he was getting ready to leave on a mission to Iraq."

She remembered the time. "You're right. Liam was distracted back then. Actually, for a while. At first, I wasn't so worried. You know how Liam throws himself into his mission to the point of being consumed by it. But his behavior became increasingly more withdrawn as the weeks went by. Then he showed up at my house…and you know the rest." She shrugged. "I think Iraq was just a staging location, though. He was heading behind enemy lines."

"It makes sense. The fewer people who know about where an agent is going, the better chance they have of surviving. The last time we talked, he told me a little of the same things he told you. About this new player coming onto his radar. He seemed really worried and alluded to the fact that if they couldn't find out his identity soon, it could have deadly consequences."

Rachel shivered at the implication. Had Liam tracked the identity of the person and found out it was one of his own people?

As they rode along, a tree branch snapped close to

the edge of the trail, immediately drawing Rachel's attention back to the moment. Was it just an innocent animal roaming the woods nearby? Or had an enemy found them and was closing in quickly?

Alex reined in his mare and listened carefully. Nothing but silence followed. The sound had come from just up ahead. Slowly, he dismounted and drew his weapon. Rachel did the same.

Close by, the dog growled and headed for the woods in the direction of the sound, sniffing the air.

"Stay, Callie," Rachel ordered and stopped the dog with that verbal command. Callie sat back on her haunches, her guard up.

"Stay behind me," Alex said and then eased into the treed area. Once inside, he stopped for a second to take stock. At one time, he had known these woods like the back of his hand. He and Liam had hunted just about everything the forest provided since they were kids. Alex could recognize the different sounds made by animals that roamed the mountains, and the noise he'd just heard earlier didn't belong to any of those animals.

To the right, another twig snapped, riveting both their attentions that way. A mule deer stood frozen in place not far from the spot, staring at them. Rachel let go of a breath, relieved. Yet Alex couldn't share in it, because he was positive the previous sound hadn't come from the deer.

Rachel turned to look at him and saw the truth in his eyes. He barely had time to shake his head before something charged from the bushes nearby and right for them.

A man dressed completely in black, with a ski mask

covering his face, hit Alex full force before he had time to react.

The momentum of the man broadsiding him sent both of them sprawling across the rocky ground. Alex's weapon flew from his hand. The man had slung an assault rifle behind his back.

As Alex struggled for control, his attacker temporarily gained the upper hand, and they wrestled back and forth. In the hand-to-hand combat that ensued, the man's assault rifle slipped off his arm. They were now both unarmed. Alex was relying on physical strength alone.

Out of the corner of his eye, Alex saw Rachel struggling to get a clear shot off. With them grappling back and forth, there was no opportunity.

Alex managed to free one hand and he slugged his attacker hard. The man's head spun sideways and he yelped in pain. The fury in his eyes was pure evil as he clutched Alex around the throat, trying to strangle him. Alex fought free and punched the man hard once more. This time, he slumped to the side, stunned by the blow. It was enough for Alex to get away. Jumping to his feet, he searched the ground for his Glock. He recalled the general direction it had landed, but it was nowhere in sight.

Rachel fired off a warning shot as Alex's attacker regained his senses. "Stay where you are," she ordered. The man didn't listen.

Before Alex located the weapon, the man lunged for him once more. This time Alex was prepared. He set his feet and grabbed hold of the man's arms.

His assailant was yelling at the top of his lungs. It

wouldn't be long before his buddies zeroed in on the direction of the noise and came to his aid.

Before Alex could slug the man again, Rachel slammed the stock of her gun hard against the man's temple. He didn't have time to register what had happened before he slumped to the ground at Alex's feet.

It took a second for Alex to gather his breath and then he knelt next to the man. Yanking the mask off, he recoiled when he got a good look at him. He recognized the man from somewhere.

"Do you know him?" Rachel asked in amazement, seeing his reaction.

"I'm not sure." A quick search of his pockets produced a driver's license with the man's name on it. Alex wasn't sure what he'd been expecting. Certainly not that something about the man's face would be familiar. The name, on the other hand, was elusive. He stared down at the man, racking his brain to come up with how he might know him, but he just couldn't place it.

Alex handed the ID to Rachel. "It says his name is Victor McNamara. Does it ring a bell to you?"

She studied the photo for a second, then shook her head and handed it back to Alex. He shoved it in his pocket and then slung the assault rifle over his shoulder.

"Let's go. The way he was carrying on, everyone within a two-mile radius will have heard him."

They hurried past the waiting dog, who leaped to her feet. Once they were both back in the saddle, Rachel nudged the mare forward, and Alex followed.

While the horses made their way across the uneven countryside, Alex tried to make sense of what had just taken place. Why did this man look familiar? He was positive he recognized him from somewhere. He needed to figure out where and soon. Their lives and Liam's depended on it.

The fact that they were coming after Rachel with such force gave him some hope that Liam might still be alive and had gotten away somehow. They'd need her to find her brother. Yet if Liam were still up on Midnight Mountain and if he was hurt, he could be in danger from more than just the men hunting him. The temperature at night up at the higher altitude could plunge well below freezing.

On the back of the capable mare Esther, Alex took in the passing countryside as they steadily climbed. It amazed him that through it all, Callie kept a careful stride behind them. The dog reminded him a lot of a mutt he'd had as a kid. He'd loved that dog until the day she'd passed away.

Alex took a second to gain his bearings. They were almost to the top of Plume Mountain, one of the many mountains neighboring Midnight Mountain.

He couldn't figure out how Victor McNamara or any of the events that had taken place related to Liam's disappearance. He was positive the name was a fake.

Frustrated, Alex shook his head. It was beyond him at the moment. Right now, with the steady climb, it took all his skills and concentration to keep on the mare.

After they'd put sufficient distance between themselves and the men hunting them, Rachel slowed the horse's speed and Alex caught up to her.

Her brown hair was windblown. Her cheeks flushed from the ride. And she had never looked more beautiful to him...or more worried.

"Are you okay?" Alex asked when he got a good look at her expression.

She shrugged. "I don't know anymore. What was that about back there, Alex? Why do these people want us dead? And why is someone trying to kill Liam? Liam is a patriot. He would never compromise his loyalty to our country for anything. So, if those men are CIA, why do they want him dead?"

"I don't think it's a matter of Liam compromising his values, but someone else compromising theirs. That man back there, to name one. I'm not sure what Liam uncovered, but he's in serious danger because of it." He hesitated before voicing his concerns. "Rachel, we can't do this alone, especially when we really don't know what we're up against. We could both end up dead. Let me call in my team." He pressed when she didn't answer. "I promise we can trust them."

She stared at him as if he had lost his mind. "We can't. Even if we can trust your team, who's to say that someone won't mention what's happening here to a colleague? We could all end up dead because of it. Please, we can't reach out to anyone connected to the CIA."

He understood her reluctance was because of what Liam had scribbled on the back of the map, but that didn't change the fact that they were grossly outnumbered.

"All right, I'll go along with it for now, but the sooner we get some breathing room between us and those thugs back there, the better." He expelled a weary sigh.

She smiled over at him and squeezed his arm. "Thank you, Alex. And thank you for coming so soon. I know it couldn't have been easy."

To be honest, he hadn't even thought about it. He'd just come. Her call had left him shaken. He'd gone against every instinct screaming inside of him that told him he was making a bad decision by not looping in his CIA Scorpion commander, Jase Bradford. He'd simply left Jase in the dark as to why he needed a few days off for personal time. Then he'd borrowed his buddy Aaron Foster's plane and left Colorado right away, because something had happened to Liam and Rachel needed him.

"You know I'd do anything for Liam and for you. You guys are like family." He watched her draw in a breath, her eyes clouding with some unnamed emotion he'd give anything to understand. There was a time when he knew what her every little expression meant. Back before he'd screwed things up.

"We should probably keep going. They could have men stationed farther up this mountain," she murmured, looking away, breaking the spell.

Before he could answer, Rachel nudged the mare and headed up the trail once more. After a moment, he followed, while rebuking himself over letting his emotions get the better of him. He had to stay focused. The past was over and done. He was here for Liam.

So far, it didn't appear that anyone was following them, but Rachel was right. They could have men everywhere. Until they had a better handle on what they faced, they needed to stay on the move. They'd be harder to track that way.

It took more than a heart-pounding hour before they summited the top of Plume Mountain, one of the lesser mountains that was part of a chain of them stretching through the area. There was still a long ways to travel before they reached their destination of Midnight Mountain. Rachel reined to a stop and took out the binoculars once more to scan the area below them where Willow Creek was located before handing them to him.

"I don't see anything. Not even Tom." She got off the horse and stretched out the kinks in her back.

After he'd checked the area and was satisfied they were safe for the moment, he did the same back stretches. He had finally gotten a sense of where he was again. He'd been away for years. It took a while to reacquaint.

"He should have been here long before us. I don't see his truck and trailer." She turned to Alex. "I don't like it. What if he was being held hostage? What if they followed him here?"

He went over to where she stood and placed his hands on her shoulders. He could feel her grow tense in reaction to his touch and he hid his hurt with difficulty.

"Hey, we don't know anything's happened yet," he said, and yet as much as he tried to reassure her, Rachel was right. By vehicle, the drive shouldn't take more than a half hour.

"Where would he normally park?" he asked while trying not to show his concern. If these people were somehow CIA, they'd have the full resources of the Agency at their disposal. They could make people disappear...for good.

She pointed to some trees close to a trailhead. "Tom and his wife come here quite often. When my husband was alive, he and I would ride horses with them up here. Tom always parked over there."

The mention of her husband was a painful reminder of the things that could have been his. He found himself being jealous of a dead man. Pitiful.

"Let's not think the worst until we know for sure.

Anything could have happened. A flat tire. Maybe it took him longer to load the four-wheeler than usual." Alex tried to sound positive, but his worst fear was that the men coming after them had gotten to Rachel's friend.

"Wait, I see something." She pointed down below, then took up the binoculars once more. "That's him. But he's riding the four-wheeler... I thought he would pull it on a trailer behind his truck," she said with a bewildered frown. "Something's not right."

Rachel headed back to the horses, ready to ride down into the valley, but he stopped her.

"Hang on a second. We still don't know if he's here alone or by his own will, for that matter. Like you said, something's not right."

She stared at him for the longest time. "There's no way Tom would set us up."

He didn't break eye contact. "Maybe not willingly, but he may not have had a choice."

She drew in a breath. "All right. What do you suggest we do?"

He scanned the area below them once again. "Let's leave the horses up here and go the rest of the way down on foot." Alex pointed to the left. "There's plenty of tree coverage through there. If there's someone else with him, we'll be better able to take them by surprise."

"Okay," she agreed, and then led the mares into the woods to find a location where they could tie them off with plenty of grass for grazing.

Once they'd strapped on their backpacks, with Callie glued to their heels, Alex took the lead. "Stay close to me and if anything happens, get back here and ride out as fast as you can," he told her, knowing she wouldn't do any of those things. She was a soldier at heart and a soldier would never leave a fellow comrade behind.

The hike down the opposite side of the mountain proved just as treacherous as the summit had. All the while, Alex couldn't get the man who had attacked him out of his head. Was he CIA? They were sworn to protect, but it wouldn't be unheard of for one of their own to go rogue. Still, why come after Liam unless he'd uncovered the traitorous threat? Was it possible this new terrorist had gotten Liam involved in something way over his head?

Once they reached the valley, Alex stopped long enough to bring out the binoculars and scan the area. There didn't appear to be anyone else around but the man who had dismounted the four-wheeler and stood looking around with a rifle in his hand.

The dog had stuck close to them the whole way down, as if sensing something was off.

"I don't see anyone but your friend." He drew his weapon and turned to her. "Just in case," he said in response to her raised brow.

They stepped from the cover of the trees close to the man with the four-wheeler who stood at full alert. His body language alone seemed to confirm something had gone wrong.

Callie spotted Tom and galloped toward him, tail wagging. A twig snapped beneath the dog's paw and the man whirled at the sound, shotgun ready to fire.

The moment he spotted Rachel, he visibly relaxed, then reached down and patted the dog's head. When he saw Alex with a gun in his hand, his demeanor changed immediately. He clutched the rifle tighter. Alex had no doubt he was skilled at using it.

"It's okay, Tom. He's my friend," Rachel said, and then rushed over to give the man a heartfelt hug.

Alex watched her with the older man and it was easy to see that she loved him.

She stepped back and turned to Alex. "Tom, this is Alex Booth. We grew up here together. He and Liam are good friends."

Alex tucked the Glock behind his back and shook the man's hand. "Good to meet you, sir."

"You, too," Tom said with a firm handshake. He watched as the dog went to explore a nearby plant. Alex could tell the man seemed distracted by something.

"Has something happened, Tom?" Rachel obviously saw the same thing he did.

After a moment or two of silence, Tom looked at Rachel. "I wasn't able to bring the truck. I used the four-wheeler to slip out the back way." The man shook his head. "I'm not really sure what to make of it, but it scared me. I haven't seen anything like it in my seventy-plus years."

He paused for a breath and Rachel shot Alex a worried glance.

"Right before you called, a couple of men showed up at my place asking a whole bunch of questions about Liam and you." The concern in Tom's eyes was real enough. "They had IDs." He shook his head. "They said they worked for the CIA... Rachel, they said Liam did something terrible. They said he wants to hurt a lot of people."

All the color drained from Rachel's face. "That's not true. Tom, you know it's not true. Liam would never hurt anyone."

Tom's expression softened and he managed a smile

for her. "I know that. I'd trust Liam with my life. Jenny, too. But these men seemed determined to lay the blame on him for something. They said he betrayed his country." Tom spat the words out and shook his head. "Jenny was in the kitchen when they showed up. I wasn't going to let them inside, but they pretty much forced their way in. Something about them just worried me. When you called, I went in the other room. That's why I couldn't talk much."

He stopped for a second. "Anyway, Jenny told me after they'd gone that she's pretty sure she saw at least a half dozen more men in the woods surrounding the house. They were coming from the direction of your place. She said they were armed to the teeth."

He blew out an uneven breath. "They're coming after you, too, Rachel. And they're not going to stop until they find you and Liam. And I don't think they care if that's dead or alive."

THREE

It felt as if the ground had been yanked out from beneath her feet. Was it possible that this whole thing was all about someone trying to frame Liam for a crime they had committed? What were they trying to cover up?

"You saw their IDs? They were definitely CIA?" she asked in shock.

Callie trotted back from her exploring as if sensing her owner's unease.

Tom nodded. "I did. They looked like CIA to me, or a very good forgery."

Alex pulled out the driver's license they'd taken from the man who attacked them. "Is this one of the men you spoke with?"

Tom took the ID and studied it before shaking his head. "Nope, that's not one of them. The two who did the talking were both dark-haired. Average looks. Around the same age as this guy, though. They were definitely trying to be intimidating and let me say, they accomplished it." He handed the ID back to Alex.

Perplexed, Rachel turned to Alex. "It could be the same man from this morning. Was one of them injured?" she asked Tom.

Tom appeared alarmed. "No, at least not that I could tell. What happened this morning?" His concern was obvious. Rachel gave him the amended version.

He shook his head. "Unbelievable. I told Jenny I thought I heard shots pretty early this morning. I'm sorry I didn't come to your aid, Rachel."

She patted his arm. "I'm glad you didn't. They might have killed you."

That chilling reality hung between them, keeping everyone silent for a while.

"Still no word from Liam?" Tom asked, breaking the quiet.

"No." And she was terrified for Liam's well-being, especially after what the man who broke into her house had said. She had no idea how many days her brother had actually been missing or if the person he'd gone there to meet had set him up. The only information she had was where he was going, a dangerous location near the top of Midnight Mountain.

"Do you need me to help with the search?" Tom asked, and his generous offer came as no surprise even though she knew she couldn't accept.

"Thank you, Tom, but it's too dangerous. We'll be okay." Rachel wished she felt as confident as those words sounded.

Tom bowed his head. He had been so protective of her since Brian's passing.

Alex touched her arm. "I hate to say it, but we should probably get going. Those men know the general direction we're heading. They'll keep coming after us."

She swallowed deeply. She hated to let Tom go. Would she see him again?

Please, God...

"You're right." She faced the older man again. "We left the horses up on top of the mountain." She didn't want to leave them in the elements too long.

"Don't worry about it. Callie and I will fetch them and take them home with me," Tom assured her. "You two get going. The less time spent out in the open like this, the better. Jenny packed you food in the four-wheeler's storage compartment."

Tom stared at her for a long time with worry creasing his face. She knew he was concerned for her safety and so she tried to ease his mind.

"We'll be okay, I promise. Thank you for the use of the four-wheeler. And thank Jenny, as well."

Tom and Jenny had been like family to her since her own parents passed away three years ago. Without them and Liam, she wouldn't have gotten through losing her husband.

After years in the trenches of a different and terrifying kind of warfare, Rachel had thought she'd left behind the dangerous life she'd once led. Yet here she was right back in the thick of it again, and suddenly she wasn't so sure she could survive this time.

She hugged Tom one more time, hating to leave him, but Alex was right. Tom needed to get home to Jenny and they'd need to put distance between themselves and the men hunting them. And she had no idea what they'd face once they got up on the mountain.

"Be careful, Tom. Those men could still be close and watching your place."

Tom stood up a little taller. "Jenny stayed behind in case they came back with more questions. She thought it might look suspicious if we were both gone. She's a better shot than I am and can handle herself in any situation. If they know what's best for them, they'll steer clear of her. And don't worry about me. I know this countryside better than anyone. I'll give them the slip if they're still hanging around my property. You two just watch your backs."

Alex pulled out a piece of paper and wrote something down. "If anything comes up and you feel threatened, call this number. Ask for Jase Bradford. Tell him what's happened and he'll send help right away. He's a friend and you can trust him," Alex said, and she believed it was just as much for her benefit as for Tom's.

"I will." Tom put the number in his shirt pocket and then hugged Rachel once more. "Stay safe. And find Liam."

"We will." She drew in an emotional-riddled breath and turned to Alex. "It's been a while since you've been up on the mountain. Do you mind if I drive?"

He smiled at her and some long-suppressed memory resurfaced of a time they'd spent together on a moonlit night. He'd looked at her much in the same way. She'd been crazy about him back then. She still loved the way he smiled.

"I'm fine with that. In fact, I'm happy to act as lookout. But the sooner we get on our way, the better. We have a long trip ahead of us, and this machine can only take us so far."

She got on the four-wheeler and he hopped on behind her. Suddenly having him so close was a little too unsettling. It reminded her of all the times they'd spent in each other's company in the past, both here and in the field. It made her want to protect her heart from the inevitable time when he left her again…and he would.

They were still some distance from Midnight Mountain. With a final wave to Tom, Rachel headed the machine off in the same direction her friend had entered the valley.

The four-wheeler's powerful engine took the steep incline easily enough, but Rachel was concerned that once they reached the higher altitudes, the snow and ice would make it a dangerous trek. They'd be on foot and vulnerable. She just hoped the weather held.

They said Liam did something terrible...

There was no way she'd ever believe her brother would hurt anyone without cause. So why was someone so determined to brand Liam a traitor? What exactly had he uncovered?

If someone from the CIA was a double agent, then they'd stop at nothing to keep their crimes from being uncovered, and chances were, they hadn't acted alone.

Alex leaned forward so that she could hear him over the roar of the engine. "We may have a bigger problem. There's no way we can conceal the noise this thing makes. And the location where Liam indicated on the map is close to nine thousand feet in altitude."

Rachel had considered the same thing, too. "You're right. We'll need to find a place to leave it once we reach the base of Midnight Mountain. How are you at hiking these days?"

When they were younger, the three of them had hiked this mountain dozens of times. There was one spot in particular that they loved to camp at. The mountains at night were breathtaking and the stars appeared close enough to touch.

Alex chucked softly, the sound sending chills through her nervous system. "Don't worry. I'm not that out of shape. I think I can still keep up with you."

He certainly appeared fit enough. Outdoorsy as ever, Alex would always be the most handsome man she knew. Yet being close to him brought up emotions she'd just as soon not deal with.

She'd been crazy about him for as long as she could remember. The three of them had been determined to stay close after high school, and so they'd attended the same university. Deciding to join the CIA had been a joint decision, as well. They had all excelled at the job...for a while.

But soon, the stress of the life of an agent became too much for Rachel. Her world consisted of one dangerous mission followed by another. She found herself needing more than the adrenaline rush. She wanted a life beyond the spy games they played. A family. And she wanted all those things with Alex. She just hadn't expected his reaction. He didn't share any of her dreams.

Now, Rachel found herself wondering about what his life had been like over the past five years. Liam had told her that Alex had taken a different job within the CIA, a more specialized detachment, but he hadn't been able to talk about it much. Was Alex involved with someone new, or was he still married to the job?

Somehow, Rachel let go of the past. No sense crying over spilled milk. Neither one of them could go back in time and change things.

"We're almost to the base." Her voice sounded less than steady. It was just the past. It had a way of coming to the surface no matter how hard she tried to keep it buried. Right now, she had to find a way to shove it aside. She needed Alex's help to bring her brother home.

"There's a group of scrub brush to your left. They'll make for a good cover for the machine." Alex pointed to the left side and she eased the four-wheeler in that direction.

When they were close, Alex got off and she followed. They pushed the four-wheeler behind the scrubs and then piled extra brush all around until it was completely obscured from view.

Rachel watched as Alex slipped into his backpack. Just seeing him back home made all of her young girl wishes resurface. She turned away and grabbed the extra backpack filled with supplies and then opened the storage compartment on the four-wheeler and smiled at the sack full of sandwiches, chips, fruit and water Jenny had packed.

Alex came over to where she stood and peered over her shoulder. "Looks like a feast. Remind me to thank her in person when we get back." The words were out before he really thought about them and their eyes locked. Would they make it out of this thing alive?

As she looked into his eyes, Rachel fought to keep her equilibrium. She couldn't get sucked back into Alex's charm again. He was her past. If they survived this, perhaps they'd be able to resume their friendship, but that was all it could ever be.

She wasn't ready for anything more after losing Brian. Even though they both knew his death was inevitable when they'd married, losing him had still brought her to her knees emotionally. There wasn't anything left inside her to give to someone else, and she couldn't put the pain and heartache Alex had caused her in the past aside, no matter how hard she tried.

The wind kicked up. On it Rachel caught the faintest of sounds. Voices? Multiple ones. Someone else was up here.

Before she could get the words out, Alex heard what she did. He pulled her close and whispered, "We need to get out of sight." He glanced around the area. "Over there. A small opening in the mountain. It might be enough to keep us out of their view."

They hurried over to the entrance, looking into what appeared to be a pitch-black gap in the side of the mountain.

"I don't think it's a cave as much as a small crevice," Alex said in a low voice before they stepped inside. He took out his phone and shone the light into the five-foot-deep mountain flaw. "It's not much. If they're paying attention, we'll be sitting ducks. Let's hope that doesn't happen. Here, get on the other side of me." He tugged her deeper into the crevice and as far away from the entrance as possible.

Rachel could feel her heart echoing in her ears. She glanced up and saw Alex watching her. He was probably wondering if she was up to the task at hand.

"Do you think we hid the four-wheeler well enough?" She whispered her concern aloud. If the men spotted the machine, they'd know someone else was up here. If they were deliberately searching for them, then she and Alex wouldn't stand a chance.

"Unless they're really looking, it'll be fine. The camo paint on the machine will help it blend."

She said a prayer in her head as outside, multiple rocks dislodged and rolled down the path. Someone was close. It took everything inside her not to react.

Alex drew her close. She held her breath. More footsteps followed, too many to count. It sounded as if they'd stopped just outside the crevice.

Rachel remembered that they'd forgotten to cover

their footsteps. Would the men look down and spot them? If so, they'd know they were right under their noses.

Outside, a cell phone rang. A man answered it. "Yeah." He sounded less than thrilled.

Alex held her closer and she hugged him tight.

"There's no sign of them here. The noise could have been coming from the adjoining cattle ranch. We're heading back your way again," the man said in a sharp tone.

Rachel waited until the men had moved away and it was quiet outside, then she let go of the breath she'd held on to. "They didn't see the four-wheeler, but that was close."

"I counted at least five sets of footsteps." Alex glanced down at her in the darkness. She could almost feel his tension. "I don't understand what's going on here, but I sure hope we find Liam and get some answers soon."

"Me, too. Do you think it's safe to get out?"

"Let me take a quick look around first. Wait here." He slowly slipped out and she felt his absence completely in the oppressing darkness.

Her pulse hammered every single second Alex was gone. When he returned, she resisted the urge to hug him again.

"It looks as if they're heading back toward Plume Mountain, probably to your husband's place. I'm hoping the rest of them are still there."

Rachel followed him out again and stared up at the mountain, which was partially hidden by cloud coverage. A chill sped up her spine.

Where are you, Liam?

In the past, she and her brother always had a special connection. She could almost sense his presence in her heart. Rachel didn't feel him now. She was terrified they were already too late.

"It'll be dark soon. We need to find a place to get out of the elements. We're almost to Midnight Valley. We can camp there and head out again in the morning," Alex told her after they'd been hiking for hours. He felt the exhaustion of the miles they'd covered, fueled by his fear for Liam's safety, catching up with him.

Rachel appeared ready to drop, as well. His heart went out to her. He loved Liam like a brother, but Liam was her flesh and blood. She probably hadn't gotten any sleep since Liam's disappearance.

They reached the top of the peak that looked down on Midnight Valley. The moon had slipped from its cloud coverage and made an appearance for the first time. He could see Midnight Lake in the middle of the valley below them.

Alex lifted up a prayer of thanks for their safe passage so far. They'd battled rough terrain and fear all the way to this point.

Rachel stopped next to him and their gazes held. Alex found himself unable to look away. Even worn-out and disheveled, she was lovely. An old memory from the past resurfaced. The three of them had been chasing an arms dealer for months near Kabul. They'd finally tracked the man's location to a mountainous region in Afghanistan. Alex remembered the area had reminded him of this place. The air had been crackling with electrical tension back then. It was the first time Rachel mentioned leaving the Agency. He'd seen her fear. Realized the toll the job had taken on her. At the time, he couldn't fathom walking away. Now, after being with the specialized CIA Scorpion team for several years, he understood. The team was close and they were doing good things. It wasn't about the high for him anymore. Even so, there were times when he could almost imagine himself back here living in the small town of Midnight Mountain again.

Unexpectedly, he took her hand, and she froze briefly before turning to him. Her blue eyes were huge pools in the moonlight. The unasked questions were all there, and he couldn't bring himself to answer a single one of them.

Through the years, there hadn't been a day that had gone by where he hadn't regretted letting her go. Now, he realized it was too late for them. He'd lost her for good. They weren't the same people they once were.

He squeezed her hand and then let her go and cleared away the regret from his throat. "We'd best keep going. We're going to need to make a fire to stay warm. It's getting colder by the minute."

Something bordering disappointment shadowed her eyes before she nodded and headed down the steep mountainside. After a second, he followed.

Once they reached the valley, Alex glanced around for the best spot to build a fire without it being seen by anyone above.

He pointed to a treed area. "Let's set up camp over there."

Alex took off his backpack and leaned it against a tree. "I'll gather some wood. Let's get a fire going and then dive into those sandwiches Jenny made. I'm starving."

With the beetle infestation of recent years, there was plenty of dead timber around. Alex gathered an armful and found a good spot for the fire.

Once it was roaring, he and Rachel unrolled their sleeping bags and Rachel took out the food and handed him a sandwich and some chips along with a drink.

"There's fruit if you want some." She took a bite of her sandwich.

Alex didn't answer. He said a prayer of thanksgiving in his head and then dug into his meal with relish. A simple ham sandwich had never tasted so good.

Rachel must have spotted his reaction because she laughed. "It's the mountain air. It makes everything taste better."

He put down his sandwich and watched her. "I remember. All those picnic lunches we used to enjoy. Good times." He swallowed back his regret. He'd give anything to go back to that simpler period in his life.

Alex studied her expression in the firelight. He could almost swear he saw her blush.

She brushed a crumb from her mouth. "They were good times, weren't they? When I first left the CIA and came back home, I used to come up here all the time. I think it was just being in touch with something I loved from childhood that helped ground me."

He understood. He felt the same way.

Alex hesitated, needing to tell her something that could prove touchy. He hadn't been completely honest with her when she'd asked about the last time he'd had contact from Liam. For unknown reasons, he'd chosen not to mention the strange letter he'd received from his friend. Now, more than ever, they needed answers. Maybe something about it might make sense to her.

Alex stared at the fire, unsure of how she would take this new piece of news. "I need to tell you something, Rachel." He glanced her way. Immediately he could see he had her full attention. "A few days before you called, I received a letter in the mail from Liam." Alex stopped and shook his head. "I don't know what to make of it. It's nothing but ramblings to me. Liam talked about our childhood here in Midnight Mountain and some of the places we used to explore together. One in particular is underlined."

Alex took out the letter and handed it to her. When he'd gotten her call, he'd shoved the letter inside his jacket pocket and brought it with him. She unfolded it and read through it, a tear slipping slowly down her cheek.

"I have no idea what he's talking about," she whispered sadly, and then handed him the letter back. He tucked it back in his pocket, the desire to comfort her running deep. Alex reached over and touched her face gently, brushing aside the tears.

Before he could voice the regrets of his heart, a noise close by had them both jumping to their feet, weapons drawn.

A woman and man emerged from the shadowy woods. The woman spotted their weapons right away and quickly raised her hands.

"Oh…we're so sorry. We didn't mean to frighten the two of you. We just lost our way in the dark. When I saw the fire, I was so relieved," the woman said with the tiniest of giggles, her voice accented.

Dressed in dark clothing, she was tall, almost six feet. She stepped closer and Alex got a better look.

Her dark hair was pulled back in a ponytail; she wore a baseball cap that covered part of her face.

The man hung back a little ways in the shadows. He held his hands up, too. There was something familiar about him, too, and an uneasy feeling sped through Alex. What was going on here?

Alex moved closer to Rachel's side in a protective gesture that came naturally. "It's okay. We just weren't expecting company tonight." Like her, Alex hadn't lowered his weapon yet.

"We're really sorry to bother you, but would it be okay if we camped out with you tonight? We're both exhausted and I promise we won't be any trouble."

There was something in the woman's voice he couldn't place. Fear. Some type of warning. He was unsure, but Rachel's reaction to hearing the woman speak triggered all sorts of alarms. Was it possible that she recognized the woman?

Rachel reached out and clasped Alex's hand, squeezing it once, then letting go. She was definitely trying to warn him of something.

"Why don't you both come warm yourself by the fire?" Alex said when Rachel stood, silently assessing the woman.

The woman glanced oddly at Rachel, almost as if she knew her. She moved over to the fire and warmed her hands. After a brief hesitation, her partner joined her.

Once Alex got a closer look at the man, he was positive he recognized him. He had no idea how.

Slowly Alex lowered his weapon. Rachel did the same and the woman let out a breath, relieved.

"Sorry to draw down on you like that. We thought

you might be a bear." Alex came up with the best explanation he could.

The woman smiled again, but it didn't seem sincere. "No problem. I'm Michelle Mullins, by the way. This is my husband, Peter. We're from Colorado. We've been hiking all the mountains in the Midnight Mountain Range."

Alex strove for calm and eventually found it. He held out his hand and she shook it. Her husband wasn't nearly as friendly.

The woman turned to him. "Peter, shake the man's hand. They're keeping us from freezing to death," she said with another laugh.

The two seemed to be communicating something to each other. After another second, the man smiled and took Alex's hand. "Nice to meet you both."

"You, too," Rachel said with an attempt at a smile once he'd shook her hand.

"Thank you so much for saving us. We got caught up in the spectacular views from the top of Midnight Mountain and lost track of the time. A foolish mistake, I know." Michelle shook her head. "And one I'm embarrassed to say we made. We've been hiking for years. You'd think we'd know better."

Rachel's gaze met Alex's briefly. He could see she was troubled.

"It's no problem," she said. "Are you two hungry?"

The woman smiled genuinely. "Starving. I'm afraid I didn't pack enough food for the evening meal. I wasn't expecting to be up here." She shrugged.

"It's okay. We have plenty." Rachel brought out some extra sandwiches and a bottle of water and handed them to Michelle.

"Thanks." She took it and gave Peter one of the sandwiches.

"It's easy to get lost up here at night if you're not careful," Alex told the two while keeping a close eye on Peter. Where did he know the man from?

Peter nodded without answering and took a bite from the sandwich.

"Do you guys have sleeping bags with you?" Rachel asked, and looked around at the gear they carried.

From the looks of it, they had prepared for a long stay in spite of what Michelle had said.

"We do. It just makes good sense to be ready." Michelle unzipped her backpack and brought out a sleeping bag. Alex caught a glimpse of what looked like a pistol before she closed the bag again.

He wondered why such knowledgeable hikers would allow themselves to get lost at night. Their story didn't add up.

"So what did you say you did for a living, Alex?" Michelle asked, pinning him with her sharp gaze.

"I didn't." Alex didn't elaborate. He wasn't even trying to pretend anymore. These people were not who they said they were, and his mind had already begun to try to figure out a way to get Rachel and himself out of there safely.

How had they known where to find them? Not for a second did he buy they'd been atop the mountain. He believed they'd been deliberately searching for him and Rachel. The path Alex and Rachel were on wasn't the most direct way to the meet location. In fact, only the locals knew about Midnight Valley, so they didn't just happen here by accident.

"We should probably get some more firewood," Alex

told Rachel. "We don't want the fire to go out overnight. Why don't you come with me?"

Rachel nodded and they headed for the woods behind the camp when Michelle stopped them. "Wait, why don't you let us help you?"

Alex believed she was trying to keep an eye on them. "There's no need. We can handle it. You two stay warm. You must be frozen."

He waited until Michelle sat back down before he and Rachel headed a little deeper into the woods and out of earshot.

"I don't know about the man, but she looks familiar. I only got a glimpse of the woman who showed up at my house this morning, but I think Michelle might be her. I recognize the voice." Rachel stepped closer, keeping her tone low. "She's armed, too. I'm sure he will be, as well. We need to get out of here as fast as possible. We don't know if they've called in backup yet."

Alex couldn't let go of the feeling that he knew Peter from somewhere. Was it just a coincidence that there were two bad guys who appeared familiar to him?

"You're right. There's no doubt that they know we're onto them. We'll have to find a way to neutralize the threat they pose." He glanced back at the couple by the fire.

"I have an idea. We said we were going for wood, so let's get some." She quickly gathered a few nearby sticks, as did Alex. "We should get back before they become too suspicious. Follow my lead and keep your weapon close."

Alex nodded and she drew in a breath and led the way back to the camp. As they neared, Alex could see the couple whispering to each other. They glanced back and saw them and broke apart guiltily.

"There you are. We were wondering if you two had decided to take off," Michelle said, and Alex attempted a smile.

"Now why would we do that?" While Alex didn't see a weapon, he suspected that they had them close by, which wouldn't leave him and Rachel much time to disarm them. He sure hoped her plan worked.

He watched as Rachel dropped her logs close to the fire. Alex placed a couple of sticks on the blaze itself, waiting for Rachel's cue. She held the final log in her hand and moved around the fire, pretending to stir it. She was now closest to Peter.

Without warning, she swung the log hard and hit Peter across the face. He keeled over backward, out cold.

Right away, Michelle searched beneath her sleeping bag, no doubt for a gun.

"I wouldn't if I were you." Rachel drew down on Michelle, her voice reminding him of when they'd worked missions together.

With Rachel standing guard, Alex went over to the woman and grabbed the weapon she'd hidden, then checked under Peter's sleeping bag. There was a second gun.

"We were just worried for our safety. You guys were acting strangely," Michelle said, trying to convince them.

Alex ignored what she said and snatched up both backpacks. "We need to tie them up," he told Rachel. "I'll see if I can find some rope and secure him first."

Rachel kept the gun trained on Michelle's head.

"Don't try anything foolish," she warned. "Or I promise you'll regret it."

Peter had just begun to regain consciousness when Alex retrieved some rope from one of the bags and forced Peter's hands behind his back, then secured them.

The minute Peter realized what was happening he fought against his restraints and raged. "How'd you let this happen?" He glared at Michelle and the woman actually shrunk away from the animosity on the man's face.

"That's enough," Alex ordered, and then moved to the woman. Once he'd tied up Michelle, he did a thorough search of both backpacks. What he found in one of them scared the daylights out of him. A phone. He brought up the number. It was the same phone that Liam had called him from. They had Liam's phone. What had they done with his friend?

FOUR

Across the burning fire, the look on Alex's face was alarming. He held Peter's backpack in his hand. Something was wrong. What had he found inside?

Please, don't let it be bad…

She held her breath. Their gazes locked and he silently tried to communicate something. He dropped the backpack and came over to where she stood, every step bringing more turbulence to her pulse.

"What is it?" She managed a whisper. The thought of losing her brother was terrifying.

Alex still held something in his hand. He silently motioned for them to step a little ways from the camp.

When they were out of earshot, he showed her a cell phone. She didn't recognize it. She shook her head. She didn't understand.

"I checked the number." His tone was tense, so unlike Alex. Rachel braced for bad news. "This is the same phone Liam called me from before."

She stared at him as the implication of those words finally dawned. "Why would they have Liam's burner phone if they didn't know where he was?" When Alex had no answer, without thinking, Rachel charged back to Michelle and yanked her to her feet. "Where is he? What have you done with him?"

Taken aback, Michelle stared at her with fear in her eyes, struggling to get away. "I don't know who you're talking about. Let me go."

"You'd better keep your mouth shut." Peter glared over at his partner. Michelle visibly flinched. She was clearly terrified of Peter.

Alex went over to the man. "You're in no position to try to intimidate her. If you want to help yourself, you'd better start cooperating."

Peter wasn't swayed. "I have nothing to say." He shot Michelle a venomous look. "And neither does she."

"She can speak for herself." Alex took Michelle by the arm and pulled her away from Peter's hearing.

"Don't try anything foolish while we're gone," Rachel warned, and then followed Alex.

"He can't hurt you anymore," Alex told her. "We'll protect you, but you have to tell us what's going on here. Who are you working for? Where's Agent Carlson?" Michelle's brittle laugh cut through what he'd said.

"You have no idea what you're talking about," Michelle said in a hushed tone. She was visibly shaken and immediately seemed to regret her outburst. "My husband and I told you who we are. We came to you because we were lost and needed help, but you two have all but taken us hostage and we've done nothing wrong."

Alex held up the phone. "And this? I found it in Peter's backpack. It belongs to a friend of mine who's gone missing up here. A federal agent. How did you end up with his phone?"

Michelle glanced back at Peter and then looked Alex in the eye. "I don't know what you're talking about. You two are the first people we've run into. Maybe there are others here. People with bad intentions aimed toward your friend…and you."

Rachel sucked in a breath. "What do you mean by that?" She was convinced Michelle was trying to tell them they weren't alone up here. Or was she simply trying to dodge the question?

Michelle turned back toward Peter. "I have nothing else to say to you. And I would suggest you get out of here before you find yourself facing far worse trouble than you've seen so far."

Shocked, Rachel riveted her gaze to Alex. There was no doubt in her mind the woman was trying her best to warn them without giving away too much.

Alex took Michelle back to where Peter was silently fuming. Then he motioned to Rachel and they stepped out of earshot once more.

"We need to get out of here now, Alex. I don't know what her intentions were for saying what she did, but I believe she was warning us there are others up here, searching for Liam and probably for us, as well."

Alex nodded then glanced over her shoulder to where the two sat. Michelle still looked afraid. Peter appeared to be browbeating her. "I think you're right. Their driver's licenses seem to back up their claim of who they are, but they could have been forged. And I'm positive I know this guy Peter from somewhere."

This bit of news was unsettling. He'd said the same about the man who had attacked them earlier. Did Alex recognize the men because they were part of the same organization as he was? It was an uneasy thought.

"Do you have any idea how?" It was too big of a co-incidence that Alex would know two of the men that were hunting them down. They really needed to figure out why they were being chased so aggressively. Perhaps in the process it would lead to answers into Liam's location.

He shook his head, obviously frustrated by the elusive recollection. "I wish I knew. It's on the edge of my memory, but I just can't bring it out. Anyway, you're right. If what Michelle alluded to is correct, they could have men on the way here right now."

Which meant their window of escape was rapidly closing.

"What do we do about those two? We can't leave them up here in the elements."

"We stoke the fire and get out of here as quickly as possible before the people they've called catch up with us. Make no mistake—they didn't just happen upon us."

He was right. They'd probably been stalking them for a while.

"You need to let us go now." Peter talked in an overly loud voice once they'd returned to camp. Was he trying to alert his comrades to their location? "You can't leave us here. We'll freeze to death."

Alex ignored the man's raging and piled enough wood on the fire to last until morning.

"That should get you through the night. I'll be calling the authorities to let them know where they can pick you two up as soon as possible. I would suggest you tell them the truth."

"You can't leave us here," Michelle pleaded with Rachel. She could almost swear there was real fear in Michelle's eyes. Was it just an act? She'd had her chance to talk and had refused.

"You'll be fine until the authorities arrive," Rachel assured her. "The fire will keep any predators away."

Alex gathered up their phones and camping supplies. Rachel slipped on her backpack and they headed out in the opposite direction from where they believed Liam's meet had happened, trying to throw the two off as to where they were really heading.

Once they'd gone some distance from the campsite, Alex slowed down. "How are you holding up?" he asked.

Rachel glanced up at the sky filled with stars. "Okay, I guess. But I hate trying to make our way up to the top of Midnight Mountain at night." She thought about Michelle's warning. "I don't doubt for a second that Michelle was warning us there are more people up here searching for Liam and us. They probably called them to let them know they'd found us before they came into the camp."

Alex nodded. "I can't figure out her motives. She seemed genuinely scared, but when given the opportunity, she chose to back Peter. It could all be an act. Right now, we can't afford to trust her."

Rachel placed her hand on his arm and he turned to look down at her. "We can't really call in the authorities, Alex. We don't know who's really behind Liam's disappearance. You saw the note Liam left. It's too dangerous."

Alex looked around the area uneasily. "I know. There's no doubt in my mind that there are others out there. I think Peter was trying to warn them of our exact location by talking loudly."

She'd thought the same thing. "We should be far

enough away by now to circle back in the right direction."

They started off in the different path that would take them up to the top of the mountain. "It's getting colder by the minute." Alex turned the collar of his jacket up.

He was right. It felt as if the temperature had dropped at least ten degrees. Rachel rubbed her gloved hands together. "We need to keep walking just to stay warm."

The rugged mountain terrain made it impossible to keep up a good pace. Not to mention that they were traveling in the dark, unable to use flashlights to illuminate their way. They'd be sitting ducks if they were to happen upon the enemy.

Rachel's thoughts churned out questions by the dozens. The fact that Peter had Liam's phone wasn't a good thing. "How do you think they ended up with Liam's phone? There's no way they just happened upon it."

Alex stopped and faced her. In the darkness, she couldn't make out his expression. "No. They had him at one time. The fact that they're still searching for him gives me hope that Liam managed to get away. My gut is telling me he's still up here somewhere, though. The only question is, where? There's a lot of territory to cover and we have no clue as to where he might be hiding."

Rachel tried to hold on to some small amount of faith that Liam was still alive. She couldn't imagine her life without him. She searched her memory, going over every conversation she and Liam had had recently for anything that would give them a clue as to where he might be. She recalled something that Liam had told her once about one of his buddies from high school buying one of the logging camps up on the mountain. Was it possible that Liam had made it down to that area and was hiding there?

Please, Lord…

Alex was a few steps in front of her. Before she could tell him about what she'd remembered, he stopped dead in his tracks, putting his arm out in front of her to keep her from going any farther.

He turned back to her and whispered, "Voices." Then he placed a finger over his lips. She heard it, too. The voices were coming from some distance ahead of them.

Alex pointed to a group of trees close by and they eased that way as quietly as possible.

Rachel tripped over a log, her foot rolled sideways, and she froze. But it was too late. The noise it made echoed throughout the still night.

"I hear something." A man's voice reached them. In the moonlight Rachel caught a glimpse of four people moving through the woods just a little ways from where they'd been walking.

She held her breath, praying that they hadn't been spotted. She and Alex were trained agents, but it was dark out and they were outnumbered.

Rachel tucked behind the closest tree, a pine that was barely large enough to conceal her from view. Alex had reached the group of trees he'd pointed to. Her gaze glued to his. Her heart pounded in her ears, drowning out all sound.

A flashlight's beam shot past the area where they were and Rachel sucked in her breath.

Please don't let them see us.

"There's nothing out there but a bunch of animals." A different voice than before snapped the words out. The flashlight hovered close to where Rachel was hiding. She tried to keep as still as possible. If she moved an inch, she'd be in the light. "They're waiting for us."

The man with the flashlight didn't make a move to obey. "I heard something." He kept the beam focused on the tree close to her for a second longer.

"And I'm telling you there's nothing there. He's waiting on us. You know how angry he gets when someone doesn't follow orders."

After what felt like an eternity, the man finally gave in. "Yeah, yeah, I'm coming." The light searched the area one more time and then she could hear them heading away. The same direction she and Alex had come.

Thank You, Lord, she whispered and struggled for a calm her heart wouldn't allow.

Once the men were safely out of the area, Rachel pointed up ahead. They needed to put as much space as they could between themselves and the men. When they reached Peter and Michelle, they'd know something was wrong. They'd put two and two together and realize the man had been right when he thought he heard something.

After she and Alex had covered more than a quarter of a mile, Rachel stopped for breath. "That was close. They're heading right toward where we left Peter and Michelle, as if they know exactly where to find them."

"I'm sure they do." Alex confirmed her belief. "I'll guarantee they called them in before they came out of the woods and confronted us. It won't take them long to reach those two and when they do, they'll come after us. We need to get out of sight as quickly as possible."

Once her heart finally stopped racing, Rachel remembered what she was going to tell Alex before they'd spotted the men.

"With everything that just happened, there wasn't time to tell you before. I remembered something Liam said to me not too long ago. I don't know why I didn't think of it earlier." She told him about Liam's friend buying one of the old mills.

"Do you remember which one? That could be where Liam is hiding out," he said in relief.

There were numerous logging camps up the mountain. Most were being reclaimed by the woods in which they were carved.

"There are several. We'll have to search them all." Not exactly the ideal situation, but they couldn't risk overlooking any of them on the off chance that Liam might be hiding there.

"Do you think you can find them in the dark?" Alex couldn't hide his doubt. He could barely see more than a couple of feet in front of him. Finding a bunch of deserted logging camps seemed like an impossible task in his mind.

"I think so, but I'm going to need the flashlight. We can't risk walking off the side of the mountain." She didn't sound nearly as positive as he had hoped.

"Lead the way," he told her, and she clicked on the flashlight and headed out.

While they walked, Alex couldn't shake the impression that he knew Peter from somewhere. He just couldn't pull the answer out of his head. That he seemed to recognize two bad men in one day told him he was onto something.

Rachel stopped to gain her bearings and he stood next to her. She brushed hair from her face. Even exhausted to the bone, she was beautiful. And every time he looked at her, he was dogged with regret. He'd messed things up between them. He'd been foolish enough to think that life revolved around the job. He'd been so wrong.

Thanks be to God, for working on Alex to help him see what was truly important. Still, it was a bitter pill to swallow that it had come at the expense of his relationship with Rachel.

"This way." She pointed a little farther up. "I remember Liam telling me once that his buddy hiked up here a lot before buying the place. He said it was one of the few camps on this side of the mountain."

They headed in that general direction, his thoughts keeping him quiet. Alex realized that he knew so little about her life now. Was she happy? Did she have regrets?

"Do you still hike the mountain?" he asked, mostly because he wanted to know more about her and he didn't want to bring up their touchy past.

Her steps faltered a little at the question. "Sometimes. Not as often as I'd like." She shrugged. "I feel so free up here. It's as if all the world's cares just melt away and it's just me alone up here with God."

He looked at her in surprise. Growing up, none of them had really been religious. He recalled attending church only at the big holidays. He hadn't paid much attention back then. He mostly just wanted the time he spent in church to be over. Yet everything had changed when he lost Rachel. He'd hit rock bottom for a while, doubting everything in his life. It was why he'd chosen to make a career change. He'd been searching for something different. Something more meaningful.

Joining the Scorpions, he'd found a tight-knit family where he belonged. Each member openly discussed their faith in God. He'd fought against the tugging at his heart for a bit, but the moment he gave in and realized he needed God in his life more than ever, the peace he felt inside at that decision was amazing.

He'd started attending a local church near their headquarters, and had grown closer to God ever since.

"I know what you mean," he told her quietly. "That's kind of how I feel when I hike the mountain near our compound. It's as if you can see God in everything."

She looked at him curiously. "Liam told me you'd joined a different branch of the CIA after I left. He said you seemed different. More at peace."

It surprised him to hear that Liam had noticed the change in him. "I guess I am." He didn't look at her. "Before, well, the job was everything to me. I couldn't imagine life without it." He shook his head and realized he had her full attention.

"What happened to change that?" She seemed genuinely interested in his answer.

"God happened," he said, and grinned over at her. "This new team that I joined, well, everyone there is a Christian, and they believe the work we are doing is God's work. When I joined, I was skeptical at first. You know I wasn't raised as a Christian. Back when we were kids, attending church felt like a chore, so I did it as seldom as possible."

He chuckled. "But then I realized these people were sincere. Soon, I started attending the church close to town and then I knew what was missing from my life. Now, I can't imagine where I'd be right now if I hadn't found the team."

She smiled up at him. "I get that. I was pretty messed

up when I came home. Then I met Tom and Jenny and started attending church with them." She stopped for a second and he realized there was something more than she'd told him. "If it hadn't been for God, I'm not sure where I'd be right now."

Guilt tugged at his heartstrings. He didn't doubt for a moment that most of the reason why she'd been heading for trouble was because of him.

That he'd hurt her was painful to accept. It was hard letting go of their burdened past, but he did. She had married someone who could give her the things she'd needed. Things he couldn't. Best to leave that door closed.

His thoughts went back to the two men he seemingly recognized. They both appeared to be highly skilled. He had no doubt they possessed military training of some sort. How were they connected to Liam's disappearance and, more important, why did both men seem so familiar?

He considered what Rachel had said about Liam believing the person he'd been chasing might be CIA. Was that how Alex knew them? Had he run into the men as part of his job?

Alex pictured the two men in his head again. He focused on each one's facial features. It was on the tip of his tongue, just out of reach…and then it finally hit him why they both seemed familiar. He stopped dead in his tracks, drawing Rachel's worried attention back to him.

"What's wrong?" she asked.

Was it possible? He couldn't even believe it. His mind didn't want to go there.

He took a deep breath and voiced his fears aloud. "I told you that I thought I recognized Peter and the other man, Victor McNamara, who attacked us?" She nodded, her gaze plastered on his face.

"Well, I just remembered from where." He blew out a breath and shook his head.

Rachel saw how concerned he was. "How do you know them?" she prompted when he didn't answer right away.

"From CIA headquarters in Langley, Virginia." He tried to get the realization to make sense to him. It was absurd, surely.

"Langley?" She was clearly confused. "I don't remember either of them being at Langley."

He shook his head. "That's because we didn't train with them." He stopped and clasped her shoulders, needing a moment to fit it together in his head. "Rachel, those men are honored on the CIA's memorial wall. They're supposed to be dead. They were killed while on a mission a few years back. They aren't supposed to be alive anymore."

FIVE

Rachel stared up at him, trying to make sense of what Alex had just told her. "Why would they fake their deaths?" It was unimaginable.

He shook his head and they continued walking. "I can't imagine. I don't remember much of the details, only that their entire six-man team was killed while on a mission in Iraq. Peter Mullins and Victor McNamara are not their real names, though."

"Do you think they faked their deaths as part of their cover? Maybe they're still on a mission? They could be deep undercover with some really bad guys?" Even as she said the words aloud, the idea didn't make sense.

Alex shook his head. "No way. If they're up here chasing some bad guys, why are they trying to kill us and Liam?"

What Tom had told them earlier about Liam doing something bad chased through her thoughts, wholly unwelcomed. There was no way she would ever accept that her brother had gone rogue. Yet she couldn't dismiss what Alex had said about the men supposedly dying while on a mission in Iraq. That was the last place Liam had gone overseas. It couldn't simply be a coincidence.

Try as she might, Rachel couldn't seem to fit the pieces together. Exhaustion wasn't helping. She hadn't slept properly in days; she'd been too worried about her brother. She glanced around the wooded area. The first logging camp was still a good distance away. What would they do if those men had been there? Maybe they'd found Liam already? Would they be wasting precious time by searching the logging camps instead of going straight to Liam's last known location? If her brother were up there injured, he could be dead by the time they reached him. Her thoughts swam.

"Alex, what if he's still up there on the mountain somewhere, hurt and alone? Maybe we should keep heading up?"

He shook his head. "I don't think he's still up there, Rachel. Think about it. It's been over a week since we believe he went missing. These people have been searching up there all this time and I don't doubt for a minute that they knew about the meet location. If Liam were still up there, they would have found him by now."

Unless he were dead… She couldn't voice her deepest fear aloud. It didn't matter. Alex saw what she was thinking.

"Don't go there. If Liam were truly dead, they wouldn't still be up here. They'd have what they wanted and they'd be long gone. He's still alive and he has the advantage. Liam knows this place like the back of his hand. All of the mountain's secret hiding places. These men do not. Liam would know where to go to disappear until it was safe to leave."

Rachel hung on to that promise with everything inside of her. Alex was right. Liam could find every cave up on the mountainside in the dark. If her brother were injured, it would slow him down. Depending on how serious his injuries might be, it was possible he couldn't leave by his own strength.

"How much farther to the first camp?" Alex asked while keeping a careful eye behind them. "Those men must have reached Peter and Michelle by now. They can't let us go because they believe Liam may have told you something critical that they don't want made public."

The implication was frightening. These men were willing to kill to keep their secret.

Exhausted and barely hanging on, she and Alex didn't have the luxury of taking a break.

"It's still a little ways from here." She hated telling him the next part, but he needed to know. "Alex, there's some pretty rough terrain standing between us and the camp. The loggers used to reach the camp by coming up from the opposite side of the mountain where it's more accessible."

"What's standing between us and the camp?" he asked, as if dreading her answer.

It had been a while since Rachel visited the area, but if she remembered correctly, there was a creek that ran through here. It fed off the spring thaws and it would be raging at this time of the year.

"Water," she answered. "There's a creek a couple of miles before we reach the camp. We had a lot of snow this year. It's going to be running pretty swiftly."

She could see this wasn't exactly the best news. "Let's hope it's still pretty frozen up here. Otherwise, we're going to get wet, and with the temperature close to freezing, we could be in serious danger of hypothermia."

* * *

Alex felt the exhaustion of the day seep into his limbs. He was working on next to no sleep. He couldn't imagine what Rachel was going through.

"The creek is just past this next ridge." He glanced at her. She was shivering from the cold.

They wouldn't be any good to Liam or anyone else if they died up here from the elements.

Rachel stopped suddenly and listened. "I hear it." She turned to him. "We're almost there, Alex. It sounds like it's running pretty strong."

Crossing a fast-moving creek would be next to impossible under the best of conditions. In the dark and ill prepared for the crossing, it might cost them both their lives.

They reached the top of the summit. Alex could see the white water rushing below them. It appeared as if the creek had overflown its banks. The worst possible scenario. His heart sank. "Maybe there's an easier way to cross. We have to try."

He and Rachel made their way slowly to the edge. At one time the water had been much higher. There was evidence of flooding all around them. Alex's feet slogged through thick mud as they neared the edge of the water.

He stopped once they got as close as the rushing water would allow. There were charred trees all around. Not too long ago, there had been a fire up here, no doubt from a lightning strike. It happened frequently in the mountains. The fire had taken out most of the trees in a wide swatch on either side of the creek bank. Only a couple of trees still stood and they were as charred ghosts tottering on the edge of the bank.

As he surveyed the opposite bank, Alex had an idea.

"There's still some rope in one of the backpacks. If we can lasso that tree across the creek then tie onto this one here, I think we can make it across the water."

It was a long shot, but it was their only option. They couldn't stay here until morning, and to try to find another way around the creek would cost them precious time.

"How are your lassoing skills?" Rachel asked with a weary smile. Even though she was exhausted and travel worn, looking at her still had the power to make his pulse race. He'd do just about anything in his power, lay down his life if need be, to protect her.

"Rusty, but I think I can manage. I'll need some light, though."

She shone the flashlight his way in response.

"Thanks. I know it's risky, but otherwise we could be here for a while."

She followed him over to the edge of the creek. Rachel shone the light across the creek to where a single tree had survived the fire.

It was a long shot at best. *Lord, I need Your help*, Alex prayed.

"I think I can hook it around that branch up there. It's tall enough to keep us out of the water, at least."

Rachel took out the rope and handed it to Alex.

As a kid, Alex had loved to rope just about anything in sight. He'd given up on becoming a professional bull roper when his interests turned to other things as a teen…mostly Rachel.

Holding the greater portion of the rope in his left hand, Alex swung the lariat above his head. It took five tries, three more than it should have in the old days, to lasso the branch in question.

"You haven't lost your touch." Rachel smiled brightly. "And I'm sure glad you haven't."

He jerked the rope tight and tested the branch for stability. Having survived the fire, it could be compromised, but they were all out of choices. It was this or turn around and head back the way they'd come and risk running into those men.

"It looks like it should hold our weight. We just need to tie it off on this end." The remaining tree on their side of the bank wasn't nearly as sturdy looking.

"Let's hope it holds up," she said and shone the light on the charred tree. She was right. If the tree fell, they could be in serious trouble. If they landed in that water, they'd be swept downstream before they had a chance to save themselves.

Alex looped the rope around the tree and started tying it off. Before he'd finished, he heard voices coming from just over the ridge.

Rachel glanced behind them. "Alex, they're almost here. We have to hurry." He took her hand and they headed to the edge of the creek.

"You should go ahead of me. I'm positive it will hold your weight. I'm not sure about mine. If they reach me before I can cross, cut the rope and get out of here. Find Liam."

He didn't get to finish before she shook her head. "I'm not leaving you behind. We're in this together."

His gaze clung to hers. So many unspoken feelings weighed on his mind. He had to protect her.

"Rachel, I…" He wasn't sure what he wanted to tell her, only that he needed her to understand that he still cared about her.

She placed her finger over his lips. "No, you're going

to make it and I'm not leaving this area without you. We're going to find Liam and this is all going to be a bad memory someday."

He knew it would be pointless to argue. Time was precious. While the voices still sounded a little ways away, it wouldn't take them long to reach the creek. Crossing the water by rope was going to be time-consuming.

She tucked her weapon behind her back. Alex gave her a boost up to the rope. Rachel put one hand in front of the other, slowly pulling her way across past the bank and over the raging water. The process was excruciatingly slow. The creek wouldn't normally be as wide to cross, but with the additional water running, it had doubled in capacity.

Behind him, multiple voices grew nearer. Rachel was barely midway across the creek. He didn't dare start across until she was safely on the opposite bank. With his weight, it could snap one of the tree branches and they'd both land in the freezing water.

Keeping a careful eye on Rachel's progress, Alex glanced behind him. He could see several flashlight beams bouncing across the night sky.

Hurry, Rachel…

She was almost to the other bank. Like it or not, he had to start making his way across.

With his gloves on, Alex jumped as high as he could and managed to grasp the rope. Working as quickly as he could, he placed one hand in front of the other until he was over the water. He heard the tree make a cracking, groaning noise. Was it about to snap?

On the ground now, Rachel watched him make his way over the water. "Hurry, Alex. They're coming down the ridge now." She took out her Glock and fired on the advancing men while Alex did his best to double his speed. He was still a little ways from the bank when the men returned Rachel's shots. He was caught in the cross fire. One stray bullet and he was dead.

With a couple of feet still left between him and the bank, Alex took out his knife. While balancing with one hand, he cut the rope behind him. Immediately, he plunged toward the creek. Alex jumped with all his strength toward the bank's edge, barely hitting it. Then he tucked and rolled.

"Let's get out of here," he said the second he was on his feet again. Together they kept low to the ground as bullets continued to whiz past their heads.

"Get some rope," one of the men behind them yelled. "If they can cross that way, we can, too."

"We can't let them get across," Rachel said as she continued firing at the enemy.

With his thoughts struggling to find a solution, only one came to mind. He'd need to find a way to pull the tree over. He remembered there was a small ax among the camping supplies.

"This is the only tree for them to tie to on this side of the bank. If I can get it down, they won't be able to cross." Like it or not, it was their only chance to stay alive.

SIX

Rachel glanced back at the tree. "You'll be exposed. They have nothing to lose. And I hate to point this out, but even with using the weapons we took from Peter and Michelle, we don't have an unlimited amount of ammo."

They had both brought extra clips of bullets and had the confiscated weapons, but if they had to continue to defend themselves like this, their supply wouldn't hold out long.

His gaze held hers. "It's our only choice. I'll be okay."

She slowly nodded. "Okay, I've got your back. Do what you have to do."

Alex grabbed the small ax from the backpack and slowly edged his way over to the tree in question. He had barely left the area where they were hiding before the men spotted the movement and began firing right away.

From her vantage point, Rachel engaged the men. She glanced back over her shoulder. Alex had reached the tree and was on the backside, as out of sight as possible. Because the ax was so small, she knew it would take longer to bring the tree down.

As she continued to return fire, she saw the tree give way ever so slightly out of the corner of her eye.

While the men continued shooting, she felt the blowback from bullets close by. She couldn't hold them off for long.

"Hurry, Alex." Time was running out. She watched him gather his strength, and with one final swing of the ax, the tree came crashing down, barely missing him.

He hurried back to her. "That should buy us some time. We need to make it to those woods over there. Go ahead of me. I'll cover you."

She ducked low and ran for the woods while Alex continued to fire at the men. Once she'd reached the trees, he charged for the woods while Rachel covered him.

"Let's get out of here," he said. "I have no doubt that they'll find another way across soon enough."

They hurried into the wilderness. Rachel glanced back briefly. The men were slowly coming out of their hiding places. How long before they crossed the creek?

After they had covered more than a quarter of a mile through dense foliage, the woods begin to thin out slightly.

"We must be close to the camp. We need to search this area quickly. If Liam's here, we won't have long to find him and get out of here."

Alex nodded. "Let's just hope this is the right camp."

Rachel stopped once they reached the edge. "What if he's not here?"

"Then we keep looking. Let's take a quick look around the place and see if there's any sign of him."

Working as fast as they possibly could, they searched the crumbling camp, but Liam wasn't there.

Rachel couldn't have been more discouraged. "This can't be the camp Liam mentioned."

Alex touched her cheek. "We can't give up. You said yourself there are several other camps up here. We just need to find the right one."

She nodded. Alex was right. She had to keep fighting for Liam. She struggled to recall the particular layout on this side of the mountain. "The next one should be a little ways up the mountain from here."

"Good. Let's keep going. Perhaps, if those guys come this way, they'll think we kept heading downhill. How are you holding up?" Alex asked when she stumbled slightly.

"Tired, but I'm okay. Don't worry, I can keep up." She wished she felt more confident. She wasn't used to this kind of pace.

"Let's stop and rest for a moment." He pointed to a fallen tree and she sat down. Alex took out one of the water bottles and handed it to her.

"Thanks." She took it gratefully and drank deeply.

Alex looked around the desolate area. "It doesn't look as if anyone's been up here in a long time."

He was probably right. The camp they'd just left was overgrown; the woods had reclaimed most of its remaining buildings.

"Liam said that's why his friend wanted to buy the camp he did. It hadn't been used in years, so he got a good price. He wanted to make the camp a working lumber mill again."

She handed Alex the water and he took a drink, then put the bottle back in his backpack.

"There's certainly enough timber up here to run several mills, especially if it's been years since the area has been harvested." He blew out a sigh. "As much as I hate to say it, we need to move on. We don't know if they've found their way across the creek yet."

As they headed deeper into the woods, getting into the higher altitude forced them to slow their steps down tremendously.

Rachel found herself listening to every little noise around them. She'd been in the woods since she was a kid, but this was different. She'd never been chased by people intent on taking her life.

As she had so many times since Liam's disappearance, Rachel thought about her brother's last visit. Liam had alluded to the fact that someone from the CIA might be involved with the terrorist threat he'd been chasing. His comment on the map he left seemed to indicate he believed it, and now there were presumed CIA agents combing the area looking for Liam. All things pointed to the same conclusion Liam had come to.

What if these men were somehow working for the same terrorist that Liam had been chasing? She voiced her concerns aloud. "If Liam discovered the connection, he could pose a threat to any further attacks."

Alex's expression was grim. "What are they doing here in the US? There's no way they'd travel all this way just to track down Liam because of something he knows. They'd risk blowing their cover. There's something more going on."

A disturbing thought dawned on her. "Unless Liam has something they want."

Alex stopped and stared at her. "What would be worth coming out of hiding and risking their lives for?"

Rachel shook her head. "I don't know. Whatever it is, it must be big."

"Let's just hope we find Liam at the next camp. We need answers, Rachel, before this thing escalates any further."

It felt as if they'd been hiking for hours and they still hadn't come across the camp. So far, there was no sign of the men, but she didn't doubt they would have found a way to cross the creek. They weren't about to give up, especially if what she suspected were true and Liam had taken something important from them.

As she walked, she kept going back over what had happened. One thing bothered her. "Did you see Michelle or Peter back there?" Where were they?

Alex shook his head. "No. I have no idea where they are. Right now, you're the only connection they have with Liam, so why not put every man available into capturing us?"

"Unless they're searching for something else... Maybe whatever Liam took."

He stopped dead in his tracks. The dawning of what she'd just said registered an alarm. "You think?"

"Somewhere here in the US could be their next target. What if they planned to attack someplace here and Liam discovered it? Liam tracked them here, found whatever they brought in to do the attack with, and hid it somewhere up here. They would be desperate to get it back. They have nothing to lose."

If what Rachel said were true, then this thing was much bigger than either of them had originally believed. They needed help.

"Rachel, we're in way over our heads. Let me reach out to my commander for backup." When she didn't answer he pressed. "We're outnumbered and certainly outgunned. Our ammo supply won't last past another confrontation. We have no idea how many more men these guys have up here searching for Liam and whatever else they're looking for. We could die." He hated pointing out the obvious, but the truth had to be faced.

He could see from her mutinous expression that she wasn't ready to give in. "We can't. You said yourself these men are CIA. We don't know how deep their connections go. Even if your people aren't involved, they could still inadvertently tip off someone who is. We can't risk it now. Liam's life is on the line."

Her answer didn't surprise him and he certainly couldn't blame her, but he had a feeling at some point they'd have no other choice but to reach out to Jase and the Scorpion team for help. He just hoped he could convince her to do so before it was too late.

Rachel took out the binoculars and activated the night-vision function, homing in on something off in the distance.

"Do you see something?" he asked.

"Yes, just up ahead. I think it's the second camp." She handed him the binoculars.

From what he could tell so far, nothing about the second camp was reassuring. It appeared as overgrown as the last one. Alex chose to keep his misgivings to himself. "Let's hope we find Liam there. Then we can get out of here and figure out what's really going on."

The exhaustion of the hike had begun to take its toll on his body. His legs felt like rubber. He was fit and used to the rigor. He couldn't imagine how Rachel was feeling.

Once they reached the opening leading into the camp, Alex stopped to take in their surroundings. In the dark, it was hard to tell much about the place, only that it appeared as if it had been years since anyone had been there. The surrounding woods had already reclaimed parts of the camp. But then Rachel had said that was one of the reasons Liam's friend had wanted to buy the place.

"We can't afford to use the flashlight. We could be walking into a trap." The hackles along his neck stood at attention. He didn't like it. "Maybe you should wait here. Let me check it out first."

He didn't have to look at her to see her reaction. "As I told you before, Alex, we're in this together, I'm coming with you."

He touched her face gently. Losing her again was an unbearable thought, but he knew it was useless to argue.

Please keep us safe…

"Ready?" he asked, the weight of what he wanted to tell her roughening his voice.

She covered his hand. "Yes, I'm ready."

Alex shoved branches away and stepped into what had once been a camp.

When they were in the clearing, he stopped for a moment to listen. Only the sounds of the night could be heard around them. Still, the uneasiness in the pit of his stomach had him on full alert.

"Let's start over there." He leaned in close and whispered so that only she could hear. The last thing they needed was to alert anyone with deadly intent. He pointed to a particular area. "There's a couple of buildings still standing. He could be in one of them. Stay close. I don't like this."

Alex could see the uneasiness he felt reflected in her eyes as they slowly advanced into the camp. The first building they came upon had collapsed in upon itself. It appeared to be where the trees were milled at one time.

"I can't see anything on the inside." He took out his flashlight and shone it around the dilapidated building. "There's nothing here."

An unsettling thought occurred. What if the camp were empty? They'd have no choice but to keep climbing up the mountain to Liam's last known location. By coming this way, they'd cost themselves several hours of valuable time. If Liam were injured, it could mean the difference between life and death.

The next building appeared to be living quarters of some type, mostly intact. Alex stopped next to the door. It took several tries for it to free itself of years of decay.

Once it screeched open, he and Rachel eased inside. It took a few minutes for his eyes to become accustomed to the darkness enough to make out shapes.

The place consisted of a single room. What appeared to be a broken-down table was shoved into one corner. On the opposite wall a bed was set up. There was nothing else. Alex's heart sank. It didn't appear that anyone had been here in a while, either.

Frustrated, he turned back to Rachel. "It's empty." He barely got the words out when a noise that sounded like a wounded animal came from the area where the bed was located.

"What was that?" Rachel asked.

Alex whirled around to survey the area. "I don't see anything." He slowly advanced to the bed with his weapon drawn. Had some animal gotten injured and crawled inside the cabin to seek refuge?

There was nothing but a ratty old mattress on top of the bed. He realized the noise was coming from under it.

He indicated that Rachel should cover him. Alex clicked on the flashlight and counted off three in his head. Then he grabbed the bed and shoved it out of the way.

Huddled beneath it was a badly injured man who had clearly been shot. But the most disturbing part was the fact that Alex recognized this man, too. He knew him. Had worked several missions with him. This was the legendary CIA agent Deacon Broderick.

SEVEN

Rachel tucked her weapon behind her back and hurried to the man's side. He seemed to be caught somewhere between consciousness and unconsciousness. It took only a cursory exam to realize he was in bad shape. "He's been shot in the shoulder and leg. He's lost a lot of blood."

Alex knelt next to her and undid the man's shirt. "Someone's bandaged the wounds," he said in amazement. "Still, he needs proper medical care right away."

"Do you know him?" Rachel asked. She'd seen the way Alex looked at the man.

He searched the man's pockets and come up empty. "Yes, I know him. I've worked with him before. His name is Deacon Broderick." His gaze slid to hers. "He's CIA, Rachel. And he's a legend at that. Deacon has helped take down some of the biggest threats around the world."

She couldn't believe it. If this man was CIA, then what was his connection to the supposed deceased agents? "Do you think he's working with the others?"

Alex shook his head. "No way. Deacon is a stand-up guy. He may know something about Liam's disappearance, though."

His attempt to rouse the man proved futile. Deacon continued to mumble incoherently. "He's delirious. We need to get him help."

Alex was right. It was time to reach out to the Scorpions for assistance. A man's life was in danger. Liam was still missing and they were way outmanned. "You should call your command. Tell them where we are so that they can send help. We can't let Deacon die."

Alex clutched her arm and smiled. She could see his relief. "I'll make the call. Can you try to keep him as comfortable as possible?"

"Go. I'll see what I can do to help Deacon."

While in the field, Rachel had gotten used to dealing with medical emergencies, especially gunshot wounds. She had no idea how long Deacon had been lying here injured, but there was little doubt in her mind that without further expert attention he wouldn't survive long.

She eased his shirt away from the wound to get a better look. Whoever had bandaged the wounds had done a good job. She glanced around for something to use as a bandage and noticed that there were extra strips of cloth matching the ones used. It looked like someone had ripped apart a flannel shirt to use. Next to the cloth, there was a half a dozen empty water bottles there, as well.

Rachel took it as a good sign that perhaps Deacon hadn't been this bad off when he'd reached the camp. She slowly eased the old bandage from the wound and examined it. Deacon moaned in pain. It appeared that the bullet had gone straight through. A good sign. It didn't look as if infection had set in yet. Once she'd cleaned the wound with the water, she wrapped it as tight as she could.

Alex returned and helped her with Deacon's leg injury. It was just a grazing shot and not nearly as bad.

Once they'd finished, she and Alex stepped away.

"Did you get in touch with your team?" she asked anxiously.

He shook his head. "The phone service is nonexistent here. I'll need to see if I can find a spot higher up. Maybe I can pick up a tower from there. Will you be okay by yourself for a bit?"

"Of course." She looked into his eyes and her breath caught at what she saw there.

He stepped closer, his voice rough with feeling. "Rachel…"

She believed she knew what he was going to say and she couldn't let him. It was best not to open that door again. She shook her head. "No, it's okay. You don't have to say it."

Regret reflected on his face and she turned away. She didn't want to hear his regrets.

The door closed quietly behind him. Rachel drew in a shaky breath. Her feelings for Alex had no place in the hunt for Liam. She had to keep her focus on finding her brother. And Deacon needed immediate medical attention.

She shoved her own regret down deep and went back to the man. He was perspiring and mumbling to himself, unaware of what was going on around him.

Rachel touched his arm and lifted up a prayer for his safekeeping.

Someone had obviously cared for Deacon's injuries. If it were the enemy, they would have left him wherever he was to die. Was it possible that Liam had done this? Her brother wore flannel shirts similar to those used as the bandages.

The sight of it gave her hope that her brother had brought Deacon here to keep him safe. Perhaps Liam had tried to hike out to get assistance. Did he have a cell phone with him? Deacon had nothing on him, including any form of ID.

She bunched some of the remaining strips of cloth under Deacon's head as a makeshift pillow, then got out the extra jacket she'd brought in her backpack and placed it over him for warmth.

One thing was for certain—they couldn't stay here long. Those men could show up at any moment and every second they were here meant Deacon's condition could worsen.

Lack of sleep and the physical strain of hiking the mountain had taken its toll. Not to mention the emotional roller-coaster ride she'd been on since Liam disappeared. Nothing made sense. Once they were on safer ground and they found Liam, maybe they could figure out who was behind this horror.

When Alex returned a few minutes later she hoped he had good news.

"I was able to reach my commander. He's dispatching several choppers right away, but we may not have that long." He had a worried look on his face. He nodded toward Deacon. "Rachel, we need to get Deacon out of here right away."

Alex was right. The man's life was on the line. "What do you suggest?" she asked.

"I saw an old logging truck out back. If I can get it running, we can head down the mountain to Hendersonville. There's still a hospital there, right? Let's hope these men won't be looking for us there. Then, once Jase and the team arrive, we can continue our search for Liam."

She knew it was the best plan to save Deacon's life, but the thought of abandoning Liam even for a little while tore at her conscience.

He seemed able to read all of her thoughts. "We're not leaving him up here. We are just saving Deacon."

She slowly nodded. "You're right. He needs our help the most."

Rachel could tell there was something else on his mind. "Did you find out something?"

He heaved a sigh that spoke volumes. "I did. I talked to Jase about the agents that were supposed to be dead. He remembered hearing the story behind the agents' deaths from another former Scorpion commander by the name of Kyle Jennings." Alex hesitated as if recalling the conversation. "Kyle told him that the men were in Iraq on a mission, searching for the Chemist, an elusive man who had perfected the recipe for sarin gas and was selling it on the dark web to the highest bidder. The team was spearheaded by a senior agent by the name of Blake Temple. Jase said Blake seemed to have an unusual interest in bringing down the Chemist. Kyle assumed he was just dedicated to the task at hand. I don't know if that's the case."

How did the missing agent's reappearance and the story of the Chemist fit into Liam's disappearance?

"Now I understand why Peter looked particularly familiar to me. Rachel, he's Blake Temple." He held her gaze. Saw the surprise she couldn't hide. "If these men came out of hiding, it has to be for something big."

He was right. There was no way they'd risk being captured unless they were desperate. "I wonder how Michelle fits into all of this."

"I have no idea. I couldn't get a good read off her." He shook his head. "At least we have help on the way. The sooner we get Deacon out of here, the better, though. I'll go see if I can get that truck running before Temple and the rest of his thugs catch up with us."

He turned to leave, but she caught his arm. She wasn't ready to answer the questions she saw in his eyes just yet. "Please be careful," she said in a whisper of a voice.

"I will." The hint of a smile was filled with sadness. He'd expected more. She wished she could give it to him. After she was alone, regret crawled into every fiber of her being. Alex wasn't the same person he'd been earlier and that was easy to see. But was there a chance for them? She couldn't let herself go there. She'd lost her heart to him once. She couldn't afford to do so again.

Rachel checked on Deacon once more. He seemed to be resting somewhat more comfortably. It was still hours before daylight. If Alex could get the truck running, they might be able to leave the area before sunrise, which would give them a better chance at escaping the men chasing them.

"Where are you, Liam?" she whispered into the cold air, but her only answer was the mutterings of the injured man close by.

Rachel went over to the window behind the cabin and glanced out at the darkness. She could see Alex's flashlight beam as he worked to bring the truck to life.

Where were the men? Had they actually bought their

decoy? As much as she wanted to believe, she didn't. These men had survived for years without detection. They were highly trained agents just like she and Alex. They would think in the same way. They'd keep coming until they found them.

"Liam! Get down!" Deacon called out in a panic. Rachel whirled from the window. Deacon knew about her brother!

She was still trying to make sense of it when Alex came back inside.

"It won't make it far, but I think we can get down the mountain in it if we're careful…" He stopped when he got a good look at her shocked expression. "What happened?"

"Deacon just mentioned Liam by name." She told him what Deacon had said. "Alex, what if Deacon is Liam's asset?"

Alex stared at the unconscious man. "I guess it's possible. But why was Deacon working with Liam?"

Rachel shook her head. "I wish I knew. Do you know what type of work Deacon was doing recently?" If Alex knew what he was working on, maybe they could figure out why Liam had asked to meet with Deacon.

"It's been a while since I worked with him. But I do know that Deacon was responsible for bringing down some major players in the terrorism game."

Maybe Deacon had information about the agents or the Chemist or… She had never felt so frustrated before. It was like trying to fit together a puzzle with half the pieces missing.

Alex came over to her and tipped her chin so that she looked into his eyes. "We'll never figure it out without Deacon's or Liam's help. But we *will* figure it out. Liam's a survivor. He's been in far worse circumstances than this."

She wanted to believe that. "If he brought Deacon down here, why wouldn't he hike out on foot to get help?"

Alex shook his head. "I don't know. But right now we need to concentrate on saving Deacon's life."

As worried as she was about Liam, Deacon needed their help immediately.

"I'll bring the truck around and then we can get him into the back seat where he can lie down."

Alex still held her, searching her face. She struggled to bring enough air into her lungs. With another intense look, he let her go and went to get the truck. She was grateful to be left alone because she so needed to control her racing pulse. Alex had a way of getting to her like no one else. She'd loved him so much. Part of her heart would always belong to him, but she needed to keep her focus on helping Deacon and saving Liam. If her thoughts wandered back to the past it wouldn't benefit anyone.

As hard as she tried, Rachel still couldn't settle in her mind why Liam had brought Deacon all the way here and then left him. Something must have forced Liam to leave in a hurry.

Before she could try to bring her chaotic thoughts together, the noise of gunfire coming from the woods nearby exploded all around. Rachel grabbed her weapon and hurried to the front of the cabin where the shots seemed to have originated. Her hand had barely touched the door handle when it flew open and Alex rushed inside and slammed the door closed.

The fear she saw in his eyes scared her. "What's happening out there?"

"They've found us. We have to get out before they surround the cabin and have us trapped inside…" He stopped for a second before adding, "I don't think it's wise to take Deacon with us under these conditions. The hectic pace would be too much for him."

They'd have to leave Deacon behind. But if those men found him here, they'd finish what they started and kill him.

Rachel hurried over to the injured man. "What should we do? What if they search the cabin? They'll kill him."

There was really only one option. "We'll cover him with the bed again. I have an extra jacket. Hopefully, between the two, he can stay warm enough until Jase's team arrives. If we can successfully lead them away from here, he should be safe enough."

Alex put his extra jacket over Deacon and tried to make him as comfortable as possible, then together they placed the bed over the top of him. Alex prayed that Deacon would be safe until help arrived. "We have to hurry, Rachel. They're not far."

They grabbed their gear and headed out to where Alex had left the old beat-up truck running.

Rachel slid in the driver's side and Alex followed. He shoved the truck in gear and turned the vehicle toward the rudimentary road that had been carved out of the woods.

"Hang on," he told her. "I'm afraid this is going to be one hairy ride."

He was right. Rachel clung to the door handle as the

truck bounced over downed trees and debris left from years of logging. Alex kept his attention on the road ahead as it tested all his skills. Where were the men he'd spotted in the woods? He was pretty sure he'd hit one of them, but by his best account there had been at least half a dozen others up on the hill above the camp.

The headlights of the truck were so bad that he could barely see where they were going. He was forced to slow the truck's speed down to a crawl as he rounded a curve.

Ice still clung to the road in places where the sunlight didn't reach. The truck slid sideways and close to the mountain's edge. Rachel stifled a scream in response.

Somehow, Alex got the truck back on the path, but his hands shook from the close call. Doing his best to dodge downed trees, he continued to weave down the mountainside.

Without warning, the front windshield exploded. Both Alex and Rachel ducked as glass flew everywhere, narrowly missing their eyes.

Another round riddled the passenger side of the truck. Alex could barely see where he was going as the shots continued to ricochet off the truck, and he was forced to stay low. He managed a quick glance ahead and saw five men emerge in front of them, weapons aimed at the truck.

Alex slammed the brakes on hard. The men kept advancing. They were all out of options. If they continued forward, they'd be shot. Desperate to keep them alive, Alex shoved the vehicle in Reverse and tried to keep the truck on the trail.

"Get down." He barely got the words out when the men opened fire. Alex whipped the truck around and headed back the direction they'd come.

"We need to find another way out of here. Otherwise, we're trapped." Alex glanced over at Rachel. She was white as a sheet. "They're on foot. We're not," he said without feeling nearly as confident about what he'd said. He'd scouted the area briefly. This was the only road he'd seen. "Do you remember the layout of what's just below this camp?" The road in front of them quickly disappeared and was replaced with overgrown brush.

"Alex, there's no road past the camp. There's nothing." She confirmed his worst fears. "We'll never make it down this way."

He barely had time to process what she said before he realized they were now surrounded by armed men. There would be no escaping now.

EIGHT

Alex hit the brakes as the men circled the truck.

Rachel watched the men advancing on them. "What do we do now?" she forced out.

She saw the reality of their situation reflected in his eyes. "We give up."

She couldn't believe what she heard. They were still no closer to knowing what had happened to Liam than when they'd first started. "No, Alex, we can't. We have to keep fighting."

He shook his head. "If we resist, we'll be dead. We have to stay alive. It's the only way to save Deacon and find Liam."

Tears filled her eyes. She knew he was right. She didn't want to die here. Not without knowing what had happened to her brother. Not with things still unsettled between herself and Alex.

"They wouldn't be coming after us this hard if they'd found Liam," Alex reasoned. "I believe they still need us. They won't kill us if we don't resist. Maybe we can buy enough time for my team to arrive."

As she looked at his handsome face, there were so many things she wanted to say, but now was not the time. She would fight with everything inside her to live another day because she wanted to have the chance to tell Alex everything that was in her heart.

With a smile of encouragement for her sake, Alex yelled, "Hold your fire. We're coming out." To her he said, "Do what I do, okay?"

He waited for her to confirm, then he slowly opened the driver's-side door. With his hands in the air, he got out. Rachel hesitated a second longer before doing the same.

"Search them," one of the men shouted, and someone jerked Alex forward and quickly patted him down. They took his gun and phone right away. Their backpacks with all their supplies were still in the truck.

Another man forced Rachel to turn around, then he searched her. Alex tried to free himself to get to her side, but his captor slugged him hard in the gut. He dropped to his knees. The man reached for him again.

"No, stop. Don't hurt him. We're cooperating with you." Rachel was terrified they'd kill Alex.

The person looming over Alex hauled him to his feet.

"Get them back to the cabin," said the man who had ordered his men to search them. She and Alex were forced into the bed of the truck, along with several armed men, and driven back to the cabin where they'd left Deacon. What they'd tried to prevent was happening.

Don't let them find Deacon.

The man holding Rachel's arm in a viselike grip shoved her hard, and she flew into the cabin, almost losing her balance.

Alex freed himself from his restrainer and hurried

to her side. "Are you okay?" he asked while glaring at the man who'd shoved her.

"I'm fine." She touched his arm and forced his gaze to her. "I'm okay, Alex."

The anger slowly evaporated from him. They both needed to keep their wits about them if they stood any chance of surviving.

The leader stepped forward, inches from Rachel's face. With his arms crossed, he stared her down. "Well, we finally caught you two. I'll admit you gave us a good run. Just not good enough." His smile held no humor in it. Right away, Rachel recognized him. It was the former CIA agent Victor McNamara.

"Why were you trying to kill us?" Rachel demanded.

McNamara smirked. "If we were trying to kill you two, you'd be dead by now." McNamara's words seemed to confirm what Alex said earlier. These men had no idea where Liam was.

One of the men handed McNamara Alex's driver's license. He stared at it and then Alex while Rachel held on to her breath. If he recognized Alex as a CIA agent, no matter what he'd claimed earlier, he'd kill him.

"How do you fit into this?" McNamara demanded, but Alex kept silent. McNamara motioned to one of his thugs, who grabbed Alex and slugged him hard once more.

"Stop," Rachel cried out as Alex doubled over in pain. She tried to come to his aid, but someone grabbed her arms, holding her in place.

"I'll ask you again. How do you fit into Agent Carlson's crimes?"

Agent Carlson's crimes… The words settled over her.

"What are you talking about?" Rachel demanded.

She wasn't about to let them sully Liam's name. "My brother hasn't committed any crimes."

McNamara turned his full attention on her. "Ah, the sister," he sneered. "You clearly have no idea who your brother really is." She had to struggle not to take the bait. "Your brother, along with Deacon Broderick, has stolen some very deadly weapons. My team and I have been searching for them for quite some time. We had them surrounded up on the mountain, but they both managed to give us the slip. Not without being wounded first, I might add. They won't get far on their own. I believe you know where your brother might be hiding. Why else would you be up here? For his own well-being, I suggest you tell me where, so that we can find him alive."

McNamara was talking as if he were still an agent. He had no idea they knew the truth.

"Tie them both up." He barked the order to one of his men, who grabbed Alex. Forcing his arms together, he wrapped the rope tight around his wrists. Another man did the same to Rachel, and she winced in pain.

"Who are you? Why should I tell you anything?" Rachel tried to hold on to her composure when McNamara stepped to within inches of her face.

"I'm the only person who can keep your brother from facing the death sentence for treason."

Treason. "How can *you* charge Liam with treason?" she exclaimed, astonished. She had to hear him say who he was.

"Because I'm working for the CIA and I've been trying to bring down a terrorist known as the Chemist for a long time. Turns out, your brother knew him all along. They've been smuggling large amounts of sarin gas into the States together. Who knows to what deadly purpose?"

She couldn't afford to give anything away. "That's a lie. My brother did nothing of the sort."

McNamara's smile sent a shiver down her back. "You really don't know how deeply involved in this thing your brother really is." She raised her chin, refusing to give in to his bluff.

With a shake of his head, McNamara went back over to his men. He said something to them that she couldn't discern. She had the impression that they were waiting on something...or someone.

Rachel eased closer to where Alex was restrained. Just being close to him helped to steady her frayed nerves. She turned slightly and he did the same. As she glanced at him, so many raw emotions surged through her. She'd spent so long trying to deny what she felt for Alex. The anger and bitterness in her heart didn't cover up the truth. Alex was important to her. Her entire past was mingled with his. How could she just write him out of her life simply because things hadn't worked out between them? She smiled up at him and for a second, it was just the two of them. And she was sure that she saw the same feelings she felt for him reflected on his face.

The look in her eyes warmed his heart. So many feelings had been left unsaid by them. He believed she still cared for him, no matter how ugly he had let things end between them. Was there still a chance? He was going to do everything in his power to find out. He wasn't about to let these men take that chance away, or lay the blame for their crimes on Liam. He'd die first.

So far, McNamara had no idea Alex was CIA, and

he planned to keep it that way. He glanced briefly at the bed covering Deacon. So far, Deacon hadn't made a sound. Alex wasn't sure if that was good news or bad.

Hurry, Jase.

He wondered where Peter—aka Blake Temple—and the woman called Michelle were. McNamara was acting as if he was the boss, yet Alex didn't believe Temple would allow that to go on for long. From what Jase had told him about Temple, he wasn't the type to let someone steal his glory.

"We ran into two of your people in the woods earlier. Peter and Michelle. They were easy to capture." Alex hoped to get some reaction out of McNamara.

Something slipped briefly on McNamara's face, assuring Alex he knew Peter and the woman.

"I don't know who you are talking about. We don't know anyone by those names. Maybe they're working for Carlson."

McNamara motioned to several of his men and they went outside, leaving two more to stand guard. What were they doing?

He noticed Rachel's attention kept going to the bed where Deacon was hiding. "We have to help him," she mouthed.

So far, the two men guarding them didn't appear interested in what they were doing. As Alex's thoughts churned in a dozen different directions, he struggled to recall how many men there were in total.

If he was remembering correctly, it had to be more than twelve all together, which meant they were grossly outnumbered. With their hands restrained in front of him, there was no way they could take them all on, yet they desperately needed to draw the men's attention away from the cabin and Deacon.

The door opened once more and McNamara and the other men returned. "Just go along with them for now," he mouthed to Rachel. They needed to see what McNamara had up his sleeve. He prayed they weren't making a huge mistake by not making one final stand.

McNamara didn't waste time. He strode up to Rachel, his anger evident in each step. "Time's up. Where is he?"

She squared her shoulders and didn't answer, fueling McNamara's rage.

"If you don't want to go to prison yourself, I suggest you start talking. Where is your brother?" he demanded, his face flushed with anger.

As a trained agent, Rachel knew not to react to his anger. "I don't know where Liam is. He didn't tell me where he was going."

McNamara clearly didn't believe her. "Don't give me that. You're lying. I know Carlson visited you. He told you something. What was it?"

Alex could see Rachel struggling to come up with a believable answer. He had to help her. "I'm Liam's friend. He never mentioned anything to me about where he was going, either. What you're accusing him of is preposterous. Liam would never betray his country."

McNamara gave him the once-over. For a moment, it was almost as if he recognized Alex, yet Alex was positive they'd never met before.

Still, McNamara's interest was now on him. "Then why are you here, if your friend did nothing wrong?"

"I'm here to help Rachel look for her brother," he told

the man. "She hasn't spoken to Liam in over a week. She was worried."

McNamara's gaze narrowed as he continued to stare at Alex. "You're from here then?"

Alex hesitated before answering. "Yes, originally."

"Then perhaps I should be asking you where your friend is hiding. It would be better for him if he comes in peacefully. If we have to hunt him down it could turn…deadly."

The threat was clear. Before Alex could answer, a noise from where Deacon was hidden took McNamara's attention from him.

He stared at the bed. "What was that noise?"

Alex had to think fast. He couldn't let them examine the bed. "Wait, I think I may know where he is." He turned to Rachel. "You remember that one place where we used to hunt up here as kids?"

He watched her struggle to grasp the meaning of what he was trying to tell her. They'd hunted deer since they were kids, but only a couple of times up this way. Alex remembered the one time when they'd tracked some deer up to a particular spot.

It wasn't much to run with, but if they could talk McNamara and his men into going there, they'd get them away from Deacon. Possibly find a way to overpower the men left behind.

"Oh, right," Rachel said, as if it had finally dawned on her. "Liam loved that place. It would be the perfect place to hide, too. I can't believe I didn't think of it."

McNamara's interest riveted back to them. He'd forgotten all about the noise.

The man looked first at Rachel and then Alex as if smelling a trap. "You'd better not be trying anything

or I'm telling you both, you won't like the outcome."
The warning played uneasily through Alex's thoughts.

"We're not trying anything." Rachel pulled off the
story completely. "But you have to promise you won't
hurt my brother."

McNamara snorted. "I can't make that promise. Your
brother will get what he deserves."

"Then I'm not telling you the location." She looked
him straight in the eye.

McNamara stepped closer, once more trying to intimidate. "You are in no position to make demands as
I see it."

Rachel didn't waver and eventually McNamara gave
in. "All right, we'll do our best to keep him safe. Now,
tell me where he is." Unfortunately, it was a hollow
promise, given by a thug. Alex had little doubt that
they'd kill them all once they had what they wanted.

"There's an old lodge up here that used to be popu-
lar when we were kids. It's been vacant for years now.
It's warm and there are plenty of places to hide out. I
think he would go there."

McNamara still wasn't convinced she was telling the
truth. "Then you'll show us where it is." He yanked her
toward the door.

Without thinking, Alex went after him. "She told
you what you wanted to know. Let her go."

McNamara shoved him away. "You think I'm that
naive? You two are planning to escape the minute we're
gone. She's coming with me. That way I know you'll
be here when I get back. You'd better not be lying," he
barked at Rachel.

The man started for the door once more. Alex wasn't

about to let him leave with Rachel. He didn't trust Mc-Namara not to kill her. "Then I'm coming with you."

McNamara turned, looking at Alex as if he'd lost his mind. "If you're taking Rachel, you're taking me, too." Alex stood his ground. There was no way he was leaving Rachel at the mercy of these thugs.

NINE

"No, Alex." Rachel's gaze locked on Alex. She was terrified McNamara would shoot him right where he stood.

McNamara continued to glower at Alex while Rachel's heartbeat hammered against her chest.

Please don't kill him... A disjointed prayer sped through her mind. She wasn't even sure what she was praying, only that she was certain God knew their needs and would protect them.

"Fine, you'll come with us," McNamara said in a deadly low tone. "But you'd best remember that you're expendable. I wouldn't suggest you try anything funny." Rachel's gaze clung to Alex. She would give anything to be able to understand the unspoken emotions simmering in his eyes right now. Would there ever be a right time for them?

Please, God.

McNamara nodded to one of his men, who grabbed Alex by the arm. They were both forced outside.

When the final man left the cabin, Rachel found comfort in the fact that McNamara and his thugs hadn't discovered Deacon. At least he was safe for the moment.

Outside, the predawn had finally arrived and bits of filtered light pierced through the trees.

Two black SUVs slowly made their way to the camp. One of the drivers got out and hurried over to McNamara.

"We haven't found either of them yet." Rachel just managed to catch the man's words. Were they still looking for Liam and Deacon? If so, then at least there was hope that Liam was still alive.

McNamara was clearly irritated by the news. "Have your men keep looking. They can't have disappeared into thin air. Find them."

The man appeared scared of McNamara. He nodded and hurried back to the SUV.

McNamara turned his annoyance to Rachel. "Your brother has caused us enough trouble. You'd better know where he's hiding, otherwise it won't be good for you." Whatever it was that Liam had taken, McNamara was consumed with getting it back.

He opened the back door of the remaining SUV, flipped the seat down, and shoved her inside to the third-row seating. Seconds later, Alex was thrust in next to her. There was barely room for both of them to sit. Two men climbed into the back seat, keeping a careful eye on them.

With McNamara in the passenger seat, he pinned his gaze on Rachel once more. "Now, tell us where this lodge is and don't try to pull anything."

Rachel inched closer to Alex. She wasn't alone. No matter what happened, what they faced from here on out, she wasn't alone. "It's down road we were on, halfway back to the town of Hendersonville. This road hasn't been maintained in years, though. We may not be able to make it the entire way by vehicle."

McNamara didn't answer. He motioned to the driver, who put the SUV in gear and slowly eased it down the slippery road.

Alex touched her hand and she looked at him. "We have to create a distraction to get away," he mouthed. She understood. Once they reached the lodge and discovered Liam wasn't there, McNamara would know it was a ruse.

Rachel struggled to recall the layout of the land, looking for something that would give them an edge over their captors. This side of the mountain usually got a lot more snow and ice accumulation. The patches she and Alex had run into earlier while fleeing would make traveling difficult.

Still, they needed help. God's help. She desperately prayed for divine intervention.

The driver didn't appear familiar with driving in the icy mountain terrain. His nervous reaction each time he hit a slippery spot on the road made it clear he wasn't comfortable with the conditions.

As he rounded one of the tight curves in the road, the vehicle began to slide. The man quickly overcorrected, heading them straight toward a sheer dropoff. He struggled to regain control of the ride while McNamara was screaming at him. The driver finally managed to rein in the vehicle, but not before blowing a tire after he drove the SUV over several jagged tree stumps.

When the vehicle finally came to a jarring stop, Mc-

Namara commenced verbally berating the driver for his failings.

"Well, what are you waiting for? Someone get that tire changed. Time is running out. We need to find him and get the…stuff." McNamara caught himself before giving more away.

The two men in the back seat hopped out along with McNamara and the driver, momentarily leaving Alex and Rachel alone.

Alex turned to her. "This is our chance. We have to get out of here now. It won't be easy with these." He held up his hands.

Rachel glanced behind them, where one of the men had unloaded the spare tire and jack from underneath the SUV.

"I think they left keys in the ignition. If I can get up there without them seeing me, I'll try to drive us out of here. It'll be slow going, but they're on foot. We have a chance."

It was a long shot, but one they had to take. "I'll keep watch for you."

Alex slowly eased to the front seat undetected. He got into the driver's seat. "The keys are here. Hold on, this is going to be a rough ride."

Alex locked the doors, grabbed the keys, which proved difficult enough with his hands tied together, and then fired the ignition. He shoved the vehicle into Drive.

"They're getting away. Stop them!" McNamara yelled.

Rachel watched as all four men charged after them. "Hurry, Alex. They're coming."

Alex floored the gas pedal. The SUV lurched forward, the blown tire and his restraints making the ride ten times worse.

"Can you make it up to the front seat? We need to find a way to get these ropes off."

"I'll try." Rachel struggled to ease over the seat with her hands tied. She landed halfway between the seat and floor and righted herself. After fumbling with the glove box, it finally opened. "There's a knife, a flashlight and a lighter inside."

Alex somehow managed to keep the vehicle moving forward in spite of the tire.

Rachel peeked behind them. The men were still coming after them. With the SUV's slower speed, they'd never get away from them like this.

She couldn't get the knife into a position to loosen her ropes. "Let me try to get yours free." With the blown tire and the rough road, the knife almost flew from her hand several times. Finally, she was able to cut through the rope and free his hands.

Alex rounded another curve and the road stretched out in front of them. Even with the bum tire, they were able to put distance between themselves and the men.

"I'm not sure how much farther we can make it in this thing. The engine's overheating because of the stress of pushing it so hard." He glanced behind them. "At least we appear to have lost them for now." As if in answer to his words, the engine sputtered and coughed several times before dying.

Alex took the knife from her and cut her free.

"Let's get out of here while we still can," Rachel said.

Alex shoved the knife and lighter into his pocket

and grabbed the flashlight. Once he was by her side, they raced into the woods for their lives.

Alex grabbed her hand and they took cover in the nearby trees. "If we can stay out of sight, we might stand a chance."

"What should we do about Deacon?" Rachel asked. "He really needs help, Alex."

The men had taken their weapons and phones. They had no way to contact Jase or anyone else to get aid to Deacon. "We can't go back and risk leading them to him again. Let's just hope Jase was able to get airborne and will reach us soon."

Rachel grabbed his arm. He glanced at her and she pointed to the right. "I hear them," she whispered.

Alex froze where he stood. His arm circled her waist, tugging her close. He could hear McNamara yelling at his men.

"They can't be far. The SUV's right there. Search the woods. Find them!"

"Alex, we can't get captured again. They'll kill us."

"Let's get out of here," he said, and they headed deeper into the woods at a fast pace, while behind them, Alex heard the men enter the treed area.

Rachel stopped suddenly and he turned back to her. "Do you remember the summer we discovered that one cave up here?" she asked. It took him a minute to recall what she was talking about.

"I do. It's not far from here, if I remember correctly."

She nodded. "It is. If we can make it there, we can get out of sight. We'll disguise the entrance so that they won't know where we've gone."

It was a good plan and it just might work. When

they'd discovered the cave, they'd spent the day combing through its tunnels and had never reached the end. It would make the perfect hideout. Would they find Liam there?

They were almost right against the mountainside now. Alex gathered his bearings. For the life of him, he couldn't figure out the direction of the cave.

"Which way?" he asked, hoping she knew.

She looked around. "Over there." She pointed to the right and then glanced behind. He could hear the men coming. They'd be right on top of them soon.

"They're almost here." He took her hand and they ran the rest of the way.

Finding the entrance after so many years wasn't easy. It took a few minutes but he finally located it.

"Here, take the flashlight and go inside. I'll do my best to cover the entrance before they get here."

She took the light from him. "You won't have much time. Hurry, Alex."

Rachel went inside and he gathered armfuls of nearby brush and brought it over. He stepped inside the cave and piled the brush in behind him.

Please let it be good enough.

Rachel flashed the light down one of the corridors. "Let's get as far away from the entrance as we can just in case they spot the opening and check inside."

They headed down the corridor together. "Do you remember where this one goes?" he asked, and watched her smile at the memory.

"I do. There's that underground pool a little ways from here. Remember, we spent that same summer coming up here to swim. Liam never did figure out where we disappeared to."

He remembered that summer as clear as if it were yesterday. It was when he and Rachel had first started dating and they'd wanted to spend time alone. Liam had grumbled, feeling neglected by his best friend and sister.

"I remember Liam was so mad at us," he said, and chuckled quietly. As he recalled, there was no way out beyond the pool and he told her this. "We need to go another way. It wouldn't do to get trapped in here."

They backtracked slightly and headed down another path.

"I was close enough to hear the exchange between McNamara and one of his men. He said they hadn't found it yet. They're looking for something other than Liam."

It certainly made sense. "I'm guessing this has something to do with what Liam took from them. That's why they need to find him."

"That'd be my guess, too." She shook her head.

They'd been walking for a while when Rachel stopped and listened. "Did you hear that?"

He did. It sounded like wind rustling close by. "Maybe there's another way out that we never found." They hurried toward the noise.

"I sure hope so. We need something to break our way."

Alex stopped in front of a small opening in the side of the mountain, barely large enough for them to squeeze through.

"We should be okay." Rachel looked up at him. "From what I can tell, we should be on the south side of the mountain. Some distance from where we last saw them."

He sure hoped so. Alex eased through the opening and looked around. Nothing stirred beyond the wind. "It's safe."

Rachel followed him out. "Looks like we've lost them for now, but they could have other men searching the woods. Alex, this thing is way over our heads."

He understood her frustration. He wasn't sure what the men were after, but he had a feeling it was deadly.

"We need to get to a phone and try to reach my team. Let them know the woods are crawling with men. They could be flying straight into an ambush."

TEN

Rachel's unsettled thoughts were torn between making sense of what they'd been through so far and untangling her feelings for Alex.

"Rachel?" She realized Alex had been trying to get her attention for a while.

"I beg your pardon?"

Something unreadable crossed his face. It made her wonder what he was thinking. "I said what if Liam actually *is* hiding at the lodge? We could be leading them straight to him. We need to reach the lodge before they do."

She hadn't considered it when she'd told them about the lodge, but it was possible. Liam loved the old place and there were many times when he went there to seek solitude. "I sure hope not. It depends on whether or not he's injured."

"I'm pretty sure Liam was the one who took care of Deacon. He'd try to get help. If McNamara and his men took Liam's phone and obviously Deacon didn't have one on him, then the only option for Liam would be to hike out…unless he couldn't."

They were racing against the clock, unarmed and

running for their lives. If they didn't get help soon, those men back there would quickly catch up with them.

Rachel struggled not to let the helpless feelings overwhelm her. She'd been in countless situations just as deadly before, but she wasn't part of that life anymore and going back to it was difficult. She had to stay focused on saving Liam's life because the thought of losing her brother to these thugs was unimaginable.

"Hey." Alex stopped walking and took her hand, tugging her closer. He'd clearly seen all her fears. "Help is on the way and there's no way on earth we're giving up on Liam."

She forced a smile. "I know. I just feel so frustrated." She looked up at him. The expression in his eyes made breathing painful.

Alex gently framed her face. "Rachel," he whispered so softly and then leaned his head against hers. "I've wanted to tell you something for a long time now…" He hesitated, unsure. "I'm sorry for the way things ended between us."

She flinched as if he'd struck her. His regret was the last thing she wanted. She tried to pull away but he didn't let her.

"No, listen." The urgency in his voice made her want to hear what he had to say. "I should never have let you go," he whispered with so much passion that she believed him.

But did it matter anymore?

"I was messed up back then. I thought my life revolved around the CIA and you wanted me to walk away from all of that." He shook his head. "I was wrong. So wrong, and I've regretted the decision every day since."

Five years ago, she would have been thrilled to hear

him say that. Now, it was just another reminder of what was lost.

Rachel moved away. Slowly, he let her go. "It's okay. Things happen for a reason. Maybe we wouldn't have worked out. I wouldn't have met Brian and I couldn't imagine my life without him. I think our lives turned out the way God wanted them to."

She watched him try to cover up the hurt. "I guess you're right," he murmured, and then turned away. When the awkward silence between them became too much, Rachel started walking again. Best not to reopen those old wounds again. Especially when their lives and Liam's were still in danger.

In the past, she'd tried to hold on to the fond memories of her life with Brian and shove aside the heartache of losing Alex. Although her husband had never questioned her about the relationship with Alex, she'd told him everything.

"How did you two meet, anyway?" Alex asked after a while, probably to fill the uncomfortable silence between them.

Rachel didn't really want to talk about her husband with Alex, but he had asked. "At church," she told him. "Brian attended the same church as Tom and Jenny. After I'd been home for a while, the Reagans invited me to go to the service with them." She stopped, remembering that dark time in her life.

She'd felt so lost. Couldn't believe it was possible to move forward with her life after losing Alex. Brian had taught her that no matter what circumstances you were going through, you could overcome them with God's help.

Brian's exuberant personality always made her smile.

"He had leukemia when we met and yet you would never have known it from the way he presented himself. He was always smiling and happy. He was dying and he knew it but he never let it bring him down. He was an amazing man and I miss him terribly."

Rachel hadn't realized how much she'd loved Brian until he was gone. If his death had taught her anything, it was that it was possible to move on with your life no matter what you faced. She knew Brian wouldn't want her to be sad forever. In fact, that had been his dying wish—that she not mourn for him too long. He wanted her to get on with her life. Be happy. She'd been trying to fulfill that promise to him ever since his death.

Seeing Alex again had brought all the old hurt to the surface once more. Was it possible for them to be able to move beyond the pain and regain the friendship they once shared? Could she accept being friends with Alex after everything they'd once had? She still cared for him, there was no doubt about it. Theirs had been a passionate romance. Could she settle for anything less?

Alex swallowed back the ache he felt when he looked at the love in Rachel's eyes for another man.

He could see she was still hurting. It was evident whenever the conversation returned to their past. Would there ever come a time when they could talk about what happened? He sure hoped so.

"We should be getting close to the lodge," she told him, and he roused himself.

He managed a nod. "Good. Let's hope Liam is there and that he's not injured too badly. We'll need to get him out as quickly as possible before McNamara and his men show up, which is only a matter of time."

"I can't even imagine what they're planning." Rachel shook her head. "And where are Temple and Michelle?"

He didn't want to say it aloud, but he believed whatever Temple had planned, it would involve deadly sarin gas.

"Right now, nothing makes sense and I'm too tired to try to fit the pieces together," Rachel said. "I'll leave that up to your team."

Under the best of conditions, the hike up Midnight Mountain was a physically challenging test. Having to run for their lives tripled the strain of the journey.

Alex stopped when he spotted the full round-log lodge in the clearing up ahead. "There it is." It had been years since he'd last been up here. Even back then, the place had been showing signs of decay.

They hurried past the overgrown parking area and stepped up on the porch. It had more boards missing than were still intact. Alex peered through one of the grimy windows. Years of dust and cobwebs blanketed the floor and the remaining furniture inside. He tried the door. Locked. The windows, as well. Were they wrong about Liam being here?

The temperature outside had dropped considerably with the growing cloud coverage, and the threat of snow loomed. It had to be well below freezing.

He and Rachel trudged through piled-up snow on the north side of the lodge around to the back and tried the doors and windows. All locked, yet someone had broken one of the windows.

Please let it be Liam.

Alex carefully removed the remaining slivers of glass and crawled through the broken window. It was only slightly warmer inside but at least it offered protection from the wind and snow. Several hours had passed without any sign of the men who'd taken them hostage, and yet he didn't doubt for a minute that they were still coming.

Alex unlocked the door and opened it for Rachel. "We need to search the place quickly. We won't have much time before they get here."

She glanced around. "There are so many rooms. We'll need to split up."

Rachel was right. They'd never get through the place otherwise.

"I'll take the upstairs. You search down here." She started to leave, but he reached for her hand, holding her there. All of her uncertainties were reflected on her face. "Be careful. I don't want anything to happen to you, too."

She swallowed visibly and then slowly smiled. "I will. You be careful, too."

While she began the downstairs search, Alex took the crumbling stairs two at a time. He and Rachel and Liam had been here many times in the past, so he knew there were only guest rooms up here. The time sitting vacant had taken its toll on the place, even more since the last time he'd visited it. Everything was showing signs of deterioration, and there were patches in the ceiling where Alex could see the sky. The weather and the elements were slowly reclaiming the place. A few more years and there wouldn't be much left.

After a thorough search of the rooms, there was no sign that anyone had been up there in a while. Was he wrong about the broken glass? It might have been broken years ago. Maybe Liam never made it this far?

Alex hurried back downstairs to help Rachel finish the search. He'd reached the kitchen area when he heard it. A footstep!

He found Rachel. Before she could say a word, he held his finger up to his mouth then pointed outside. She understood and frantically looked around for someplace they could hide. An enormous stone bar covered the length of the room, dividing it from the great room. She indicated the bar and they ducked below it. Someone stepped up on the front porch. Liam? Another set of footsteps proved him wrong.

"I'm not so sure they'd come here," McNamara growled. "I think they were bluffing, trying to throw us off."

After a moment of silence, the second man said, "Looks like someone's been in there. They broke out the window."

McNamara said something unintelligible, then, "Hang on. The boss wants us to stand guard. The rest of the team is on their way. They have something."

If he and Rachel wanted to stay alive, they had to find another way out before the other men arrived.

Alex pointed to the hallway and Rachel nodded. They crept as low to the floor as they could while heading down the long passage. He opened the first door he came to as quietly as possible. It was a small bathroom with only a slatted window above the sink. Not enough room to escape.

Rachel opened another door. It led to what appeared to have once been the laundry room. There had to be another way out beyond one of the remaining doors. There was no way he was letting these men take them again.

Alex tried the final door on their left. It opened up to

a large bedroom suite with French doors leading out to a wraparound deck outside. If his bearings were correct, they should be at the south side of the lodge facing the woods. Opposite from the men on the porch.

They moved to the doors and looked out. Alex couldn't see anyone. He said a quick prayer for their safe passage and slowly unlocked the door. It creaked as he opened it and he froze for a second.

Alex listened to make sure McNamara and the second man hadn't heard the door. He could hear them talking quietly. A good sign. He hoped it stayed that way.

ELEVEN

Rachel eased out behind Alex and around to the side of the lodge. She peered around the corner. Not a sound could be heard beyond the sporadic conversation from McNamara and his goon.

"We'll have to go slow, otherwise they'll hear us," she whispered.

Rachel stepped off the porch and Alex did the same. The snow lay deep in the woods behind the lodge, making the going slow. There would be no way to cover their tracks should someone happen this way, but the white blanket helped muffle the sound of their footsteps.

They'd barely covered any distance when the noise of an engine broke the silence of their surroundings. They stopped long enough to catch their breath.

Rachel's lungs burned from the cold air. "That must be the rest of McNamara's people."

"This place will be crawling with men in a few minutes." He looked at her, seeing the exhaustion she couldn't hide. "We have to go faster. Are you up to it?"

She wasn't so sure she was, but the alternative was impossible. "Yes, I'm up to it."

"The minute they find out we're not inside, they'll

fan out and search the entire mountainside. We have to keep ahead of them."

They started walking as fast as the deep snow allowed through the woods. It took her a few minutes to realize they were heading back in the same direction as the camp.

"Do you think it's safe to go back into the camp?" Would they be leading the men back to Deacon?

"Probably not. But it's not safe to stay out here like this, either."

From the tree coverage where she stood, Rachel could still see the lodge. An SUV was now parked in front. It looked like the same one that had left the camp earlier.

As they watched, a second similar vehicle pulled up. Two people got out. Rachel recognized them right away. It was Blake Temple and Michelle.

"Alex, look." She pointed to the two. They watched as McNamara came out to meet them. From McNamara's body language alone, it was easy to see Temple was the real person in charge. McNamara had lied about not knowing Temple.

She couldn't make out what they were saying but it was obvious Temple wasn't pleased with the turn of events, and everyone was feeling the effects of his anger.

Several men who had been inside the lodge came out. She turned to Alex. "We need to get out of here. They know we're not inside."

He pointed in the direction of the cave they'd recently left. "I hate to keep backtracking, but it seems the safest and they don't know about the cave yet. At least we'll be out of sight. It will give us the advantage."

He pointed to their footprints in the snow. "But first, we'll have to try to find a way to lead them away from the spot. They'll see our tracks and follow otherwise." Alex scanned the surrounding countryside. "This way." He pointed to their left. "There doesn't appear to be as much snow there and we can circle back to the cave easily enough."

They'd been able to slip through the cave unnoticed before. She hoped the same could be said for the return route.

"How much longer before your team arrives?" Rachel prayed it wouldn't be too late for Deacon and for them.

The bleakness in his eyes did little to encourage. "Depending on when they were able to get in the air, I'd say we have at least another four hours to survive."

Four hours! A lifetime when facing down death.

Alex saw her reaction and tried to be encouraging. "It could be sooner. Let's just get to the cave and out of sight as quickly as possible."

He was right. They were both unarmed. They needed to stay hidden.

As they hurried through the thick woods, a noise grabbed Rachel's attention. It sounded like…footsteps close by.

Alex heard it, as well. "Hurry, Rachel." He took her hand and they started running as fast as they could.

"Wait. Over there. I see them," someone yelled nearby. More than one set of footsteps could be heard stomping through the woods after them.

She glanced behind them. "They're gaining. We'll never make it to the cave."

Gunfire split the air and a round of bullets flew past her head. Rachel ducked low along with Alex.

Alex still held her hand. She looked into his eyes. "On my count," he said in a steady voice, and she slowly nodded. Once he'd counted off three, together they raced through the woods at breakneck speed with the men coming after them full force firing along the way. Were they trying to kill them? McNamara had said no, but the men's behavior spoke differently. If they no longer needed them alive, then had they found whatever they were searching for? Where did that leave Liam?

Alex stopped short when their path was blocked by a fallen boulder. It was the size of a small car and had sloughed off the mountainside.

Rachel stopped next to him. She couldn't believe it. They were trapped. "What do we do now? They're almost here."

"We surrender." She couldn't believe she'd heard this warrior beside her correctly. They'd barely escaped with their lives the last time. "If we want to live long enough to find Liam, we have to find out what this is really about once and for all."

Alex had just gotten the words out when four men came to a halt in front of them, weapons aimed at their heads.

"That's far enough," McNamara snarled at them. "You two, get them." He nodded to the two men on his right. One of the men rushed over and yanked Rachel by the arm, pulling it behind her back.

Anger boiled deep inside of him. Rachel had suffered enough at these men's hand. "Leave her alone." Before he could reach her, the second man grabbed his arm, restraining him. "We're coming with you, okay? There's no need to hurt her."

"Be quiet." McNamara fumed at him. "You are in no position to tell us what to do. You two have caused enough trouble already…along with Carlson. You'd better hope when we locate him that he's willing to talk. Otherwise, none of you are walking out of here alive."

Rachel's gaze flew to Alex. He'd heard it, too. They didn't know where Liam was and whatever he'd taken was still missing.

As he'd learned so many times in the past, when your back was against the wall, God worked wonders. Alex prayed for God's intervention with all his heart.

"Search them both," McNamara ordered. Right away, the knife Alex had in his pocket was discovered and taken along with the flashlight.

"Get moving," the man holding Alex's arm ordered. "You've wasted enough of our time thrashing through the woods like this."

Rachel stumbled to the ground. The man gripping her arm dragged her to her feet. "I'm okay," she whispered to Alex when she saw the fear in his eyes he couldn't hide. "I'm okay."

She managed a smile, but he could tell she was running out of strength and hope. He understood. He was, too. It seemed that everything they'd tried so far had failed. They had no idea where Liam was and Deacon was in danger. Still, he wasn't ready to die here, and he certainly wasn't going to let anything happen to Rachel. He'd fight to his last breath to save her.

"Get them back to the lodge. He's angry. We need to get this thing settled now. Before they arrive," McNamara blurted out, and Rachel slid Alex a look. Someone was coming here? He tried to digest the meaning but he couldn't.

With two men restraining them and two others pointing weapons at them, Alex didn't believe he and Rachel stood a chance at taking them out. They'd be forced back to the lodge.

After what felt like forever, it came into view. Blake Temple stood on the porch. Where was Michelle? She'd been his constant companion and now she was no longer with him.

Rachel saw Temple as wel, and her footsteps faltered.

"It's going to be okay. Remember, they need us." Alex hoped that was still true.

Temple spotted them and hurried down the stairs. The men holding them captive released them and shoved them forward.

"So, we meet again." Temple's menacing smile told Alex the man was going to enjoy getting even. "Well, this time the tables are turned." He addressed Rachel directly. "You will answer our questions now. Otherwise, your friend here will die."

Standing close to her, Alex could sense all her fears. She'd been through so much. He'd hurt her badly. She'd lost her husband too soon. She deserved to have the chance to be happy again, and he was determined to give it to her even if it meant losing his life to save hers.

"Where is he?" Temple got into her face. She couldn't keep from flinching. "We've searched the lodge. He's not here. Start talking."

While Rachel struggled to come up with a believable answer, he had an idea that just might work. "I know where he is," Alex told the man, immediately drawing Temple's glaring attention to him.

"What do you know? Who are you, anyway?" The man was clearly doubtful.

So far, no one appeared to know that Alex was CIA. He just needed to come up with a convincing story to buy them more time.

"Liam is my friend. He called me a few days before he went missing. I think I know where he would be hiding."

Faint interest showed on Temple's expression, yet he wasn't fully convinced.

"A friend, you say. What else did he tell you?" He was trying to figure out how much of the real story Alex knew.

"Nothing. Only that he was coming up here for a few days to fish in one of our old spots." The swimming hole in the cave. If he could convince them that Liam was in there, he and Rachel would have a shot at escaping through the labyrinth of passages the cave provided. The man who searched him earlier had taken the knife and flashlight, but had overlooked the lighter for whatever reason. They'd have the advantage. They knew how to get out. These men did not.

"Don't believe him. He lied to us before," McNamara told his boss.

While Temple didn't quite buy the story, whatever he needed from Liam had made him desperate. He was willing to go along. "And where exactly would that be?" Temple asked in a bristled tone. "And keep in mind, you'd better not be leading us on again…otherwise…" He left the threat hanging.

"I'm not. I want to live. I want Rachel to live. I know where Liam's at. I can take you there." Alex held on to a breath as the man continued to watch him, trying to determine if he was telling the truth.

"And why would you give up your friend?"

Alex struggled to make his answer seem believable. "Because I care about her and I don't want her to die because of something her brother did." He turned to Rachel, with his heart in his eyes. As he watched, a tear spilled down her cheek.

"Touching," Temple mocked. "Then you'll make sure you don't try anything foolish, because if you do, she dies." Temple turned to one of the men standing nearby. "Take him to the vehicle. I'll be there shortly." He faced Rachel again. "You'd better hope he's telling the truth. Otherwise, I'll kill you myself."

Temple motioned to one of his men, who grabbed Rachel's arm and started toward the lodge. There was no way Alex was letting Temple separate them. Staying together was their only chance at surviving.

"Hold on just a second. I'm not going anywhere without her." Alex stood his ground. He meant it. He wasn't budging without Rachel. "If you want my help, she comes, too."

Temple glared at him for the longest time. Alex was certain he'd call his bluff. "All right," he said at last. "But she stays in the vehicle, and if you're lying, I'll have my man kill her without thinking twice about it. Understood?"

Not exactly the answer Alex hoped for, but at least Rachel would be close. He struggled through exhaustion to come up with some way to get them both free. He couldn't help but feel time was running out. For them. Liam. Deacon. He couldn't imagine how bad

Deacon's condition had deteriorated in the hours since they'd left him.

"Get them both in the SUV. We've wasted enough time. We have buyers counting on us."

Alex's blood ran cold. *Buyers counting on us…* Had Temple just let it slip that whatever it was they were trying to locate, possibly sarin gas, he had a buyer waiting impatiently for it?

He looked over at Rachel. She'd heard it, too.

"You men come with us. McNamara, try to reach them. Let them know everything is going according to plan," Temple told the man. "Apparently I can't trust any of you to do the job correctly. I'll need to go there in person to make sure Carlson gives up the location for the stuff."

Two men grabbed them by the arms and forced them into the back of one of the nearby vehicles.

Temple got up front along with a driver. The remaining two men sandwiched Rachel and Alex between them. They wanted to make sure they didn't try to escape.

Turning in his seat, Temple demanded answers. "Well? Where is this place? And keep in mind, I'm at the limit of my patience. If you can't produce your friend, you are no good to me."

The warning settled over him like a storm cloud. He knew what Temple meant. If they didn't come up with Liam soon, they'd be dead.

Alex told the driver where to find the entrance of the cave. "The vehicle won't be able to make it the entire way there. We'll have to go the rest on foot."

Temple clearly wasn't pleased by this, but he motioned the driver to begin. Once the SUV reached its limit, the driver stopped.

"Bring him with us," Blake ordered to the man closest to Alex. "You, keep an eye on her. If she tries anything, kill her."

"We'll get through this." Alex turned to look into her eyes. "Just like we did before." Realization dawned on her face. Praise God, she understood. If she could overpower her captor, she'd need to head to the second entrance. He'd try to meet her there.

He was forced out of the vehicle. There was just enough time for one final searching look between them before he was hauled away.

Temple stood in front of the vehicle, staring at the nearby mountain. "I don't see any cave," he muttered once Alex was forced to stop next to him. "This better not be another runaround like the lodge. This is your last opportunity."

"It's no runaround. The opening is hidden by grown-up scrub brush. It's this way, if I remember correctly," he added, so as not to tip the man off that he and Rachel had already been through the cave earlier and Liam wasn't there.

"Then what are you waiting for? Find it." Temple was furious. No doubt he had promised something that he was in danger of not being able to deliver.

After another quick glance back at Rachel, where he was almost positive he saw the tiniest of nods, Alex headed for the entrance to the cave with Temple and the other two men in tow.

He took longer than necessary to uncover the opening, while his limited options ran through his head. Once he'd shoved aside the brush they'd piled in front of the entrance, he noticed that their footprints were still there. He sure hoped Temple didn't spot them.

With the opening exposed, one of the men shoved Alex inside. He hit the opposite wall hard and winced in pain, holding his injured side.

"Well, which way to this fishing spot of yours?" Temple demanded as all three men entered the cave.

"To the left."

"Then lead the way," Temple ordered. "But I'll warn you again, if you're lying, I'll kill you right here and she'll be dead soon after."

The chilling reminder of what was at stake shot through Alex's sleep-deprived mind. "It's dark this way. I'll need some light."

Temple stopped next to him. "You wouldn't be trying to warn your buddy now, would you?"

"I'm not trying to do anything but let you know there are some spots up ahead that can be hairy. If you're not watching what you're doing, you could break a leg."

After another glaring assessment, Temple motioned to one of his men, who used his phone's flashlight app to illuminate the cave.

The pool was still quite some distance from where they were. Alex headed that way while his brain started to formulate a clearer plan of attack. It was three against one. He needed something to level the playing field.

He remembered all the times he and Rachel had come up here in the past. The pool had been a surprise at first. He'd told Temple that Liam came here to fish, but that wasn't the case. The natural underground pool was cold as ice and there were no fish in it.

If he was recalling correctly, there was a small space just off to the right side that they'd only explored once a long time ago because it was unstable even back then. The walls were literally crumbling. If he could convince them to search in there…

When they reached the pool, the man with the flashlight app shone the light around the area. When it became evident that Liam wasn't there, Temple rounded on Alex. It was clear he was enraged. "You lied. There's no one here. And no sign that anyone has been here before. Enough. Kill him," he ordered one of the men standing close to grab Alex. The man reached for him.

It was now or never.

"I said he told me he was going fishing up here. We used to fish in this spot many times in the past. Maybe he gave up or… Wait, I think I hear something over there." He pointed to the small area.

Temple stared at the small dark space and then at him. "I don't hear anything."

Alex didn't look away. "I did. If he's injured, he could be hiding in there."

Temple motioned to the man with the flashlight. "Check it out."

The man didn't seem thrilled at the idea. Reluctantly, he did as his boss suggested.

Temple grabbed Alex's arm and hauled him along with him. The third man followed.

"Do you see anything?" Temple asked the man with the light. He let go of Alex and peered into the darkness.

Alex eased backward; the third man was now at his left side. His weapon was within reach. If he failed, he'd be dead…and so would Rachel.

In a split second, Alex grabbed the gun and shoved the man on top of Temple, sending them both sprawling into the room. Then he opened fire on the crumbling wall. It took only two shots before the ancient rock collapsed upon itself, entombing Temple and his men.

The world around him rumbled and shook. The place was unstable. He needed to get out of here as quickly as possible before the entire cave went down.

Alex stumbled in the direction of the entrance. The rumblings stopped. Dust boiled all around him. It wouldn't take long for Temple and his men to dig out. He had no doubt that the man guarding Rachel would have heard the noise by now.

He hurried out of the opening and spotted the man. He'd seen Alex. He jumped from the vehicle and began shooting.

Alex ducked behind a nearby tree. The man was coming his way. He returned fire, forcing the man to take cover behind the vehicle. One of Alex's rounds ricocheted off the front of the SUV. Right away, Alex could see fluid spilling out. The radiator was shot. The SUV was useless.

While the man continued gunning for him, in his peripheral vision, Alex saw Rachel ease from the vehicle. Before the man realized she was there, Rachel shoved him hard. He went sprawling across the frozen ground, his weapon landing in front of him. Rachel raced for the gun. The man grabbed her ankle and she fell. As she crawled and clawed for the gun, the man, still holding on to her ankle, reached it first. He snatched it with his free hand and pointed it at her head. She'd be dead in seconds.

Alex charged the man. When he spotted Alex, he turned the weapon on him. Before the man could get a single shot off, Alex fired once, striking the man through the heart. He fell backward, limp.

Now freed, Rachel grabbed the man's gun then felt for a pulse. "He's dead." She searched his pockets. "Alex, he doesn't have a phone." Frustration laced her voice.

"It doesn't matter. Let's get out of here while we still can. The SUV's useless and it won't be long before Temple and his men come after us." As they headed away from the site, Alex told her what had happened inside the cave. "We just have to stay out of sight for a few more hours. This is almost over."

He didn't say as much, but if the chopper ran into any obstacles along the way, it could be even longer before Jase and the team reached them. And he wasn't sure how much longer they could survive up here on the mountain on their own.

TWELVE

They couldn't keep running around without direction. Going back down the mountain wasn't an option with Temple's men still stationed at the lodge. She told Alex as much.

He seemed to be reading her thoughts. "We can't head back to the camp. That's one of the first places they'll look. I would if it were me. I just hope they don't find Deacon this time." He looked around the area, frustrated.

Rachel stopped dead in her tracks. "Wait, I can't believe I didn't think of it before now. The ranger station is up here on this side of the mountain."

He stared at her for a moment, not seeing the significance. "You mean the one on top of the mountain."

"Yes, but there's a radio up there. We can use it to reach the rangers and have them contact your people. Let them know where to look for us. We can get Deacon the help he needs." She didn't believe there was any way Temple's men would be looking for them up there. "They'll be expecting us to try to get off the mountain, not go farther up."

"You're right, they won't be. The only problem is it's

at least a three-hour hike uphill and we're worn-out. My team may arrive before then…and I'm not sure Deacon has that long."

She shook her head, discouraged. "What other choice do we have? If they catch us again, they'll kill us, and it's too risky to try to get Deacon out of there on foot."

They'd be sacrificing Deacon's life by making the wrong decision.

Alex stopped next to her, apparently seeing all her concerns. He drew her close for a moment. "You're right. It's our only option. God didn't bring us this far to let us die. We have to hold on to that promise."

As she looked into his eyes, she believed him. Alex had dropped everything to help her find Liam and now, faced with death himself, his faith never wavered.

A breath separated them. As she lost herself in his eyes, something shifted inside of her. All the wishes she'd buried deep in her heart rose to the surface. She would always care for Alex no matter what happened in the future. She cupped his face. Everything she still felt for him was right there in her touch.

The years melted away, and it was like turning the clock back to the time when they'd dated. Her heart beat crazily against her chest. She'd give anything if this moment were happening under different circumstances.

She pulled away and stared up at him. She didn't want to hide her feelings any longer.

He gently stroked her cheek. "We should keep going. It's too dangerous to stop now…" Yet he didn't move.

Rachel swallowed visibly. Would there ever be a right time for them? The past seemed to determine that there wouldn't be.

She stepped away and he let her go. Regret was in his eyes.

"You're right. We have to keep moving." Rachel turned and stared up at the top of the mountain, where the ranger station was situated, trying to reclaim her composure. She'd loved him for as long as she could remember, but it seemed as if circumstances were determined to stand in the way of their having a life together.

As they continued hiking at an exhausting pace, Rachel struggled to think of where Liam might be hiding. Her gut told her he was still up here somewhere. Otherwise, the entire area would be crawling with agents by now. They'd covered many of the places Liam liked to go as a child, and yet her brother was still missing. She had little doubt that Liam was the one who had brought Deacon to the cabin and then he'd disappeared into thin air.

With no answers coming, she shifted her attention to what they'd overheard. "Temple said he wanted McNamara to let someone know that things were going according to schedule. He had to be talking about selling whatever Liam had taken from him. My guess would be sarin gas. Yet I don't understand how they managed to get it here in the US?"

They had to figure out who Temple's buyer was before it was too late. She was out of breath and running on her last ounces of energy. Thinking clearly was a near impossible task.

Alex looked about as worn-out as she was. Once they reached the ranger station, they could radio for help, but if Temple's men tracked them, there was nothing but a sheer drop-off behind the station. She didn't want to think about that possibility.

"What if they didn't bring the gas here?" Alex's voice interrupted her burdened thoughts. "What if they made it themselves?"

The possibility of Temple manufacturing the gas himself hadn't crossed her mind. She remembered Alex had told her that Temple and his men had been chasing the Chemist, the person responsible for manufacturing sarin gas.

"What if they found the Chemist and killed him? Decided to take over his business? They'd have his recipe for creating it," Alex said.

A shiver ran down her spine. "It's unimaginable that someone who is sworn to protect would do such a horrific thing."

"Yes, but there's no doubt in my mind that Temple and his goons are dirty. They've been doing who-knows-what unimaginable things since they faked their deaths. They're capable of this and a whole lot more."

She didn't doubt it for a second. "How do you think Liam got turned onto their crimes?"

Alex stopped for a breath. "Probably through his investigation of the new terror threat. That led him to these guys. I'm guessing Deacon may have been responsible for bringing them together."

It was beginning to add up. Liam had been searching for a link to tie the gas to his new threat. Deacon might have been working undercover with the Chemist or even with Temple.

"What about Michelle? Where does she factor into all of this?" Rachel asked as they started walking again. It was hard just putting one foot in front of the other.

Alex ran a hand across the back of his neck. "Her I can't figure out. I felt as if she was frightened of Temple and yet when she had the chance, she didn't accept our help. In other words, I don't know." He barely managed a shrug.

Guilt tore at her. He'd put his life on the line and they were still no closer to understanding what was happening than when they'd started on his mission. She touched his arm and he stopped, looking at her curiously. "I'm so sorry I got you involved in this. I didn't know who else to trust. Liam's note scared me."

His handsome face twisted in pain. "No, Rachel, don't apologize. Liam is my family...and so are you." His green eyes softened as they swept over her face, the look in them reminding her of the man she'd once loved...the one she still loved.

You never forget your first love...

She swallowed back the hurt that realization brought. He stepped closer. She did, too. He was going to kiss her. She so wanted to feel his lips against hers again, but she was barely hanging on as it was. She wasn't ready to face the truth just yet. She stepped away. Saw his wounded reaction, but she couldn't go there. Not now. Not yet. She wasn't even sure they would survive the day, much less if she could survive Alex's leaving her again.

"I'm sorry," he whispered in a broken tone. "Are you okay?"

She couldn't look at him. "I'm fine. It's just...working with you again has brought up some old feelings I thought I'd dealt with."

He didn't say anything. The uncertainty in his eyes had her full attention. This was not Alex. He had never seemed so unsure before. "What is it?" she asked.

His gaze held hers. The pain she saw there was real.

"Being with you again has made me realize what I lost when I lost you."

With her heart breaking, she bit down on her bottom lip to keep from crying. "We both made mistakes, but that's all in the past. We can't go back and fix it now, can we?" She loved him, but she couldn't open her heart up to that much hurt again. She'd lost too much in her life.

"I guess you're right." Regret hung in his voice. She understood. She had regrets, too. "We still have a long ways to go. At least we'll have decent cover at the ranger station. It'll get us out of the elements for a while."

Rachel couldn't answer for the longest time. It was a struggle to keep back the tears. It felt as if they were saying goodbye to each other all over again. "I guess you're right," she managed, and they both started walking again.

The farther they climbed up the mountain, the more the snow piled up. Little sunlight got through the denseness of the wilderness up here.

Exhausted and barely hanging on, Rachel lost her footing on what appeared to be a downed tree. She started to slide back down the mountain but Alex caught her.

Without the proper hiking gear, they were at the mercy of the mountain. Yet one thing working in their favor was that the men chasing them didn't seem any better equipped for the hike than they were.

She looked behind her to see what she'd stumbled over and somehow managed to stifle the scream before it could escape. It wasn't a log. It was a man.

He'd been shot in the back of the head. There was a gaping hole there where his skull had once been.

Alex knelt and rolled the man over. Rachel recognized him. "That's Seth Jamison. Liam's handler. Alex, they killed Liam's handler. Which explains why I haven't been able to get in touch with him. What was he doing out here?" Her voice trailed off as the truth became apparent. Seth was the person on the inside helping Temple and his men.

"My guess is he was working for Temple. Something must have happened. Maybe Seth got a conscience and threatened to turn them in. They killed him because of it."

Rachel was in shock. "I can't believe it. Why would he do such a thing?" Something else occurred to her. "He betrayed Liam. Alex, he must have told Temple about Liam's meet. That's why they were ambushed. Seth almost got them both killed, and for what?"

Alex stared at the dead man. "I don't know. I can't believe someone Liam trusted was corrupt. But it explains a lot. Once Jase and the team arrive, we'll send someone down to retrieve the body. His family will need to be notified." Alex got to his feet and looked at her. "How are you holding up?" It was freezing cold and she was beginning to perspire. They couldn't afford to become hypothermic.

She shrugged, resigned. "I'll be okay. The sooner we get to the station, the better, though."

Alex didn't look convinced. "It's at least another hour if not more before we reach it. We need to find a place to warm up. Otherwise, we'll never make it."

Weary to the bone, she looked around, but there was no shelter from the elements. "We really need a fire."

Alex dug into his pocket and pulled out the lighter the men hadn't taken. "Let's see if we can find some sheltered trees to a build a fire so that we can warm our frozen limbs."

The sight of the lighter in his hand was like a prayer answered. "Oh, thank you. I can't feel my feet anymore."

He looked around, trying to find a safe place for the fire that would be obscured from sight. "Over there." He pointed to a group of trees. "It looks secluded enough. They shouldn't see it if they happen this way."

Alex dug out a spot in the snow to put the fire while Rachel gathered what loose branches she could find.

When the fire finally caught, they both moved in as close as they dared. Rachel could feel its warmth as she leaned in closer. Never had a simple fire felt so good. She closed her eyes with joy. "That feels wonderful."

Alex chuckled at her expression. "You're right it does. But we can't afford to stay here for very long. We have to keep one step ahead of them if we're going to make it out of this. And there's always the chance they'll see the fire and come check it out."

She understood, but she hated to leave the warmth. It was funny the things you took for granted. Like being warm enough.

"How much longer before your team members arrive, do you think?" she asked again, and couldn't quite keep the desperation from her tone.

"Not too much longer. The only problem is they have the coordinates for the camp. They won't know how to find us up here unless we can radio them from the tower."

He focused on the fire, no doubt weighing their impossible options. Rachel glanced his way. Alex was still the most attractive man she knew. He fit the part of a true hero right down to tall, dark and handsome. And she would always love him.

Alex caught her watching him, and her chest grew tight at the tenderness she saw in him. There was no denying the feelings still ran strong between them. But would it matter in the end if neither of them were able to walk off Midnight Mountain alive?

There was no doubt in his mind that he loved her. He'd never stopped loving her. She wasn't ready to hear those words from him. Would she ever forgive him, or had his actions all those years ago destroyed any hope they had for rekindling their love?

It was a hopeless feeling to be caught up in a situation so out of control and bordering on impossible like the one they faced right now. In his heart he believed that God had answered his prayer and was giving him a second chance to prove to Rachel how he felt about her. They just had to survive long enough for him to have that chance.

"How are you feeling?" he asked, trying to take his mind off their grim situation.

She turned to stare up at him, then slowly smiled. "Better, thanks. The fire really helped." Her smile still had the power to brighten his dark day.

"I'm glad. Are you ready to finish this?" She didn't hesitate before confirming with the smile still in place.

Together, they tamped out the fire then threw snow on top of it to cover the smoldering ashes. Once Alex was satisfied they'd hidden all evidence, they started up the mountain again.

Just having time to warm up and rest did wonders for his drained energy. He was ready to finish this thing once and for all, to find out the truth behind Liam's disappearance and hopefully convince Rachel to give him a second chance.

He still couldn't believe that Liam's handler had been working for Temple's crew. How long had Seth been betraying his country? Had he been involved with Temple's plan to fake his death? With Seth dead and Liam missing, the only chance they had for getting answers was through Temple.

Alex hadn't been able to get Liam's letter out of his head. There was no doubt in his mind that Liam was trying to tell him about the one specific location he'd underlined for a reason. He believed it was where Liam had stowed the sarin. He told Rachel his suspicions.

That realization dawned on her face. "It makes sense. I can't believe I never considered it before now. Alex, we can't let Temple and his men find those weapons. If they reach the cave before we do, then they won't need Liam or us."

Those frightening words hung uneasily between them. "Let's just hope they haven't found them already. They certainly have enough men out here to search the entire mountainside."

"Where is Liam?" Rachel shook her head, and Alex could see her frustration. "I can't help but believe he's up here somewhere still. There's so much territory to cover up here. It could take weeks to locate him. By then it will be too late."

He stopped walking and faced her. "You can't think like that. We need to trust God to take us to where Liam is." He did his best to sound convincing, but it was hard to keep positive after everything they'd been through.

He wanted to believe God was directing their footsteps, but his faith was faltering.

Help my unbelief. The last thing he wanted was for Rachel to see him give up.

"You're right. I'm sorry. I'm just tired. Liam wouldn't give up on either of us if the tables were turned. I won't give up on him, either."

He tucked her hands in his. "Good. I can't help but think Liam had a backup plan in place when he came up here. Maybe he even had some supplies stashed somewhere. I know Liam. He's a stickler for details and he always was the most prepared of the three of us."

She smiled at the memory. "Yes, he was. He left me the map and his phone for a reason. The same way he left you that letter. Of course he'd be prepared for whatever came his way. He'd be expecting trouble. He *was* expecting it."

Her confidence in her brother was well deserved. Liam was a seasoned agent. He would be okay and so would they. Once they reached the ranger station, they'd radio Jase with their location. Praise God, this thing was just about over.

The thought had barely cleared his head when a noise nearby captured both their attentions and sent them running for the cover of a nearby grove of spruce trees.

Alex could make out voices. More than one and they were almost right on top of them.

"The boss said he saw smoke over this way. I don't see anything, do you?" There was no mistaking McNamara's voice.

Alex tugged Rachel closer. Her eyes were filled with an uncertainty that he couldn't begin to assuage. His own pulse was threatening to explode in his chest.

"Did you hear something?" one of the men asked in a somewhat uneasy tone.

"No, but you two check it out," McNamara ordered. "We can't afford to let them get away. Too much is at stake."

Alex heard footsteps coming toward their hiding spot. One of the men was almost directly in front of them. If he turned slightly, he would see them. If they were found now, his gut told him they wouldn't walk out of the wilderness alive.

He prayed with all his heart and left the fear in God's hands.

"There's nothing here," the man closest to them grumbled. "Come on, it's freezing up here. I don't see anything that resembles a fire, anyway. The boss must have been mistaken."

The second man stared straight at the tree they were standing behind, then abruptly turned on his heel. He and his partner headed back to where McNamara and another man waited.

"Let's get out of here. Chances are, they headed back down the mountain another way," McNamara told them. "We can still head them off before they reach the town and we have men waiting there if they give us the slip."

Alex clutched Rachel close as the noise of the men's footsteps slowly disappeared.

When he felt it was safe, he eased out from behind the tree with Rachel still tucked in his arms.

"That was too close," she whispered, her breath fogging the air between them.

"Yes, but it sounds as if they aren't expecting us to be here, which means they won't be looking for us up at the station. That's something," he managed without really feeling confident.

"It should give us time to finish the climb without looking back over our shoulder. Either way, let's keep pushing forward. We're almost there, Alex. We're almost there."

He brushed back some escaping hair from her face and looked into her eyes. There was still a lot of danger between them and getting the answers they wanted. He needed her to listen. He'd been holding these feelings inside for way too long and there was no promise of the future. They faced armed men, the elements of the mountain and physical exhaustion. There were no guarantees.

If they were caught, if they didn't walk out of this thing alive, he wanted her to know the truth. He loved her. He wanted to be with her. And he'd do whatever it took to convince her he was serious this time.

THIRTEEN

She held her breath, waiting for him to say something. Hoping he did. Praying he wouldn't. She couldn't lose her heart to him again.

His hands still rested on her shoulders. She couldn't take her eyes off him. "Rachel, I know things ended badly between us before because of me. I know I hurt you terribly, but I want you to know that I learned a lot after you left."

She tried to pull away, but he didn't let her. "No, wait."

She couldn't do this now and not fall apart. "Alex, please..."

"Rachel, look at me." Slowly, she did, because in spite of everything her heart desperately wanted to hear what he had to say. "I know I messed things up between us, but I'm not the same person I was back then. I've changed. *God* changed me," he amended, and she believed him. She'd seen this change in him.

"I'm not asking for you to forget what happened, and I don't expect you to answer me now, with our lives on the line like this. I just want you to know that I still care about you. I never really stopped caring."

Tears filled her eyes. She turned away and he let her go. Why now? Why did he have to tell her these things now, after all the heartache and pain she'd gone through? Why couldn't he have loved her the way she needed him to back then?

"Alex, I can't do this now." Her voice was little more than a broken whisper.

When he didn't respond, she looked at him. Her answer couldn't be the one he'd hoped for, yet he slowly agreed.

"Okay." Without another word, he started walking and, after a much-needed moment to regain her composure, Rachel followed, her thoughts disjointed. Her heart was in her throat.

Through the clearing in the trees, she could see the ranger station up ahead. They were almost there.

"Alex, look." She pointed up ahead and he followed her direction. The relief on his face was easy to read.

Just seeing the station gave them both an extra boost of energy. They were almost to the building when a debilitating thought occurred and she grabbed his arm.

"What if someone is waiting for us in there?" Rachel could tell he hadn't considered it.

They ducked behind a tree. "I can't see anything, can you?"

She squinted hard but could see nothing in the twilight of the wilderness. "There's no movement that I can tell. What do you want to do?" She was grateful that at least they were both armed now.

"Let's ease up to it. Try to stay in the cover of the trees as much as possible."

She nodded and waited until he'd made the first move and then she followed. Each step echoed in her ears. So far, there was nothing out of the ordinary. Still, they'd been through so much already. What if there were men waiting inside to finish the job?

Still some distance from the station, Alex stopped suddenly.

"Did you hear that?" He barely got the words out when the silence around them was shattered by an assault rifle discharging.

Rachel dove for the cover of the closest tree, with Alex in tow.

They hunkered low as the shots continued to ring out. With the distance between themselves and the person firing on them, it was impossible to make out anything about him.

"I only hear one shooter," she told him.

He listened for a moment. "You're right. Whoever it is, they're alone. Can you cover me? I'll try to circle around behind the station and go up that way. Maybe I can take him out."

She nodded, but before he left the protection of the tree, she stopped him. "Alex, wait."

He turned to her, those piercing eyes undoubtedly seeing what she could no longer hide. "I still care about you, too. I always have... I always will."

The joy on his face sent her heart soaring. Alex took her hand and slowly raised it to his lips. He held it for just a second longer and then slowly let it go.

She was more fearful than ever before. She had so much to lose. "Be careful," she urged, and he smiled down at her.

"I will."

She watched Alex run for the next tree up. The person firing on them was quick to spot his movements and another round of bullets kicked up the dirt near where Alex stood.

Keeping as flat as she could, Rachel edged around the tree and opened fire. She caught a glimpse of a man standing in the open station window before they ducked out of sight.

Alex took advantage of the down time and rushed to the back of the building. Once he was in place, Rachel would draw the shooter's attention away from him.

She aimed for the opening and fired off several rounds. She could see Alex slowly easing up the stairs. If she could keep the man's attention on her, Alex might be able to take him by surprise.

Rachel fired off several more rounds, giving Alex the time he needed to charge the station. She heard a brief scuffle, then silence. *Alex!* He needed her. She ran as fast as she could to give aid.

With her heart pounding out the rhythm of her footsteps, she took the steps two at a time.

Once she reached the landing, she was boosted by adrenaline every step of the way to the open door. The station consisted of one circular room that afforded a three-hundred-sixty-degree view around them.

Through the filtered light, she saw two men standing close. Something was wrong. There were no weapons drawn. Alex jerked toward her. As she drew near, the look on his face was one of sheer disbelief.

"What is it?" She barely managed to force the words out.

And then the second man slowly turned to her. Two things quickly became apparent. He was injured, his shirt covered in blood. She couldn't tell the extent of his wounds, but he'd obviously lost a lot of blood. The man staring back at her had Rachel dropping her weapon and running into his arms.

This was her brother. They'd finally found Liam and he was alive.

Alex watched as Rachel hugged Liam, and his exhausted mind struggled to take it all in. Liam was here. He was alive.

Liam staggered under Rachel's embrace and she pulled away, somehow managing to catch her six-foot, one-hundred-seventy-pound brother before he could fall.

"You're hurt." She slowly eased him to the floor. The amount of blood on his shirt was alarming.

Alex tucked his weapon behind his back and knelt next to Rachel as she carefully unbuttoned Liam's shirt.

"I'm okay. I bandaged it up, but we need to get out of here as soon as possible. They can't find it." Liam tried to get up but slumped back onto the floor.

Alex tried to quiet his friend. "We will. Help is on the way. I just need to let them know where to find us." He glanced around the circular room, looking for the radio. He spotted a flare gun and quickly pocketed it. But then he saw something that threatened to take away his last bit of hope. Someone had deliberately smashed the machine. His spirits sank.

"What happened to the radio?" he asked Liam.

Liam shook his head. "It was like that when I arrived. They must have beat me here. I guess they wanted to make sure I didn't have a way to call out for help." Liam winced in pain as Rachel did her best to secure the wound once more.

Alex had to know what Liam had found out. "Who are these people? Why are they after you?"

Liam seemed to be fighting to keep from losing consciousness. He'd lost a lot of blood and the exertion of trying to defend himself had taken its toll. "Former CIA," he murmured, before he closed his eyes. "They're all supposed to be dead."

The statement pretty much confirmed what he and Rachel had suspected.

Before he could ask another question, Rachel's worried gaze met his. "He needs immediate medical attention and I can't even imagine what's happened to Deacon by now."

Liam caught what she'd said. "Deacon? You've seen him? Is he okay?"

Alex couldn't lie to his friend. "He's in pretty bad shape, but he's hanging on. You were the one who took him to the camp?"

Liam nodded weakly. "We were attacked. I'd been working with Deacon for a while. Through his asset, he found out where the sarin gas was stored and we managed to get it to a secure location. I was supposed to meet with Deacon's asset, who would give us the names of the people Temple and his men are selling sarin gas to, but we were attacked instead. We were taken hostage. They took our weapons and cell phones. I thought they would kill us, but they demanded to know where we'd moved the sarin. Deacon and I managed to escape, but not before we were both injured." Liam closed his eyes once more, breathing heavily.

Alex squeezed his friend's arm. "Rest now. I'm going to see if I can fix the busted radio."

He got to his feet and motioned to Rachel. She made

sure Liam was as comfortable as possible and then she joined him.

"Do you think you can get it working again?" She glanced at the destroyed radio with doubt.

"I don't know. It's in pretty bad shape, but it may be our only way to reach Jase before it's too late."

"What do you need me to do?" she asked.

"Keep a watch outside. If they've been here before, and we have to assume they have because of this—" he pointed to the destroyed radio "—then there's a good chance they'll search here again. Especially after hearing the shots."

A noise behind them captured both their attentions. Something was wrong with Liam. His head slumped to one side. He was unconscious.

They rushed to his side. "Liam, buddy, wake up." Alex shook his friend gently. After an alarming amount of time had passed, Liam slowly opened his eyes. "Stay awake for me, Liam. I need you to do your best to stay awake."

Liam managed the smallest of nods. Rachel's reaction to seeing her brother's condition worsen was devastating. She was terrified of losing him.

Alex got to his feet and held his hand out to her. She couldn't take her eyes off her brother.

"Rachel, look at me." She stood as well, finally focusing on his face. "I need to see if I can fix the radio to get Liam help. I need you to stand guard…okay?"

Slowly, she agreed. She took up her weapon and went over to the opening that faced out to the grounds below. It showed the same path that they'd come up.

Alex went to work on the radio, using all his ham

radio knowledge to try to bring the busted machine back to life.

While he worked, he couldn't help but feel that time was running out. With so many loose ends tangled around each other, they'd need a clear head and safer grounds to understand what was really going on here. He still couldn't believe former CIA agents who had once been honored for their work in the field were responsible for attacking Liam and Deacon along with himself and Rachel. They clearly had nothing to lose at this point.

He tried to sort through the details he knew so far. Temple and his thugs had sarin gas here in the US, which was unimaginable in itself. Whether or not they'd smuggled it in or produced the gas themselves was uncertain. Both he and Rachel had overheard Temple talking about a meeting with someone. A possible buyer for the weapons here in the US. Alex didn't like the sound of it.

Something Liam had said troubled him. He'd told them that Deacon was working with him and that they were supposed to meet with Deacon's asset, presumably someone connected to Temple. Did Liam's handler know about Deacon?

Alex knew very little about Jamison, other than what Liam had told him. According to his friend, Jamison was a stand-up guy and always had Liam's back. He trusted the man completely. Had Liam's trust been his downfall?

FOURTEEN

Trying to keep her focus on the grounds below was an almost impossible task. All she could think about was Liam. His condition was getting worse. She glanced back at her brother. Had they found him again only to lose him to his injuries before they could get him to safety?

Please, God, no.

She'd never seen Liam look so weak. He'd been shot before, but never like this. Liam had been her rock, especially after she'd lost Brian. Now Liam needed her and she felt so helpless.

Something caught her attention below. What looked like a light flashed. She quickly ducked behind the closest wall. She was almost positive it was the reflection of a gun scope.

Alex must have spotted her reaction because he hurried to her side, careful to stay out of sight of the opening. "Did you see something?" Concern creased his brow.

"There's someone out there. They're armed."

"Did you see how many?"

She'd only caught a glimpse. "I'm not sure. I just caught sight of the one person."

He looked back at Liam. "We need to try to keep him as quiet as possible. Maybe they won't look here again since they've destroyed the radio."

She so wanted to believe it. She didn't. These men were ruthless and they had everything to lose. They would have heard the shots from earlier. They'd know the direction they came from.

Rachel eased to the opposite side of the opening, careful to keep out of sight. Alex followed. She peered out. She could no longer see anything, including the rifle scope. Had she been wrong?

She watched as Alex searched the area below them then shook his head.

"I don't see the person anymore, either. I could have been wrong." She didn't believe it, though. There was someone out there. The only question remaining was how many of them there were.

He didn't answer. His focus was trained on something below. "Wait, I see something. There's at least three men coming this way."

She looked in the direction he indicated and spotted them. "We can hold our ground against them for a little while until we run out of ammo, but it's going to call a lot of attention to us. The rest of Temple's men will be here before your team has a chance to find us. There will be no escaping then."

Alex hurried across the room and looked down below. "Nothing but a sheer drop-off back here. There's a small ledge, which barely has room to stand and no room for error."

She understood what that meant. They'd have to try to hold off Temple's team until the Scorpions arrived.

Rachel grabbed Liam's weapon and checked the clip.

He was almost out of rounds. Hers wasn't much better. It was only a matter of time before they were overthrown.

If they were going to die here, she wasn't letting that happen without telling Alex how she felt about him.

Alex headed for the opening where he'd seen the men, but she stopped him. "Alex, wait."

He turned back to her, searching her face.

Rachel slowly found the courage she needed. "Alex, we may not make it out of here and I can't die without telling you…how I feel about you."

She'd never seen him look so uncertain. He reached for her and tugged her close. His arms were everything that she remembered, but she needed to tell him everything.

"No, I need to say this."

He waited for her to go on.

"When you chose the job over me, well, it was crippling. I thought we would have a future together and then it just ended." She shrugged. She couldn't lose control now. "When I got back home, I was a wreck. I couldn't function for the longest time, but slowly, with Liam's help and the Reagans, I moved on. I married Brian because I cared about him. He knew all about you and me, but it didn't matter to him." She stopped for a breath. "I'll always be grateful for him, but I never stopped loving you, Alex. And I never will."

He framed her face with his hands and kissed her tenderly. When he looked at her the way he was right now, she was so afraid. She had so much to look forward to in life, and it might quite possibly be taken from her again.

"I'm not going to let that happen, Rachel," he said, reading her worried thoughts. "We will make it out of here, and when we do, we will have a lot to talk about. Do not give up on us." The sincerity in his eyes made her want to keep fighting with all her might.

She managed a smile for him. "I won't. I'll never give up on you again." With one final kiss, they both eased to the opening once more. The men had stopped. They appeared to be assessing the station carefully. She could see them talking, then one of the men slipped closer to the station.

"He's coming inside. If we can take him out, it might force the others to search for him. It will give us some leverage."

Rachel understood. She would act as bait for the man to draw his attention away from Alex, who would take the man down. She heard the first step below creak, followed by another. She'd been in situations like this hundreds of times in the past, yet the adrenaline rush of the life-and-death situation was always there.

A shadow fell across the door to the building. Rachel kept her hand on her gun. This was it. Their lives—their future—came down to her not losing her cool. The door slowly opened. She saw the barrel of the gun first. She waited for the man to enter. Her thoughts screamed that she didn't want to die here along with Liam and Alex without knowing what their sacrifice was all about.

Alex waited behind the door as the man eased through it. He barely cleared it when he spotted Rachel. Before he had the chance to fire off a single round to warn his comrades, Alex grabbed the man from behind in a choke hold. The man struggled like a wild animal. Alex tightened his hold around the man's neck. After what felt like forever, his struggles grew weaker. The weapon slipped from his hand. Rachel rushed to grab it before it could hit the floor. Once the man was unconscious, Alex eased him down to the floor.

"That didn't go as quietly as I'd hoped." He went to the opening and glanced down at the two men. They were definitely on alert.

Rachel joined him. "I'm not sure they heard him, but it won't be long before they come looking. At least for now, it's two against two."

It was something, he guessed, but how long before the rest of Temple's goons came after them?

Alex went back to the man and checked his pocket. He had a cell phone. "Thank You, God," he said in a grateful tone, before he punched in Jase's number. "Jase, it's me, Alex. I don't have much time." Alex knew his commander wouldn't recognize the number. As quickly as he could, he told Jase what was happening.

"We're still an hour out at best," Jase told him. "We ran into some sketchy weather. We'll head for the ranger station. In the meantime, I'm calling in the state troopers. I know you don't trust the local authorities, but these guys are state. Hang in there. This is almost over."

Alex ended the call with Jase's assurances running through his head.

He turned to Rachel and smiled. "They're close. He's calling in backup, too."

She went into his arms and held him tight. "I'm so grateful. I'm not sure how much more of this we can take on our own."

He kissed her temple and let her go. "I'll keep an eye on the guys below. You watch this one in case he wakes up."

Alex went over to the opening. One of the men had

disappeared. He searched the area below. Where had he gone?

"What's wrong?" Rachel had noticed him looking around.

"One of them is missing. He may be heading this way."

She moved closer to the door. With the butt of the weapon ready, she waited, but nothing happened. After what felt like an eternity, she glanced over at Alex.

He shook his head. The man still hadn't appeared again. His buddy was standing behind a tree, partially visible. "I don't see him. Maybe he got worried about his missing comrade and went for help." If he had, then Alex wasn't sure they could hold the men off until Jase arrived.

"We can't afford to make a run for it with Liam's condition so serious."

Liam opened his eyes as if he'd heard her say his name. When he spotted the man lying by the door he tried to stand, but Rachel hurried over, trying to quiet him. "Liam, it's okay. Try to stay as still as possible. Help is almost here."

"That's one of the men who took Deacon and me hostage," Liam managed in a whisper. He glanced up at Alex. "There are others out there still, aren't there?"

Alex had to tell him the truth. "There are. Two more that we know of. I see the one, but the second is missing. He could be anywhere. Can you keep an eye on this guy?"

Liam didn't hesitate. "I can."

Alex smiled in spite of the situation. It had been years since he and Liam had worked together. He'd missed his companion.

Rachel clearly wasn't sure. "He's too weak, Alex," she whispered so that only he could hear. "He won't be able to withstand a firefight. Is there still no visual of the other one?"

Alex shook his head. He didn't like it. "They're definitely up to something."

He had barely gotten the words out when the second man appeared again next to his friend. "Where was he?"

"Something's wrong." Rachel looked through the scope of the weapon of the man she'd disarmed. "He has something in his hand."

Before she finished talking, the man's companion opened fire and they were forced away from the opening.

After the first round of shots whizzed past them, Alex aimed at the man who'd fired on them, forcing him back behind the coverage of the tree.

"Where's his friend again?" Rachel asked. Alex glanced below. The man had vanished again.

Uneasiness coiled into the pit of Alex's stomach. The shooter opened up on them again, forcing their attention from the opening.

Alex and Rachel returned his shots, but they were using up valuable ammo they didn't have to use.

"Hold your fire," Alex told Rachel. "They could be trying to run us out of ammo then charge the station."

She did as he suggested but kept a careful eye on the man behind the tree. "He's just standing there. Almost as if he's waiting on something."

"Or someone…" Alex's gaze latched with hers. She shivered visibly.

With the silent standoff continuing, Alex kept listening for any sound of the missing man approaching. What was he up to?

The thought had barely cleared his head when something came hurling through the opening. Alex ducked to keep it from hitting him; the smell of gasoline was pungent.

Seconds later, the station exploded in fire. The man had thrown a Molotov cocktail into the building. The station went up like a tinderbox, filling the room with acrid smoke. Alex hurried to Liam's side and helped him to his feet. Their once-unconscious assailant was beginning to come to.

Alex pointed his weapon at him. "If you try anything, I'll shoot you. Do you understand?"

Coughing from smoke inhalation, the man glared at him.

"There's only three of them! You can take them!" the man yelled, trying to warn his buddies.

Alex took a step closer and he quickly shut up.

With the station now becoming a raging inferno, they could no longer go through the entrance. "We'll have to go out the back window." Alex headed for the opening that faced the valley below.

Their only plan of escape was at the edge of the mountain with no way down.

FIFTEEN

Rachel looked below them at the sheer drop that was now their only escape.

"I'll lower you down first," Alex told her. "Then Liam. Then this guy. Once you're on the ground, head right." Alex's love for her was shining in his eyes. She smiled up at him, trying her best to reassure him and herself that everything would work out, in spite of what her gut was screaming.

She tucked her weapon behind her back and climbed through the opening, trusting Alex with her life. He grabbed hold of her arms and slowly lowered her down. There was still a three-foot jump. With her heartbeat threatening to drown out all other sound, she nodded and Alex let go. She dropped to the ground and stumbled on the uneven footing. Somehow she managed to catch herself before she slid over the edge and plunged to her death.

Rachel blew out a huge sigh and stood on unsteady legs. Alex was as pale as a sheet, clearly terrified by what he'd just witnessed. "I'm okay," she quickly reassured him.

Liam's descent wasn't nearly as easy. He landed on

his injured side, the pain causing him to scream. Rachel rushed to his aid and helped him rise to his feet. They carefully made their way to the safe area. She lowered Liam against a nearby tree and went to help Alex.

The building appeared close to collapsing. "Hurry, Alex, the station won't last much longer!" she called out. Once the captured man dropped down, Rachel kept her weapon pointed at him as he headed over to Liam. Behind her she could hear parts of the station collapsing upon itself.

Alex!

"Keep an eye on him, Liam." Rachel didn't wait for his answer. She had to get to Alex. She couldn't lose him again.

"Alex!" she called out. She couldn't see anything but fire and smoke coming from the rapidly disintegrating station.

Please, be okay.

"Alex!" She screamed in panic. She watched in horror as the station crumbled to the ground. The heat from the blaze so intense that she was forced to look away. Was he inside? Had she lost him? The pain that thought brought shot through her, leaving a path of destruction like a bullet's wound.

The smallest of sounds close by had her whirling around. *Alex!* Singed and bloody, he emerged from the firestorm raging behind him. She ran to him. "You're hurt."

He winced as she held him close. "Just a few cuts and scrapes is all. I barely managed to jump out the window before the place went down. Let's hurry. We can use the fire and smoke as a distraction to get away."

They went back to where Liam had managed to stand and was keeping a close eye on his prisoner.

"Can you walk?" Rachel asked. She could see he was in a lot of pain.

Liam nodded. "I'll keep up. Let's get out of here while we still have a chance."

Rachel motioned to their prisoner to start walking. "You go first."

He tossed her an evil look. "You'll never get away. He has people everywhere up here."

"Just start walking." She wasn't letting him get in her head.

The man headed in the direction she indicated. Liam moved close so that only Rachel and Alex could hear. "He's right. They have dozens of men out here."

Alex nodded. "How did you get turned onto these guys, anyway?"

"Through Deacon." Liam confirmed what they'd suspected. "He's been deep undercover with someone close to Temple's crew for a while. That's how we crossed paths. Temple is the one I've been tracking for a while."

Rachel started to ask her brother where the sarin was hidden. Before she got the question out, they were ambushed by gunfire.

"Take cover," she yelled, and they ducked behind a small grove of trees barely wide enough to cover them. Their prisoner went running in the direction of the shots while yelling for his buddies not to shoot him.

Rachel peered around the tree. A round of gunshots sounded a little ways from them. Someone screamed. She had no idea what was happening. She turned to Liam. He was slumped against the tree next to her.

"Liam!" She could see that he'd reopened his wound and was losing blood again.

Alex hurried to help her. "Liam, are you able to walk?"

Rachel shook her head. "He can't go anywhere, Alex."

Liam flinched in pain as she did her best to secure the wound once more.

"No, it's okay, Rachel. I can keep up. We have to get out of here. We'll be trapped if we stick around." Liam words slurred. He barely had the strength to get them out.

Before she could answer, a noise close by sent her whirling toward it. One of the men from earlier had his gun pointed straight at them and was ready to fire. Before she could draw her weapon, a shot rang out. The man's startled expression was the last thing she saw before he dropped to the ground dead.

Rachel searched in the direction from where the shot had come and saw Michelle standing there with a gun in her hand. Before Rachel could fully comprehend what had happened, Michelle dropped her weapon on the ground.

"I can't believe she did that," Rachel murmured to Alex and then said, "Get your hands in the air."

Michelle obeyed and Alex grabbed her weapon. "You saved our lives," Alex said in amazement. "Why would you do that?"

But Rachel believed she knew. "You're the asset who is working with Deacon, aren't you?" Michelle managed a frightened nod. "You did the right thing. You're better off with us. Temple will kill you if he discovers you helped us out."

* * *

"Where are the others?" Alex asked, wondering how she'd managed to get away from Temple and his men.

"The two that were here are dead. I shot them. Your prisoner got away. The rest of Temple's crew will have heard the shots. They'll be here soon. We need to get out of here before that happens."

"How do you fit into all this, Michelle?" Rachel asked. She appeared just as confused by what happened as he was. "You had your chance to get away before and you didn't take it. Why help us now?"

"I couldn't before. I didn't trust you…and I was scared of him. He threatened me. But I can't let him go through with what he has planned. It's too horrible."

Rachel's gaze collided with Alex's. "Who are you talking about?"

"Peter… Blake Temple," she amended. "He's not who he says he is. He's a monster. Please, you have to stop him."

"What's he planning with the sarin gas?" Alex asked.

"How did you know about that?" Michelle looked at Alex in surprise.

"Let's just say we put two and two together. We know Temple and the rest of his men faked their deaths," added Rachel.

Michelle looked from one to the other. "Who are you people?"

Alex wondered how much they could trust her. But she had saved their lives. "I'm CIA, just like Deacon. You can trust us."

Michelle appeared unconvinced. "You'll understand if I don't. Temple said he was CIA, too, and he did terrible things. He forced me to work for him."

Before she could say anything more, another round of shots rang out close by.

"Duck," Alex yelled, and they slipped back behind their tree coverage.

"That's him." Michelle's eyes grew wide with fear. "He'll kill me. He'll kill all of us."

"We're not going to let that happen," Alex assured her.

Before Michelle could respond, the woods around them detonated with gunfire.

Rachel glanced over at him. "We can't hold them off much longer."

Alex searched their surrounding woods. "We'll have to make a run for it. Liam, can you make it?"

Liam was barely hanging on, but he was quick to assure him. "I can." Alex slid a look Rachel's way. He could read all of her skepticism, yet they were out of options.

He pointed deeper into the wilderness behind them. "That's our only way. Go, Rachel."

Rachel grabbed Liam around the waist and took off running with Michelle following. Alex covered them as best he could until he was certain they were safe, then he left his hiding spot and ran as fast as possible while shots flew past him, barely missing him several times.

Alex caught up with them. "We bought ourselves some time. I just hope Jase and the team get here soon. We can't hold Temple's men off for long."

As they hurried through the woods, Alex kept a careful eye behind them. So far, no one was following. His gut told him it was only a matter of time before that changed.

SIXTEEN

It felt like the nightmare would never end. Rachel could hear the men tramping through the woods at a fast click.

Alex glanced over his shoulder. "I see them. We are way outnumbered."

With her heart threatening to explode against her chest, Rachel could feel each breath as it burned her lungs.

She was barely hanging on. She couldn't imagine how difficult the trek had been for Liam. He looked as if he was ready to drop. Her brother stumbled and almost took her with him. "Alex, we have to find a place to hide. Liam can't take much more."

She glanced around, searching for anyplace where they might take cover to wait it out until the Scorpion team arrived.

"Over there." She spotted a thick grove of trees off to the right where it was impossible to see inside. "It's worth a try."

The four of them headed for the grove. If their plan worked, Temple's men would keep going straight.

As they entered the wooded area, Rachel could barely see a few inches in front of her.

With Alex's help, she slowly eased Liam down to the ground. She could see he was close to losing consciousness again. *Please let help arrive soon.*

Next to her Rachel could feel Michelle trembling. If Temple and his men realized she had been helping Deacon all along, they would kill her without asking questions.

Over the drumming of her heartbeat, Rachel heard the men working their way through the woods. They were almost right on top of them now.

Michelle came close to screaming. Rachel covered her mouth with her hand. They couldn't afford to be found out.

"Do you see them? They were just here." McNamara sounded as if he'd been running a marathon.

"No, but they can't be far. They have Carlson with them and he's injured. That should slow them down," answered a man she didn't recognize.

Silence followed while Rachel held on to a breath.

"Temple wants them found now. Who knows who they've contacted? We're running out of time and our buyer is waiting. If we don't deliver the sarin soon, it will be bad for us. These people don't accept excuses," McNamara said.

Rachel reached for Alex's hand and held it tight. As an answered prayer, she heard the men slowly move away from the spot.

"I think they're gone," Alex whispered. "We need to get back to the station, where Jase is expecting us to be."

Rachel looked down at Liam. He hadn't regained consciousness. Tears filled her eyes. They couldn't leave him here.

"I've got him." Alex hauled Liam up beside him. It

was going to take all of his strength to get Liam back to the station, yet he never hesitated. "You and Michelle head out. I'll be right behind you."

She shook her head. "I'll follow you. In case those men circle back. Otherwise, you'll be vulnerable."

He slowly agreed. It was their only option. "Okay. Michelle, you know the way. Don't try anything foolish."

The woman was clearly terrified of McNamara. Rachel didn't doubt for a moment that Michelle had suffered terrible things at Temple's and McNamara's hands.

With Alex all but hauling Liam beside him, it was slow going. It felt as if it took forever for them to make any time at all.

Rachel kept a close eye behind them. She was afraid the noise they were making would attract the men's attention. So far, they seemed to have bought their decoy. But for how long?

Several times, Alex had to stop to catch his breath. Michelle kept a careful watch out for them. Whenever they stopped, she did, as well. As much as Rachel wanted to trust her, she couldn't bring herself to fully. She'd worked for Temple. To what degree she had been involved in his organization was still undetermined.

Rachel eased up next to Alex and put her arms around Liam, too. "Let me help you. We can make better time together."

He nodded and they slowly made their way along the path. They were still some distance from the station, but she could see it burning above the treetops.

Behind them, Rachel heard something. She stopped, as did Alex. "That has to be them. We need to hurry."

They did everything they could to go faster, but it

was impossible. They stumbled several times and almost fell.

"We'll never outrun them. We have to find a place to take cover," she told Alex.

He shook his head. "We're almost there."

Rachel grabbed hold of Liam again and she and Alex all but ran with his dead weight between them.

"I see them. They're up ahead," McNamara yelled. "Don't let them get away."

"We have to hurry, Rachel," Alex urged.

She felt as if she were running blindly, not sure how much farther she could go.

Michelle grabbed the weapon Rachel had tucked behind her back. "Go. Let me cover you. I can slow them down for a bit to buy you some time."

Rachel glanced at Alex. "It's our only chance."

Alex slowly nodded and they took off running again.

Behind them, shots ricocheted through the woods.

Once they reached the destroyed station, they found a safe place to hide.

"I don't hear anything." Rachel listened over the noise of her pulse and the fire raging, but there was only silence.

"I don't, either. I hope she got out of there safe. Stay here with Liam. I'm going after her."

Rachel clutched his hand. "Be careful, please."

He smiled down at her and squeezed her hand before heading back to where they had left Michelle.

Rachel glanced over at Liam. Her brother was mumbling incoherently.

Lord, we need Your help…

She barely got the words out when she heard multiple shots fired. *Alex!*

Seconds later, more than one set of footsteps came their way. Rachel got to her feet and drew her weapon. She wasn't going down without a fight.

With the rifle ready to fire, Alex charged into the wooded area with Michelle close behind.

He spotted the weapon and stopped dead in his tracks. "Whoa. Hang on, there, Rachel. It's just us."

She slowly lowered the weapon. Relief threatened to buckle her knees. She was on edge. They all were. They needed the nightmare to end soon.

"They're almost here." *Where are you, Jase?* He didn't want to show Rachel how worried he was, but they couldn't hold out much longer. McNamara and his men were almost right on top of them and Liam was fading fast. If they didn't get help soon, none of them would be walking out of here alive.

"We know you're in there." McNamara stopped in front of their hiding spot. "Come out with your hands up and we might let you live. If we have to come get you, it'll be a different story."

Rachel was close enough to see all of Alex's uncertainties. He didn't know what to do. Should they keep fighting? Or give up? If they did, would McNamara let them live long enough for Jase to reach them?

McNamara ordered his men to fire on them. Shots riddled through the space where they stood, forcing them down to the ground.

Their time was now measured in minutes. Rachel took his hand and looked into his eyes. Seconds passed while he just took in her beauty. Was this the end for them?

She leaned over and kissed him tenderly. "It will be okay. We just have to keep believing."

He nodded. He so wanted to believe that, but desperation made it difficult to hold on to his faith. He loved her. He didn't want to die without letting her know how much.

Alex cupped her face. There were tears in her eyes. She understood what possibly lay ahead for them, as well. "I love you, Rachel. I love you so much."

A sob escaped and she hugged him tight. "I love you, too, Alex."

"Last chance. Surrender or die." McNamara's ultimatum interrupted the intimate moment.

Alex brushed a tear from her cheek. "I know that, and I never stopped loving you, either. I'm just so sorry I messed things up between us before. I should have listened to what you needed. I should have been there for you."

She shook her head. "No, you were right. I had no business putting demands on you. Just because I was ready to leave the CIA didn't mean you were, too. I should have listened to what you wanted. I shouldn't have run away from you."

He tugged her closer. "None of that matters now. We love each other. That's all that matters. I love you so much and with God's help, we will get through this."

She smiled up at him. She had enough faith for the both of them and he was grateful. "You're right. We will."

But they both knew there was only one option left for them. Giving themselves up was their only chance, but convincing Michelle of this would not be so easy. Alex told her what they must do.

Her reaction wasn't a surprise. "I can't. He'll kill me." Alex didn't doubt for a second that her fears were justified.

"You're right, he will. You should head out," he told Michelle. "We'll turn ourselves in. They still need us to find the sarin. Take the gun. My team should be here soon."

Michelle was stunned that Alex would let her go. "Thank you for trusting me," she said with heartfelt gratitude. "I don't know how to repay you."

"You saved our lives," Rachel said. "You don't need to repay us. But you need to hurry. We can't hold them off much longer."

As Michelle went deeper into the wilderness thicket behind them, Alex prayed he hadn't made a terrible mistake by letting a person go who was at the very least an accomplice to Temple's crimes.

When he was satisfied she was a safe distance away, he looked down at Rachel. "Are you ready for this?"

She didn't hesitate. "Yes. I'm ready. We'll get through this, Alex. I know we will." Her strength reminded him of all the times they'd fought side by side.

Alex let her go and they got to their feet. "McNamara, we're coming out. Hold your fire. I want your word you're not going to shoot us. Otherwise, you'll never find the sarin."

A tense silence followed. Alex wondered if McNamara and the rest of Temple's goons had already located the sarin. If so, they wouldn't hesitate to kill all of them.

"All right, you have my word. Put your weapons down and come out with your hands up."

Alex blew out a sigh. They hadn't found the gas yet.

Rachel didn't seem at all convinced. "Do you believe him?"

He didn't, but he didn't want her to give up. "I do. He has no idea where the sarin is. They need us. Follow my lead, okay?"

She slowly nodded. "Let's do this."

Alex lowered his weapon to the ground and Rachel followed his lead. With one final look into her beautiful eyes, and a prayer for safety chasing through his head, he took Rachel's hand and stepped out of the coverage to face five armed men.

McNamara stared at them through narrowed eyes. "Where are the others?"

"Carlson's injured. He's in there. Your friend Michelle got away."

McNamara stepped inches from Alex's face. "You're lying. She's working with you. I saw her helping you."

Alex shook his head. "I don't know what you saw, but she tried to shoot us."

McNamara motioned to one of his flunkies. "Check it out."

The man clearly wasn't thrilled to be heading into what could be a bloodbath, but he knew better than to disobey McNamara's command. He eased through the opening. He wasn't in there long before he returned. "Carlson's in there. He's unconscious. He won't be telling us anything. *She's* gone."

"You expect me to believe Michelle overpowered both of you and got away?" McNamara asked. When they didn't answer he said, "It doesn't matter, she won't get far. I'll take care of her soon enough."

Alex wasn't going to let McNamara hurt Michelle. They'd need her to help them fit the pieces of Temple's crimes together and put them away for the rest of their lives.

"So with your friend in there unable to help us find our product, why should we keep you two alive? You've been useless so far."

"Because Carlson told me where he hid the gas. If you want your product, you'd better hope we both stay unharmed," Alex told him.

McNamara didn't believe him, but he was all out of options. "All right. Let's say you know where it's hidden. Tell me where, and I'll have my men check it out. If you're telling the truth, I'll let you both live."

Alex's thoughts churned like crazy trying to come up with a believable location. There was only one that came to mind. "It's at the lodge."

McNamara grinned his disbelief. "Nice try, but we've already been there, remember? There's nothing there but a decaying old building."

Alex kept his expression blank. "That's because you didn't look in the right place."

McNamara's interest was piqued as he tried to determine if he was telling the truth. "And where might the right place be?"

Alex could think of only one option the man might buy. "Under the floorboards in the great room. Carlson told me he hid it there."

McNamara looked as if he hadn't heard him correctly. "The floorboards," he said doubtfully. "You're lying. There's nothing there."

"Am I? Do you want the sarin or not?"

Wavering, McNamara grabbed his cell phone and tried it, then raged at the lack of service—the fire must have destroyed the phone lines. He turned to two of his men. "Head back that way. Tell Blake where the sarin is supposed to be." He tossed Alex a threatening glance. "Let me know if it's not there as soon as possible."

The two men headed back in the direction of the lodge. McNamara came over to where Alex stood. Taking the butt of his gun, he slammed it into Alex's midsection. Alex doubled over in pain as air evaporated from his lungs. It took forever for him to be able to breathe normally again.

"That's for all the trouble you two have caused us so far," McNamara growled heartlessly. Alex slowly straightened, trying not to show any reaction.

"You'd better hope for your sake and hers that you're telling the truth. Otherwise, your deaths will be slow, and you, little sister, can watch your brother die a very painful death."

SEVENTEEN

Rachel put her arm around Alex's waist to help him stand. McNamara saw it and yanked her away, dragging her over to one of his men. "Keep an eye on her." To the other man he barked, "Get Carlson out here. I don't trust him out of my sight."

The man rushed to do McNamara's bidding while Rachel's mind went crazy with worry. Liam was so weak. He could have internal injuries they didn't know about. He needed to be kept as still as possible.

The man returned, dragging Liam in his arms. He dumped him on the ground at McNamara's feet.

Rachel broke free of her captor and knelt close to her brother. She cradled Liam's head in her lap.

"Leave him alone. He can't help you with anything." She stared up at McNamara in defiance.

"Then your friend had better be telling the truth. Otherwise, I'll force you to watch him die."

It took everything inside of her to hold it together. She was terrified Liam would die up here on the mountain and there was nothing they could do to help him or Deacon.

McNamara took out his phone again. "Keep an eye

on them. I'm going to try to get a service spot. I need to talk to Blake right away."

Rachel watched as McNamara walked a little ways from them. She glanced over at Alex. This was their only chance. She could see he understood.

She motioned to the man standing near her. Alex gave a tiny nod. She silently counted off three and then jumped to her feet. Before the man knew what she had planned, she struck him hard in the stomach with her fist. He bent over in pain and she grabbed his weapon easily enough.

Once she'd gained the upper hand, she turned. The man guarding Alex charged for her, but Alex grabbed his weapon and he froze.

The man she'd disarmed yelled at the top of his voice. Right away, McNamara jerked around. Seeing what was happening, he came rushing back to the site.

Alex grabbed the man closest to him and pointed the gun at his head. "That's far enough. Unless you want your friend to die."

McNamara stopped dead in his tracks, hesitating. Then he grinned. "You think I care about him?" Before they knew what he had planned, he shot the man through his chest. Alex just had time to jump sideways before the bullet struck him, as well. The man fell to the ground dead.

Alex fired one shot, striking McNamara in the upper arm near his shoulder. McNamara's weapon flew from his hand. He grabbed his wounded shoulder, screaming in pain.

"You shot me," he raged as if he couldn't believe what was happening. Alex grabbed the weapon he'd lost.

"Don't you dare try anything." Rachel kept her

weapon trained on the one remaining man. The man slowly nodded.

Rachel moved to Alex's side. "We need to get out of here before Temple's men realize we were bluffing about the sarin gas."

"We can't leave Liam here. They'll kill him," Alex said.

Rachel turned to the remaining man. "You, get him up."

"I'll help." Alex grabbed Liam's legs and the man took hold of his arms.

Rachel motioned to McNamara. "Get moving."

Before they'd managed but a few steps, Michelle appeared out of the woods.

She pointed her gun straight at McNamara. "You, you deserve to die." All of her anger and hurt was written on her face.

Rachel couldn't let Michelle kill McNamara. They needed him and she would have to live with what she'd done for the rest of her life. "Drop the weapon, Michelle." She zeroed the gun in on the woman. "If you kill him, you'll be just as guilty as he is."

"He and his buddies murdered my husband," she said with tears in her eyes.

Rachel couldn't believe it. "What are you talking about?"

"Shut your mouth," McNamara raged.

"My husband was Robert Ludwick. You know him as the Chemist. He created the recipe for the sarin gas Temple used. Temple and his men promised to pay him for the recipe and his client list. Instead, they killed him and forced me to work for them."

Now it made sense why Michelle had helped them.

"This one, he shot my husband in front of me." She waved the gun at McNamara. "He deserves to die."

Rachel took a step closer. "You're right, he deserves to pay for what he did to your husband, but don't let him destroy you in the process. He's not worth it. You still have a chance at a life, Michelle. Don't throw that away for him. It's too precious."

Tears spilled from Michelle's eyes and she sobbed, her heart breaking. Slowly, she lowered the weapon.

Rachel went over and put her arm around her. "It's going to be okay. We'll make sure they all pay for what they've done…thanks to you."

Michelle finally managed a smile as she brushed away her tears. "Promise me?"

Rachel gladly gave that promise.

"Ladies, we need to get out of here now. We don't know where the rest of Temple's goons are." Alex motioned to McNamara to get moving.

With Michelle guarding McNamara, the man in front of Alex took hold of Liam once more.

As they headed through the woods at a slow pace, Rachel kept a close eye behind them to make sure no one was coming after them. Thanks to God, they now had breathing room.

"I'm sorry about your husband," she told Michelle. "I lost mine, too."

Michelle looked at her in shock. "You did? I'm so sorry. I know how difficult it is, losing someone you love."

It had been. She'd loved Brian so much and she was grateful for the time they had together. But part of her heart had always belonged to Alex. He'd been her first love. They'd shared so much together. Like it or not, their pasts were forever linked to each other.

Rachel so wanted to live long enough to find out

what the future held for them. Yet she couldn't shake the feeling that Alex was a career agent. It was his calling and he was good at it. She couldn't ask him to leave again and she couldn't live that type of life. She was done with the shadow games. She needed to live in the light. Would he surprise her and walk away from the CIA? Or would he break her heart again when he left for the next mission? She didn't think she could bear going through that much pain again, but somehow she would manage for him. Because she wouldn't keep him from doing what he needed to do.

A noise in the distance captured his attention. It sounded like…choppers. More than one! Jase was here.

Rachel heard it, as well. "Is that…?"

His smile broadened. "It's my team. Rachel, it's almost over." He lowered Liam's legs to the ground. The man did the same. "Keep an eye on the both of them for me, Michelle."

"It will be my pleasure." Michelle moved closer to McNamara while keeping the second man in her sights. Alex glanced over at the raging inferno that had once been the ranger station. "They won't have any way to know we're still here. We have to find a way to get their attention." He remembered the flare gun he'd taken from the station before it collapsed around him. He pulled it out of his pocket. "The station was equipped with this. Once they get closer, we can shoot it off to let them know we're still down here."

Rachel hugged him close and he was so thankful that he'd thought ahead enough to grab the flare gun.

Alex spotted the two Scorpion choppers rising over the mountain edge. He'd been through some terrifying moments while on a mission, yet never had there been a more welcome sight in his opinion. The first chopper hovered above the burning remains while the second one hung back.

Alex aimed the flare gun away from the fire and shot the flare into the air.

The first chopper moved away from the fire and lingered near where they'd seen the flare. Alex left the cover of the trees and began waving frantically. Rachel followed him and did the same.

He could see his friend Aaron Foster at the helm of the chopper. Aaron banked to the left, looking for a place to land.

"They've seen us. They're landing." He hugged Rachel close once more. He was so happy. They'd survived the nightmare. They weren't alone anymore.

Aaron found a landing spot and brought the chopper slowly to the ground; the dust debris it kicked up had them shielding their eyes against the blast.

Once the first chopper was on the ground, the second found a landing spot a little ways down the mountainside.

With Rachel tucked against his side, Alex hurried toward Aaron's chopper. The door slid open and his good friend Jase Bradford hopped out, followed by several other members of the team.

Jase glanced at the towering inferno. "What happened here?"

Alex gave him a quick rundown. "I have an injured man over here who needs immediate medical attention." He pointed toward Liam. Then he explained about McNamara's injury and where he was located.

Jase motioned to Ryan, the EMT of the group. Along

with Gavin, they hurried to assist Liam and bring out McNamara.

"We need to get to Deacon, too. He's in bad shape and he's been down there alone for a while." Rachel told Jase where the agent was located.

"I'll send Ryan and Aaron down to get him. They can take him and your brother along with McNamara to the hospital right away. I have the state troopers on their way up the mountain as we speak. We'll have this location saturated in no time. Temple and his men won't get away this time."

Alex watched as Ryan and Gavin carefully carried Liam over to the chopper, with McNamara trailing behind them. Liam was strong and Alex believed God would bring him through safely. McNamara appeared defeated. He had to know what lay ahead for him. If he talked, it might help him in the long run.

"Take some of the team with you." Jase gave Aaron the location where Deacon was hiding. "We don't know what you'll find there. Temple's men might have found Deacon by now, so be prepared." Alex prayed Deacon was still alive.

The chopper carrying Liam and McNamara quickly became airborne. Jase waited until it was heading down the mountain before he turned to Rachel and held out his hand.

"Jase Bradford. It's nice to meet you." Jase smiled.

Rachel shook his hand. She seemed to be unable to grasp that they'd finally been rescued. She had a surreal look on her face. "Rachel Simmons. I can't tell you how happy we are to see you."

Jase laughed. "I can imagine it's been a crazy few hours up here."

Michelle emerged from her hiding place with her prisoner in front of her.

With everything that had happened, Rachel had forgotten about Michelle guarding another of McNamara's men. Alex explained what he knew about Michelle's role in everything along with what she'd done to help them.

Agent Liz Ramirez took the weapon from Michelle and then cuffed her prisoner.

"I appreciate you helping my people, but you have to understand, you're still a suspect in all of this until we know what truly took place." Jase indicated Liz should put Michelle and the man into the remaining chopper. "Keep an eye on both of them."

Michelle's story would get sorted out in time. She'd be treated fairly.

"We found agent Seth Jamison's body a little ways down from here." Alex filled Jase in on what he believed happened to Liam's handler.

"Unbelievable. I guess that's how Temple and his men managed to stay hidden for so long. They had inside assistance." Jase shook his head.

They'd sort through the web of lies in time. Right now, Alex's main concern was locating Temple and his men before they found the sarin gas. "We need to go after Temple's people before they get away. Or worse, locate the gas."

Jase nodded. "You're right." He motioned to the rest of the team standing by. "Fan out. Keep your eyes open. They have lots of men up here and they have nothing to lose."

Jase turned to him and Rachel. "You two should hang back. You both look exhausted. We've got this."

Standing next to him, Alex could feel Rachel ready

to protest. He was right there with her. They'd come this far. "No way. We want to see this through to the end."

Jase didn't appear surprised. "All right, but be careful."

The airborne chopper was still in sight when it opened fire on something down below.

Alex focused on the area. "It looks like they've located some of Temple's men." The team rushed for the location. Alex stuck close to Rachel. They were both drop-dead exhausted, but they'd come this far. They weren't about to give up the fight without knowing its ending.

The chopper hovered over an area, occasionally firing. Alex heard the men return shots, then silence followed.

Rachel glanced at Alex. "What happened?"

He shook his head. "I don't know. I'm guessing they realized they were outnumbered and gave up."

Once the team reached the site, the chopper took off again. There were half a dozen men standing with their hands in the air. Within no time, they were subdued in cuffs.

As Alex looked over the faces of the men who had surrendered, he realized none of them were Temple's CIA team. They'd somehow managed to get away.

Jase came over to where they stood and confirmed the truth. "Temple and the rest of the agents aren't here."

Alex couldn't believe they'd gotten away. "Let's just hope he hasn't located the gas already." Alex told Jase what they overheard McNamara say about the prospective buyer.

"That doesn't sound good. We need to find these guys and soon." Jase glanced up at the threatening skies. "It's getting colder and we're running out of daylight.

If we haven't found them by night, they could manage to give us the slip."

Jase ordered some of his team to watch the prisoners. "Let's keep looking," he told the rest. "We're losing daylight fast."

In a matter of hours, the entire mountainside was crawling with state troopers and agents. Alex didn't believe Temple's team would risk leaving the area. "They're hiding out somewhere. Probably hoping we'll think they've left the mountain."

Rachel stopped walking. "The cave. It's the perfect spot to stay hidden and Temple knows about it. There are several passages, and if they stumble upon the one that we did, they could escape."

"You're right." Alex told Jase about the cave. "I sure hope we find them before they reach the sarin. We have no idea who their buyer is, but we need to put him out of business before he can do any harm." Alex didn't want to think about the possibility of the gas falling into deadly hands. He'd seen enough damage over the past few years by terrorists wanting to promote their own agendas.

They'd lost one of their teammates because he'd gotten tied up with some very bad people. The last thing Alex wanted was more bloodshed. He'd seen enough of that to last him a lifetime. And it was why he'd come to a conclusion while up here. This was it for him. He'd gotten a second chance with Rachel and he wanted a fresh start in life with her. He was ready to come back home to the tiny town of Midnight Mountain and start living a normal life again.

EIGHTEEN

As they approached the cave, Rachel couldn't help but feel as if everything they'd gone through so far would come down to just this moment.

She touched Alex's arm. She was so afraid something bad was going to happen to take away their chance at happiness.

He looked deep in her eyes and she saw the same fears in his. But he did his best to reassure her. "It's going to be okay."

She tried to smile. She so wanted to believe it.

"Jase, we need someone around at the back exit in case they stumble on it. We don't want them to get away. Too much is at stake," Alex told his commander.

Jase agreed, "You're right. Go. You two know where it is. Take some men with you."

Alex pointed to three of the team members. His fellow patriots. They followed Rachel and Alex as they headed toward the back entrance.

Rachel's thoughts went to Liam. He'd looked so pale when they'd taken him away. She couldn't bear it if anything happened to her brother.

Alex clasped her hand briefly. Their eyes met. His

feelings for her were right there for her to see and she wanted to cry. She couldn't think of a single thing to say. Would Temple and his band of corrupt CIA agents win in spite of everything they'd fought so hard to accomplish?

"We'll get them." She glanced up at Alex. He was trying to be strong for her. She needed to be for him, as well.

"You're right. We will."

Rachel located the back entrance of the cave and pointed it out. "Over there."

They eased closer. If Temple's team was in there, she didn't believe they'd had enough time to find the escape route yet. But there were dozens of other passages throughout the cave. There could be another way out. She and Alex knew the cave better than anyone and even they hadn't known about the exit.

She turned back to the three men. "Stay here. Alex and I will check it out."

The three agents looked to Alex, who nodded. Then he and Rachel headed inside.

As hard as she tried, Rachel couldn't shake the feeling that something bad was about to happen. Alex must have sensed her struggle.

He drew her close and whispered against her ear. "It's almost over."

As they headed down the same narrow passage they'd taken before, her heart was hammering in her chest. She so wanted to have another chance at a future... with Alex.

Alex stopped and grabbed her arm. She heard it, too. Voices.

"They're CIA and she's with them. It's over, Blake.

We should just turn ourselves in and face the music," said a voice she didn't recognize.

The only answer was a single gunshot. Then the sound of something dropping to the ground. She didn't doubt for a second that Temple had killed the man. Trapped like animals, they were turning on each other. Would they kill themselves before Alex's team had the chance to interrogate them?

She mouthed, "We need them alive."

She and Alex charged Temple's men. She didn't doubt that the three men standing guard outside would have heard the shot and would follow.

Surprised, the men whirled with weapons drawn. One man lay on the ground at Temple's feet.

They stood facing each other in a silent standoff.

"Drop your weapons. Otherwise, you're not getting out of here alive," Alex ordered.

Rachel counted the remaining men. Three. There was something wrong. One of the team was missing. Had he escaped a different way or...?

Before she'd finished the thought, someone grabbed her from behind. A gun was shoved against her temple.

"Drop your weapon unless you want her to die," the man behind her yelled.

Rachel's gaze locked with Alex. She was so afraid. She didn't want to die. Not like this.

"Take it easy." Alex tried to keep the man calm. "You don't want to do that. There are dozens of agents all around. None of you are walking out of here free."

"Shoot her. I've got him," Temple ordered the man.

"I said drop your gun." Her captor's hand shook nervously on the weapon. Rachel knew if she did as he asked, she'd be at the man's mercy. That would leave Alex alone. She couldn't do it.

Alex's gaze sliced to the side. He was trying to tell her something. The three Scorpion team members were close.

She managed the tiniest of nods.

"Okay, stay calm. I'm lowering my weapon now." She held the gun out in front of her. With the man still clutching her, she managed to slowly ease the weapon down to the ground.

"Now," Alex yelled. Rachel jabbed her foot hard into the captor's shin. He let her go and she hit the ground. Alex fired; the shot hit the man in his arm. The weapon flew from his hand. Rachel fired at Temple before he could get a shot off, striking him in the upper torso.

Before the remaining men could manage even a single shot, the three Scorpion agents appeared with weapons drawn.

"Shoot them," Temple raged while rolling around in pain. "You can take them. We can still get out of this."

"Don't do it," Rachel warned. "You still have a chance to live. You don't have to die here."

As the standoff continued, the men seemed to be debating on whether or not they stood a chance at surviving. Behind them, Jase and the rest of his team reached them.

Realizing they were severely outnumbered, Temple's men slowly lowered their weapons.

"Get a medical chopper up here right away. We have injured men," Jase told one of his guys.

But Rachel was no longer listening. She ran to Alex and threw her arms around him. She was so grateful that they'd made it through alive.

He held her close for the longest time. Then he framed her face and kissed her tenderly.

She loved him so much. She didn't want to deny it any longer. She loved him and she was so afraid he would choose the job over her once more.

"Temple shot his own guy dead," Alex told his friend. "He wanted to surrender. Temple wasn't going down without a fight."

Jase came over to where they stood. "We need to get these two to a hospital. The rest of the men will be taken into custody. We'll interview them separately. Let's see if we can get one of them to talk about who was supposed to buy the sarin gas."

Rachel still couldn't believe how close to dying she'd come. "Is there any news on my brother?" She had to know Liam was okay.

Jase's smile broadened. "The cell service up here is horrible, but I just got the word. He's going to be fine. He'll be in the hospital for a while, though. Deacon's touch and go. He was in pretty bad shape when Ryan reached him."

She said a silent prayer for Deacon's recovery. He'd fought so hard to live even though his injuries had been severe. Deacon had tried to help Michelle get away from Temple. He'd done his best to bring down Temple and his thugs. He didn't deserve to die because of his loyalty.

"I know where the gas is hidden." Alex glanced down at Rachel as he spoke.

Jase stared at him in surprise. "Where?"

"The cave Liam mentioned in his letter," Alex said to Rachel. "He was trying to tell me without saying it directly in case the letter fell into the wrong hands.

Liam must have realized that Seth was dirty and was fearful he'd find the letter somehow."

"We need to find the sarin as soon as possible," Jase said. "And we need to find the rest of Temple's men. I have the state troopers combing the woods. There were some at the lodge. They'd been digging up the floor. They said they thought the gas was there." Jase shook his head.

"I guess they bought my story after all." Alex told him what had happened before they arrived.

"Unbelievable." Jase gave them both the once-over. Alex couldn't imagine how horrible they must look. "Ryan's on his way back here to take these injured men to the hospital. I want him to take a look at the both of you. You look as if you could use a little medical attention."

Once air emergency services arrived, they prepared Temple and the other injured man for the trip. Ryan and Aaron were with them.

Exhausted to his core, Alex asked Ryan to take a look at Rachel first. She'd been through so much and she wasn't used to being in the field anymore.

Alex wasn't about to stay behind until he'd found out the ending of the story. Why Liam and Deacon had risked their lives.

He waited until Ryan had finished his exam of Rachel and had treated her cuts and scrapes. "I'm going with them," he told her gently. "I want to know that the sarin is safe. Liam and Deacon deserve as much."

"I'm coming with you, Alex." But he shook his head. "No, you've been through enough. Go be with Liam. I'll find you again."

He could see all the doubts in her eyes and he understood each of them. He'd let her go once. She believed he would choose the job again.

Before he could reassure her, Ryan came over. "It's time to go. We need to get these guys to the hospital as soon as possible."

Alex nodded. "Give us a second." Ryan faded away and when it was just the two of them again, he didn't know what to say.

She leaned over and kissed him gently. "Go. I'll see you soon."

He hated leaving her, knowing that she had doubts about his love, but he'd see the mission through to the end, because in his mind it was his last.

Once Rachel had left with Ryan, Alex found Jase.

"So where's this cave?" Jase asked.

"I can take you there. It's some distance away. We can reach it by chopper faster."

"Good. Let's get back to the chopper where Liz and her two prisoners are waiting."

Liz was standing outside waiting for them when they arrived.

"Has he given you any problems?" Jase asked.

She shook her head. "Nothing I couldn't handle."

Before long the state troopers arrived and took Michelle and the other man to a location where Jase and his men could interrogate them.

Aaron piloted the chopper to the cave where Liam had indicated. Alex led the way inside. At first glance, the cave appeared empty. Alex's spirits sank. Had he been wrong? Was Liam simply reminiscing?

"I don't get it. I was positive Liam was trying to tell me something. Let's keep looking. Chances are, he wouldn't have hidden it too close to the entrance in case one of Temple's men stumbled across it."

As they went deeper into the cave, it opened up into a room that was filled almost to capacity with the sarin gas.

"What were Temple and his men planning to do with all this sarin?" Jase asked in amazement.

"I don't know, but whatever it was, it could have had deadly consequences. Thankfully, we found it before it fell into the wrong hands."

"Yes. It'll take a while to safely get this stuff out of here and stored. Do you want to be part of that? You're the one who brought it to our attention. This is big for you," Jase told him.

Alex shook his head. He had found the sarin for his friend's sake. He'd finished the mission. Now all he could think about was Rachel and the future. She needed to know what he'd decided.

"No, if it's all the same to you, I'll let someone else take the glory." He faced Jase. This man was his friend. Jase had been there for Alex when he'd needed to change jobs within the Agency. But it was time. Still, saying the words to his friend was hard.

"Actually, I think this is my last mission with the Scorpions."

Jase clearly hadn't expected this. It took a good minute for him to answer. "Oh, man, are you leaving us or the Agency?"

Alex believed Jase knew the answer already. "Both, actually."

"I'm going to miss you, buddy. Is this because of Rachel?"

Alex had never told anyone about his history with

her. Now he wanted to. "Yes. I love her and I blew it with her once. I don't want to do the same thing again."

Jase slowly smiled. "You're going to be missed tremendously. And if you ever change your mind, you have a place with the Scorpions always, but I get it. Finding someone to love you, well, that's a gift from God. You need to hold on to that with all your heart." He turned to Aaron. "Can you take Alex to the hospital?"

Aaron had overheard their conversation. He nodded quietly, regret showing in his eyes. "Sure thing, buddy. But what Jase said about missing you, well, I second that. I'm going to miss your friendship like crazy."

As they made the trip down to the town of Midnight Mountain, Alex felt the weight of the life he'd been living slowly lift away. His heart soared with the decision he'd made. There would be no regrets for him. No going back. This was the change he'd always wanted, even when he didn't think he needed one. He just prayed that she still wanted the same thing. That she wanted him for the rest of her life.

NINETEEN

She'd been sitting next to her brother's bed for a long time. Liam had wakened long enough to know that she was there and so Rachel was at peace. She'd told him they had Temple's men in custody. He'd mumbled something about Deacon and Rachel had done her best to reassure him. In spite of his injuries, he was holding his own. She'd promised to check on Deacon and had. So far, Deacon's condition hadn't changed much. Still, his doctors were optimistic. The next twenty-four hours would tell the tale.

Now, as she watched her brother resting, Rachel couldn't get the sadness to leave her heart. Alex had wanted to finish the mission, just as he had in the past. He'd been driven back then. It appeared as if nothing had changed in spite of the love he said he still had for her. So where did that leave them?

She was still sitting next to her brother when the man in her troubled thoughts came into the room.

She glanced up at him. She'd never seen him look so serious before. Had something happened?

"Did you find the sarin?" she asked when the silence between them stretched out, filled with unanswered questions.

He came over to where she sat. "We did. Thanks to Liam, the gas is going to a secure location away from danger."

"Are Temple's men talking yet?" She held his gaze.

He shook his head. "I don't know. I left as soon as we found the sarin." She tried to understand the meaning behind those words.

"How's he doing?" Alex asked and looked at Liam.

She leaned forward and touched her brother's hand. "He's going to be fine. He was awake earlier. He was asking about Deacon. It's touch and go." She answered Alex's unasked question.

Alex nodded, his gaze still on Liam. "I can't believe this is finally over." He stopped for a second and then looked down at her. "Rachel, I'm done."

She didn't understand what he meant. Done with her? The Agency? "I don't understand…"

He knelt next to her. "I'm done with the CIA. I told Jase before I came here. I want out. I want…you."

She got to her feet and moved away, unsure of what she was doing. Rachel had to be certain she'd heard him correctly. Losing him again would destroy her.

"Please don't say that unless you mean it." Her voice came out as little more than a whisper.

He came to her, taking hold of her arms. "I mean it, Rachel. I've never been more serious in my life. I want out. I've seen enough death and terror to last me a lifetime. I'm done. I want to move back home to Midnight Mountain…and I want a second chance with you. I want to love you for the rest of my life."

She'd waited years to hear him say those words. He

finally wanted the same thing as she did. She went into his arms and held him close for a moment and then she kissed him and was so grateful that what happened between them in the past hadn't defined their future. They had a second chance.

"It's about time you two got it together." They turned at the sound of Liam's voice. He was awake and grinning at them. "I was afraid you'd blow it again."

Rachel laughed at her brother's typical Liam saying and smiled up at Alex. "We did get it together, thanks to you. You gave us a second chance, Liam." She kissed Alex again. She would be forever grateful that even though they'd gone through one of the darkest moments of their lives up on the mountain, they'd found each other again.

EPILOGUE

"Babe, I'm home." Alex closed the front door against the chilly Wyoming morning and called out to his wife. It was still dark out, yet he knew she was awake.

Almost a year had now passed since he and Rachel had married. They'd settled back into her place and Alex had found his calling as a cattle rancher. This was a childhood dream both he and Liam shared.

"In here." She peeked her head out of the kitchen. Dressed in a robe, her hair tousled from sleep and seven months pregnant, she still took his breath away.

He was so excited about becoming a father. He went to the kitchen and drew her back against him, his hands splaying across her midsection. Their child. He was so happy. There was a time when he couldn't imagine ever being this happy.

"How's the little one today?" he asked and kissed her neck.

She covered his hands with hers. "Active. I think she's ready to come out." He and Rachel teased each other about whether they were having a girl or a boy. She insisted a girl, while he felt obligated to say a boy. Truthfully, he didn't care. He was just so happy to be having a child with her.

That time over a year ago had faded into a memory now. The pain and fear they'd both experienced were all but gone. Liam was safe. Deacon had recovered from his injuries, and thanks to Michelle, they had the buyer for the sarin gas in custody and Temple and his men had gone away for a very long time.

Thanks to God, he and Rachel had made good on the second chance God gave them.

"How's the ranch coming along?" she asked as she put the eggs on to cook.

He loved watching her. She was so beautiful. At times, he still couldn't believe she was his bride.

Since Liam's last mission, he, too, had left the CIA. He and Alex had decided to use the property Brian left Rachel to buy some cattle to run there, as well as keep up the horse ranch.

So far, it had been a learning experience for both him and Liam, but Alex loved it and he found himself looking forward to each new day…with her.

Rachel caught him watching her and immediately ran a hand through her hair. "I must look like a mess."

He shook his head and planted a kiss on her lips. She had no idea how lovely she was to him. "You've never looked prettier." He gathered her close. "I love you, Rachel. I love you so much. I still can't believe I'm blessed enough to have this life with you."

Tears filled her eyes. She cried a lot lately. Hormones. "I'm the blessed one. I thought I'd lost you for good. I'm so glad God brought us together again."

"Me, too," he whispered, and then kissed her gently and held her close. He'd forever be grateful to God for bringing them back into each other's lives. He thought he'd lost this part of his life for good. But God with His infinite perfect timing had chosen the right moment for them, and he'd spend the rest of his life trying to be worthy of this wonderful life he had.

* * * * *

A groan echoed in Ariel Potter's ears. Was someone
hurt? She needed to help them.

She heard another moan and decided she was the
source of the noise. The world seemed to spin. What was
happening?

Somewhere in her mind, she realized she was being
turned over onto a hard surface. Dull pain pounded the
back of her head.

"Miss? Miss?"

A hand on her shoulder brought Ariel out of the foggy
state engulfing her. Opening her eyelids proved to be a
struggle. Snow fell from the sky. Then a hand shielded
her face from the elements.

Her gaze passed across broad shoulders to a very
handsome face beneath a helmet. Dark hair peeked out
from the edge of the helmet and a pair of goggles hung
from his neck. Who was this man?

The pull of sleep was hard to resist. She closed her eyes.

"Stay with me," the man murmured.

His voice coaxed her to do as he instructed, and she forced her eyes open.

Where was she?

Awareness of aches and pains screamed throughout her body, bringing the world into sharp focus. She was flat on her back and her head throbbed.

Ariel started to raise a hand to touch her head, but something was holding her arm down. She tried to sit up, and when she discovered she couldn't, she lifted her head to see why. Straps had been placed across her shoulders, her torso, hips and knees to keep her in place on a rescue basket.

"Hey, now, I need you to concentrate on staying awake."

That deep, rich voice brought her focus back to the moment. Memory flooded her on a wave of terror. The horror of rolling down the side of the cliff, hitting her head, landing in a bramble bush and the fear of moving that would take her plummeting to the bottom of the mountain. She must have gone in and out of consciousness before being rescued. She gasped with realization. "Someone pushed me!"

Don't miss
Alaskan Rescue *by Terri Reed,*
available wherever Love Inspired Suspense
books and ebooks are sold.

LoveInspired.com

LOVE INSPIRED

INSPIRATIONAL ROMANCE

UPLIFTING STORIES OF FAITH, FORGIVENESS AND HOPE.

Join our social communities to connect with other readers who share your love!

Sign up for the Love Inspired newsletter at **LoveInspired.com** to be the first to find out about upcoming titles, special promotions and exclusive content.

CONNECT WITH US AT:

f Facebook.com/LoveInspiredBooks

🐦 Twitter.com/LoveInspiredBks

Facebook.com/groups/HarlequinConnection

HARLEQUIN

Heartfelt or thrilling, passionate or uplifting—Harlequin is more than just happily-ever-after.

With twelve different series to choose from and new books available every month, you are sure to find stories that will move you, uplift you, inspire and delight you.

Get 4 FREE REWARDS!

We'll send you 2 FREE Books plus 2 FREE Mystery Gifts.

Love Inspired Suspense books showcase how courage and optimism unite in stories of faith and love in the face of danger.

FREE
Value Over
$20

YES! Please send me 2 FREE Love Inspired Suspense novels and my 2 FREE mystery gifts (gifts are worth about $10 retail). After receiving them, if I don't wish to receive any more books, I can return the shipping statement marked "cancel." If I don't cancel, I will receive 6 brand-new novels every month and be billed just $5.24 each for the regular-print edition or $5.99 each for the larger-print edition in the U.S., or $5.74 each for the regular-print edition or $6.24 each for the larger-print edition in Canada. That's a savings of at least 13% off the cover price. It's quite a bargain! Shipping and handling is just 50¢ per book in the U.S. and $1.25 per book in Canada.* I understand that accepting the 2 free books and gifts places me under no obligation to buy anything. I can always return a shipment and cancel at any time. The free books and gifts are mine to keep no matter what I decide.

Choose one: ☐ **Love Inspired Suspense Regular-Print** (153/353 IDN GNWN) ☐ **Love Inspired Suspense Larger-Print** (107/307 IDN GNWN)

Name (please print)

Address   Apt. #

City   State/Province   Zip/Postal Code

Email: Please check this box ☐ if you would like to receive newsletters and promotional emails from Harlequin Enterprises ULC and its affiliates. You can unsubscribe anytime.

Mail to the Harlequin Reader Service:
IN U.S.A.: P.O. Box 1341, Buffalo, NY 14240-8531
IN CANADA: P.O. Box 603, Fort Erie, Ontario L2A 5X3

Want to try 2 free books from another series? Call 1-800-873-8635 or visit www.ReaderService.com.

LIS21R